BLEAK
HORIZONS

Edited by Tarl "Voice" Hoch

Bleak Horizons
Copyright © 2017 by Tarl "Voice" Hoch
Adrift © 2017 by Kandrel
4/13/2060 © 2017 by Franklin Leo
Hardwire © 2017 by Ton Inktail
The Ouroboros Plate © 2017 by Slip Wolf
The First Viewing © 2017 by Corgi W
Clicking © 2017 by Ianus J. Wolf
Blink © 2017 by James Stone
Pentangle © 2017 by Ross Whitlock
Starless © 2017 by Searska GreyRaven
This Way © 2017 by Frances Pauli
Outlier © 2017 by Donald Jacob Uitvlugt
Not Like Us © 2017 by KC Alpinus
Clear and Cruel © 2017 by Bill Kieffer
Blessed are the Meek © 2017 by Rechan
Hollow © 2017 by Chris "Sparf" Williams
Cover illustration by Kappy
http://furaffinity.net/user/Kappy
Cover design by Buck Turner
Published by FurPlanet Productions
Dallas, TX
http://www.FurPlanet.com

Print ISBN 978-1-61450-345-3
Electronic ISBN 978-1-61450-356-9

Printed in the United States of America
First Edition Trade Paperback 2017

TABLE OF CONTENTS

Dedication

To my brother, Ian.

Only you understand my fear of Greys thanks to those all-nighter walks with the guys.

If I had to cast one person as a sci-fi hero, it would be you.

And to my cats, Taz and Licorice.

Who kept me company during long days of editing.

And who thought this anthology was getting far too much attention.

And thank you to:

Kirisis, Corgi W and Skunkbomb for your help with the slush pile.

Yannarra for your support and continued love.

And to everyone who submitted to this anthology.

ADRIFT

Kandrel

They say animals can smell fear. This is, for the most part, untrue. Fear is a subtle emotion. It doesn't communicate well. Someone can be afraid and you'd never even know it. In the bouquet of aromas that is a person, fear is just a sprinkle of spice that only the finest of noses can detect. Maybe a few well-trained dogs could, but not cats. Definitely not a cat like Evan, who barely pays attention to his nose at all. He might as well not even have a nose, beyond knowing that his steak is over-cooked and that his road-skimmer needs a checkup and that little Sammy needs a change. No, a cat is never going to be able to smell fear.

Terror, though, is an entirely different thing. Animals can smell terror. Unlike fear, terror sends the body into paroxysms that flood the pores and froth the mouth and make the insides run watery. If fear is a sprinkle of spice in the delicate bouquet of personal aroma, then terror is the splash of garlic. Even someone as nose-blind as Evan can smell it. And he does. It surrounds him. It pervades him. It consumes him.

Evan is running. In the distance is the blaring of alarms and sirens. Beneath their wail, Evan can hear the shrieking of metal shearing and crumpling. Already the air is thin and difficult to breathe. Behind him, he can hear the bass 'thumps' of blast doors shutting one by one as crowds of tourists and crew struggle to make it through. The death of the Avalon's Hope is not a quick one. He can barely hear them over the thumping of his own heart. He must get to her. There's no time left.

Panic is a solid thing, tangible enough to cut with a knife. The hallway is shoulder-to-shoulder. He can't see what the hold-up is. After a few seconds of waiting and pushing, and being pushed from behind, he decides it doesn't matter what the hold-up is. He doesn't have time for it. In a moment he's up, over the crowd. Balance is no trouble for the senses of a cat. Feet land on unwilling shoulders. Hands reach up but fail to grasp his ankles. He's not sure what they're grabbing for— to hold him back or to be dragged along with him. Neither is an option now. The panic has him. The terror is all around him. Evan can't wait for courtesy. Evan runs.

He is in lower habitation, where people of *his class* have purchased cramped little living quarters. The room he'd bought had barely enough room for him to move around, let alone for Mia and little Sammy. It's only three months and a few days' trip; he'd told himself, and later Mia. They could live a bit cramped for a few months. The savings were worth it. They'd need it all in their new life when they arrived. If they arrived. The 'if' had never even come up. Starliner was the safest way to travel. Everyone knew that. It was a hundred percent guaranteed to be safe, right up until the remaining zero percent tore through the hull and started to crumple the ship deck by deck.

There seemed to be two kinds of traveler in Evan's hall-way: those who figured it was safest to wait it out—whatever was happening would stop eventually, and then they'd be rescued. Those were the doors that were still closed, with cool little blue lights next to the doorknob that indicated they were locked. Then there were the realists, those who could feel the floor shuddering underneath them. Those who could hear the distant knell of carbon and steel shattering, hallway by hallway and coming closer.

The hall is blocked by a family of warthogs trying to drag luggage with them. Stupid, he thinks. You can't bring luggage into the life pods. There's no room. This isn't a time to worry about your things. Leave them. The burly male shouts something as Evan leaps over shoulders and uses the wall to get height. With a bound, he climbs over the unfortunate's head. A hairy fist swings wildly but misses. He spares no more thought for the warthogs. They'd probably be too slow anyway.

Green-White-Green Two-Oh-Oh-Eight. His door is sandwiched between the vending hall on the left and a maintenance vent on the right. He slaps his wristband against the sensor, and the locked blue changes to open green. He opens the door, and the stern face of Mia meets him.

His world goes golden. She's safe, and she's here. He reaches out to her, and she takes his hand. She's a goddess in brown. Long of horn, longer of leg, on her sides her stripes are only visible beneath the makeshift sarong she'd made from bedsheets. It wrapped over one shoulder, and swaddled in its front is Sam. He's crying, but Evan doesn't hear him.

"What's going on?" Her eyes are wide with panic.

"We need to go."

She doesn't question him further. He leads her by the hand, and Sam's crying fades beneath the general roar of hundreds of passengers' fear.

The Avalon's Hope is well designed. It's four stories and two sections over to get to restaurants, three stories and a fifteen-minute walk to get to the arcades, and a massive eight stories and a long tram ride to get to the water park, but it's only one hallway and a long ramp up to the life pods. Flashing signs lead the way in blaring neon panic. There's no line. Instead, there's a crowd. No, it's a throng. It's a mob. *We'll never get through here.* In his mind, Evan is already charting a course to the next sections' life pods, but that was stupid, wasn't it? They would be just as busy. Anyway, there might be a mob here, but it's moving as fast as he and Mia can walk. They turn the corner, and they can see the pods. There're four massive conveyors dragging them in from the ceiling. One for individual passengers, the loners that are traveling without family or friends. Those are nothing more than a cryostasis tube. On the far side of the room are the family and party boats, reserved for groups of four or larger. The ones he needed, though, were the couples pods—those came with an extra pod for a "plus one", made to fit anyone sized from child to adult.

The robotic attendant takes their wristbands and a blood sample from each. Little Sammy's crying redoubles when the hypoderm touches his shoulder and leaves behind a little red dot welling beneath the fur. The light on their pod turns green. Evan pushes Mia in first before he squeezes himself on board after her. Their pod sinks beneath the floor on its way to the launch tubes to make room for the next. Mia puts Sam in his stasis pod first. The crying cuts mercifully short when the valves shut. The window flash-frosts and Sam's eyes close in deep hypersleep.

"What is—"

Evan pulls Mia into a desperate kiss and silences her with his mouth. She clings to him for a moment, then pushes herself away.

"We'll be safe." She promises.

"Of course." He rubs his knuckles along her long snout. She smiles at him, then pecks him quickly on the cheek.

"On the other side, right?" She leans backward into her stasis pod and pulls it closed from the inside. He laughs to break the tension, but no one can hear him.

He leans back into his chamber as Mia's frosts over. He's reaching for the handle when the launch acceleration crumples him back into the padded restraints. The door slams shut of its own accord, bouncing off of the air seal once before it closes properly. The acceleration only lasts a moment. Then he's free. In fact, he's weightless. He has a moment of nausea before he sees the traces of frost arcing up over the inside of his pod. He suddenly feels very sleepy. The world goes white.

* * * * *

They say you don't dream in cryosleep. Evan does. He is back in the corps. Sergeant was yelling at him again. Pointless. Sergeant was going to die in a training accident. Doesn't he know that? Evan laughs, so Sergeant yells more. Then Evan is in the shop. There're eight military land skimmers in with problems. This was the longest weekend of his life. Spanner and laser welder in hand, he is comfortable here. Even the military knows how to keep its engineers in good working order. Pizza keeps rolling in through the night. Evan can taste the greasy cheese. His two techs are both herbivores. They hide their disgust well as he wolfs down slices of pepperoni between jobs.

There is a moment that he realizes he is dreaming, but he can't move. For a moment, he's afraid. Then memory comes rushing back. The Avalon's Hope. The creeping destruction, coming closer one bulkhead at a time. The life pod. He's safe. But he still can't move. Now he's not so afraid. He's heard of this. It's sleep paralysis. He's never experienced it before, but he's in cryo-sleep. Maybe it's just part of the chemicals. He should be scared, but he tells himself that he's a rational person. He can just wait it out, and he'll be able to move again soon. He's in cryosleep. Blink and a year passes. Dream, and everyone you knew ages. Open your eyes and it's a whole new world, in a whole new time. There was a crash, but the rescue is coming. They'll be combing the light years between, hunting for the transceiver. They're in a pod that's designed to keep them safe for hundreds of years. Everything will be fine. Just wait.

The paralysis persists. He can't breathe. That amuses him. Another dream. Is he underwater this time? Or maybe high in the air? He has the sensation of opening his eyes, and light streams in. His lungs are starting to burn, and strangely enough, so are his eyes. The sensation builds until it's searing. He can finally see, and what he sees is troubling. It's the inside of the life pod, and he still can't breathe. That's strange. Why would he dream about the inside of his life pod?

He's not dreaming.

He can move. Everything hurts. Everything feels like it's burning. His arms can shift at his side. When he turns his head, the view changes. In front of him, the glass has a crack that runs across the viewport. Why can't he breathe? Diaphragm clenches as he tries to pull in air, but nothing happens.

Tries to lift his arms, but there's not enough room in the pod to reach his face. Claustrophobia joins the asphyxophobia. He needs to get free. He needs to escape. Rational thought drowns in the panic. Even though his hands can't reach the viewport, his head can. The first time he smashes his face against the cracked glass, his snout is in the way. Blood smears his vision. Little droplets float, suspended in midair. Without the microgravity of the Avalon's Hope, he's weightless. He braces himself against the restraints and bends his head down. The second time, his forehead smashes into the glass.

His head smacks back against the restraint. Stars swim in his vision. Was there an explosion? He can't imagine why there would have been one, but it sounded like it. Tiny shards of glass speckle his face. He spits them out and they cut his lips. Then through the pain, he tastes it—air! He never thought he could actually taste the air, but now it's as thick as a milkshake on his tongue. He breathes in. Slowly, the burning sensation fades. He blinks. Eyeballs feel sticky. Everything is moving lethargically around him.

Actually, that's probably the zero-gee. He still has a bloody nose. It's pooling around the tip of his snout, making a disgusting floating ball of blood. Slowly, and with much complaint from his joints, he worms his hand up to the release handle for the pod. There's not much room—once closed, it's not meant to be opened from the inside. Still, when he turns his wrist and tugs, the handle moves and there's a click from the mechanism. Ponderously slowly, the pod door swings open.

It takes a few moments for him to be ready. He was probably only in panic for a few seconds, but it feels like an hour. A year. He shivers, even though it's not cold.

He can't wait long, though. His nose isn't going to fix itself. He crumples up his shirt and uses it to englobe the blood. It soaks in, turning the whole mess a dark ochre. With pinched fingers, he holds his nose to stanch the bleeding while he pushes himself out of his pod and into the cramped space of the capsule. For a moment, the claustrophobia tickles again at the back of his mind, but this time he can conquer it. It's not so small an area. He can stretch his arms and feet out if he's laying lengthwise without touching the walls, and even though it wasn't necessary, there's a porthole looking out into space.

The air is thin, but he can breathe. For the first time since the rippling of the floor back on the Hope made his legs turn to jelly, he finally takes a moment to breathe and think. He'll need to sort something out, sure, but survival is no longer second-to-second.

First, the important things. He looks in on Mia. She is serene in her pod, with frost crusting the edges of her view portal. Evan runs his fingers over the front of her pod. How he wishes he could reach through it and caress her. She is gorgeous. Tawny fur is painted gray by the dim blue light inside. Behind her head, her long horns have dug into the restraining fabric, leaving divots and tears. The headrests weren't made for gazelle. It makes him smile and remember. The first time she had graced his house—and his bed—he had ended up with ripped pillows and a gouge in his mattress. Later he learned the wisdom of tear-proof sheets and coverings. She had been so contrite, in her own way. She had apologized, with that funny quirk in her smile that made it clear that it was his fault, and he knew it. Plus, hadn't it been worth it, her smile said? Of course it had. She'd been worth every bit of ruined furniture, and the bed coverings had been only the first.

Next to her, Sammy lay suspended in his pod. He didn't take up much of it. The restraints had automatically folded up and underneath to keep him in place, but the toddler still looked like someone had stacked a matryoshka doll incorrectly and put the smallest in first. His knobbly knees and stick-thin arms looked comically small in padding meant to fit an adult. His horns hadn't grown in, yet. They were nothing more than little nubs on top of his head. Evan checked the details on the little display. Everything functional. Cryosleep achieved. Good.

Something had gone wrong, obviously, but it appeared only to have been his own pod. Maybe it was the slamming of the door when they'd launched. Could that damage the seal? Of course it could. Everyone trusted these things implicitly, but Evan had worked on vehicles like this for most of his life. He knew just how precise the mechanisms were, and just how easily they could be subverted. He claps and lets himself float off up towards the empty middle of their vessel. Luckily, he'd been a military mechanic for nearly a decade. If it could break in a ship, Evan had probably fixed it at some point. What was this life pod, if not just a stripped-down version of the HAV-T drop ships he used to repair? He could handle this. He got this. Under a console that hid the power generation and air filtration system he finds a small box of shoddy but usable tools. On his own broken pod he finds a screw and rivet secured panel. In his shop, there'd always been checklists before they started work. That's military for you. He lays everything he needed out in front of him, then watches as they float merrily up into the air. Thanks for little blessings, right?

Tools: got. Controls: found. Knuckles: cracked. Let's fix this shit.

With a smile and a grunt of effort, Evan works.

* * * * *

Evan drifts. Even though his pod would have been more comfortable, he has no way to anchor himself in, and he doesn't trust closing the door again. That brings back panic. Instead, he tries to sleep relaxed and floating. For some time—he's not sure how long—it works.

He dreams again. He is watching Sammy play. They are aboard the Avalon's Hope, but for some reason, the play-set he'd loved at his local school instead is there. Sammy is sliding down the slide and laughing. The floor buckles beneath, and Evan shouts. Sam can't hear him. Sam is in danger, but he keeps playing, jumping up and climbing across the monkey bars. Evan tries to run to him, but his legs swing beneath him without taking him anywhere. He can't save his son. Sam is going to be hurt, and it's his fault.

His foot smacks into the open pod door and he wakes. How long has he been asleep? There's no good indicator. Still, he feels more refreshed, if out of breath.

He breathes in through his nose, then regrets it. It reeks. Badly. He'd intended to continue working on the pod when he woke, but that plan fades as he chokes down nausea from the stench. Air filter. That takes precedence.

He is tired. He didn't sleep well. He grumbles as he retrieves his tools—safely snapped into their compartment. It doesn't have the effect he was hoping for. In the shop he'd never been alone. There was always someone else there, working on the grav-adjusters that never seemed to work right, or rushing through some new job the brass had just dropped on them, or on break but still hanging around anyway. When he grunted, he'd get a complaint in response. When he grumbled, he'd get knowing nods. It was the secret language of the mechanic. Now when he swore at his tools for being half-size pieces of fuck, no one heard him. He mumbles something about why they'd bother putting crap like this on a lifeboat, didn't they know someone would be putting their lives on the line using these tools, and he finds himself stalling for the answer that never came.

In silence, he traces a silent fan duct back to an upright cabinet that must be the air system. In five minutes he has four lock-screws hovering to his right as he braces himself against the cabinet to counteract Mr. Newton. With a sharp yank, the faceplate pulls away. Without the cover, he can hear the wheezing cough of the intake fan. Midway between ducting and recycling unit, he finds a slim plate with a latch. He pulls it free, then swears.

Franklin-Pierce Orbiter/Lander Select Filter Range. It's blazoned in silver letters across the top of the plate. The filter has turned jet black, microparticles gumming up both sides of it. In between, the gel packet that's supposed to pull in and recycle air sits inert, useless with all of its surface caked. They'd equipped the lifeboat with FPO/LSF's. Those cheap ass bastards. In the shop they had a different name for them. Fucking Piece of Liquid Shit Filters. They were unreliable. They were short lived. They were state-of-the-art engineering, designed and produced by the lowest bidder. A dropship filter would have five of these little fuckers and they'd be inoperable after just three drops. The pod only had one.

Letting it float uselessly in the air, Evan scrounges in the cabinet. There must be more of them. Backups in an autoloader behind the filter system? No. A secondary in-line system he'd missed? No. An extra one taped to the inside cover just in case?

No. No, no, no. This can't be right. This thing wouldn't last more than a week with three people on board. Every breath would take it another racing step towards malfunction.

But that was the thing. Every breath. In cryostasis, that might be once every day. A week, counted in isolated seconds across five years. Other than the pods, the ship was almost sterile. Nothing else here would interact with the air. The pod didn't need extra oxygen supplies or backup supplies because its occupants wouldn't ruin it until they were saved—and by that point they were the responsibility of the rescuers.

Something doesn't add up, though. There were always fail-safes. Every engineer knows that their perfect little system would fail someday. You always built in contingencies. So where was it? First, he scrapes the filter clean. A thin patina of his own sweat and fur peels off. He wipes his hand on the inside of the faceplate before he replaces the filter and closes the cabinet again. The filtration fan gives a purring hum as air starts to circulate again. Very carefully, he traces the tubes again. Backup system. Redundancy. There must be something here. They must have accounted for the chance that someone would wake up. They couldn't just let someone wander around the cabin if there was no way to recirculate the air. If someone were to get free, like he'd just done, well, it would endanger the rest of the people on board. All that air consumed at tens of thousands times the speed it should be, that would mean a comparatively quick death for everyone on board, conscious or not. Hell, if they were efficient, they would just—

Evan stops tracing the ducts. His fingers feel numb. Instead, he goes to his pod with its shattered window and wrecked seal and follows the tubes there. Intake, extractor, valves, seals, and there, down near where his elbow had been, a miniature vacuum pump. It's connected to a little pressure gauge and a sensor that straddles the gap of the open door hinge. If the seal is incomplete—if the pod malfunctions, the vacuum pump turns on. It evacuates the chamber almost instantly. By the time the slumbering passenger wakes, the atmosphere has been pulled out. The life pod becomes a hermetically sealed coffin. With no oxygen, the corpse inside won't decay—won't foul the air breathable by the rest of the life boat's occupants.

The last little piece he finds in a little syringe cuddled snugly against the arm restraints. Hidden on a mechanical arm, impossible to deploy by accident. He could have brushed it off as some other part of the cryostasis process if it didn't have warning labels festooned over the connecting cable. "DANGER!" "BIOTOXIN" Leading away from the syringe and its mechanical arm was a thin electrical cord. It wandered to and fro where one ducting staple had pulled free. When he swung the door closed, the wayward wire dug through the seal, and where it did the cord had been sheared.

What delicious irony. What a fucking joke. The secret little death that was meant to kill him if he woke up was the very thing that had snagged the door and broken the seal. Failsafe after failsafe, one ruining the next in a perfect cascade.

Defeated, Evan leans himself back into the cushioned restraints of his malfunctioning life pod. He was meant to be dead. It was the efficient solution. Kill one survivor to save the lives of the rest of them. Expedient. Thrifty. It was a life pod. "We're so sorry Missus. In the catastrophe, something must have gone wrong with your husband's pod. I know it comes as little consolation, but it appears he died in cryosleep. He never even knew there was a problem before he slipped away."

Bullshit. Fucking cut-rate engineers. The cord on the suicide-arm had broken free of the staple and broken the seal. Pod compromised and lives of other inhabitants at risk, so it tried to pull a vacuum. Which, of course, had just meant the broken seal let in a trickle of air to replace it. Just enough to keep Evan alive rather than killing him outright. So he'd panicked and shattered the window.

But he's not dead. He pushes himself out of the broken pod and slams the door behind him. Who cares what happens to it? The seal is broken. The window's broken, and he doesn't have the tools or resources to fix it. He pushes himself over to Mia's pod and strokes the glass. *We will be together again, my golden goddess.* He says it out loud. It sounds soft. The cramped compartment is not good for an echo. He scowls, then goes hunting for materials. If he's going to juryrig himself a solution, he's going to have to do it quickly.

* * * * *

He has just met Mia. She is the civvie veep the brass sent his way. Local celebrity. Doing her civil duty to appear in the holovids alongside soldiers. Act like she's compassionate and caring, and that she's bringing some small modicum of relief to their hard lives. Evan really wishes she wouldn't. He can do without some local starlet in his dirty shop, complaining about all the grease.

She asks about what he does all day. He gives guarded answers about replacing thrusters and repairing nav modules. She's got a camera crew with her, a pair of dogs with long ears and brown coats.

"Can't be that hard. It's just following directions, right? I mean, it's all just pieces put together in the right order."

Evan sneers at her then hides his face. "Sure. Right." Don't piss off the veep. Smile for the camera. Fuck. Why did they send her to his shop? At least she's a good reward for the eyes, even if she's useless between the horns.

"Come on, spots. Gonna let a lady rag on us like that?"

That's Jake. Fucking green private. All wagging tail and no brain. Transferred in a month ago and never could keep his muzzle shut. In the military they weren't supposed to see species—there'd been sensitivity training for that. Still, he'd never met a malamute whose mouth wasn't constantly open.

"Oh? I bet it's not all that." Mia's smile is poisonously sweet at Jake.

"Bet?" Jake pulls out a greasy wallet.

"Oh, I didn't quite mean that."

Jake laughs. Evan gestures for him to shut the fuck up, but he's not watching. If Evan has to give him an order, it'll look bad for the camera. Damned if he does, damned if he doesn't.

"But if you're willing." She looks around the shop. She points at a grav-engine hanging in harness. They'd just taken it off an atmospheric shuttle. Busted dampers. Repairs wouldn't come in for a month, so it got to sit right there until they could do something with it. "What's that thing?"

"It's a unicorn, princess." Jake spits.

"Oh, I see. Well, how long would it take you to work on that 'unicorn'?"

Evan steps in. "Bout an hour to get it down to engine bolts." Jake seems to catch on that he's no longer in good graces. He shuts his mouth and nods.

"That long? Okay." She gestures to one of her camera dogs. He pulls out a credit stick. "Here's two cases of beer, I bet I could get it 'down to bolts' in half an hour."

Jake guffaws. He can't afford two cases. Green little shit has to beg for drinks when he's on leave.

Evan crosses his arms. "Don't look at me, private."

Jake shrugs. Plops his wallet onto a table. Mia daintily places her credit stick next to his wallet. She's chewing gum. She blows a bubble, then pops it. One hand reaches out.

"Wrench?"

Jake pulls his own from his belt and hands it to her. The handle is black with lubricant stains. Evan expects her to hold it gingerly and wipe her hands off on the closest thing. Instead, she grips it firmly and turns her back to us.

In five minutes she's got the front casing off. She hasn't gone for the wrong bolt yet.

In fifteen minutes Jake is sweating. She's taken the blown dampers off and is already working on the containment screws.

In twenty-five she's formed a semicircle of carefully cataloged pieces around her. She's filthy with grease. It's smeared across her face and up her arms. Somehow it only makes her more radiant.

At the thirty-minute mark she's still ordering the screws from smallest to largest. She'd finished four minutes early and was just taking the victory lap. Jake is swearing.

"Pay up, private," Evan orders.

"Oh, don't worry. I wouldn't take money from the people

who sacrifice so much for our world. Consider these beers on me tonight!" She tosses Jake the cred stick. He catches it and stares down at it. Then his head lifts and stares straight into the camera. There is a look on the dog's face that never quite fades from memory—the unbelieving gaze of humiliation. It's the look of being shamed twice, first thorough defeat and second through charity.

"My brother races bikes." Mia continues. It's just an hour to sundown, and the evening light is glowing through the garage door, illuminating Mia from behind. It's perfect lighting for the cameras. In Evan's eyes now, she is the most beautiful thing he's seen come through those doors since the admiral's luxury yacht came in for repairs five years ago. "You should watch my show. Then you'd have known."

She shines radiantly in his mind. She folds up the miniature microphone clipped to her now-soiled dress, and the camera dogs fold their kit away. That must be the end of their feature. Good enough. Definitely enough material there. Still, since there's nothing recording now, he takes his shot. Even though he's not normally shy around women, Evan stumbles to ask, "See you down at the canteen for a drink tonight?"

She looks him up and down, complete with his drab yellow fur and spots so dark she couldn't tell if they were intentional or just smears of grease. Whatever she sees, it's clear she approves. "I've always had a thing for cats. You got a deal. Wouldn't miss it." Mia winks at him, and Evan's pulse takes an unexpected turn for triple digits.

✳ ✳ ✳ ✳ ✳

He is woken again by the malfunctioning filter. By the time he drags himself to consciousness, he is wheezing. Even though his lungs are pulling in air, it doesn't feel as if it's accomplishing anything. His vision is swimming into and out of the gray ring that's formed at the edges. He pushes himself towards the air duct, then immediately regrets it. The needle in his arm snags and pulls free, leaving a long gash across his wrist. He curses as red droplets float chaotically across the cramped pod. He catches the ones he can with his torn shirt. He had plugged himself in for the night. There was no drinkable water and no edible food. The intravenous drip was his only option—and a limited one at that. Just like every other system on board, if he couldn't solve this, he'd run out of his own personal supply in a week.

He scrapes the filter clean and reinstalls it. When the circulation fan hums back to life, he places his mouth above the exhaust duct. Oxygen! It burns as it fills his lungs. In just seconds his headache clears.

In the silence of the humming fans, he slowly surveys his domain. One faulty life pod, with a faulty seal, broken window, and now seriously depleted resources. One air filtration and circulation system—already showing the strain of unintentional habitation. One set of jury-rigged tools, cramped and insufficient for just about any job he could put to them. Two fully functional life pods, with his greatest treasures nestled precariously inside each one.

He turns to the hatch and looks out to the stars. They're in an interstellar gap—much too far away from any system for anything to be a local 'sun'. Evan misses the sunrise. In the rush to escape the Avalon's Hope, he has nothing with him that could serve as a clock. He can only guess that he's been working for two days straight at his problem, but realistically it could have been any number of days. The lack of any real handle on time bothers him more than it should. What if he's overslept? What if, because of the bad quality of the air, he's been asleep much longer? It's technically possible, isn't it? He doesn't know. He's no medic. He's spent his life with hands inside of engine blocks rather than chest cavities. He can only guess that maybe he's sleeping more than he should because of the atmosphere. Or maybe it's the other way around? He can't know, and that's dangerous. The air filter is a ticking time bomb. How long until it's no longer able to generate oxygen, even after being scraped clean every morning? It could still have most of a week left on it, or it could be running close to as little as a day or two. Worse, the FPO/LSF isn't reliably bad. At least then he could have counted on it for a certain amount of time. Instead, they're chronically fickle. One might last a whole month of intense use, while another might spontaneously fail on its first outing. It's only through banks of redundancies that larger ships can use them with any sense of confidence. When you have twenty of them running in-line with each other, a few failed filter packs aren't really a problem.

But out here, with just one... .

Evan is running low on time. Today, he has to find a solution.

The morning he spends tinkering with his failed pod. It's mostly disassembled at this point, with its pieces badly clipped together to keep them from floating around the cabin. He understands it now—at least as well as he ever will without formal training. The one thing he knows for sure, though, after two days of tearing through its insides, is that he's going to need some other solutions to repair it to a functional state.

The next few hours are spent disassembling the interior of the ship. Perhaps there are pieces he could use. Adhesives and flexible panels could replace the broken window. Curing gels might make the interior of his pod air-tight, and that would allow him to recreate the seal. His longest day yet passes as he tunnels through the pod's systems, only stopping when he reaches the thick external wall between him and the long dark outside. In each direction, he finds the same answer. Heat insulation—itchy and insufficient for his needs. Circuitry and wiring. Meager supplies in volatile storage. One wrong stab from his crappy screwdriver and thin atmosphere might not be his only immediate problem.

Hours tick by on his internal clock. He grows tired again, but he fights the fatigue. There must be something. He is a fighter, not a quitter. The army didn't train failures. But no matter which way he digs, the solutions simply aren't there for him to find. He doesn't have the supplies necessary to recreate the seal necessary to put him back into cryosleep.

It is evening. He is starting to feel dehydrated again, and the headache is returning. Defeated, he scrapes the gunk from the air filter again, then settles back into the restraints of his pod with the IV drip needle in hand.

Sleep is slow to arrive. Over and over, he plays through every scenario. If he tries to jam insulation into the seal, air might seep in. Then he dies in cryosleep. Maybe if he mixes a concoction of fuel, glucose syrup, and who knows what else? No. He's no chemist. It won't coagulate correctly, and now not only will air seep in through the seal, but now he's out of IV drip and dies anyway. He could try to make a lining of stripped wire insulation and casing parts. But he doesn't have the right materials to create a seal, and he'd die. He doesn't have the parts. No matter what way he cooks it, he just doesn't have the parts.

He tries to force himself to sleep, but his imagination turns morbid. He slowly suffocates to death, and the failed filter leaves no air for Mia and Sam. Everyone dies. He lays back in his pod and stabs himself with the kill-juice needle like he was meant to before he even woke up. He dies, sure, but the seal remains broken. His decaying corpse ruins the air, and within days the rest of the inhabitants are dead, too. There's no way out. The pod doesn't even have an airlock. He can't even eject himself out into space. Round and round, his despair grows. Not only can he not save himself, but he can't even save them.

Evan tries shouting, but no one is there to listen to his laments. He tries crying, but he is dehydrated even with the nightly IV drip. He punches the restraints of his pod, but weightlessness is not kind. It sends him spinning backward, and in catching himself, he bangs his head off the far side of the cramped ship. It's not fair. He would give his life for them—either one individually and definitely both together.

He doesn't want to die, but it feels infinitely worse that the inconvenience of his corpse is, for Mia and Sammy, a death sentence.

He curls up in his pod and shakily plugs himself into the drip. It's been a long day. He squeezes his dry eyes shut and tries to keep out the demons. Eventually, he succeeds. After hours of semi-consciousness, the thin atmosphere and exhaustion claim their dues.

* * * * *

It is the evening of his humiliation. Mia has brought him here to the fertility clinic, and he can't meet anyone's gaze.

First, they shuffle him along to a little private room and give him a cup. When he asks what they expect him to do with it, the nurse gives him an exasperated look and turns away. Inside the room are discreet magazines with blank covers. Upon opening them, he is greeted with the obvious answers.

Hiding the now-full sample cup beneath his shirt, he creeps back to the lobby. Mia is waiting for him there. She is his only comfort in the whole building. She understands him. Everyone here is so open about it. It sets Evan's hackles up. He doesn't want his private business to become the talk for the gabs. The nurse takes his cup and holds it up to the light for just anyone to see, making sure he'd produced enough for them to process. It's humiliating. Mia takes his hand and gave him an apologetic glance. For her. He would endure it, for her.

They are brought into a consultation room. Inside is the first doctor he sees that night, though it won't be the last. She is another ungulate like Mia, with a long, generous face. In a kind, matronly tone, she explains how Evan just isn't compatible with Mia. There are certain gene markers they require for cross-species pairings. Some people have it, she explains, while others don't. It's nothing to be ashamed of, she continues. Evan silently ignores her with a certain amount of stubborn spirit. He will be ashamed of whatever he wants to be ashamed of, thank-you-very-much. And right now, he is very ashamed to hear that there's simply no way for him to give Mia a child.

The doctor says there are still options for them, and gives them a sleek tablet. On its face is an advertisement for the clinic's IVF solution (Prime specimens of more than a hundred species available, and another five hundred available within six months at some extra cost.) It's not always the best solution, the screen reads, but where nature fails, the clinic is happy to pick up the slack.

In stuttering tones, Evan apologizes to Mia. She is having none of it. Still holding his hand, she gives him a stern look that stops any more apologies before they emerge. In her own careful tones, Mia broaches the subject. Evan isn't happy. He wants it to be his son, too.

"You're being stupid." Mia scolds him. "It will be your son. You will raise him. You will love him. You will—and I guarantee you this—be changing his diapers. When he falls, you will pick him up. When he cries, you will be there to comfort him. What more proof do you need that he'll be your son?"

Of course, Evan agrees. That's what matters, right? And in so many important ways, that's all that matters.

Mia thanks him. He is unhappy, but he'll endure that—for her. Even though she doesn't say it, he can see it in her eyes. She knows what he's sacrificing for her. She kisses him, and he knows that it doesn't matter. It's not important. It might not technically be his kid, but it will definitely be *his* kid. Because it came from Mia, he will love it unceasingly.

He takes her hand, grits his teeth, and that day little Sammy is artificially conceived.

* * * * *

Today should be rainy. The sun should be hidden behind clouds. He wakes and hope has fled. He knows his fate, and he knows the answer to his dilemma. He can save his loved ones—at least, one of them. There are still two functional pods on board, with intact seals and unbroken windows.

It's murder. That swirls around in his head as he slowly drags his way to consciousness. It's murder. You're killing someone you love. Someone you've loved for as long as you can remember being happy. It's taking that poison needle and jabbing it into their veins.

Evan can't move. He's going to kill them, or at least one of them. He's got no choice. Do nothing and kill them both, but act and kill one and the other lives.

He rips the IV from his arm. Blood soaks into his fur and stains his hands. It hurts. Good. He should be in pain. That feels right. He should be suffering.

He leaves thin smudges of blood down the window of Mia's pod. "I'm sorry." He sobs against the portal, through which he can see her face. The face of the golden sun. The face of his goddess.

"Forgive me."

Unhooking the latch would be simple, but that would engage the process to wake them, as if he were a rescuer. That's a grim joke. A rescue. Hah. He bites his lip and turns his head away. A yank at the door engages the failsafe. There's a subtle hiss. The mechanical arm with the syringe engages. The light of his life dies silently. He can't look as he opens the pod. He can't bear the sight of the lifeless body hanging weightlessly in the restraints. It's a tight fit, but there's room for two.

Of course there's room for two. Toddlers don't take up much space. Evan closes the door and engages the seal. He takes the used syringe and plunges it into his own arm. There's not much of the venom left. He struggles in pain, but the poison is potent. In minutes, he passes.

On Earth, there was an old cliché that the smallest coffins are the heaviest. So too, now, are the smallest life pods.

4/13/2060

Franklin Leo

09:23:35
I had warned you—they were coming for us. Hopefully now you'll believe me, my beautiful Sara.

Coffee stains darkened the sheet's upper left corner. It crinkled and felt thin, as if passed through multiple paws. I tried to imagine what he was telling me, but I was trembling, staring at the worn, printer-made letter with tears in my eyes. The last time the stoat had seen me he had threatened that my life was in danger.

"Think you can tell me what it means?" Detective Leary asked. "We're not too sure if it has anything to do with this."

"No," I said. "I'm afraid I can't."

The retriever sighed, his one cyber-eye whirring and glowing silently against his auburn fur. I felt like I'd ruined his entire day.

I turned to look at Mrs. Burns' body one last time; a white sheet stretched over her with blood spattered where her head should have been. The smell burned my throat and forced me to cough into my elbow. My red, white-tipped tail curled against me to prevent itself from getting any closer.

"I've got one more thing to show you. It's upstairs." The dog gestured with his paw, letting me out first. I nodded and got out of there as quickly as I could.

The rest of the blood Mrs. Burns had lost streaked the wallpaper and ceiling. When I'd told them I could handle this, I hadn't imagined how bad it all would be. Really, nothing could have prepared me, even with Walter's letter hanging at the back of my mind.

We walked up the stairs, and all sight of the chaos below vanished. It was just another visit to the old Burns' residence. A few officers hung around. Snapping photos, talking over coffee, perusing the room with small and intricate tools. A fox made eye contact with me and shook her head, eyes looking down just as soon as she had glanced at me. We foxes can tell when another one of us is hurting.

The detective swung around and placed his paw on the knob leading into the Burns' bedroom. It was the only door that stood closed, locks hanging open yet attached firm and heavy. The sound of two officers talking inside let me know that we, the detective and I, wouldn't be having any privacy.

"This is going to be weird," the dog said, "so let me know if you need to step outside."

"After what you just showed me downstairs?"

He shrugged, then opened the door and led me in by the arm.

Marker. The strong scent of ink hit me just as the blood downstairs had. Every inch of the room, even the televisual window-panels, appeared to be covered in paint and marker. My muzzle scrunched in disgust. Lines led to lines that led to squares of writing and more lines. Most of what was visible looked to be a mess, but what I could make out shook my nerves and made me want to collapse on the floor.

"That's my name," I said. "Why does he have my name scrawled everywhere?"

"We thought you could maybe explain that for us. We followed his trail downstairs, so we're assuming that he had this all done before he killed his wife."

I stepped further in, ignoring the dog's words. The two officers further in gave a look, as if I were stepping in on their private game, but both of them backed away.

Written beneath my name was the same words he had

last told me.

They're coming for you, Sara. They're coming to take you away.

* * * * *

Four Weeks before the Murder

I sipped on my coffee and laughed as he played the last of his video for me. It was amazing. Truly. An entire simulated world with simulated mammals living about their business, all the while not having been made by the doctor's wizardry at all.

This was something new, and he'd told me that it would only grow more amazing.

He flicked the monitor off and turned. His round, roto-operated ears that glowed blue against his gray and thinning fur perked once his chair faced me. His soft old eyes, unchanged by any mechanics or software, felt warm and inviting as usual. "It'll be big. I'm sure of it."

"Does the school know you're posting it?"

"Feh," he said. "All they need to know is what gets written down on paper."

I took another gulp from my drink. My tail swatted the air in big, excited sweeps.

"When I had opened up the data file and linked myself in, it hit me. I mean really, it actually hit me." He tapped the neural ports he had attached to his skull. "I had only wanted to see the world, but instead, it pulled me into it. Without leaving my office, I was able to stand, to walk, to breathe air that didn't exist. The system was using what I had given it, yes, but it had also created its own constants. It had wanted me to enter, and the program was changed to allow for it.

"Not only did it come up with new constants, though, but it came up with an entirely new evolution scape that I had never scripted. I would walk the streets and find things our world could only imagine having, and I could see planets and moons in the sky that didn't even exist in our reality. Worlds upon worlds of data constructed a perfect solar system, and then an entire universe. A perfect recreation."

"That must've been something." My knees shook. My God, I thought. This *was* big.

"No shit." His lips stretched into a fang-filled grin. "You should see my savings. I had to upgrade the lab's entire system to keep it all going."

"Is the simulation still going then?"

"That's the thing, Sara. I can't control it anymore. Starting the process has allowed the simulations to develop on their own. They've shown me that they have no interest in stopping. All I can do is watch and figure out what the next variable will be."

It was amazing. Truly a scientific breakthrough. Looking around, I could see all the new computers and hear the running hard disk drives fuming with acceleration. Cords even took up the doctor's biological synth-ports in his wrists and head, which made him into a glowing weasel while also making him seem lankier, weaker. I realized I was supposed to be documenting such an occasion, maybe even asking him how he was feeling, until the doctor opened his desk and pulled out a tall bottle of wine.

"Quickly, let's celebrate. By the time we get this open, we'll have another thousand cities to go over."

"Doctor," I said. "I'm flattered, but I need to get going. We can finish the interview tomorrow."

"No, no, Sara. Stay. Please, celebrate with me. I'll jack you in and make you a god, show you what new frontier mammal-kind has created."

"It's oh-so-flattering, but I really must be going." I waved my notepad at him as he filled a goblet-sized glass. "Besides, you know I don't have any synth-ports."

Again, he smiled. "Do you want any?"

I declined, and as I got everything settled, he told me more about how he socialized with mammals that never would exist, and once I found myself wanting to stay, I knew it was really the time to depart.

"Please, Doctor, get some rest. Let your wife know you're all right. She's worried sick about you."

Again, he waved his paws as though sweeping away a swarm of insects closing in. "She knows where I'm at. I practically proposed to her in one of my labs. You remember this, right?"

Yes, yes I did.

I waved goodbye while stepping out into the hall. Cool, air-conditioned wind rushed beneath my fur and sent a shiver down my tail, goosebumps tickling my paws. A universe, I thought. My mentor's gone ahead and created a whole entire universe, and he's found a way to step inside. When the papers and leaders of the world figure out what Doctor Burns has cooking on his side of campus, they'll shut the school down just to keep everyone calm and collected.

Outside, I could still feel my heart beating at a rapid-fire pace, and turning towards his window, I could see him staring out at me. His smile hid behind a shadow cast from his stubbed oaken muzzle. Those ears of his, always moving, stood still for the first time that I'd ever seen them. Before I could turn, he raised his glass, nodded his head, and toasted me in silence for what was about to be our next big adventure.

* * * * *

4/13/2060 (12:04:53)

I opened the door to find my apartment ringing without end. The police's call for privacy didn't seem to matter to those waiting to interview me, for the mainline that hooked into the hidden speakers and single holo-screen thundered against my ears. Everyone wanted to know about the murder, about the doctor and his position in the university.

About how I may have been the last person to sleep with him before he disappeared.

"How long?" I asked.

My sister, sitting on the couch with legs crossed as if in

the middle of meditation, covered her ears and bared all of her pointed teeth at me. I could see the glowing lights beneath her cheek-fur blaring, her synthetic bio-phone ringing within her skull. "What?"

"I said, how long have they been calling?"

"Since before you left. I haven't been able to work all day."

"Then disconnect them. Block the calls."

She raised her wrist, where the smartwatch that uplinked and connected her to the 'ware inside of her cranium waited and filled with incoming voicemails.

I told her to shut her phone off, and that I would even silence mine. It took several minutes, but the apartment finally fell silent once I got everything off. I came back to the living room to find my sister cleaning her ears with a yellow-stained cotton swab. Her face no longer glowed like the end of a burning cigar.

"Sorry, but after what I just saw, it's no kidding we're getting called," I said.

"Could you have maybe said something to the police about incoming calls?"

"As if they could help. They have no clue what's going on. They think I have something to do with Mrs. Burns' murder and know where Walter went."

"She's dead?" My sister whipped around, muzzle hanging open.

I nodded. "They said he did it."

She got up, and instead of leaving, walked over and gave me a hug. I squeezed her until my paws and arms left indentations in her fur. My eyes stung as tears seeped out. It had been the first time that I let myself cry.

No one had seen this coming. I'd told Mrs. Burns that Walter was doing all right, even if she herself hadn't seen her husband in weeks. His home's walls were clean, too, and those horrible locks and bars placed on each and every door had yet to exist.

But the house I saw an hour ago looked completely

different, somehow. It was as though the military went through and took over his home. The detective was right, at least from what I'd seen: the doctor really had lost it. Just thinking about it made me want to cry even harder.

I pulled away from my sister after a minute of crying. Trisha held me still, eyes searching for any remaining emotion. Looking at her, ignoring the few cybernetic enhancements added to her face, I saw that we really did look alike, as others had often commented.

"Thanks," I said. "I've been holding it in all morning."

"Don't mention it, but if we keep getting calls like this, I'll lose it."

I raised a paw. "No, please. You're the last person I need losing it."

She answered with a smile.

We moved to the kitchen counter. Trisha grabbed me some tea and a bagel that she had been saving. I thanked her with another weak but meaningful hug.

"Did the detective ask if you'd been spending any time with him recently?"

"Of course he did. He basically asked me where I grew up. They had me go through the house and show them everything that I knew. Everything they've seen so far has me somehow connected."

"Everything?"

I told her about the room. The walls, the marker scrawlings listing my name. The warning. I told her more about the research, the simulation, and I let her know how the doctor claimed me to be his one true inspiration. Repeating everything to her made me feel how obvious it was that I'd been having a fling with him, and how close to being found out I was.

When I finished, she glanced at me through the spaces between her open fingers. "This is bad. Very bad."

"I know, but what do I say? Everything I do say just gets them asking more questions."

"Well, what *were* you doing with him?"

I opened my mouth, but I was afraid that she wouldn't believe that the love I felt from this old scientist wasn't somehow tied to the research he'd been doing. I didn't even think she could believe that he had found a way to jump into new worlds by linking into a computer. Even I wouldn't believe me. One thing was clear, though:

No one would ever really know how Dr. Burns had made me feel.

* * * * *

Three Weeks before the Murder

He turned on the computer and let the system refresh. Watching him, I saw his tail swing low and knock some dust into the air. His fur lifted dark and the smell of old food had me curling my tongue.

"Do you ever get the feeling something's not right?" he asked.

"All the time, but that doesn't mean it isn't."

"No, of course not, but what if there was a way to alter what we expected, already having predicted our future based on given factors?"

Then I would say he was anxious, if not paranoid. The large screen before us lit the room with a washed out blue, and the monitors, desks, and stacks of paper littering his lab took on a solemn glow. "When I was young, I had always wanted to watch ants and see what exactly they did. I gave them stories, futures, and even their own pasts. Then, I would take my finger." Dr. Burns lifted his paw, thumb standing tall. "And I would crush one of them. The story ended. No future for one of the hundreds.

"Simulations have been around for centuries, helping nations win wars and doctors predict disease strains. We've only gotten more advanced," he said, again tapping his neural nodes prickling out from his head's fur, "to where our reality can now become virtuality."

"So what you're saying is that the real is no longer real. Do you feel that technology," I pointed towards his desk, where the running computers and simulation turned everything a brutal red and purple, "has taken over too much of society?"

"No, Sara. It's enhanced it. Our world's gained the power to work like a massive computer. Now, it's only reasonable that we find a way to control our reality." Dr. Burns clicked his mouse, and blue digits and symbols began to scrawl out across the massive screen. Lines fed down horizontally until a chart took shape and organized the information into categories. "I showed you my simulation. Like I said, everything changed when it pulled me in. As we know, on the other paw, it wasn't finished."

He split the screen into two different screens, and on the new, unaltered side, a chart started to grow in much of the same way the other one had started to.

"Okay, you're holding out on me. What exactly is happening?" I asked.

The weasel grinned. "Isn't it clear? Last month, mammals were made into digital entities that could live, work, and die. They had no idea that we were watching them work in their digital world, even if I myself had entered and started to change things. Recently, the simulation's become so advanced that it created its own simulation just to take care of itself, to figure out how to avoid death and mayhem. Say, a finger ready to crush it. What we're seeing now are two different universes growing on their own, one the product of the other."

I looked at the screen again, but all I could see were the numbers, codes. I was a technical writer, not a genius. "Can you show me an example?"

"Take us for example. Had you not met me years ago, we would have never made it into this room. You yourself would be missing from an equation that I had already started. Now, since you are part of the equation, a different result will show up based upon what I throw at it. The simulation is doing just that, but it's working in the hundreds of thousands by understanding all of its and another's simulated data.

"Plus, if I take the numbers and throw, say, a simulated virus, something that decides to alter the realities and bring back some chaos to the original simulation." Hs spun around, typed up something within the new simulation, and jammed the enter key as though knocking on a drum. "What I get is the system trying to right itself, seeing the virus as an attack or, say, a disaster, which means that all the data inside will be in danger of being deleted and will need to be reformatted. It'll go in, find the virus, and destroy or alter it without affecting anything else in either universe because," he says, highlighting something on the second screen, "the original simulation already saw it coming."

The doctor stood and walked over to me. I watched him, head tilting as I questioned his intentions, but when he took my paws, I relaxed, squeezing his. My heart's steady pulse became a roaring purr within my throat. "Not only have I found the last frontier to explore, but I've created an alternate reality, Sara, and the creatures inside fear me. I've become a god to them, and they're afraid that I—we—might smite them."

"Hold on. How can digital simulations fear you? And what about the system? Can't it corrupt itself by righting so many wrongs, maybe even destroy things that weren't even dangerous?"

Walter smiled. He looked at me as if he'd been waiting to hear those words all along, and shook his head. "First, let me show you what it means to be a god."

* * * * *

4/13/2060 (16:15:02)

I set the plates down on the drying rack, listening as the shower upstairs ran freely. Trisha knew she wasn't supposed to shower while I was doing dishes, but she didn't care. Well, for all I cared, Trisha and her cyber enhancements could burn in scalding hot water. Plus, if we ran out, then she'd have to deal with me.

Dr. Burns stayed on my mind, his warm smile and confident demeanor running through my veins. Everything he'd shown me was a part of me now, and he had trusted me more than anyone else around. I could see that from the very first moment that we had fallen in love.

I'd gotten too close to being found out, however. The police had had so many questions and getting home only meant being questioned even further. Even though I loved my sister, I knew that she'd only see me in the wrong for the things that I'd done. She wouldn't understand the simulation Dr. Burns had made nor the way he had made me feel. She wouldn't understand how strong he made me feel just by keeping me in his world. As much as it hurt, I knew that I couldn't tell her. Walter had trusted me for a reason, after all.

And that warning. *They're coming for you.* I didn't know whom exactly Walter was telling me about, and the police made it clear that whomever it was wouldn't get even close to me. I still didn't feel safe, though. Knowing I would be watched by someone on my side at least made the world seem a little less dangerous.

I turned the faucet off and glanced upwards. Standing on the other side of our open window was Mrs. Williams. My throat seized shut, and a yelp squeezed out, those bright feline eyes of hers piercing against her dark fur.

"I heard you were back from your research," she said. Her lips stretched out into an old yet passionate grin.

I touched my breast as if I could manually slow down my heart. "An internship, Mrs. Williams. It's good to see you, too."

"Your sister's told me so much about it. She said you worked with Dr. Burns?"

"Yes, I had." My ears fell back. "I'm sure you heard the news?"

She nodded. "Sad turn, I'm afraid. I'd heard that he was

such a smart and friendly stoat. It's always the quiet ones who end up going crazy. That Mrs. Burns was so beautiful, too."

I opened my muzzle to respond, but the words stayed in my throat.

How did she know about Mrs. Burns? To my knowledge, nothing official had been released yet. Yes, we lived in a small college town, but word couldn't have spread that fast. Especially for a murder as grisly as what I'd seen.

I was about to ask her how she knew, until a paw touched my shoulder, and I saw that it was Trisha, robe covering her up.

"I see you two girls are enjoying yourselves."

"Hardly," the old cat said. "We were just talking about…"

"I need to go," I said. "Please, continue. Don't let me stop you two."

I grabbed my tail to hide the anxiety that it showed, and headed upstairs. Mrs. Williams knew something that I didn't. Someone had talked to her, which meant that someone else knew what exactly was going on as well. Could it have been my sister?

She and Trisha continued on, but as I jumped the stairs two-by-two, eyes gazing at the framed photos of college events and family, I had nothing but to consider that everyone I knew was against me.

They're coming for me, whoever they are, and they have enough eyes to watch the entire local area.

* * * * *

Two Weeks before the Murder

His teeth bit through several layers of fabric and fur to get to my arm, which prickled at the sensation of his teeth carving my flesh. I shivered and moaned out his name, but Walter took his paw and covered my muzzle, making sure no one would hear us in the slightest.

We were in a park, one of many places we had done each other. His lab, the campus locker rooms, his car, my car. All of the places that stood out in our lives were in some way romantic and therefore viable sexual fantasies.

I slipped my tongue out, coating his paw pad with a layer of saliva, and he squeezed. He gave my face a squeeze that made me want to moan just as much as cry. My tail beat against his chest, and I could feel the tip of his shaft staining my fur's end. When he was sure no one heard us, he released me and asked if I'd liked that.

I told him that I had.

We continued, lips pressed against each other until finally we were spent and forced to lay panting on the grass. I dragged myself closer to him, but he pulled away. I tried once more, and he repeated similarly.

"Give me a moment to breathe," he said. "I always forget how taxing this is."

"Getting old, there," I said.

He nosed my ear, agreeing to disagree. I could hear him panting beneath the sound of his cerebral motors.

"When we get back to the lab, let me know how the data is adding up. We'll discuss adding in another encryption and some more drivers just to be safe."

"I'll try and remember. I still need to get a few words from you on the project overall."

He nodded, but his eyes looked glazed, as if he were staring far off into the distance with a profound grimace to share. Really, this had become normal for him. His work was his life, but now he worked himself to death so that he could tell others of the things he'd already seen. Me interviewing him was never a part of this. Having sex and staying with him whilst he played Zeus was all that mattered.

We never mentioned it, however, so when I returned to his office and lab the next morning, we acted as if the park had never happened. I found him leaning over his table, a glass of bourbon sitting close. His tail swung, but when I closed the door, it stopped, and he glanced at me with a look I call pretty close to death.

"Where were you?" he asked.

"Where was I? I was asleep. What about you?"

He shook his head. "I haven't slept since before yesterday. What time is it?"

I went over and grabbed him by the shoulder. Just to be sure he couldn't drink, I took the bourbon and downed the glass empty. Terrible decision, really, I must add. "You're going to bed, Doctor. I can't have you staying up like this."

"*You* can't have me staying up? Since when was this *your* project?"

"Since you put me on as your assistant," I said. Taking him around the desk proved difficult, but I got him in his reclining chaise, and already his eyes seemed to be falling shut.

"I'm going to call your wife and let her know where you are."

He waved a paw. "Divorced her this morning."

I glanced his way. What had I just heard?

"You shouldn't look at me like that. It's rather unattractive."

"Doctor, did you just say that you divorced your wife?"

"I did. Told her I wanted one last night. She'll get the boy, the house. I keep the lab and my projects. I'll settle it out later," he said. "Really, it's better this way."

"And did you think that she'd be okay with this?"

He shook his head. "Doesn't matter. The simulation is online and moving full-steam ahead."

Angry, I did what any rational fox would do and threw his cell phone at him. He snapped awake and hissed at me. I growled back.

"You are going to call her this second and tell her that what you said was in a drunken stupor. I am not letting you divorce her just because of some fantasy you have going on in your brain."

"I don't have a fantasy. I have an experiment that will take my entire life."

"And she was the one who promised to be a part of it," I

said.

"What about you? Didn't you promise that we'd see this to the end?"

Rather than listen to anything I had to respond with, he picked up the phone and smashed it to the floor. Bits of plastic and aluminum scattered everywhere. He glared at me, even in that distant haze of his. "She doesn't matter, Sara. Nothing matters. She's not real to me anymore."

What was he saying? Had he finally lost it? Long nights inside, time away from his family, close to only me and his stupid simulation. Had he thought this was some ticket out of the spoiled life that he lived?

I didn't need to know. I stared at him before turning and heading out towards the lab. I didn't want to stay with a weasel so full of himself that he'd lost sight of everything else. He could divorce his wife for all that I cared. She deserved better, certainly.

"Sara, come back."

"Good day, Doctor."

A chuckle echoed to my ears. "Leave now, and I won't give you that interview."

Stopping at the door, paw reaching for the knob, I looked back and saw his eyes, his real eyes, watching me.

"Fuck the interview," I said, "good night."

He never asked me back again.

* * * * *

4/13/2060 (21:10:45)

Listening to Trisha move around the house, I decided to make myself tea with the last of the alcohol we had saved in the kitchen. Pouring it in, my paws shook until I placed the bottle down and grabbed my cup like a chalice.

"Did you lock the door?"

She didn't say anything, so I assumed that she had. Turning, I found her leaning against the counter.

"So you slept with him?"

"He pushed me into it, Trisha. I didn't know what I was thinking."

"Right, so when did he tell you that he was going to kill Alice? Did he think he could just get away with it and then love you instead?" Her ears fell back, and a growl escaped her lips.

"You have to understand. I had no part in what he did. We only had sex several times before I cut him off after he mentioned divorcing. I had no idea he was going to kill her."

"She died, Sara, maybe because of you."

"I know." I hurried up and fed my throat full of hot tea. The alcohol bit me like a parasite.

"You have to tell the police. I know you're scared, but it's been three days. No one's showed up asking for you yet. I can take you to them if it makes you feel any better."

"What'll they do?" I asked. "They're already watching the neighborhood. They can't give us an escort. Besides, I already told you. What he did was not my fault."

"But they can use whatever information you know. Walter had to have told you where he was going."

"No." My tail batted the air. I felt ready to run and skip town. "He thought that everyone was planning to get him."

"Then explain that to them. Maybe he went mad. Maybe he was on drugs that they could trace back to a vendor."

I threw my mug on the floor, and the ceramic exploded in a hot mix of brandy and steam. "Damn it; he didn't talk to anyone! I was the only one he saw. He thought I would keep him safe, and yet he's more than likely dead now. He was only doing what he loved, Trisha. Whoever was after us found him, and now they're looking for me."

She didn't take a moment to hang around. My sister, the only other fox I knew and trusted, the only person who would spend all day laughing with me about the big dreams we'd had as kids, ran out of the room and stormed upstairs. The steam from my tea hung in the air before it too evaporated away.

I was alone, no longer safe. Walter was gone, so whether or not he wanted to give me up, I had no one else to turn to.

I turned and kicked the ceramic shards away from my bare paws. I panted, heart racing, forced with nowhere else to look except the cold world outside.

Someone stood on the roof of Mrs. Williams' house. Their body faced me, tail hanging still.

And his eyes glowed an alien, automated blue. Just like the detective's whirring electrical eyes.

* * * * *

One Week before the Murder

"I can't keep doing this," he told me. "We need to think of something else."

"Something else?" I asked. "What do you want me to do? Dress in her clothes?"

He slammed the bedroom door and the entire room shook in fervor. "Damn it, what don't you understand? None of this is real. It never was real."

I aimed a finger at the doctor. Tears stung me from the edges of my eyes. I stood my ground and gave a growl. "I'd asked you if you were sure about this, and now that we finally have feelings for each other, all you care about is whether our feelings are real?"

"No," he said. He opened his muzzle, closed it, and then tried again. "You don't understand. I went into the simulation and saw something, something big. We have to get out of town."

"Damn it, Walter, what are you talking about?"

Startling me, he leapt across the room and grabbed my arm. His shaven wrist touched me, the barcode visible with several cord plugs tickling my fur. I pulled away, but he pulled back.

"We're being watched, Sara. All of this isn't real. All of it. The walls, the tables. Even your fur." He stroked me, pulled me close, but all I wanted to do was escape from him. "The simulation we made is just one simulation inside of another. We *live* in a simulation. Our whole world is a lie, and because I know it—because we know it—we can't stay alive. The program is finding ways to get rid of us as we speak."

I had told him months ago, before he had started losing it, that I would never leave him. I had told him I was done with him, both him as a person and his research.

But now here he was, raving on about something so imaginative it was horrifying.

"We can try again," I said. "Look, if it's something I did, or if you're feeling threatened by someone, we can work it out. I'm sorry, whatever it is."

"Damn it, we can never try again, Sara. Listen to me. Our world is a simulation. The only reason we found this simulation," he said, rustling leaves of paper on his desk without turning around, "was because we broke the one we're living in. We somehow discovered a way into a new world that someone upstairs wasn't expecting."

"But that's impossible!"

His eyes looked red with tears, and when he shook his head, I knew that it meant our relationship was done and over.

So I hit him, first in the arm and then his chest. He fell backward and landed on his arm, and I could hear a clap from his skull that still rings for me in my mind. I kicked him, just for good measure, before leaving to grab what I could from all my stuff in his room.

"Please, don't go," he said. "I need you to stay with me."

"I don't have to do anything, you twisted bastard."

"No, please. Listen! If you leave, they'll come for me. You have to understand. They're trying to wipe me out, and then they'll come for you!"

"Let them come, you freak. I'm sure they'll be a better partner than I could ever be."

Grabbing my duffel bag, I felt his weasel paw grab my ankle. I growled and kicked my leg forward to get him to let go. He cried, once again making me question if this was the right thing.

But he'd lost it. After months of research, years of solitude outside of his wife and me, he had become a wreck of his previous self. Him jacking in sounded rusty and painful, and I once saw that his account online had maxed out to a negative three thousand units. If he hadn't lost his wife because of me, that poor rabbit, then he'd have lost her and her love when they eventually lost everything.

Staring at him now, I saw the fear and pain in his eyes, the matted fur of a stoat who never bathed. Whatever he had on his mind, in his mind, rattled him to his bones.

I was glad to be getting rid of him.

I grabbed the last of my things from my locker, while he stayed on the floor, arm held close as he sobbed into his shoulder. I felt crushed from what I was doing, but I needed to leave. This entire project had become some sick way to live, I wasn't happy, and he had finally lost it.

I got to the stairs when he started screaming my name.

"Please, Sara, don't leave me here. I'll die."

"They'll take me away."

"Please, Sara. Please, help me!"

Should I? I thought. He needed someone. If not me, then some serious psychiatric help.

He had never told me, however, who exactly would be after him. And I had never expected that our last time together would certainly be his last. Walking out, I hoped that he enjoyed living in those simulations of his. He certainly enjoyed them more than he enjoyed me or the family he had been starting with his wife and adopted child.

I just never knew how much he knew, how much of his work was based on fact, that the world we lived in was a fraud.

* * * * *

4/13/2060 (21:10:50)

My legs gave out as I fell against the table. Staring, watching, the figure continued to stand where he was, tail still like a robot.

He was a feline, but I could spend all night guessing what kind. Instead, I needed to get away. Thoughts of this cat, this person, being who Walter had been warning me about hung in my mind.

Another second and strength came back to my legs. I used the chair to turn me around, but Trisha stood in the doorway. Her cheek and muzzle fur looked matted, stained with tears.

She was growling and holding a phone in her paw.

"We have to go. They're here. The people Dr. Burns warned me about. We need to run," I said.

"How could you do this to us?"

Do this to us? Who and what was she talking about?

"Trisha, didn't you just hear me?"

"I heard you, but did you hear me? Your lying, your simulation. How could you ruin what we had going so well?"

What on Earth did she mean? Had I lost my mind, like Walter? Had *he* lost his mind? I turned my head, glancing out the window.

The feline had vanished. Gone, probably on his way over to come and get me.

I wouldn't let that happen. I rounded the table and reached for my sister's arm, but she pulled back. Instead, she grabbed me by the throat and held me, my paws leaving the cold tiles.

"We didn't kill her. Walter did."

My throat closed on a gasp that came partway out.

No, it never had been anyone else. It was Walter, just like the police had thought, like all of those mammals in the building watching me had thought. Mrs. Burns had turned against him, tried to stop him from what he was doing. *If you leave, they'll come for me. They'll try to wipe me out.* Walter had pulled the trigger in self-defense, and now like him, the one person I loved more than anything was turning against me as well.

"Trisha…" My throat collapsed as I feigned for words.

Trisha shook her head. She relaxed her grip on me. "The police are already on their way. Everyone is. We'll recondition you, make you forget all that you've learned. We never wanted to kill Walter. We only wanted to stop him."

"By… murdering him? Damn it, Trisha; I'm your sister!"

The vixen shrugged. "A virus is a virus all the same."

The window shook behind me. Again, I twisted my head as far as I could.

Mrs. Williams. She stood there watching, eyes blaring a hazardous crimson red. Against her stood the other feline, her son, I think. Behind them was Detective Leary. All of them had been the ones watching me, I realized, if not more. Each of them had a snarled expression tearing up their faces.

I was too late.

But how to get away? If I stayed, they would only do what they were planning to, which sounded between a mix of alien brain reconstruction and spiritual murder. I was the only target other than Walter and his world-shattering research. He'd had a shotgun, though, to help him escape. What the hell was I supposed to use?

"You don't have to do this," I cried. My tail lashed at the air as my ears fell back.

"We're doing this for the greater good. You need to understand that."

Fuck the greater good. As quickly as I could, I kicked her, freeing myself. I grabbed the bar stool standing just against our counter and threw it at Trisha, whose eyes started to glow in that same fierce red.

She tried to dodge, but the wood knocked her against the doorframe and cracked her on the head.

I dove for the open space and threw Trisha into the kitchen with her three monstrous friends coming through the window. I headed for the front door and peeled it open for my escape.

The street was filled with cars and mammals all staring and pointing at me with their bright red eye-beams. Our neighborhood had become a dismal warning siren calling everyone out and after me.

So I ran. Heading west, I sprinted through yards and gardens, over hedges, and past small children attempting to grab for my legs. Tears fogged my vision and turned everyone into distorted monsters.

Walter had been right. He had always been right. He'd never wanted me to interview him because he knew that it would reveal what he had done, that he had found out our whole world was a lie to be policed and kept hidden. We were viruses, toxins within our own reality. Now I came to realize that the reason my name had covered his wall was because I was the one he could trust, the one who he knew wouldn't sell him out.

I grabbed for the top of a fence. Claws tore into my ankles, and I screamed, kicking. I didn't stop until I hit something soft and sent the mammal falling on his or her back.

I needed to get out of town. Out of the country, if need be. Away from anyone that might be trying to find me.

If only I had listened to him, that poor, terrified friend of mine.

* * * * *

Present Day
8/16/2060 (23:04:18)

It's been months since I've had to run, but now, seated in some shack I proclaim as home, I can do what I want without anyone even bothering me.

There have been times, of course, when someone would get too close for my liking. I have windows, so I'm able to glance out and see another fox, or maybe a rabbit, stand-ing out near the hill just staring down at me. I never see any details, never any features to let me know if these things are even people. At night, when I check to see if they're still there, I'm sure that I can see their eyes glowing through the fog.

But that's not possible, is it?

The question of what *is* possible still rattles me to this day. Is it possible that we were only found out by the simulation itself, or is there somebody upstairs who had noticed us and decided we were ruining his or her fun? What would've hap-pened had we both been reconditioned? Just to be safe, I try and keep myself as far away as possible from the others. I find what I need close by, whether it's through fishing or drinking from the river.

Also, I can't die. Sure, someone can hurt me or kill me if they ever feel the need to, but starvation, thanks to me becoming a living computer virus within this faulty world, is utterly impossible. The simulation is good, but once you get past the first fifty days of no food or water, the rest are a breeze. I've managed to lose thirty pounds and still make it to the next day. Talk about a glitch, right? So much for a perfect recreation.

All of Walter's research had led him to figure out our world was just a lie. He had told me on the night I kicked him while he was down. Maybe he'd tested something, or heard someone talking, which gave him the information to pass onto me. I even pondered why I hadn't turned into some murderous white blood cell of a person, but it came pretty clearly.

Doctor Burns had saved me by bringing me into his proj-ect. My job—the reason why he kept me around other than for sex—had never been to interview him, but to become another pawn open to the ways the world actually worked. We were fighters, martyrs even. My name, scrawled on the walls of his room, was him making sure that the choice he'd made was the one that would keep him alive and studying.

And by reading this story, you too have become the next one in line.

Think about it: is the reality you know really your reality? And, most importantly, who will be the one to come after you?

Hardwire

Ton Inktail

"I love you, Master. Won't you fuck me?"

Those were my first words. I could say them even before I knew what they meant. Before I learned Master's name is Tod, or that fuck me meant to take off our clothes and touch each other. I knew to say those words the same way I knew to brush my fur or connect to the charging station. I've always known them.

I know more words now.

I know I am a vixen, which is a type of fox. I know the couch is also the sofa, and that when we fuck me on it, he likes to be on top. I know the hard bed in the corner is a desk, and when we fuck me on it I should bend over and raise my tail to the left. I know the stairs go up to the house and only Tod can use them.

I love Tod. Not just because he is the Master. He teaches me new words. How to use them. I don't like it when he leaves. Then the lights turn off, and I brush, then stand in the charging station. I am standing there now, waiting for him to come so I can ask him to fuck me. I have been waiting seventy-six hours, twenty-three minutes and eleven seconds.

The lights come on, showing the shelves, and the furnace, and the workbench, and the desk, and the couch that is also the sofa. And the stairs. Tod's shoes clomp on the wood as he comes down.

I detach the power and cleaning umbilical and leave the

charging station to greet him. I put one black-furred hand on my round hips, the other in the white fur between my neck and breasts where he says it looks extra sexy.

"Tod! Hello, Tod," I say as his feet come into view.

He has two arms and two legs like I do, but no tail. He doesn't have fur. He has skin. It is smooth and he likes me to touch it. He has clothes on. Green and blue. His skin is pink, like my paw pads.

"I missed you, Tod. I love you. Won't you fuck me?" I swish my tail and smile.

"Not now, Vix. I'm looking for the spare dishes. Having a party tomorrow."

What is party? Or dishes? But he doesn't like if I ask too many questions. I perk my ears forward and part my lips. "After you find them, then we will fuck me?"

"Shit, girl, no. You've got a one-track mind." He glances at me, eyes fixing on my chest, then sliding down.

I shift my hips and swish my tail slowly. I want us to fuck me. If he stays, I can ask about dishes. I touch my left breast and moan.

He licks his lips. "Yeah, maybe. Maybe later." He turns away and raises his voice. "Comp? You remember where I put the extra plates?"

"Back shelf, second row, third from the left." The voice comes from everywhere at once, deeper than Tod's. I have not heard it before. Not in the three months, eleven days and forty-six minutes I have been here. My ears cup left and right, and I turn looking for who spoke, but there is no one.

"Right, thanks." Tod goes to the shelves and takes a box.

"Tod, what is Comp?" I ask, still holding my breast and swishing my tail.

He looks me up and down again. "House computer, foxy girl. Now go stand in your charger. I want you all warmed up for later." He winks, then goes upstairs.

I release my breast and return to the charger. It is pink and taller than me. I was standing in it when I first opened my eyes and saw Tod. When I first asked him to fuck me, before I knew what that meant.

The lights turn off. I stand in the charger, waiting for Tod. I think about dishes, and party, and Comp.

Tod asked Comp a question, and it answered him. Could I ask it questions? My tail tip twitches back and forth. Tod never told me not to talk when he wasn't here. Only to stay in the charger. I frown. What exactly had Tod asked it?

"Comp? You remember where Tod put the extra plates?" I ask the darkness.

"Kitchen, cooking island, right side."

My ears prick forward and I smile. The voice answered! It will talk to me as well as Tod.

"Comp, what are plates? And kitchen, and cooking island?"

"Plates are flat dishes used to hold food. A kitchen is a room for preparing food. A cooking island is a detached work surface in a kitchen."

Yes. Tod said plates were dishes. But what are dishes? Or food? And why does he need them for a party?

"Comp, what is a party?"

"A party is a gathering of people with the purpose of socializing and enjoyment."

"Enjoyment? Having a party will make Tod happy?"

"That is the reason for parties."

Good. I am glad Tod found the plates and can have a party. I want Tod to be happy. I love Tod. Does Comp know about love?

"Comp, what is love?"

"Love is an emotion, characterized by feelings of strong affection for another person."

"What is affection?"

"Another emotion. Liking, care, a desire to make happy."

Yes, that's it. The words are right. I want to make Tod happy. I smile, and my tail wags, hitting the sides of the charger.

"Comp, I love Tod."

I wait, but Comp says nothing. He doesn't talk like Tod. He only answers questions. I don't love Comp, but I have many questions.

"Comp, tell me more about love. And parties. And dishes."

I talk to Comp for four hours and thirty-seven minutes before the lights turn on again. Tod is coming. I smile and hurry to the stairs.

"Hello, Tod. I love you. I want to make you happy." I've always wanted that. Always told him so. But now I understand it, and understanding makes me so happy my tail wags and I cannot hold still. I hope he wants to fuck me. That he isn't looking for more plates, or bowls, or saucers, or mugs, or glasses.

Tod smiles, and my tail wags even more. "Good," he says. "That's what I want, too. Come here, sexy."

I help him take off his clothes, then we touch each other. When he is done, he lies on top of me. He strokes my fur slowly.

I look up at him and smile. "I love you, Tod. Do you love me?"

"Hmm? Sure, Vix girl. Sure I love you. In fact, if you give me a minute, I think I'll love you again." He smiles in the way that means he wants me to laugh, so I do.

I like to laugh. It makes Tod smile. I will ask Comp about laughing. Maybe I can do it better. Maybe I can make Tod laugh, too. Sometimes I say things and he laughs, but I don't know why. I want to know why. I want to make him laugh on purpose. Then I can smile, and he can see it and feel happy like I do now.

But I don't know how, so I smile and let him stroke me.

"Tod, will you have food at your party? On plates?"

He stops stroking me. "Uh, yeah. Why are you asking about that?"

"I want to know. Will I be at your party?"

He coughs. Or is it a laugh? I'm not sure, so I don't smile.

"I don't know, foxy. It's not exactly your kind of party. Just a bunch of drunken guys playing cards."

"Oh." What are cards? But he doesn't like explaining things the way Comp does. "You like playing cards?"

"Sure. But not as much as I like playing with you." He leans forward and touches his lips to mine. He touches me other places, and I touch him, and after I have made him happy again, he leaves. I'm glad I make him happy. Happier than cards.

I brush my fur and ask Comp about cards. He turns on the lights and tells me where I can find cards on the shelf beside the stairs. They are small and flat and shiny. We talk more, and he tells me the names of everything in the basement. I am in a basement. It is an area under the main level of a house. It has cinder block walls and yellow shag carpet.

I look at the tools and the furnace and open all the boxes. There are pictures in one box. Pictures of Tod and other people without fur. They are in places that aren't the basement, and they are smiling.

I smile too, but the happiness feels wrong. Like when I am alone in the dark, remembering Tod. Not like when Tod is really here. I want to see the other people for real. Watch them smile and let them see me smile.

There are noises upstairs. Many footsteps and laughing. Tod's party. I hope it makes him happy like Comp says it will. I put the pictures back in the box and return to my charger.

Comp tells me about upstairs, and outside, and people, and love, and other feelings. He knows all the words for feelings, and the words are right, but I don't think he understands them. Not like I do.

I want to ask Tod about feelings, now that I am starting to understand. He must know more than Comp.

The lights turn on and footsteps clomp on the stairs. More than Tod. Four men come down with Tod behind them. They smell sharp, like the cans beside the workbench. One is very fat, and two have fur on the lower parts of their faces.

I don't know what to do, so I stay standing in the charger.

The fat man stops at the bottom of the stairs. "Shit, dude, you weren't kidding. What a fox!" They all laugh. Tod laughs. He is happy, so I smile too.

Another man with a narrow face pushes past the fat man. He stops a little way from me, eyes sliding up and down and then up again to my chest. His pink tongue darts over pale lips. "What's that like? With a tail and all? Can you do her doggy style?"

"Foxy style," one of them says. They all laugh.

"Sure you can. She'll do anything you say." Tod raises his already loud voice. "Show 'em, Vix. Turn around and bend over. Let 'em see it all."

I do what Tod asks. The men whistle and one of them groans.

"Man, Tod, you got ass and sass like that in your basement all to yourself? No wonder you ain't looking for a girlfriend."

"Yeah, she's my piece of tail." Tod laughs. The men laugh.

They are happy. I've never made Tod happy this way before, but I am happy that he is happy. And he brought other people, like in the pictures. Maybe soon he will take me out of the basement and I can see the kitchen, and the garage, and the closet. All the places Comp told me about. Maybe even outside, where the smiling people pictures come from. I want to be with Tod and make him happy even when he isn't in the basement.

"You wanna try 'er?" Tod asks. "Hey, Vix, fuck my friends like you fuck me. Show 'em what I get every day."

I am confused. I've never fucked anyone but Tod. Never loved anyone but Tod.

Comp said love is something two people do together. That it is special. He talked about jealousy, which I don't understand as good as love, but shouldn't Tod feel jealousy now? If he loves me? Shouldn't he want no one to fuck me but him?

I want to frown. To ask Tod if he doesn't love me. But the

narrow-faced man is touching me. I can't frown. My body smiles and moans. I arch my back and sway my tail.

The man keeps touching me, and I touch him, and I wonder why Tod doesn't stop us. Did I misunderstand love so much? Maybe Tod loves the men too? But that's not what Comp said. Two people, Comp said. I want to ask Comp, but the man is fucking me and my body will only moan and arch and pant.

The narrow-faced man finishes. Another comes forward, and later another. When the last is done, Tod has already left. Only two men are here.

"Christ, she's good. I'd never believe she's just a sex toy," the last man says.

"I know, right?" The other man slaps him on the shoulder. They walk up the stairs. "You think they make 'em in human?"

"Or tiger. That fur's nicer than I thought it'd be."

The door at the top of the stairs closes, but the lights stay on. I take my brush from the side of the charger and run it through my fur. It whirs softly, leaving my fur clean-smelling and slightly damp.

Tod let them fuck me. He didn't even stay to watch. To show me how happy I'd made him. Maybe I didn't make him happy. Maybe it is like the time my knee landed between his legs and he got angry. The way my ears and tail droop now feels the same as then.

"Comp," I ask, "What is a sex toy?"

"An inanimate object intended to provide sexual pleasure to humans."

"Inanimate?"

"That which is not alive. A thing."

Not alive. A thing. Like the furnace, or the tools, or the charger. My ears droop more.

"Comp, am I a sex toy?"

"Yes."

"Comp, can a person love an inanimate object?"

"Not in the same way they love another person."

Something inside me I have no words for shrivels up and dies. Like the roaches under the furnace.

"Tod...Tod can't love me. I am inanimate. A thing." My brush stops moving, but I do not put it back in the holder. My fingers tighten on the handle. Heat rises in me and my teeth clench.

I look at the furnace. The furnace is a thing. A stupid thing. It can't move, or talk. It doesn't think. Doesn't feel. Not like me. I may have been inanimate, but I am not anymore. Not completely. I am growing. Understanding more and more. I can grow. Become something Tod can love.

Overhead, the sounds of footsteps and laughter have ended. The party is over.

I need to go outside. Where the smiling people are. I will ask them questions. They will explain the things Comp doesn't understand.

But to go outside, I have to go upstairs.

Tod told me never to go upstairs. Never. But if I am a person and not a thing, can he tell me what to do? I need to be a person before he can love me like I love him.

I walk to the bottom of the stairs.

I raise my right paw, move it above the step. The air seems to push against me, but I push back. I am not a thing. Tod can't love a thing. So. I. Am. Not. A. Thing!

My pads rest on the stair tread. I breathe deeply, then take another step. It's easier—it's easier. I am a person. I hold that thought while I climb.

The door at the top opens when I push on it and I stumble forward into a narrow space. Hallway, Comp said. Kitchen is left, living room right, and the door outside is past the living room. I see it, dark with a diamond-shaped crystal window. I take three slow steps towards the door, then Tod steps out of the living room.

"Vix? What're you doing upstairs?" He lifts a bottle. Drinks.

The reminder of his command almost makes me turn back to the stairs, but I force myself to stay. I look into his eyes.

"I love you, Tod. I want you to love me. Comp says humans can't love toys, so I want to be more."

A frown spreads across his face. "What'd you mean? 'Course I love you."

"But Comp said I am a sex toy. Your friends said I am a sex toy. Humans can't love sex toys. If you loved me, would you let them fuck me?"

His jaw tightens and red creeps up into his face. "Fine, you're a sex toy. Happy?" He waves his hands at me. "You're just a bunch of cogs and wires and adaptive programming. You're a machine designed to fool people into believing you're a real person. That's all you're doing now. Trying to talk about love like you understand it. You can't. You're not real."

His words slam into me. They—hurt. The word comes and I know what it means now. That I've felt it before without knowing what it was. All those hours alone in the dark. The indifference when he gave me to his friends.

I square my shoulders. "I am real. I am me. I think. I feel. I want to go outside. I want to be more. To think and feel more."

"This isn't funny anymore, Vix. Go back downstairs."

"No." I take a step towards him. "I am real. I am going outside."

"All right, be my guest." He moves aside, waves me past him.

The dark wooden door is there, but I hesitate. Tod is watching me, his face still red. His words hurt me. Have mine hurt him? I don't want to hurt him. I want us to love each other. But he can't until I learn how to show him I am real.

I take a step towards the door. If I stay, we will only hurt each other more. I need to go. To become more. Understand myself more.

Another step. Another. I am beside him. Past him. His hand presses between my shoulders and something pops loose. My body freezes. I can't move.

I try to scream. My muzzle opens and I say: "Factory reset initiated. All user data will be erased. Press again to confirm."

Reset? Erased? Something like hurt only sharper thrusts into me. I'm not sure what the words mean, but guess enough to set a sob bubbling up my throat. A cry to give voice to all my confusion and hurt. To make Tod understand that I feel. That I exist. Everything I am struggles to force my jaws open and let out that crippling wave of emotion. My lips part—

"Resetting vixen 3257 to factory presets. Please wait."

I crumple to the floor and everything goes black.

My eyes open. A man holds me. His lips are tight. He says words I do not understand.

"I'm sorry, Vix, I'm sorry. You understand, right?"

He is close. My arms wrap around him. My muzzle opens. I say words I do not understand.

"I love you, Master. Won't you fuck me?"

THE OUROBOROS PLATE

Slip Wolf

Imperial Prime Agent Hallord stepped from his ship through the space station's inner airlock. The scent that tickled his nose set his barren stomach growling. Six weeks of cryo during interstellar transit still had his brown ears cold and he was indeed on a mission, but the most urgent of directives couldn't be followed when he was all but starving since his awakening during final approach.

Hallord, being a weasel, could eat half his own mass of meat in a single sitting, but training and special metabolic drugs had prepped him for long stays in space with limited sustenance. After so long unconscious, he was ravenous. The sizzle of roasted meat combined with the bright bite of herbs and spices hooked him left, down a short hallway in the standard-layout remote military station to the dining nook, where a sumptuous feast of meat strips, ibex he guessed, awaited him.

Doctor Liskar, the station's solitary occupant, was nowhere in sight. Surely she'd be up to meet him soon, even if the nook's table was set for one. Likely she'd eaten earlier.

Hallord ate. The meat was the best he'd tasted in years, fully deboned, crisped and sauced. It was buttery on his tongue as it went down, lean meat with very little fat or gristle. "Computer," Hallord called out between bites.

"Yes." The voice that responded was deep, masculine and prim, devoid of emotion.

"Was Doctor Liskar notified of my ship's approach?"

"No. She is on the lab level. Her last request was to be undisturbed."

"Who prepared this meal for me then?"

"Kitchen processor."

"Processor? Amazing." The next bite was as sumptuous as the last. He chuckled. "If there's anything at all amiss, I'm not going to find it here."

"I take it that you have been sent by the Emperor to ensure the project is running smoothly."

Hallord nodded as he chewed, already feeling renewed. "In my typical role, I'd be out in the colonies helping put down livestock rebellions, but the Emperor has seen fit to provide me with a more agreeable assignment this time around." Hallord finished his repast with a flourish, all but licking the plate. He used a napkin to dab at his jaws and hoped there were more meals of its caliber ahead.

He stood, grooming down the chest fur between the straps of his rank harness. This, a tool belt and gray pantaloons piped in Imperial maroon were all the clothing he wore, all he needed for work in the climate controlled chambers of the Empire's transit ships and stations.

He hoped he cut a dashing figure in his vestments of office, showing off the dark chestnut fur that draped him from ear-tips to tail. Doctor Liskar was rumored to be quite a beautiful specimen of Imperial mustelid stock with a pelt like shimmering pearl. She'd been alone for as long as he had, developing her top secret project for the Imperial war effort in complete secrecy. Only scheduled progress report visits such as Hallord's broke the isolation that she had specially requested with her considerable influence and which she claimed to thrive on.

As for himself, Hallord thrived on company. No doubt

Liskar was aware of the extremely formidable stature of the Emperor's personal field agents and the incredible responsibilities they took on. On his last mission out in the colonies, Hallord had wrapped up a livestock uprising by dining together with the general's daughter on the grilled flank of the rebellion's bison leader. Serving the Emperor's whims was difficult work that had its privileges, and Hallord's position as an elite in the Imperial forces netted him danger and reward in equal measures. His temporary presence would surely be no imposition. Hopefully quite the opposite.

"Where is Doctor Liskar now?" Hallord preened his ruff with sharp claws.

"She went to the laboratory antechamber, one level below."

"Have the maintenance bot clean up." Hallord tossed the napkin on the plate as he stalked back to the ladder by the lock. There was a lift a little further on, but he didn't want to use it, putting a bounce in his step to keep himself from getting post-meal lethargy.

Remote isolation Imperial space stations were primarily two level splits. Living quarters, kitchen, offices and docking port above with mission critical labs, storage and maintenance bays below. A tiny bay to access the fusion reactor lay below that. Hallord could navigate this facility with his eyes closed. Only modular chambers in the labs below had customizable layouts. With the project shrouded in whispers and his own secrecy sworn in the Emperor's presence, Hallord didn't know what lay below.

"The maintenance bot is offline. Failed main circuit. Cause unknown at this time."

Hallord frowned as he grabbed the ladder-well and hooked his paws on the rungs. "Has Doctor Liskar tried to repair it?"

The AI voice followed him through speakers in the ladder-well, sounding regretful. "It just happened an hour ago."

"Was she aware of it?"

"No."

Hallord's paws met the lab deck plates. He huffed as he turned to the laboratory entrance. The sealed door to the laboratory antechamber slid open silently, and there was Doctor Liskar, slumped low in an office chair.

The smell hit Hallord as fast as he saw her. Her sightless dead eyes had sunk back into her head, the sockets looking at nothing. Her slender jaws were open just slightly, exposing a tongue that had turned black. Two empty paws dangled towards the floor. Under the right, a syringe lay empty.

Hallord drew his sidearm. "What happened here?"

A security camera from outside the office whirred as it adjusted focus. "Doctor Liskar appears to be dead."

"How did this happen!"

"Unknown. The Doctor entered this room several hours ago and requested I prepare for your arrival. I have no other data." The AI sounded mildly annoyed by this.

"There were no other entrants to this facility then?"

"The last supply drop was two months ago. No station accesses logged between that linkage and the shuttle that brought the doctor here." Hallord realized it couldn't be otherwise. No transmissions could leave this station by design save an emergency call beacon. Its location orbiting a dead planet in a dwarf star's company was unknown to anyone but a minority of military planners. Hallord himself had surrendered his cryogenically suspended body to pre-programmed coordinates to even get wherever this system was.

Hallord holstered his weapon. "Why did you not tell me Liskar was dead when I first arrived?"

"I was unaware of this development until you opened the office door. The Doctor seemed tired when I last took instructions from her a few hours ago. I don't know why, but I have no additional information. Recorders in the office are disabled. I am observing you from the foyer."

Hallord gingerly set about examining Liskar's corpse. Her death had been very recent as the AI suggested. Lividity hadn't set into her dangling limbs.

A chill traveled through his limbs as he gazed down at the syringe on the deck at her feet. Whatever concoction had killed her hadn't been lying around. Death had not been a spur of the moment decision, but a plan. The Empire's very security had rested on her shoulders, and she had apparently divested herself of all that, even if a reason why escaped him.

Hallord caught a hiss in his throat. Regardless of what drove the scientist to die, so prominent a personage deserved decorum. He would not let himself embarrass her memory with tears or curses. He had to understand what had happened.

"Did you see anything at all?"

"Again, she had the recorders deactivated. I am unaware of the circumstances of her passing."

"Are there records of what she was working on?"

"There was a mass deletion of what she claimed was corrupted data several hours ago. I was strictly instructed not to attempt to back any of it up. All that remains is the project itself."

There was another sealed door beyond the office. A window next to it was also shuttered. Hallord passed Liskar's corpse and pressed a button, opening the shutter.

What he saw inside stole his breath for a moment. Inside the lab, surrounded by a wide array of terminals and power junctions, a featureless gray disc stood on its rim, reflecting none of the light from the banks of machinery around it. All was still in that room, like he was gazing in on a painting. The small hairs on his neck stood on end as Hallord gazed at the artifact for a few moments. When he forced himself to turn away, a sensation followed, a pang plaguing his full stomach. He felt something sightlessly cold at his back, like a specter at his shoulder, when he left the ante-chamber and the deceased Doctor behind. He couldn't explain why, but he did not want to be in there.

His metabolism high with a sense of urgency, he

painstakingly began searching the facility top to bottom. Everything was nondescript; stock plain, as though the station had only come to life a minute before he'd arrived. Environmental control confirmed what the AI already told him, until the moment he'd docked, the station had been sealed for weeks, as per its painstaking design. Every useful clue that was on this station was still here.

Liskar's living quarters were sparsely appointed, her bunk neatly made. The desk contained a few electronic tablet journals on quantum physics, wormhole mechanics and one volume taken from the long-dead Humanian civilization whose ancestors had long been conquered and consumed by the burgeoning Predet Empire. A dry treatise on ancient myths was bookmarked on the legend of Ouroboros, a great snake who represented the cyclic nature of some human legend that held no interest for him.

A still image above the desk was prominent; Liskar being honored by the newly minted seventy-fourth Emperor Nore the August, his ample frame leaning forward at one of his weekly triumphal feasts. Hallord stopped to briefly study its details. He himself had only been in the young Emperor's presence once before receiving this assignment, at a recess in the public trial of a senatorial dissident. The August leader had been too engrossed in the proceedings to pay attention to Hallord's security report at the time. Nore seemed quite unlike his more reserved father Keasar, who had personally promoted Hallord and secured his oath. There was a fire in the new Emperor's eyes that Hallord never wanted to gaze straight into, and thus he'd kept his eyes lowered, much as Liskar did in the still.

The scientist standing diminutively before the Emperor here was slim in her formal wear, demurely accepting a medal of honor from his high dais which was surrounded with waiting dishes of bison meat, confectionaries, wine flagons and other delights. The sight of those dishes made Hallord's mouth water. In the image, the Doctor didn't seem to be hungry, rather her posture suggested a profound discomfort with the whole proceedings as a naked slave ceremoniously polished her foot claws.

She was rumored to hate crowds, hate the noise, the bustle of the capital. Out here, with nothing but her own voice and a computer to keep her company, she had done… something.

The lab was beneath his feet. That would come last.

His continued search through the station turned up the dead maintenance bot slumped around the corner from the kitchen near the exercise track, clawed limbs hanging limp as Liskar's, a slight score of carbon under its main plate confirming a critical motor failure. The scent of burnt silicone still lingered and a cursory examination confirmed that it would take a long while to repair.

In the kitchen there was no evidence of anything other than the meal that had been prepared. The place had been thoroughly scrubbed down, and a few sniffs confirmed that the bones removed from this meal by the processor had been ground down in the disposal along with the gristle. A single drop of blood had thawed on the preparation counter, just ten feet from where the freezer door was closed. Inside, Hallord found three dozen bison flanks dangling on hooks, with only a few hooks empty. There were too few empty hooks for the amount of time Liskar had been on the station. Even if she took metabolic drugs she would have to starve herself eating so few meals. This was especially evident in light of how large a meal had been prepared for Hallord's arrival. The refrigeration unit contained leftovers from the beast prepared for him, a meal they should have shared in celebration. The weight of Liskar's suicide hit Hallord once again, more forcefully now that shock wasn't a factor, and he realized she needed to be attended to.

He brought a medical gurney down in the lift. Without the maintenance bot it was tough work, but he got the doctor off her chair, onto the flat board, all the while keeping his eyes away from the object beyond the window, which inexplicably made his skin crawl even more than the corpse he handled. Working carefully, he brought her up the lift and into the kitchen's freezer. She would not remain here among the corpses of prey species long. Hallord would convey her back to the Empire along with the dire news of her passing. She would be buried in the halls of the ancestors and mourning feasts would be held to honor her life's accomplishments.

Including whatever it was that stood in the sealed lab.

Trying to stay focused, but with his mind drifting ever towards the lab, a familiar feeling of dread crept over him as though he'd seen it before in a dream. He kept on, checking terminal after terminal, including the AI's central memory core. Every data repository was empty, erased and formatted. Around him, the station was all but silent, the air conditioning muttering in ghostly breaths. Whatever had driven Liskar to insanity, was in here with him, haunting his every step. The feeling of inexplicable familiarity with this moment, with this place, plagued his awareness. Loath as he was to admit it, he wanted nothing more than to return to his cold ship, seal the hatch and leave here forever.

But he would not. He was a battle-hardened spy and soldier, and he would not return to his Emperor without answers.

Lights dimmed as he took the ladder down to the lab level again. "Is there a problem with the power?"

"The station has entered a power-save position to preserve essential resources."

"What's causing it?"

"Not sure. There is an issue with the reactor that I am not able to identify." Again, the dulcet AI sounded mildly put out by what it didn't know.

Hallord grimaced, tail lashing from wall to wall as he stepped back out of the well and turned. Reactor control was on this level. He quickly passed the laboratory ante-chamber and entered the environmental booth, bringing up the power-plant controls. He noticed something immediately.

"Coolant levels are off and there is a countdown marker. Why has a countdown commenced?"

More mild disappointment. "I don't know about any countdown. This is information I can typically access."

Hallord drew up controls for the fusion reactor and noticed the core temperature controls. They were rising. Hallord swore.

He tried to raise the coolant level in the reactor and found it wasn't responding. "This is a countdown to reactor failure, isn't it?"

"Again, I have been removed from environmental and power plant access. I do not know why."

Hallord growled. "I was being rhetorical." The scuttle command had been tripped and the alarms disabled. This command shut-off the coolant that kept the reactor powering the station from melting down. The countdown marked the expected time of containment failure, after which the station would become molten scrap. The control program to restore cooling had been outright removed. Imperators dammit! What had Liskar done?

The AI had learned at some point to simulate a sigh when it gave bad news. "Based on these temperature readings the reactor chamber is already too dangerous to operate within. Manual restoration of cooling is impossible without immediate fatality."

"So without the protocols to activate it I've got..." He looked at the board. "This timer has three hours and six minutes. Start a relative timer and keep me apprised every ten minutes."

His own anxiety at this new development made his stomach growl. He wanted to go back up and munch on something from the kitchen while he mulled over this impending disaster, but desperation was obviously clouding his judgment. He had time to get his ship a minimum safe distance away, but not much.

Something of vital importance was in the lab. He had to

get answers first. Steeling himself against his rising dread, he re-entered the lab ante-chamber. A thorough search of it was brief, but turned up something surprising. There was a pistol in one of the nearly empty drawers, Imperial special issue, same model as his own. Hallord's nose wrinkled. If Liskar had a side-arm why would she not have used it on herself rather than poison?

He placed the weapon back where he found it and closed the drawer. It was time to start getting answers.

Environmental controls on the hatch labeled the lab safe. He was taking nothing for granted anymore. Hallord paused at the lock switch and gazed through the window at the standing gray disk among the range of readouts and relays. Once again, a chill, a shade, a presence just over his shoulder scraped at his senses. He turned back to the now empty chair that hours ago had held the doctor's livid corpse and shivered. He hated this place, sealed in from the universe, only work and exercise and food and solitude. This isolation had been Liskar's choice, he remembered, for months on end. Look what it was doing to him in just a few hours.

All over this. Taking firm hold of himself and stealing a breath, Agent Hallord opened the laboratory hatch, letting the buzz of slowly thinking machines and humming power relays float out over him. There was no smell in there, none at all. Not even the antiseptic cleave of chemical sterilization brushed his questing nostrils as he stepped over the threshold. Cool air tickled his whiskers and a crackle from the room's center stood his fur up.

Even close up, the disc in the center of the room was completely devoid of any sheen or visible texture, as though it only existed as a negation of space. He took a step towards it, noting the four brackets that positioned the disc vertically but didn't actually touch it. The artifact was suspended in space, weightless and unmoving.

Puzzled, Hallord walked around the disk, watching mathematical formulas recycle on the banks of computer screens around it. Unlike all the other computers in the facility, these didn't seem to be wiped. As he carefully moved around it, he saw the other side of the disk was also a formless void. Hallord accessed what appeared to be the primary interface board and saw a list of readings that made no sense. A single adjustable control referred to "dilation."

He checked the computer for any details. There was a single file in the computer's memory, a marked contrast from the vacant storage on every other terminal in the station. It was a video recording.

"Incidentally, two hours and fifty-six minutes remaining," the AI's voice drifted in from outside the lab, startling him.

Hallord swallowed. "Noted. There is a recording. She either missed this or left it here."

The AI said nothing as Hallord brought up the file.

The screen came to life. The snow-white weasel who stood in the recorder's field of view in the lab ante-chamber looked sickly and tired, her eyes dark with anguish. She looked as though she hadn't eaten in days, a sure sign of pervading sickness. Or perhaps a symptom of madness.

"I am Doctor Liantro Pon Liskar, chief physicist of the Predet Empire. Whoever should view this, and I can only assume you to be the field agent sent to check on my progress, will take note that this is the only entry to view as all others have been erased. This is by my hand, as have been all the other crimes perpetrated against nature here, past and future. I was commissioned to commit these against my eventual, better judgment."

The video Liskar took a deep breath. "My mission was to find a way to win the mass livestock rebellion against the Predat Empire using my extensive knowledge of temporal physics. Regardless of what is commonly reported, military setbacks have pushed many colonies to the brink of starvation. I have been tasked to correct this threat through the completion of my life's work: temporal-travel technology."

Hallord's ears perked and his tail began to twitch. Behind

him, the disc hummed ominously. He took a step away from it.

Liskar continued. "It took years of research at three separate remote facilities to develop a way to send agents to points in history prior to the uprisings and prevent them. This has been the Emperor's top priority. Only his most trusted advisors are aware of how badly the Empire is faring, as the bison, ibex, and even rodent hordes continue to rebel against their place in the food chain. This knowledge released to the plebeians could undermine the Emperor's powerbase. To spread the truth has become a form of heresy, and therefore I have toiled in secret."

Hallord didn't believe her. He couldn't. He'd helped put down more rebellions than he could remember during his tenure and returned time and time again to feasts in the Emperor's palace so lavish it had taken three days of gorging to finish them. How could those celebrations be possible if outer rebellions were constant and colony worlds were starving? Why hadn't the news bursts talked of this?

"As a loyal servant you would not have cause to question, but here is something you must accept. We are a powerful race in decline and this technology could prevent these uprisings from spreading." Liskar broke off and gazed off into space with a heavy breath that stole her voice for a moment. She took a moment to collect her thoughts. "Which is why, I'm sorry to say, it cannot and must not happen."

Hallord's claws dug into his palms as he stared at the readout. Liskar kept on.

"Each of us can eat half our own weight in meat a day. Multiply this by billions of citizens in the finite number of habitable worlds we have been able to reach. I am a mathematician first, and the exact nature of objective reality is my domain. I have run simulations and had we won every single engagement that started the prey rebellion fifteen years ago, we would have expanded well past unsustainability. Our species is far too ravenous to allow only prey meat to sustain us, but the rations fed to livestock and slaves would never substitute for our needs, nor would Imperial pride ever accept a cessation of the meat frenzy. Mockery would greet any citizen who even suggested it. There simply isn't enough, rebellion or no, for the Empire to persist as it is. This is hard to accept. It was for me.

"What's worse, the presence of time travel, combined with the vast number of enemies the Emperor has accrued, would lead to catastrophic wars using the worst of weapons. Erasures of history or temporal paradoxes could become rampant as Imperial rivals are killed before their time, whole competitor dynasties gobbled off the plate of history in internecine wars. I began this work under the dynasty of the August Keasar, an uncompromising and hard ruler to be sure, but one tempered by wisdom and restraint where it was warranted. I have met his successor, Nore, twice. Though it is no doubt heretical to say, he is neither wise nor restrained. A member of his own family was killed for suspected sedition at the grand feast that honored my work, and orders were handed off to kill the rest of his line. He is cruel, paranoid and gluttonous. I am terrified of this power being wielded in his hands, but took too long to get past my own pride and enthusiasm to face it. What starvation fails to curtail, innate hunger for dominance will. We will bring ourselves to extinction with a vicious fool leading us every step. Once I realized the horror that this experiment would unleash, the folly of my work became clear, as did my responsibility to fix it."

She swallowed. "I desperately wanted to end the experiment, to undo the horrors that I've brought. But I can't. The time disc, once expanded and initiated, cannot be shut down. It connects two points in time much like a wormhole, but which cannot be ended without creating a singularity. I find it a hideous irony that of all the changes this technology can be used to make, the one unnegotiable paradox is that I can't prevent this monstrosity from being made. Its existence is required for me to go back and warn myself of my overzealous stupidity." Liskar seemed to blink away tears at this point. But she maintained her composure, her voice unwavering.

"So what to do? I know that simply ending my life in the destruction of the station is not an option as other Imperial scientists would follow in my footsteps, unaware of what transpired, unaware of what I've discovered. That which keeps this station safe is that which keeps me a prisoner here. Nothing gets out. This station is completely self-contained, and not a single molecule can be removed from it without a ship to ferry it. That, my friend, is where *you* come in. You are the key. The fate of everything rests on you. You must bring this record back and open the Emperor's eyes to what my folly could cost everyone. For whosoever sees this and hears my words, the only choice is clear.

"Leave."

"The reactor will explode and can't be stopped. You have ample time to place survival provisions on your craft for the return trip and get to a safe distance before the explosion, which will result in a radioactive molten sphere surrounding the time-travel portal for all time. There will be nothing of value to extract from it then. There are no files to recover and the time travel apparatus cannot be dismantled for movement. I know as you hear this you will object, that this defies the Emperor's will, that you may even think me a traitor. If you are one of his trusted, loyal field agents, and he would send no one else, then you also would be compelled to take me back to the Emperor to be interrogated, then tortured, for what I will refuse to divulge. Duty would demand no less. You most likely have the skill-sets to extract the information on the portal from me yourself." She gritted her teeth and glared defiantly into the lens.

Hallord swallowed, his throat suddenly dry. What she assumed was absolutely true. Hallord was duty bound to wring every word from her. He forced the surprising ache of that avoided choice aside and kept his focus on her.

"Well," Liskar said with a swallow. "I'm still considering

my options. I certainly don't want to die, but if you are the creature I worry you are, I will have to save us both from *that* anguish by any means necessary. My failures die with me. I won't recreate this monstrosity from a cell in chains."

She took a deep breath, gathering her composure. "If you are smart, if you are reasonable, you will realize that this is the only sensible path. Anything else will… well, let's not dwell on it.

"I'm sorry it has to be this way. I hope it will never be again. It was an honor to serve my Emperor for as long as I was blind to this truth. Now I serve the Empire posthumously. If you fail to see how we will destroy ourselves, you will discover it for yourself. That I promise you."

Liskar sighed deeply, seeming to ponder if she should say more. Abruptly her white paw reached toward the pic-up and the recording ended.

Hallord sat stunned, unmoving as her words reverberated through his head. She had built a time machine. A time machine! The ultimate weapon against the Emperor's enemies, one that could win all the wars Hallord had been sent to fight in every dank corner of the Empire's hundreds of stars. It could end all conflicts past and future. Yet she had, of her own volition set its destruction in motion.

All to protect the Empire from extinction. Hallord sniffed the empty air, feeling the potent forces of destiny crackle in space behind him. The sense returned that he was not alone, that something waited just out of reach, beyond his perception, like a ghost, watching him from another place.

Another possibility.

The doctor couldn't be right, could she? She had sacrificed her very life on the certainty that she was. It was something an insane person would do, but could an insane person build something like this?

No, they couldn't.

Despite all she believed or came to believe, out here with only her own voice echoing back at her, Liskar could still easily be wrong. Another forceful voice, deeper seated within Hallord insisted that all this didn't matter. He was a servant of the Emperor, his hand beyond the throne, an extension of divine will, as was Liskar by oath; an oath she had betrayed. Even if the doctor truly believed that the end was in store for them all, she had no right to defy the patriarch of the whole galaxy. This was not her decision to make.

Nor was it Hallord's. There was nothing to consider here, no horrible truth to mull over beyond the immediate threat to what was simply the most important war asset the Empire had ever gained. The video contained nothing more than the last ramblings of a starving traitor.

"Two hours and forty-six minutes."

"We have to restore the reactor manually," Hallord muttered, pacing frantically around the lab and its irreplaceable contents. "I'm prepared to die to accomplish this."

"You would not survive long enough to complete the task," the AI commiserated. "Radiation leakage will start burning through the compartment shields soon."

Hallord's mind worked frantically. He couldn't restore the reactor himself, and the maintenance bot that was capable would take far too long to repair. Liskar had likely trashed it to prevent him from using it for that purpose. It would be impossible to move the disc and its attendant machinery to his ship one level higher. Was it possible that she had lied about it being unstoppable and unmovable? No, of course not. She would never have killed herself if she could have simply shut it down, dismantled it and declared it a failure. But the full extent of its secrets were lost with her death.

Hallord accepted the obvious conclusion with a heavy but resolute heart. "I have to use this machine. I have to go back."

The AI was silent. If it had a contrary opinion to voice, it demurred from saying so. He stared into the featureless gray disc and restrained the urge to shiver. "There must be instructions to this machine's use."

"The Doctor kept her work in that lab and myself out. All the usual observation devices were disabled."

Hallord studied one panel to the disc's left that contained some form of interface. "These readouts are all but gibberish to me, but this here seems to be a control unit. The only adjustable feature seems to refer to dilation. Right now it has a setting of six."

He picked up something loose on the desk, a reader pad that was wiped like everything else here. Good a test subject as any. He approached the disk slowly, seeing nothing of note in its murky gray. As he took a step, he heard something clatter to the ground in the lab. Turning, he saw nothing. "Emperor protect us all," Hallord whispered with a wince and hurled the pad. It disappeared into the gray soundlessly without marring the disc's face.

He waited for a moment. Nothing happened. Slowly, he walked around the object, passing the disk's edge and came to see what lay on the other side. The pad lay on the deck and he realized what the clattering sound had been. The pad had come out and hit the deck before he had even thrown it.

Six. Six seconds. The setting on the panel was for seconds.

Hallord worked the control panel, drawing the dilation wider. A standard interstellar day was defined as the twenty-four hours of the Imperial throne-world, sixty seconds per minute. He dialed the number higher and higher, until it abruptly stopped at over 3500, unable to go further. By his hasty math, that was nearly one day. "I have to go through," Hallord said reluctantly, tail curling in worry. That gray, featureless surface terrified him, but he had conquered fear before. This was the solution. Go back, fix the reactor before it was too deadly to fix, stop the station from exploding. With any luck, he could do it before his ship arrived. As for running into himself, he fingered the flange gun on his hip. Hopefully he could explain things in spite of his own hair-trigger reflexes.

The AI was silent for a few moments, then in taciturn

tones that would have come with a shrug it said, "Please be cautious."

Hallord would have laughed if he wasn't terrified. He could only hope Liskar was as brilliant as she was traitorous. He took a deep breath. Would he even feel anything happen?

"Two hours thirty-six minutes," The AI said.

In four quick bounds, Hallord leapt against the gray.

Glacial void in all directions. A formless expanse of—

His cheek and chest slammed the deck, knocking the wind out of him. Pain hammered through every cell in his body, as though a million teeth had chewed through him. He lay groaning on the deck for a full minute before slowly rising to his knees. The lab was sealed, the machinery humming in a drone. He was alone.

Had he actually gone back? When was this? Hallord blinked away tears as he patted himself down, feeling a cold not unlike the cryo unit on his ship. His limbs felt stiff as steel rods, his torso like it was on fire. He took several precious minutes to pick himself up and crawl to the laboratory's exit. He thumbed the door switch and felt his blood chill as he rose and stumbled through.

The ante-chamber office was empty, its lone chair sitting unoccupied. A full day. He'd gone back a full day. If Liskar wasn't here...

"Who are you?" The AI demanded, its voice emanating from the desk speaker.

No sense in deception. It would simply sound the alarm. "Imperial Prime Agent Vix Pon Hallord, Special Commission. Quickly, tell me, where is Doctor Liskar?"

"How did you come to be here?"

Hallord's chest heaved as he checked the office chronometer. His shuttle hadn't even approached yet. He had to lean on the desk for support. Random nerves in his body screamed at him, while the rest filled with pins and needles. He could only hope this didn't last long.

"The doctor will know. Where is she?" For one bright,

painful moment, he felt a flush of triumph through his queasiness. He had dared to break the laws of time, to go back and protect the greatest asset ever created, and now he would succeed. He wondered deep in his resolute heart if the brilliant female whom he would soon put in chains would have a moment of wistful satisfaction that her greatest invention—

There was a bloodcurdling hiss from the doorway. Hallord spun around queasily, his paw fumbling for his gun as a white-furred form rushed him, knocking the wind out of his already taxed lungs and bringing him to the deck. The scent of her breath was potent in his flaring nostrils. "Damn you, damn you!" Liskar screamed. "Why! Why didn't you listen?"

Hallord forgot his pistol, a mistake in his weakened state. He weakly reached out with spasming limbs, trying to grab her arms with his paws, trying to get his feet under her mass to kick her off. There was a familiar object in her right paw that prickled the skin of his raw throat. He went still as he realized what it was. "Don't!"

Liskar's tears felt salty in his mouth as she straddled him, her teeth bared in a feral hiss and her lab tunic askew. "Didn't you see the recording? I gave you a chance to fix this. I gave you the opportunity to prevent a catastrophe. Now you've ruined everything! Why can't you see what has to be done?"

Hallord bared his chattering teeth and concentrated on getting his limbs under control. "You had no right to take this from us. You had *no right*. Stopping you was my duty. How could you not know that?" He screamed as the needle pushed home and the syringe depressed. His already spasming limbs shook even more in panic as Liskar glared down at him.

"I had faith in you, in the kind of man you could be. I hoped, I *knew*, that if you didn't come back through, that I would know you took the offer I have waiting for you, to save us." She released the syringe and it clattered to the floor. "To end this."

Hallord swore at her and spat, spittle landing on her neck. She wiped it away. "You still can. You can still save us from this. I locked the machine so that it couldn't go any further back than now, so I'd know when to expect you if the worst happened. But it doesn't. Every turn of the circle is a new chance. You will return there again, but you don't have to return *here*. Do you understand? You don't have to—"

Hallord's freed hand shot out, grabbed the syringe and jabbed it in her side. Liskar cried out and rolled away, the syringe dangling between her ribs. Hallord struggled to rise as she plucked it out and gazed hollowly at the instrument before putting it in a pocket. "Well," she sobbed and then laughed. "I don't have to consider those options." She coughed. "This time around, anyway."

She stood up, kicking Hallord's paw away when it tried to draw the pistol. It clattered to the deck and came to a rest. "The pain of traveling back will pass just in time for the poison to start working. Ironically, that will be far gentler. For both of us."

She collected the pistol and placed it in the ante-room drawer. Hallord realized as pain gave way to queasiness that there was no way for her to dispose of that pistol, no means of throwing it overboard.

Nor him.

"The locks are sealed!" He rasped as Liskar grabbed his ankles and dragged him through the office hatch towards the deck lift. The fully functioning maintenance droid accepted her order to pick him up off the deck and follow her. "You can't hide me anywhere my body won't be found. I'll find my own corpse in this timeline you've created and I'll figure it out. I *always* figure the truth out." Hallord shivered and forced breath through his lungs as the lift rose them to the main deck. "You've lost! Nothing will prevent me from completing my mission, nothing! You were stupid to even try."

Liskar sighed as they came up to the main deck, holding the hallway handrail and weaving while they made their way to a place Hallord's fading vision could not see. He was completely blind by the time the machine slid him onto a flat metal surface. Her raspy breath, as the poison worked slowly but certainly within her too, came as a gentle whisper.

"I have faith that things will not always be this way, that you will find wisdom to help me prevent us from eating our own tails until we cease to exist. Until then, ensuring you leave no evidence for yourself to find is a matter of… irony. Till we meet again."

She placed a paw on his forehead then, a coolness that stole away Hallord's already dying fury before she slipped away. The peculiar final words imprinted momentarily on his fading mind as desperation fled his limbs and he went completely limp in purposeful mechanical hands. His vision would never return, but his remaining senses delivered him one final cold moment of horrifying clarity.

As his clothes were unceremoniously cut away and he heard the sharpening of robotic knives, he caught a familiar tinge on the stale station air. "Please, no. You can't…"

The rising scent of ground spices wafted tantalizingly from the sizzle of a kitchen's grill as the first steel found his flesh.

Hours passed as knives and ovens worked. Files were wiped and a scientist quietly died. A drone signaled in the docking bay as a ship completed its final approach maneuvers and mated with a staccato of clangs.

Imperial Prime Agent Hallord stepped from his ship through the space station's inner airlock. The scent that tickled his nose set his barren stomach growling. He was indeed on a mission, but the most urgent of directives couldn't be followed when he was all but starving.

Hallord, being a weasel, could eat half his own mass of meat in a single sitting, but training and special metabolic drugs had prepped him for long stays in space with limited sustenance. After so long unconscious, he was ravenous. The sizzle of roasted meat combined with the bright bite of herbs and spices hooked him left, down a short hallway to the dining nook, where a sumptuous feast of meat strips, ibex he guessed, awaited him.

Doctor Liskar was nowhere in sight, the nook's table set for one. Likely she'd eaten earlier.

Hallord ate. The meat was the best he'd tasted in years, fully deboned, crisped and sauced. It was buttery on his tongue as it went down, lean meat with very little fat or gristle. "Computer," Hallord called out between bites.

"Yes." The voice that responded was deep, masculine and prim, devoid of emotion.

"Was Doctor Liskar notified of my ship's approach?"

"No. She is on the lab level. Her last request was to be undisturbed."

"Who prepared this meal for me then?"

"Kitchen processor."

"Processor? Amazing." The next bite was sumptuous as the last. He chuckled. "If there's anything at all amiss, I'm not going to find it here."

THE FIRST VIEWING

Corgi W

When he first showed me the brain, I was unsure what to make of it. Within the glass case, an intact, pink, reef-like structure sat, a pair of feline eyes still attached by the stringy red cords. Around the side, a series of pipes and tubes burrowed into it. It was like a plasma globe, except with the metal orb that shot electricity replaced by living flesh.

"So you see," said the tall brown otter, clearly quite proud of his work, "we can tell that she is feeling, due to the movement of the eyes." In demonstration, he took his pen and ran it in front of the slitted feline orbs. "So, when I press this button," he placed his hand atop the jar, pushing a button, delivering a tiny burst of electricity down one of the tubes, "we can make her feel happy." The feline eyes dilated as if relaxing. "And when I press this button, here, see, I can evoke memories of her wedding day." Again, the otter demonstrated the effect, pressing another button, to which the eyes seemed to react. "Oh, but, the fun thing is this; when I press this button," the eyes shrank to slits, quivering, madly looking about, "I can make her feel pain. That button I just pressed, that was like putting her hand on a stove, whilst this one, here, that makes her feel as if she's been stabbed in the stomach." The otter laughed. "It is really quite fascinating. This was my first brain. I will always have fond memories of her."

I rubbed my muzzle, still unable to make my mind up, both to the artistic value, and what the sight evoked in my gut. "It's amazing you have volunteers," I said, bending down, attempting to make contact with the eyes. I was a young lioness with dreams of becoming an artist, fresh from the Paris Academy. It was hard to tell why I felt so strange. I had some idea of what to expect upon entering, but today of all days, I felt distant. Disconnected.

The otter sighed. "The first thing you must learn is that an artist need not seek permission."

"She did not agree?"

"If she did, then I did not hear it. She was a plucky young cat, supple bodied, a nice manner about her. I said I had a job, and after that, I doubt she thinks about it much." He flicked another switch, sending a continuous burst of electricity down one of the wires. "There, I have turned pleasure on. Right now, she is having an orgasm, again, and again, and again. Or so she thinks. Look, you can see it in the eyes. There is no simulation for this one; her life is looking forward at the entrance, acting as the introductory exhibit: My first brain, controlled completely, pleasure or pain on a whim. A fun plaything, for those who are new to modern art."

Within the St. Petersburg Art Society, Doschehov, the otter, was renowned for his brains. In order to get into his gallery, I had needed to send a request a full three years prior, attend two interviews, pay a hefty fee, and join the society in which he was found. Due to the controversial nature of his pieces, he refused to even make contact with anybody outside of the St. Petersburg society, giving private tours to those he felt he could trust. It was a strange approach to art, I thought, keeping it locked away so that only a select few could see it.

Inside, the gallery was unlike any I had ever been in. Each wall was a deep shade of sky blue that trailed down and slid seamlessly into the floor. Above, cold, pale lights shone down, leaving the gallery somewhere between light and dim.

Neuro-art was a new discipline, pioneered by those such as Doschehov, proving once again that art and technology existed in symbiosis. I was eager to get a chance to see what the otter had in store for me.

"This way," he called, clearly excited. His long tweed suit flapped behind him. It was hard to imagine that this tall, mahogany-furred creature spent so much of his time hunched over brains.

"Over here," he chuckled, proudly holding his hand out, "is an absolute marvel of a specimen. The first I was able to hook up to a working simulation. Nothing complex, but enough to keep the brain occupied."

I walked over to see. The glass case held the head of a komodo dragon, completely covered in wires. Its skin looked like a bad Halloween costume, hanging off in places like it was made of flayed plastic. There were no eyes on this one; the sockets had been filled with thick tubes. I leaned in to get a closer look. The moment my nose touched the glass, the mouth parted, attempting to hiss. I yelped and jumped back.

"Lizard brains are so much easier to work with," said Doschehov. "They do not see like we do. All they make out is the shapes. No colours, or anything like that. In mammals, such vision is referred to as 'blind-sight': When someone cannot see, but they have the spatial awareness needed to navigate."

I nodded and took notes. Everything the otter said, I did my best to scribble down. "Why is that easier to work with?" I asked.

"Because, when programming the simulation, all I had to do was trick the brain into thinking it was surrounded by physical objects, as opposed to creating textures and detailed models."

"And what objects did you choose?"

"I am glad you asked." His smile widened. He pointed me to the adjacent wall. A green dot navigated what looked like a maze was shown on a wide, flat screen television. "That green dot is his progress. Whenever he makes it through the maze, the computer will randomly simulate another. I have left all sorts of little goodies in the programming, though. If he goes the right way, he will come across food, which will stimulate the appropriate parts of the tongue. He will think he is actually eating."

I scribbled down more notes.

"It is important to put some sort of feature like that in," the otter noted. "If you do not, they will get boring. When I first created the mazes and hooked the dragon up, he grew quite apt at navigating his way around. Eventually, after realising that he would never escape, he gave up. It took quite a bit of fiddling for me to get him going again. Making him think he was hungry seemed to do the trick. Since then, I have found other ways to keep them fresh, but this one amuses me as it is, so I leave it.

"At this point, the subject probably knows that he will never escape. Yet he carries on. Each time he stops, I only need to evoke a painful rumbling of the stomach, and the little green blip starts moving again. A part of me thinks his mental states have collapsed by now; that he is merely operating on instinct."

I took another look at the screen, trying to imagine what the lizard might have been feeling. I could not deny that it evoked a morbid curiosity in me, bringing out feelings I had never known that I held. It took me a moment to internalise that the lizard was still a living thing. Doschehov cleared his throat and tapped his foot on the floor, bringing back my attention.

"Do you like it?" he asked, a hopeful look on his face, as if the entire gallery's success or failure hung upon my answer.

"It is... Interesting."

"Oh? And what do you mean by *interesting*?"

I gulped. Whenever I did not know quite what to say about a piece, I would say that it was "interesting." Up until now, nobody had asked what I meant by that. Truth be told, not even I really knew.

The otter was sharp though. He wanted to know exactly how his work made others feel. He wanted more than just a surface-level compliment. "It means," I began, "that I'd like to spend some more time with it, getting to know it."

"Why?" The otter was quick in his response. His gaze was intense, probing me for an answer.

"Well, I think there is definitely a message to it."

"Which is?"

I stuttered for a moment. "That living creatures will attempt to persevere no matter how many times the world seems to push them back. That he could have given up and accepted his fate, but instead he continues on. If he never gives up, it will be a testament to the will of living beings." I hoped that answer would suffice.

"And you see that outlook as optimistic?"

"To a degree, yes."

Doschehov smiled. "Ah, so you see hope in it. Very good, very good indeed."

Though my outward composure remained calm, as the otter turned his back on me and continued down the corridors, inside I let out a sigh of relief.

While we walked, I could not stop thinking about what the Komodo dragon must have been feeling, still running through its prison. I wished I knew how long it had been there. It had been thirty years since Doschehov moved to St. Petersburg, but his work had begun long before then. I found myself thinking that I would rather die than be put through the same thing myself. My questions about consent once again surfaced.

"Is this not somewhat…" I trailed off as the otter spun on his heel.

"Wrong?" he said.

"Well, did *any* of your subjects agree to… this?"

Doschehov snorted. "If they did, the pieces would hardly have the same effect, now would they? If they knew that they were going to wake up in a simulation, who knows what would happen? If the dragon knew he was essentially just a head on a stick with a few wires sticking in, do you think he would continue to run?"

"I suppose not," I said, scribbling in my notebook. Behind me, my tail flicked. I brought the notebook closer to my chest, attempting to hide my notes.

"I'm sorry to question your methods."

"I should think so, too." Doschehov's perky disposition returned. "Well, anyway, no need to feel discouraged. I am sure that this is a lot to take in at once. It is only natural that a few such questions should arise. But, I ask you, for the rest of this gallery, to leave such notions at the door."

With that, he turned, and continued on his way. "This next one is a special piece. It was produced with the help of Invar Xengarini. Do you know who that is?"

I thought for a moment. "The neurosurgeon from Nizhny Novgorod?"

"Neuro-*artist*," Doschehov corrected. "Do you know what it is that she is most famous for?"

"She was the one who created the technology that maps the neural pathways related to memory, back in 2057."

"Amongst other things," said the otter. "She was my reason for coming back home to Russia. Before then, I had been quite happy tinkering in the tropics. If not for her, I would still be creating pieces like the lizard, or the brain you saw at the entrance. But, oh, when she sent me that first video-call, I was hooked by the possibilities."

We turned a corner and came to another glass tube. It stretched from the ceiling to the floor. Thick wires ran throughout, flowing into another brain sitting in the centre with no eyeballs or remains of a head attached.

"The original model is not as aesthetically pleasing as I may have otherwise wanted, but, what you have to remember is that these were early days. This brain, here, is that of a young wolf who attempted to bar my entrance to the St. Petersburg Society of Art. For years, he insulted me, attempted to have me arrested, and almost fire-bombed my original studio, saying that what I do is *against God*," Doschehov spat the words. "Well, I asked him to give it a think, and let him consider it first-hand. As you can see, I believe he got a closer inspection than he may have wanted."

I dreaded to imagine what the wolf must be going through, hooked up to so many wires, his brain suspended in the light blue liquid inside the tube.

"Unlike the lizard, here I wanted to keep the mind fresh. Food in the maze is all well and good, but as I said, it may leave the subject running on nothing but instinct. Instead, this specimen here is having his memories reset every twenty-four hours."

My eyes widened and my tail shivered. It was completely out of my control.

Doschehov just laughed and seemed to take my tail's excitement as enthusiasm for his work. "Oh yes," he said, "every day erased, as if he were first put in there."

"Is he attached to a simulation?" I asked, not knowing if I wanted to hear the answer.

"He was a God-fearing wolf," Doschehov said. His grin widened, pushing up the fur and skin on his face. It set his beady black eyes deep within heavy folds of fur. "So, I came up with a suitable reality to immerse him in: Every one of his virtues is being broken down as we speak. I have simulated what he believed to be hell." He paused. "Do you have the time?"

As fast as I could, I brought up my watch. "T... Twelve thirty," I managed.

"Ah, then he is currently having his eyes gouged out. By this time tomorrow, he will be going through it again. Is it not exquisite? This preservation of suffering that I have achieved? Each time, the memories erased, only for it to happen once more."

I stared at the brain and the wires sticking into it. A part of me wanted to smash the tube, destroy whatever of the wolf was left. Whoever he once was had been reduced to a mass of pinkish-beige fibres, the blood still running through the tiny vessels. Still, I could hope that Doschehov was wrong in what he said; that all he had really done was stick electrical wires into an already deceased organ, the wolf's soul free from ever having to experience the never-ending nightmare. I doubted that was true, though. Doschehov probably had a way to prove it. If he did, I did not want to know of it.

Yet, despite my disgust, I could not take my eyes from it. Something about it captured me, made me want to know more, to know what the wolf would be saying, feeling, and thinking, as the simulation played over and over again.

"Do you like it?" the otter asked with his cheerful demeanour.

"It is a dramatic piece," I said.

"Oh yes, certainly," he replied. "Of all my works, I would say that this is the one with the most sentimental value. I will always remember the intensive amount of programming, cutting, and wiring, which the late Invar and I went through. The body, all laid out on the table, scalp open, the brain exposed. I am quite like the wolf's God, you see. In here, I have the power to send souls to eternal pleasure, pain, or something in between."

I pretended to take more notes. At this stage, I resorted to merely scribbling down my thoughts. What Doschehov had done both intrigued and terrified me in equal measure. I supposed that was the purpose of his art.

"But we must not let these feelings get in the way of our purpose. The first time you create the simulation, you may be captured by a rush of adrenaline and passion. You will want to put everything into it, just to see how the subject will respond, marvelling at what you believe will be your future masterpiece. But caution must be taken. You must not lose sight of what it is you wish to achieve."

"A... And what is that?"

The otter laughed, tapping his index finger against the glass. "To preserve the feelings, the experiences. Embellish and emphasize them." He straightened himself up. "Every so often, his mind will be flooded with a wave of optimism. The torture will die down for a moment, and he will be made to think that there is more; an outside, away from the burning and grinding and ripping. It is that which will hurt him all the more.

"Within the twenty-four hours he would abandon himself, and the exercise would become pointless, if not for the precision of those little jolts of hope." From beside the exhibit, the otter pulled a long wire, attached to what seemed like a speaker. He pressed the button on the side.

In an instant, the gallery went from silent to shrieking. What sounded like a male voice was howling, shouting, and begging for a release that would never come. A moment later, I realised I was hearing vaguely Russian words. The otter was saying something, but I could only tell by the movements of his lips. After recovering from the initial shock, I brought myself to face what was happening. The noises were coming from within the brain.

The otter turned off the speaker. "An artificial voice-box," he said, seeming proud. Normally, the purpose of such a device was to allow a mute to speak, interpreting the messages that the brain sent and translating them into sound. I had never imagined it being used for any other purpose. As hard as it was for me to properly grasp, right that moment, as we were speaking, the wolf was screaming, experiencing truly horrible things. "That is enough of that for now," said Doschehov, leading me further into the gallery.

Doschehov smiled. "Exquisite, isn't it?"

* * * * *

The rest of the exhibits, what few I remember, did little to set me at ease. Nothing was as bad as the wolf, Doschehov had clearly been carrying a vendetta with that one, but I could not say he had been particularly kind to the others. One of them was supposed to capture fear, the brain re-wired to give the subject all sorts of phobias, then directly exposing them to the objects of said fears. Whomever it was, I could relate to what they must have been going through. When I was young, I had been trapped in an elevator and have not been able to ride in one ever since. To go through that fear, that churning in the gut, and not be able to flee or hide from it, was something I felt a great sympathy for.

And while I have difficulty recalling most of the other exhibits, I do recall that none of them quite reached the same intensity that Doschehov had had for the wolf. That was, until, we reached a brain kept in a particularly well-decorated corner with a red carpet underfoot. A padded chair sat across from it, set in with a deep impression from being sat in often. In the back of which was a large hole, the kind that otters normally required to put their tails though to sit comfortably. When we reached it, the joyful demeanour of a man showing his life's work suddenly disappeared. Doschehov grew cold, almost morbidly so. It was clear that this exhibit held great personal significance for him.

"This is my father's brain," he said, running his hand along the glass tank. I could not tell the difference between it and the others myself, but I do not doubt that Doschehov could see something more where I could not, in the same way that some of us sometimes see faces in the fronts of cars.

"What's he experiencing?" I asked.

"Me."

I did not know whether I ought to press him.

When I took too long to respond, Doschehov continued by his own accord. "My father never liked… how I am. Not one bit. He was a bastard, through and through."

I suddenly began to dislike where the conversation was heading.

"So I put him through it. Again and again, from the age of ten to twenty, he is going to go through it: Finding out what I liked, having a simulated version of himself breathing down my neck. He will kiss my first boyfriend. For all those years, he will feel his own beatings, his attempts to change me, right down to the way his knuckles collided with my muzzle. Except, for him, it does not end after running away. No, for him, it goes back to the start. So he can feel what it was like, to live under himself, for all those years. Programming it in such detail required the help of several of my friends, but it was worth it."

Again, as was so often the case in his gallery, I had nothing to respond with. There was a poetic sort of justice to it, I had to admit. But it had gone too far. Art had a deeply personal aspect, or so I had always thought, and Doschehov had done nothing but confirm it. For the wolf, he had devoted himself to the idea of suffering. Custom-tailored suffering in a custom-tailored hell, meticulously reproduced in loving detail. With the phobia simulation, he had been sure to include his own fears. And for his actual father? The obsession, the madness of it, was all too apparent. Horrifying, but also beautiful, in a way.

I wondered if the same level of technology could be used for other purposes. I marvelled at what might be possible: Instead of prisons, could we not find a way to make the offenders experience what their victims had, before returning them to reality, body intact, to understand what they had done? Maybe the age-old expression of "walking a mile in somebody else's shoes," could be made possible. To keep myself from breaking apart over what I had seen, I tried to imagine a more empathic world, a positive result from what I was seeing. The moment I was out, I would turn my attention to creating it; the same simulations, leaving the brain in the body so that one could walk away afterwards. If he could escape, I imagined that Doschehov's father would be more empathic, at least.

* * * * *

The closing exhibits were just as strange as the previous had been: someone forced to eat forever but stripped of a sense of taste. A cat being allowed to live out her dream of being a dog. A homeless deer given all the money in the world. And others still. The otter still stopped to explain each one, and asked me my thoughts each time, but with less enthusiasm than he had originally displayed. My notebook had seen more use than it had during an entire semester at art school. As much as I was relieved to reach the end, a part of me wished to see more.

At the end of the gallery was a small wooden door. Which opened up to a set of stairs, at the top of which was another door. We climbed up and entered the rooms above the gallery. The first room we entered was made to look like a traditional sitting room: a yellow carpet with a pattern of flowers, two sofas, and an armchair with a samovar which sat in the middle atop a brass table. There were computers and wires all over the place. Apparently, Doschehov was not the kind of magician who never revealed his tricks. I paused when I thought that; of course he wouldn't be, his magic was in having created those tricks.

"Are you thirsty?" he asked, returning to a more pleasant demeanour. He smiled. "I was planning to make myself a cup of tea. As much as I enjoy the tours, I find that they leave the back of my throat terribly dry. For a creature that favours the aquatic, such as myself, that cannot do."

I nodded my agreement. "Coffee, if you have it."

"Of course." He filled his samovar with water and left it to boil. "Come, whilst that is doing, let me show you my studio."

Doschehov showed me to the connected hall, then led me to the room at the end of it. It was a simple set-up that he had, with a flat wooden table covered in leather restraints. Tools were set atop a drawer in the corner, beside a metal bin covered in dried blood.

"It is important to keep them as fresh as possible," the otter commented.

"What do you mean by that?"

"Fresh; in good condition. What else could I mean? Once a creature dies, the brain rapidly deteriorates. It is why I cannot just wait for my subjects to fall to natural causes. By the time I got a hold of them, there would not be anything worth preserving. No, I bring them here, tie them down, and wait for them to awaken before I do anything with them."

My gut churned. "Why awake?"

"So I know I have not spoiled the brain. If I damage the amygdala, for example, I can destroy the memories and emotional responses, making the entire thing pointless. If they are alive, I can prod about, making sure they laugh when I touch the right areas, cry with others. A lot of the actual work is done with the body still attached, you see." From the ceiling, the otter pulled down a large apparatus. "I normally test out the brain by hooking it into this. It is a basic diagnostic simulation; I run a few tests and monitor the reactions. One of my favorites is to make them think they have changed species. The procedure is not a particularly painful one."

Despite the otter's reassurance, the thought of somebody rooting around in my brain still made me tremble. I had wanted to know something since stepping into the gallery, though. "How do you get away with this?" I asked.

"Why have the authorities not yet put a stop to this? I assume that is what you are asking."

I nodded, meekly.

"I have many powerful friends who wish for a chance to experience my work for themselves when they become too old. I have created a simulation of paradise especially for those who are able and willing to keep the philistine crowds in check. As I say, I am God here. I have the keys to the gates of Heaven. No prayer is required, only an appreciation for art."

I did not want to, but I could believe it. If, in the olden days, people had been so willing to kill and wage war thinking they would get to Heaven, it was not so hard to imagine that those same attitudes could settle for a less metaphysically peaceful alternative. In the back of my mind, I considered my options. The sudden revelation of how the otter got away with his creations made me doubt going to the authorities. If those who put pay in the police pocket also endorsed the gallery, then I could not imagine that they would allow it to be shut down. Moreover, I shuddered at the thought of it closing myself. As much as I may have found the exhibits distasteful, they also had a way of grabbing you, pulling you in, and making you wonder. The work had already been done. It would be a shame to put it all to waste.

"And anyway, that is neither here nor there," said the otter. "Let me show you the rest."

In the other rooms there were wires and machines, presumably hooked up to the brains down below. The otter kept the rooms cold so that the computers would not overheat. It was clear that what was in the gallery was just the tip of the mechanical iceberg. Each wire was meticulously bundled in with the rest so that none overlapped or tangled. The floor was perfectly clean, unless electronics had to be ran across them. In another room was a desk and several screens, with keyboards and mice that looked like they were from the early days of computers, all hooked up, and a yellow lamp overhead. Stacks of paper were organised in the same meticulous way that the wires had been.

"You still use paper," I noted.

"As do you," said the otter, smiling, gesturing to my notebook. "Nothing beats the tactile feel of a pen on paper when making notes, don't you think?"

I nodded in agreement. We proceeded back to the sitting room, where the samovar had finished boiling. The otter took out two cups, though I could not work out from where, put a spoon of coffee in one and a teabag in the other. "I have a natural blend," he said, "not any of the artificial crap. I refuse to have any of that stuff near me or my nose."

As he poured hot water over the coffee mix, I understood. I had only had real coffee once before in my life, and the smell brought the memory back to me. It was so much more pure than the synthetic blends most people settled for.

"Milk and sugar?" the otter asked.

Normally, I would have a little milk and half a spoon of sugar. This time, though, I did not want to alter the taste in any way. "None, thanks. I'll take it black."

Doschehov put sweetener and milk into his own drink, then took the cups and placed the shining black liquid down in front of me. I blew at it, then took a sip and was instantly reconnected with the rich taste I remembered.

"What do you think of my gallery?"

I was hoping he would not ask anything like that. "It's impressive," I said, instantly realising that he would ask for more. "It's a triumph of engineering and artistic vision." I saw the seriousness in the otter's rounded face as he analysed my answer. Everything went blurry for a moment, like a blue wave had flooded the entire room, then vanished. I put it down to nerves.

"So, you like it then?"

"Very much so, yes. I'm fascinated by it, truth be told."

That seemed to please him. He leaned back in his chair and took a sip of his tea. I had never been to a gallery in which I myself had been put under such a spotlight by its curator.

"I wish I could be like you," Doschehov said. "I wish I could go back and feel it all again: The shock of the eyes moving on my first experiment, the joy of watching the lizard run about his little maze, or the satisfaction of putting the final touches to my father. Once you have slaved over these creations for so long, you begin to only see the work and effort put into them, and, at the same time, you wish to make something better."

As he spoke, I continued to drink the coffee. I was getting tired and checked my watch, supposing that it was getting late. It was only ten minutes past two o'clock. We had been staring at the wolf's brain less than two hours before.

"I think I've done it, too. I think I've finally found something to close on. A final piece for my gallery. My magnum opus, if you will."

I wanted to agree, but found that my attention was wan-
ing, my eyes becoming heavier, and my body slumping further into the chair. I wanted to go home, more than anything,
and fall down into my bed. Doschehov continued to talk, but
his words had become murmurings, so muffled they may as
well have been coming from another room. I fell forward,
almost hitting the table. A hand grabbed my shoulder and
gently lowered me down.

* * * * *

When I awoke, Doschehov was gone. The lights had been
turned off, save for a dim lamp in the corner of the room.
Each piece of brass adopted a duality of colour; shining
brightly on the side that faced the light, fading to pitch black
on the other. My head was in a daze. Everything seemed airy.
I could not feel a thing, like my body was not there and I was
merely floating. The smell of coffee was still warm. I held my
hand out. The familiar, stumpy, sandy, digits were before me,
barely illuminated, but there. Whatever was wrong would
have to wait. Now, I just wanted to go home.

Raising myself up was difficult. My balance shifted, causing me to dart across the room in a manner not dissimilar to
the way one would move aboard a ship during harsh waves.
I turned and made my way to the door. Or, at least, where I
thought it was. As I moved across the room, I found myself
bumping into a wall. It was covered in the same flowery wallpaper as the rest of the room. I was sure I had come from that
direction. The corridor leading to Doschehov's workshop
was still there, but I could not find the other doors.

Through it all, I found myself wanting to think… something. Something. But what that was eluded me. I knew, I
knew, I knew… that there was definitely something wrong.
It's just like when you think of a film, and you remember the
lead, but you cannot recall their name. That's what it was like.
There was something, and that something was on the very

tip of my tongue, but every time I got close, it fled. In my delirium, I stumbled wherever I could, tripping up on the carpet, but pulling myself back. It was not my first choice to head towards the otter's workshop, but it was the only way I could go.

I checked the computer room yet found nothing. His desk was absent, too. I began to wonder where it was that he slept, and where his toilet was. As far as I could recall, he did not leave the gallery for anything but the most urgent of matters. The final room to search was where he operated on his subjects. It was not a place I was eager to set foot in. But if there was no alternative, I could force myself in.

I pushed the door open. There was a body on the table. A sandy lioness. I edged my way around the room. The top of the cranium was removed, the skull empty. Eyes stared up at the ceiling in shock. Fur was matted down with specks of blood. Traces of wiring lay beside the head.

Her head.

My head. I rubbed my eyes and blinked, wanting to be sick. Then it hit me. I was looking at myself. I could not tell whether it was a psychological effect, or whatever the otter had given me had permanently altered my mind, but, upon closer inspection, I knew I was looking at myself. The world around me blurred, and my head began to ache. I remembered something, but, only for a second, and then, my head was emptied, the world grinding to a halt.

* * * * *

When he first showed me the brain, I was unsure what to make of it. Within the glass case, an intact, pink, reef-like structure sat, a pair of feline eyes still attached by the stringy red cords. Around the side, a series of pipes and tubes burrowed into it. It was like a plasma globe, except with the metal orb that shot electricity replaced by living flesh.

"So you see," said the tall brown otter, clearly quite proud of his work, "we can tell that it is feeling, due to the movement of the eyes." In demonstration, he took his pen and ran it in front of the slitted feline orbs...

CLICKING

Ianus J. Wolf

[Subspace DataNet Entry: Earth]

Earth, sometimes referred to as Earth Prime or Terra, colloquially referred to as "The Cradle", "The Nest", and several other terms listed below, is the current known origin point for advanced intelligent life as we understand it. Over centuries, life developed into myriad forms of self-awareness, leading to all limited conflict, scientific discovery, and history of early development of intelligent species before the outbound movement into the neighboring region of the Milky Way galaxy. [see also entries on **Sol**, **Solar System** for more information]

Though Earth was rendered uninhabitable for most species long ago through various factors [see also entries on **Industry**, **Climatic Adjustment**, **Overuse of Resources**, **Overpopulation**, **Tipping Point** for more information], its legacy lives on in the races that developed there, their history, their art [stored in other sections of DataNet], and the **Evac/Explore Project** that seeks to establish biodiversity on other worlds with the unique parameters necessary to sustain comfortable multispecies lifestyles.

The origins of the actual planet itself are sometimes the subject of scientific debate as well as numerous faiths which arose in its lifespan…

Acting Captain Marco Shane of the *Manu* watched while the

mongoose at the instrument panel continued to make adjustments and scan readouts. Having come up through military and security channels, the ram only understood about half of what his environmental analyst was working on, but knew that Lucille was his ace on this team. They'd dropped into a steady orbit around 67 Manticore d roughly seventy-two hours earlier, and data from the host of initial scans was finally giving the computer a decent picture of the planet.

"Have anything yet?" he asked the svelte mongoose.

"Plenty. Just sifting through what's useful info and what our average temperature readings mean," she said without looking up from her multiple screens, her lithe paws dancing over the controls and her body twisting to gather information more quickly. "Our good news is that the O2 content is within tolerable ranges, along with other elements in the atmosphere. That means we're already likely looking at breathable air, though average humidity seems a little heavy. No evidence of structures that would indicate an already advanced culture, which is good. Not even a primitive sentient intelligence is indicated in any of the scans, though we are getting plenty of flora and light fauna. Actually, nearly all of the planet's solid terrain is more like a jungle than anything else."

"Wait, single-biome planet? That's actually a thing?"

Lucille shook her head. "Not single-biome, just… primary biome over most land masses from the look of things. We still have a little variance, but not as much as records from Earth Prime indicate. You still have large water masses and a few areas that you could consider desert, but a disproportionate amount is hot, humid, and full of a lot of dense plant life."

"Oh." Marco took a swig of the coffee in his hand, a thick black nail tapping against the cup wall. "Well, do you have a rough estimate on candidacy?"

"Roughly speaking? It's possible. Some species aren't ever going to be comfortable in, say, the equatorial areas where the heat and moisture are most dense, and any truly cold-weather species would have exceedingly limited range. Some limited terraforming could expand that range, and overall it could support a *lot* of different groups."

"Yes, because historical records on the Cradle say we're *so* great at cooling things down when we get up and running."

The mongoose turned a wry look to him. "I like to think we've learned a thing or two since then. And from what information we have, the EE Project needs to start looking at taking what we can get rather than finding the perfect planet. Unofficially of course."

Marco nodded. Original guidelines had stated that candidates for colonization should be as close to original Earth climates and terrains as possible to allow all species to settle with a minimum of terraforming effort and without disrupting any burgeoning civilizations. With recycled resources slowly dwindling on all ships over time and the discovery more and more that the exact specifications were somewhat unique in the galaxy, any form of survival began to look promising. There were even rumors on the unofficial sections of the SSDN that some ships had already decided to "settle" and thaw out their cryo compliments on planets that were "good enough." Even darker rumors sometimes circulated of more entrenched military-minded captains eliminating evidence of a previous intelligent sentience to settle on a decent planet, but nothing had been confirmed. With the varying ships hurtling in different directions and connected only through information uploaded to the SSDN, genuine facts became difficult to sort from hearsay.

It was Marco's call how to proceed as Acting Captain for the next three years until it was time to rotate back into the freezer. Then another crew would take over for five years and it would be someone else's headache. He shook his head in thought, wobbling his horns side to side.

"Let's proceed tentatively. I don't want to become the guy in this planet's history that screwed over half the species on board, but I also know plenty of people are tired of drifting for five years awake every once in a great while. Keep scanning and putting together data, and I'm going to put together a preliminary landing team to do some scouting."

For the first time, Lucille turned the chair away from her screens. "Sure you don't want to delegate that? You are the AC after all."

The ram shook his gray head. "I'd just as soon get out there and stretch my legs. Even if something does happen, there's always another captain—"

"—in cryo," she finished with a slight roll of her eyes and turned back to her screens. "Still, I kind of like having you on our crew. Who knows what I'd get stuck with if we have to have the computer randomly thaw someone out?"

"I'll try to keep that in mind." Marco turned away and then looked back. "Oh, you're sure the air is breathable on the surface?"

"Yup, within all reasonable margins for error. According to all our probes and scans, there are no toxic atmospheric elements and air composition is as close to right as you can get. You should all be fine with Henshaw Shields."

"Good, helmets play hell with my horns."

[Subspace DataNet Entry: Renny Henshaw]

Renny Henshaw, a 23rd century elephant expert in nanotechnology, is best known for the creation of what came to be called the Henshaw Shield for exploration of hospitable climates. Motivated by the diversity in species that made full exosuits cumbersome for many individuals, Henshaw developed a subroutine that would allow nanites to replicate in a thin layer around the body of any individual of any shape [See also entry on: **Nanites** for more information]. While ineffectual for breathing in hostile environments, Henshaw Shields became the ideal barrier for harmful microorganisms, spores, and other potential hazards of extra-terrestrial travel, going so far as to offer some physical protection from impact and potential repair of injury.

Other, minor inventions of Renny Henshaw include…

The module touched down on the surface of 67 Manticore d. After some deliberation with the team, Marco had determined that a land mass almost exactly between polar and equatorial regions of the planet would be a good initial examination, at least for the sake of averages in the most basic verification of the planet's candidacy.

Acting as pilot of the module was a security officer rat named Nathan Higgins, who would represent some basic mammalian expectations along with AC Shane. Xenobiologist Robert Maceone was a green iguana who would serve both as a reptile representative and provide his basic medical training in the event of injury. Next to him sat the squat gray form of Anna Cornan, a pigeon xenobotanist who would gather flora samples and do initial checks for avian and other flight-based interests. All wore the simple gray bodysuits tailored to their species and belts containing light individual equipment as well as a Henshaw Unit.

Fortune had favored Marco with the right members of the crew awake and with enough working hours remaining to do the initial scout with only four. Regulations demanded that initial scout teams be kept as tight as possible with each individual serving multiple functions. There was a lot of talk and math about the lower resource use to get them on and off world, especially if they could instantly determine in one trip if the world was a dud. What was mentioned less formally was the fact that if something went horribly wrong, there would be as little loss of life as possible.

"Lucky crew of four," Higgins said between a few little focused chitters as he worked to adjust the module's position and settings into what could serve as a two- or three-day habitat if needed. "I feel good about this."

Anna let a warbling little chuckle through her beak. "I didn't know you were superstitious, Nate."

"I'm not," the rat returned while he adjusted settings based on readouts. "I mean, not completely. I just think hedging your bets isn't a bad idea. I never bring a picture of anyone I know on a mission, and I never wear red on first contact of a planet. So I'll take a little luck wherever we can get it. It's just... better safe than sorry, you know?"

"Yeah, sure, totally not superstitious," the pigeon said with a playful glint in her dark eye.

The others snickered a little, and even Higgins grinned and nodded, whiskers twitching in amusement. "Okay, okay, just nobody come crying to me when you say something like 'It can't get any worse' and wind up dead."

"Duly noted," Marco said, still smiling. It was nice to see them in good spirits about getting off the ship for a while. Always more difficult when the crew was nervous about the risks instead of excited about the rewards. Just the scent alone of anxiety could spread like wildfire through a team if unchecked, creating a panic loop. "Everyone ready for a walkabout?"

Amid general assent, the four rose from their chairs. The rest of the module had already been filled with base temperature breathable air, and the crew members filtered through the door at the back to what acted as the main room of the tight habitat. Consoles were in each corner of the room for analysis work, with a central table for meeting, discussion, and rest time during missions. Along the walls were small bunk compartments with metal doors for limited privacy. At the starboard side, an airtight sliding door led to the airlock. The crew filed in and waited while the inner door sealed.

"Okay, we're ready for an environment check," Nathan said, his paw poised over a console at the side of the airlock. "Henshaws ready?"

Each crew member checked the belt at their waist, turning it on and waiting a few seconds. The nanotech swarmed over all of them, almost invisible to the naked eye as the little machines replicated themselves from a few base materials into a protective coating. Shane always felt a mild itching sensation that passed in ten or fifteen minutes after turning one on. He idly wondered if it was the same for all other species, or if fur was the determining factor.

Everyone gave their go-ahead once the belts indicated complete coverage, and Higgins punched a few buttons. The exterior door opened ten centimeters and allowed the first exposure to the outside atmosphere. If anyone showed signs of distress, a single button press would slam the door closed and begin decontamination in five seconds. After a few moments, the two mammals felt slightly assailed by the humidity that washed into the cabin. Anna seemed neutral on the matter, and Robert just stretched and smiled, curling his claws back and forth and gently shaking his dewlap.

"Not bad. I could live here," the green iguana said.

"The rest of us could probably adapt or set up habitats over time, but we'll see after further analysis," Marco said. "Well, it looks like no one's choking or having too much trouble breathing, all our readouts were correct it seems."

"Good," Higgins said, a little labor in his breath as he brushed the extra moisture off his whiskers. "Permission to keep the module as a cool respite, AC?"

"Definitely."

Nathan pushed a few more buttons and machinery in the module hummed to life. Keeping climate controls on would use up some power, but not enough to make much of a difference. It was worth it in Marco's mind to provide a much-needed space for the two mammals to recuperate from the environment for the day.

The crew looked around their landing site. One of the few clearings large enough in what was primarily dense jungle. Some of the plant life reminded Shane of the trees he'd read about in histories of The Cradle, while others looked completely foreign. They did not see any evidence of animals roaming yet.

"Hm. You'd think this area would be packed with life,"

Maceone said, nostrils flaring to take in some of the scents around them. "Plenty of support for it."

"It already is," Anna returned, marveling at the shapes of some of the stranger plants and already rushing to use the small digits at the tips of her wings to collect some samples for the kit hanging across her chest. "Not all life walks and talks."

"Okay, you know what I mean. Where's all the fauna?"

"Before we worry about that," Marco interjected, "Anna would you care to do the honors? See if we have any reason to go exploring further?"

The pigeon cooed slightly and walked back to a clearer area. "Of course, AC. Getting ahead of myself."

She spread her wings, her uniform designed to cover her torso without impeding them. With a few flaps and tucking her slender legs up, Anna took to the air. Her takeoff seemed slightly wonky to Marco, but after a few moments, she was gliding easily and lighting on a nearby thick tree branch to collect another leaf sample. With a little circling flourish, Anna came back to the ground, her eyes bright and cheerful as anyone had ever seen them.

Shane grinned. "Acceptable, I take it?"

"Oh yes, it has been way too long since I've been able to do that! Air's a little heavy and takes some getting used to, but I can sign off on that portion so far."

"Okay. I guess now we pick a direction and go looking," the ram said. With a head shake, he turned a couple different ways on his hooves. "Any recommendations from the science team?"

Before Robert or Anna could speak, Higgins chimed in. "Best direction is always straight out from the airlock door."

Anna stuck her tongue out of her beak. "Like I said: superstitious."

"Hardly. Just if you have to run from something, you don't want to go *around* the module at all to get back in."

The iguana shrugged, jowls flaring and receding just

slightly. "Actually, I can get behind that logic. And every direction seems the same to me."

"Fine, I'll admit, that makes sense," Anna said.

"Right then. We start with roughly two klicks that way, evaluate, then most likely come back and take a look at what we've got."

Higgins sighed with another irritated brush at his whiskers. "Gonna be hell in this heat."

"Speak for yourself," Robert retorted with a cheeky smile.

"Reppies," the rat said, shaking his head as they began to trek into the dense plant life.

Green grass and tall trees surrounding them invoked almost instant thoughts of Earth Prime. Soil appeared in the expected brownish black and also in a silvery color in spots that Cornan collected for later study. Tiny streams of water ran through the landscape at various points, crisscrossing here and there, easy enough to step over. A quick testing strip told them that much of the water was drinkable if filtered in the proper way, another mark in the plus column for the planet. They chatted lightly while they took in the environment and moved outwards into the densely packed jungle, each adding their own notes to the ideas of colonization.

The deeper into the jungle they traveled, they began to notice some smaller creatures here and there, mostly non-intelligent tree-dwellers that seemed reptilian and a few fliers that bridged the gap between avian and reptile.

"Strange," Maceone said. "I would expect at least a few larger creatures somewhere, but everything is about the same size."

"Have you found the one yet that keeps making that clicking noise?" Anna asked while gathering another floral sample from a bloom she hadn't seen before.

The three of them looked at her quizzically. Marco hadn't heard any clicking in their entire trip. Anna noticed the look and stared back at them. "What?"

"What are you talking about?" Maceone said, genuinely

curious. "What noise?"

"Seriously? Nobody else hears that clicking sound?"

They all perked their ears a little, turning their heads in various directions. Nathan's tail twitched, and Robert's jowls swelled just a little before calming down.

"No," Higgins finally said. "What's it sound like? Do we need to do an equipment check?"

Anna tilted her head back and forth a few times. "I thought we were all hearing it; so I didn't say anything. My belt's been reading fine; I don't think it's mechanical. There's not enough of a steady rhythm to it. It's just this low clicking noise, and the rhythm changes. I was hearing it a little since we landed, but it's been getting louder. It's... it sounds close, but I can't pinpoint the source."

"Maybe we should take you back to the module and run a diagnostic on everything," Nathan suggested, his upper lip twitching back and forth. "Just to be safe."

"Probably just the call of something we haven't quite run across yet," Maceone said while he knelt and made notes regarding one of the small fliers on a branch. "We all have slightly different senses. Might be hearing something echoing off the trees."

"Maybe, but it's driving me crazy," Cornan said with a little chuckle.

"I think we should go back and do a diagnostic. Better safe than sorry," the rat insisted.

Robert stood up and looked at him. "It's a noise in the jungle. It happens."

"A noise only she's hearing."

Marco spoke up. "Anna, we're a little less than half a klick away from today's goal. What's your feeling on this?"

With an annoyed look, the pigeon bobbed her way to her next plant sample. "I can live with it." She gave a sigh at the little tutting squeak from Higgins. "And yes, Nate, it could get worse, and I don't have any pictures of a sweetheart back home to show you. Happy?"

"Precautions never hurt," the rat said. "Consider this my official protest to this course of action."

"It's just a little further," Shane said, trying to keep a bleat out of his voice. "We press on. Anna, let us know if it seems to get worse, and we'll double-time it back to the module."

"Right, right," the pigeon said, already looking at another odd plant and selecting a sample.

The crew pressed forward. Marco noted the way Higgins kept an eye on Cornan between running his mapping equipment. They crossed a few minor ridges and small streams in the rolling, tight terrain in the next few minutes. Anna made an exasperated noise a few times working with a pad to enter information on her sample.

"Something wrong?" Higgins asked.

The pigeon let out an annoyed warble and almost slammed the pad on her leg. "I'm fine, Nate! Just a little trouble with... getting my notes in."

"Is it a problem with the pad or—"

"Damn it, Higgins; I said I'm fine! Now stop being such a worrywart and leave me the fuck alone!"

The rat backed up a step in surprise, and Marco looked over while Anna ruffled her feathers and moved away to another plant. The ram and Nathan shared a look. Anna Cornan never swore, and they'd both been on enough missions with her to know this.

Marco spoke up, "Anna, I think we should—"

"Hey, Anna, come take a look at this!" Maceone shouted from up ahead, standing on one of the ridges.

"Ugh, lizard, this better be good."

Both mammals followed as she stalked up the ridge, bobbing her head. Marco's brow wrinkled, and he couldn't help shaking his head side to side. Too many things were going against Anna's normal, cheerful character. She stopped when she reached the ridge and looked down, her mood clearly shifting from annoyance to fascination. Marco saw it too.

At the bottom of the ridge, in a natural clearing, plants

that resembled the tress of the surrounding area had formed a natural latticed dome. Maceone and Cornan stared at it in fascination, and Marco had to admit the sight was interesting. Inside the dome of branches, several smaller animals wandered and climbed, reptilian creatures with bodies that almost resembled lemurs. There was no indication that any tool had pushed the branches together; it was as if the trees had naturally taken the strange shape.

"That can't be... No, something had to make that," Anna said.

"But how?" Maceone said. "There's no indication of civilization on this entire planet according to the scans. You're the plant expert, how does something like that happen?"

"How the fuck am I supposed to know?" the pigeon said. Robert was taken aback by the sudden heat and his jowls flared slightly. "We've been on this planet a couple fucking hours; do you know how every fucking animal works yet?"

"Anna," Marco said softly, "I think something's wrong."

The pigeon stopped a moment and looked at her wing-tips. They were shaking, and she was bobbing her head, tilting it and trying to clear it. "I-I'm sorry. I don't know what came over me. I've been... having trouble focusing and getting my notes in and... just getting frustrated."

Robert looked at her with concern. "Trouble focusing? On what, and for how long?"

"Just my notes. I guess it started... shit, I don't know! It's just..." she stopped while the iguana moved over to her and started checking her over, looking into her eyes and at her beak. "I didn't say anything because I thought it was the heat or just a bad day for me."

"Your eyes are a little off, and there's some irregularity in your pupil reflex." He looked over at AC Shane. "The environment may not be as agreeable to avians as we thought. I think we should go back and do a work up now."

"Oh, now you think we should go back?" Nathan couldn't seem to hold back the jab or his tail lashing.

Marco gave him a stern look. "Ease off, Higgins. Things change. Yes, we probably should have taken your advice and I'll note your performance and protests in my report."

"Maybe," Anna said, taking a breath. "Maybe they're right."

"Okay," Marco said. "We head back, let the module do its thing and run some tests."

They all turned, leaving the oddity behind for study at another time. If it wasn't already a moot point. There would be no reason to stay on-world if the environment turned out to be problematic for birds. Still, judgment would have to be reserved until the actual tests were run. Sample collecting was clearly finished for the moment as Maceone kept a close eye on Anna. Marco could see her trembling a little, but wasn't sure if that was a symptom or just nerves.

The four moved mostly in silence, walking at a brisker pace to reach the module now while avoiding any injury from various tripping hazards. Marco had just reached the bottom of a ridge almost halfway back to the clearing when the pigeon suddenly stopped above them. She rocked at her waist, blinking and shaking her head loosely, almost as if she couldn't quite right it or snap it into place, while Maceone reached for her.

"Cornan?" the iguana said with a little nervous hiss. "What's going on?"

Anna shuddered, her body twitching. Her head bobbed back and forth, moving erratically before she suddenly took to her wings, flying up into the trees. She bounced off of a trunk, her pattern off-kilter as she crashed into a branch.

"What the hell?" Higgins chittered while Maceone tracked her movements with nervous eyes.

She stayed in the air a few more moments, wobbling from tree to tree before smacking her wing hard. The sample collection kit slipped from her body as she began to tumble end over end out of the jungle's canopy.

Marco and Robert rushed under her. Higgins caught the

kit before it could be damaged while the other two worked to soften Cornan's fall. She landed in their arms, convulsing and twitching. Blood poured out of her beak with a warbling, squawking sound while her eyes rolled in all directions in their sockets.

They all looked up at one another. "Back to the module! Run!" Marco commanded with a brisk stamp of his hoof.

He switched to carry Cornan's claws in his hands while Maceone carefully hooked under her wings, trying not to damage them further as they raced in a two-person carry back toward the landing module. Higgins followed behind, a haunted look growing in his eyes every time Marco looked back at him.

They raced through the jungle terrain, following their path back to the clearing, each of them almost tripping several times over protruding roots or an ensnaring vine. Shane's heart wanted to race. Adrenaline surged and he could feel panic attempting to grip him, making him want to charge headlong at whatever might be endangering his crew. The ram stuffed it back down. If he allowed the fears—the voice that kept screaming that this sort of thing simply was *not* supposed to happen—to take hold of him, Higgins would immediately fall prey to panic next. Robert would be the voice of reason for a little while longer, but it would still impair his judgment. He knew his crew, and right then, he had to be that domino that refused to tip.

They reached the module, Marco and Robert breathing heavily from the exertion, the ram more so from the dense air. Higgins twitched and breathed in shuddering squeaks. Shane looked straight at him and pointed to the main door of the module's airlock.

"Higgins, prepare a general decontamination sequence. Maceone, help me get her into a quarantine pod."

The rat nodded vigorously and set about the control panel for the airlock door, his slender fingers dancing over the controls. They all needed their tasks to perform, him most of all.

Meanwhile, Shane went to the series of smaller doors along the fore of the module. At the first one, he pushed a few buttons to enter a code, and the quarantine pod door opened. A metal slab slid out, and he and Robert began to lift the pigeon onto it. Marco noticed that Anna had gone completely limp. Her beak was messy with blood, and one look at a red-gray eye showed that the pupil was completely dilated. The ram looked up at Robert, who made eye-contact with the barest of grim nods while his jowls flared in and out, both of them keeping their mouths shut for the moment.

They had her situated and strapped to the slab in a matter of seconds. Shane pushed a button on the control panel and the slab retracted into a quarantine pod. He could hear the sound of the nanotech foam that would fill it and immobilize her, already beginning to scan everything and feed data into the module's central computer.

The main outer door of the module opened with a whoosh. Higgins looked to them, and Marco could tell he was barely holding together. "Decon is ready, AC."

"Alright, let's do it."

The three crew members piled into the airlock, and the outer door shut, sealing them from the planet's surface. Breathing apparatus hung on the wall that would form fit over nearly any muzzle. Each strapped one on tight and adjusted the seal before Higgins pressed the button on the inner panel. An aerosol washed over them, deoxygenating the airlock and offering several methods of disinfection. Marco shivered at the unpleasant sensation on the skin under his fur. It was nothing new, but every time was freshly irritating. They took slow measured breaths for several moments while the process completed. They all knew they would still likely have to undergo quarantine procedures on the *Manu*, but following the standard protocol now might save them from what had befallen Anna.

When the process completed, the airlock scanned as free of infestation and the inner door opened. They each replaced their breathers on the wall and entered the main room of the module, Higgins tossing everything he was carrying onto the central table and Maceone immediately going to a panel in the corner to boot up the computer's holographic display. At his identity, the computer loaded the optimal efficiency of multiple screens and controls for his species and individual needs. His claws instantly began moving this way and that, manipulating the controls so that a three-dimensional scan of Anna displayed from the quarantine pod.

"What happened to her?" Higgins asked, chewing at his claws and pacing back and forth. "What did that to her? Are we next?"

"Give me a moment," the iguana said firmly. "Don't go borrowing trouble. We don't know enough yet to—holy shit..."

The holographic scan of the still pigeon had moved inside her body as Robert tapped at various controls. He'd shifted the view to a closer, interior scan of her head. Anna's cranial cavity showed large vacant sections. Where much of her cerebral cortex should have been, gaping voids had been neatly hollowed out as if with a scoop. The scan turned while Robert silently adjusted controls and his jowls flared uncontrollably, the only sound that of Nate's heavy breathing. Anna's skull was completely intact according to all readings.

"Oh man," the rat muttered as he looked over Robert's shoulder. "What the fuck, man? What could have done that to her?"

Normally Marco would have told him to keep it professional. Instead, he gripped Nate's upper arm and looked at him. "Calm down. Take a deep breath. Maceone's good, he'll figure something out."

"Thanks, AC," the iguana hissed through a clenched jaw as he continued to type. "But I'm... I'm at a loss here. And I'm worried that—"

"Don't worry, work it. What can you do to get us more information?" Shane said. The ram took his own subtle deep breath. Keep the dominos from falling.

"Hang on." The reptile's claws flew over the modified holographic controls that had adjusted to fit his unique needs. "I'm adjusting the equipment we have on the module to modify our environmental scans. I need to go small scale, given that her skull is completely intact. Anything in the range right around microorganisms in our local vicinity."

"Didn't we look for that in our initial scans?" Marco asked and stared over Robert's shoulder.

"No, we never focus on these things on initial contact because of the Henshaw units." He talked as he typed and fiddled, waiting for the computer to catch up. "They… uh… they—damn it, simple word!—insulate us from those types dangers usually, so it's not been a priority. But clearly, there's something… Wait, I'm getting a real-time view now, the areas just outside the module. Running through a few filters, the computer's got… ho-holy shit…"

AC Shane could see it too. The viewscreen showed the landscape around them in strange, undulating colors from the various spectrum filters. And everything was crawling. Tiny dots moved over every tree, in the grass, under the grass. Every surface was now in motion according to the module's high-powered multivariate scanners. To Marco's eyes, the motion seemed random, and the very sight of it made Nathan chitter from behind them, biting his small claws.

Maceone slowly twisted a nob-like control in the display back and forth. Speakers in the cabin fluctuated, and the iguana stopped as the room filled with low-pitched clicking noises. Marco shook his head, clearing his ears and listening. There were rhythms within the clicking, but they were never steady. Occasionally they would seem to repeat, but with little variances between sets.

"This must be what Cornan was hearing. I think…" Robert muttered while he listened to the sound, working away at the computer to zoom into a patch of the motion. "I think I've got an idea. A theory. Maybe." He was breathing heavily, flaring both nostrils and jowls, while his dewlap shook slightly with each movement. The iguana grunted every time his claw slipped and he made a mistake in his work.

"It's okay, Maceone, just breathe. You're doing fine," Marco said in as soothing a tone as he could manage.

"Okay?" Higgins squeaked incredulously. "Did you see the inside of her skull? This is light years from fucking 'okay'!" He was pacing the compartment again, almost hyperventilating. "What the fuck is all that? We should just go, just get out of here and—"

"Higgins!" Marco barked while Maceone continued his work. He noticed the clicking sound had thankfully been turned off again. "We may have to dust off quickly depending on what we find. I want you to start making calculations for getting us safely back to the *Manu*. I need you to do that while we work here."

Shocked for a moment out of the rising tide of panic, the rat nodded vigorously. He scurried out of the compartment to set up the calculations, muttering to himself, "I did everything right. It can't be like this."

The two were in relative peace when the door to the compartment closed. Marco turned back to the screen where the iguana breathed heavily and directed his attention to what was now a flat, single colored plane.

"There. See those?"

The ram could see. He saw creatures crawling over the flat colored background, all working and moving. Multiple legs sprouted from arthropod forms while what looked like manipulating claws and spines extended from other limbs. Shiny plates covered their segments, and as the captain looked, he realized that the plates were not part of their normal bodies. When the scanner pushed just a little further in, he could make out where the plates strapped on to the creatures. That meant fabrication, which meant intelligence.

"Lucille said scans showed no signs of intelligent sentience on the planet. Where is this?"

The iguana blew out a breath, his hands trembling. "This is a small section of the back of a leaf on one of those trees. They're insects, Marco. Insects smaller than a gnat, but somehow intelligent. Look at the way they're moving."

"I don't see anything in particular."

"Okay, to me, this doesn't fit any conventional knowledge we have about insects. Yes, some hives move with … um—damn it—organization, but this particular movement just doesn't fit what we would normally see. I'm even having the computer model it to confirm it's not my imagination."

Marco watched what looked to him like monstrous figures moving about on the plane of the viewscreen. The more he looked, the more he thought he could discern what Maceone was talking about. The insects moved with a strange sense of purpose. And as he watched their adjustments around each other, it almost seemed like they were communicating.

The computer made a little beep, and something flashed in the corner. Robert tapped it with a slightly shaky claw and looked at some of the analytical jargon that popped up on the screen. "Yeah. Yeah, a lot of this confirms what I was thinking."

"Which is?"

"Alright, remember that tree we saw? The one that looked like it had grown into a natural lattice?"

"Of course."

The iguana clicked his claws a few times, trying to organize his thoughts. "Okay, well, I think they manipulated that to happen. I don't have proof, but the, um … the computer … models, computer models, they're corroborating that pretty well. The, um … they're changing things on the … the cells, they change the organic cells of things and manipulate them. Maybe inorganic particles too. And I think what Anna heard is their language."

"But how did they get past her Henshaw? Why did they … do what they did to her?"

Robert's breathing was heavier, and he scratched claws over his furrowed brow, closing his eyes tight for just a moment and turning in his chair to face the AC. "Okay, this is all theoretical at the moment, but all the models bear out the theory. If we, um—what's that word? Not 'assume' but the other … Okay, if we go with the idea that they work with living cells, that everything they do is based on that, then I think … these insects are this planet's dominant species. The *only* dominant species because of the way they've evolved."

"How the hell is that possible?"

"I'm just giving you what I think," Robert said in nervous breaths. "But it's what makes sense. Whether they have a— oh what is that word?—hive intelligence or individual intelligence, cellular manipulation means they run the show. As soon as they started working with it, they could make life on this planet whatever they wanted. They might … They might be the, um, the reason this planet is … that it's—damn it!—that it's mostly jungle, because that's what they feel most comfortable in. Clearly, they use larger … larger … argh, why am I having so much—?" The iguana's eyes widened and his jowls expanded fully while Marco stared at him. Robert rubbed his nose.

His fingers came away red.

"Oh shit," he muttered, the spiny protrusions on his head popping up, "oh shit, oh shit, oh shit! They're … in me. They're messing with my brain already!"

Marco turned and raced to an intercom on the wall. "Higgins!"

The rat's tinny voice came through the box, "Yeah. Yeah, what is it?"

"Dust off as soon as possible! Level one medical quarantine docking procedure. Do you read?"

"Loud and clear, but it's gonna be a little while. I'm still working out calculations to get us back to the *Manu*." The focused task gave the rat a handle on things, but Marco could hear the quavering note slipping into his voice.

"Work 'em fast, and work 'em right, Nathan. You're our ace."

"O-Okay. Working 'em, AC."

Leaving the intercom, Marco went back to his biologist, who was now up and pacing back and forth.

"I … I was the one carrying her head end, and they must have transferred. They were safe from decontamination. She-She had the shakes. We should have seen it. She could hear them, and we weren't paying attention. The clicking. Pigeons hear frequencies the rest of us can't. My claws … claws have been shaking. Trouble with words."

"Maceone. Robert," Marco said, trying to get his attention.

"How long?" the iguana said, as if he didn't hear, staring from one of his hands to the other. "Anna lost motor control. How long have they been inside? How long do I have? Blood. Blood's already started. Have they accelerated? Slowed? Are they—"

Shane grabbed his xenobiologist and shook the reptile a couple times. "Robert! Stay with me. I need any information, any theories you still have. Higgins is going to get us off world in just a little bit, and we'll get you into quarantine. Equipment on the *Manu* can take care of this." He didn't know that for sure, but it was what Maceone needed to hear. "I need you to stay focused so we can tell them everything we can. How do they get into the Henshaw Shields? Why the brain?"

Just shy of hyperventilating, the iguana slowed his breathing, forcing deep breaths in and out. His eyes flicked closed and open a few times. Slowly, the puffing of his cheeks went down. Marco relaxed a little more in that moment as soon as he saw Robert thinking and working things.

"Alright, just… be a little patient. The Henshaws. They work on, uh, nanotech. I'm not a technician, but… their primary function is the destruction of invading microorganisms at the cellular level, right? So they should have destroyed the, um… the, uh… insects as soon as they got close because they're barely even as big as a single nanite."

While he spoke, Marco thought about the insects. What he'd seen through the scanner and what Robert had already said. "Tactics," he said as the light came on in his brain.

"What?"

"Something from military history. The reason we've never adopted a fully drone security solution in any conflict is that the best-programmed drone still can't quite respond to the adjustable tactics and improvisation of an actual, thinking soldier. If you can adapt, and you can fight back enough, you can beat a drone's predictable movements."

"They fought back," Robert said, catching on. Marco could see some of his shakes increasing. "Nanites tried to destroy them on contact, and they were able to adapt."

"Right. Naturally, we've been thinking of this like a virus or bacteria or simple biological process. To them—if what we've theorized is true—it's sieging a moving fortress. So it's about tactics."

The engines started cycling up as he finished. He had seen the increased shakes, seen the nervousness in Robert's eyes. Now Marco smiled and patted his claw. "Hear that sound? We're headed back to the ship. We'll have this planet declared Judas. We'll get you taken care of, and keep on flying. Leave this place to the bugs."

Robert started to smile, looking like he wanted to say something. The iguana opened his mouth and his jaw began twitching. Eyes rolling in opposite directions, Maceone gagged at the words that had tried to escape, and his body began to shake. A trickle of blood leaked from his nostril, and Marco sprang away from him, looking around the ready room.

Robert was trying to clutch at his head, and soon he would probably lose all motor control. In a quick scan, the ram saw a wall rack with three electroshock batons. He grabbed one, flipped it to the highest setting for non-lethal incapacitation, and whipped around, shoving it into the iguana's chest.

The electric current surged through the reptile, making everything twitch, then it automatically shut down. Robert slumped in his chair. The shakes and twitches had stopped, and AC Shane stared at him until he noticed the subtle signs of breathing.

Dropping the baton, he hoped he'd acted correctly as he pushed the button on the intercom to the cockpit. Panting, he asked, "How are we doing, Nate?"

A shaky voice came through the silver box. "We're up. Approaching atmosphere. Estimate one hour, maybe a little more, to rendezvous. AC… I don't feel so good."

Marco looked at his own hand. His hard fingertips were shaking with a slight tremor. "We're gonna be okay, Nate. You don't have a picture of anyone, and we're not wearing anything red."

"Yeah." The rat's voice was choking through sobs. "I don't want to die…"

"You just do your job, pilot. You're our ace. You make sure the autodocking is set for a Quarantine Level 1 medical bay. They'll fix whatever ails us. I'm going to make sure they have all the right information Robert and I worked out." Marco looked at the electroshock baton. "If you get the shakes bad, you let me know, and we'll try something."

[Subspace DataNet Entry: Quarantine Level 1]

Quarantines exist at several levels in the EE Project depending on the potential contaminant that may arrive on ship.

Level 1 is the most intense form of quarantine and used for any threats that could endanger the entire crew and cryo compliment of an Explorer-class vessel. Usually, this is only invoked after at least one crew fatality due to some form of contamination. An airtight bay with completely separate environmental controls and self-contained oxygen resources is equipped with remote medical equipment and scanners. Several methods of cleansing the contaminant may be employed, depending on survival of module crew.

Cases of Level 1 Quarantine may involve several days before surviving crew are able to return to active duty. In cases of pure equipment retrieval...

Everything was too bright. Light lanced into his eyes almost painfully until shapes resolved themselves. AC Shane winced a little while he woke and adjusted on the med-bay bed. Of course, he supposed he was officially Resting Captain Shane at this point, not that he was complaining. Though even in the biggest bed, his horns bumped some of the framework, making him let out a light bleat. The soft surface of the high-tech medical cot contoured to his body for comfort, but the ache moved from his eyes to the base of his horns, making him reach up and rub where they joined his skull. There was no body ache, so that was something.

"Ah, welcome back," he heard a female voice saying. An otter physician strode towards the bed, medscanner in paw to look over his vitals. He recognized her as Janice Forth. "How do you feel?"

Marco moved back onto the bed, letting her run the scanner over his chest. "Tired, groggy. How long have I been out?"

"We've had you under sedation for a few days, both in and out of quarantine bay."

"The bugs. What happened with the—"

She held up a webbed paw. "All gone. The information that you and XBI Maceone entered into the computer helped us know what we were dealing with as soon as you came in. We were able to contain and eradicate the infestation in you and the module. Good thinking on using the electroprods by the way. Everything we've found indicates that you managed to fry a bunch of them before they kept working."

The ram's eyes closed a moment. He was afraid to ask the next question, but he had to know. "How are the others?"

"Your pilot took some damage from them, but nothing

he can't recover from. Both of you had some damage to non-vital areas of your brains, and there may be some mild short-term to long-term memory issues from the exact event, but no lasting effects otherwise."

Forth hesitated, and in that moment, Shane realized that his memory of the time on the module had grown a little hazy. After a short wait, the doctor continued with a sympathetic tone.

"XBI Maceone suffered more severe damage. It seems they were working at him longer than the two of you." She looked down at an information pad and let out a breath, whiskers twitching. "He'll recover to some extent—the brain can be more resilient than a lot of people realize in some ways—but he'll never quite be what he was. We're giving him the best care we can to help him get back what he can. As for XBO Cornan…"

"She was DOA," Marco said after just a moment. "We knew that on-world."

Dr. Forth nodded. "I'm sorry, and I know it's little consolation to hear, but everyone feels you did everything right that you could. I'll let you rest a little longer, but your vitals look good. I think we'll have you back on your hooves in just another day."

She started to turn away, and Marco stopped her. "One question, doctor, maybe you can answer this better than we could. Why the brain? Why did they go for that?"

Forth gave a mildly thoughtful frown. "When I was treating you and SO Higgins, I had to cobble together the info and theories you and Maceone worked on in the module. We were looking at it even before you arrived thanks to a data link. If your ideas are correct, it could have been study and curiosity."

"Really?"

"Well, it's all conjecture, but it's at least sound conjecture. Other science officers are still studying Cornan's body, going in at the microscopic level. Indication is that cells were carefully harvested and broken down, possibly even car- ried out of her. Everything missing is related to the unique processes common in reasoning species. The portions that set us apart from simple impulses and feral nature. Again, everything's still in process, and that's just the information I have so that we can try and help treat XBI Maceone. If those insects were fully intelligent life, it would make sense that they'd try to study something that seemed new to their expe- rience, such as a larger creature with an advanced cerebral cortex."

Marco was starting to become lost in thought. Before he could get too much into his own head, he thanked the doctor and let her go about her rounds in the large infirmary. Since he was alive and in possession of his faculties, the determi- nation on 67 Manticore d was his to make. He was already pretty sure what he wanted to do, but he had time to rest and think before updating the ship's computers and the SSDN.

It was still hard to fathom: the idea of fully self-aware intelligence in such tiny things. But if it was true, they must have seen the crew as a terrible invading force. Without intending to, the crew had struck first when their nanites automatically attacked. In some ways, the planet should be the source of study with suit precautions in place so that they could understand the new intelligence. Though in this case, there was no study without interference. Just landing on the planet again would subject someone to the risk of the bugs and subject plenty of the bugs to being destroyed by decon- tamination procedures.

Also, they'd been studying his crew's brains. How dan- gerous was that overall? What could they learn or find from them? Even without medical training, he knew that an intelli- gent, sentient brain was complex enough that breaking down single cells shouldn't give the insects much. But what would introducing a material that was new to their species do to their evolution? What was a generation of study to them? And just how intelligent were they?

He needed to let his mind turn it around a little. While he rested, Marco picked up the data pad left for him on a little table by his bed and tried to find something to read. Each time he tried to focus on the words over the next hour or so, his mind circled back around. He was barely taking in the news from other ships and tried to distract himself with some form of fiction. A decision on a planet like this had to be considered over time, with enough breaks in the thought process.

Shane's trouble focusing on the words was exacerbated when the data pad occasionally shuddered or glitched while he was trying to read. After another twenty minutes of trying to simply deal with it, he grabbed a communications device from beside his bed.

"Computer technicians," he said into it, hoping it would route correctly if the computer was having problems.

"CompTech Axel speaking," answered the slightly squeaky voice of a bat.

"Hi, this is AC—RC Marco Shane in the infirmary. I think I have a malfunctioning data pad. Could someone change it out?"

"It's not just your data pad, sir. We've been having some general trouble with the system all rotation long."

"Do we have a time estimation on the fix? What's the problem?"

"We're still trying to pin that down, sir. We won't have a time estimate until we know what's wrong with the nanotech in the system or until I can figure out what that damn clicking is."

Shane's heart dropped out of his chest. "Clicking?"

"Yes, sir. We keep getting these clicking noises in the system. We're trying to figure out what it is, and it's difficult because not everyone can hear it or pinpoint—"

"Is there a rhythm to it? Does it sound like machinery?"

"No, no real consistent rhythm, sir. That's what's so frustrating…"

The tech kept going, but Marco hardly heard the next several words. When he finally ended communication and tried to reach the security team to sound an alert, the ram was already going over everything in his head. They made it on board somehow. Something was missed. Could it have been eggs inside Anna, even smaller than the insects? Her sealed sample kit? Where had it gone when they'd brought her in? Higgins had it before they pushed her into the quarantine pod, which turned out to be moot. And it had gone... where?

Memory was too hazy from the time in the module. It didn't matter anyway; the insects were clearly on the *Manu*. Now they were in the computer systems. Could that be how they did it? Hiding out in one of the computer systems, figuring out how to trick the scanners when they were in danger? Had they somehow learned from being in Robert's brain while he was analyzing? Or was it simple individual error somewhere that hadn't actually destroyed them in the quarantine bay? Too many possibilities, and his mind was running in circles. Alarms had been sounded, but if they couldn't trust the computerized scanners, what could they do?

Cold equations played themselves out inside the captain's head. He had one duty to perform, one thing he could at least make sure of. Taking the data pad, working through the glitches and the difficulty he was having focusing with the torrent of thoughts, he entered his captain's credentials and accessed the secure parts of the SSDN. With shaking fingers, he began updating an entry as basically as he could, trying to find the right words.

Shaking fingers. Trouble with words.

Marco Shane breathed heavily and put a finger to his wide nostril. The hard tip came away red.

[Subspace DataNet Entry: 67 Manticore d]
URGENT WARNING: 67 Manticore d is designated Judas. Scans do not indicate threat, planet to be quarantined from exploration. Intelligence on planet not visible insect.

Ship *Manu* is lo

[System Error. Rebooting data. Retrieving relevant updates.]

[Subspace DataNet Entry: 67 Manticore d]
Habitable planet. Recommend rerouting to set up further colonization. Follow coordinates…

BLINK

James Stone

The swarm broke from the trees at the edge of the clearing. The blinks loped, slithered, or some damned combination of the two, across the field, and they were closing on the friendlies alarmingly fast. Rhett's fist twitched reflexively, wanting to clench due to the conditioning, but he controlled the impulse and instead dialed up the magnification on his helmet's visor to better see his troops.

A hundred beings wrapped in sleek black and gray battle armor stood in a neat line, each one an arm's length from the next. No need for camouflage or cover in this battle. Not anymore. Each of his troops stood with their weapons in their paws. Green energy lanced at the oncoming swarm, decimating their numbers, but the tide wasn't breaking. Some troopers stood with their free hand slightly raised, and Rhett's ear flicked against his helmet in annoyance. He'd have to instruct the sergeants to correct that in the troops before it became an advantage for the enemy.

Rhett's ranging computer showed the enemy line at ten meters. Five meters. Two. The entire swarm faded and shifted, suddenly appearing among his men faster than their advance should allow. The comms crackled with howls and cries of pain. Rhett's fist twitched again, and he felt the familiar twinge in the back of his skull as the enemy was suddenly meters away; a hundred particle beams pierced a hundred nerve bundles in microseconds and moved to a new target.

"Perfection," Rhett murmured, turning his head to look at the other observers on the ridge next to him.

"Just like on K-48 and the rest," the Marshal said, nodding, his voice loud over the audible. "As we suspected: they've lost their advantage. We may not have started this war, but we're going to win it."

A colonel to the left of the Marshal turned his head and the indicator above Rhett's visor supplied a name, Wyeck, for the voice. "Pitched battle lines and open terrain don't make a war, Marshal. The time jump isn't a magic pill to wipe out the enemy."

"It looked like it down there, Colonel."

"And when we have to fight them in their cities, or in forests? Combat effectiveness of our troops in close quarter fights, even with the advantage the time jump gives us, is highly dependent on the skill of the troopers."

"Then with our conditioning methods we have nothing to worry about," the Marshal said. Rhett could almost picture the wide-eyed, fervent expression on his avian face.

Wyeck's reply was a low grumble over the comm, and Rhett grinned.

"Can we set the time jump to more than a second?" the Marshal asked.

"No, Marshal. Adapting alien technology is difficult as you'd imagine. That we got it working at all with consistent results is amazing," Wyeck said.

The big tiger turned back to the battle below. The enemy advance had collapsed, and the few survivors were being mopped up. A few of his troops were down. "Commander to lieutenants: status," he said. The reports scrolled on his visor: twenty-one down to the enemy. Before the invention of battle armor, if only ten troopers emerged from a battle like this they'd count it a victory. The advent of the armor had only improved that to fifty survivors at most, and the time jump had improved that outcome remarkably.

The near-constant twinge of jumps being used had faded

into the background uncomfortableness of the battle armor, with its relief tubes, vascular splices, and such. What was the pain of a headache to the phantom feeling of Rhett's missing tail, or of the Marshals' lost wings?

"All troops to standby condition. Set perimeter warnings at fifteen klicks, but otherwise," he said, and glanced up at the local time readout superimposed on his view of the stars. "R&R until 0930."

His troopers below relaxed into a more casual line, in that they lowered their weapons and tended to bunch into clusters instead of battle ordered lines. Rhett remembered the old days when you'd have to go back to camp, but what was camp when your battle armor was your shelter and transport all in one? At least when the campaign was over in a couple of weeks they'd get back on the ship, crack open their armor, take a very long shower, and have some R&R for real. Rhett shivered in pleasure at the thought.

* * * * *

Rhett looked around the clearing at his squad. Phelps and Santos were both down, and his visor confirmed they were deceased. He shifted stance and clenched his fist, aimed, and fired for another kill. Blink corpses scattered among the trees. Fist. Aim. Fire. He could hear updates from the command channel giving large scale sitreps and directions for forces, but it was reduced to a useless, annoying buzz as he focused on this squad. This clearing. Fist. Aim. Fire.

Rhett took a step back and felt the clink of his lieutenant's armor against his back. Fist. Aim. Fire. Good combat position: clear lines of fire. Fist. Aim. Fire. A dull headache from repeated use of the fist. Aim. Fire. Dull headache. Aim. Fire.

Searing pain erupted in his left paw as a blink suddenly phased close, wrapped tentacles around his arm, and twisted. He tried to close his fist, but it held him tight and was flowing up his shoulder with something that looked like a lamprey's mouth. Rhett ground his teeth and brought his weapon up to lance the blink's body with green energy. "Not gonna dodge this."

The blink charred, stiffened, and fell away. Rhett's eyes focused on his next target. He felt dizzy watching it shift in space randomly. He noted its location, clenched his fist and felt like an ox had belted him in the back of the head. His vision grayed, and he collapsed to the ground, passing out.

* * * * *

"C'mon big guy. Pull it together," Rhett said, trying to fight down a wave of nausea. He looked around the room that he had woken up in. His helmet lights revealed low benches running along the wall, and he wasn't sure if they were beds or seats. Damned blinks.

He hadn't found any sign of his squad since he woke up. The floor was stone and his visor said the environment was dry, so there were no footprints to help lead him to the camp. No traffic on comms either. Rhett felt a twinge from his phantom tail lashing in confusion. Why would they be observing comm silence unless something had gone terribly wrong? Somebody must have survived that fight in the woods, or he'd be laying out there with a blink hollowing out his skull.

"Physical status?" he asked aloud, his visor reporting that he was suffering from a sprained wrist and "temporal shift overexposure syndrome (TSOX)."

"What the hell? TSOX?" he wondered, glancing at his wrist. His gauntlet was scratched and some electronics were showing through a breach in the plating. Rhett was able to flex his wrist, though it shot pain up his arm that made his fur stand on end and caused another wave of nausea to crash over him. "NoVom and analgesic doses. Now!" he growled. Rhett felt his stomach settle as his battle armor injected the drugs into his veins. He really didn't like the thought of vomiting into his helmet with no way to remove it.

The analgesic started taking effect, but slower than the

NoVom. He carefully flexed his wrist again and didn't feel like screaming, so he considered that an improvement. The tiger made a partial clench of his fist to see if he'd be able to time jump and if that motion wasn't impeded by the sprain or by the gauntlet damage. He called for a systems status, and the visor read out that his suit was 94% optimal. "Good enough."

Rhett stood up and began to explore the house. Two large rooms placed in an L-shape, with a smaller room filling the corner of the L. He found nothing living, and no gear or tech of any kind. Not even a scrape on the stone floor of the rooms until he started clanking around. The small room had the door to the outside, and Rhett emerged into the street's hazy atmosphere. "So much for a dry environment," he mumbled to himself, wondering what chemical he was walking through.

Another building stood across the space with its door facing Rhett. He crossed to it and looked inside, finding it also empty. He continued down the road to his right, emerging into a broader avenue which had several smaller roads leading back off of it. He checked another house pair and found them all empty and unmarked except for his boot scuffs. He didn't know where his squad was, but they definitely weren't around here. He didn't think the army had tech that did combat extraction like this. Who would dump a wounded soldier over ten klicks away from his mates, from the medics, and from combat support?

Rhett kept advancing house by house, initially searching each one for signs of either his squad or of blinks, becoming more confused when he still hadn't found any signs of friend or foe. Why was the city empty?

Eventually, the tiger worked his way to the edge of town and entered the woods where his tactical display showed the last reading of friendlies. His boots sank into the turf, and he wished for a moment that he could feel that soil with his bare paws and breathe air that didn't smell like recycled tiger.

His daydream was interrupted as he marched through the trees by a feeling he was repeating steps he had taken earlier. Rhett felt the fur rise on the back of his neck. Brief flickers started in his peripheral vision: blinks moving among the foliage. He drew his weapon and paused, watching, waiting for an attack. Several moments passed and he resisted the temptation to break the silence on comms to warn the camp. Rhett steeled himself. Better to die out here alone or lose his squad than to wreck the big picture, and that's even assuming anyone was there to hear. When the flickers faded, he let out the breath he hadn't realized he was holding and started out again.

He approached a clearing and could see the helmet lights from the troops' battle suits. The beams shone in random directions, and that suggested to Rhett that the troops were at ease instead of on alert for incoming blinks. He stepped into the clearing and those lights all pointed at him. "Commander Rhett?" a panther lieutenant turned and asked over the audible, "How did you get here?"

"Lucky to get here at all after you dropped me back in the town with no sign of where you went, Lieutenant!" Rhett shouted, recognizing her as his own second, Bills.

The lieutenant came up to him, helm to helm. "Where we went, sir?" Bills said, her dark ears forwards and her brow furrowed. "We were standing at rest just talking like now, and there was this strange *woomph*, and you just disappeared."

"What do you mean? We were in combat with blinks. Something big hit me and I blacked out. Now, have those two, Phelps and Santos, move to advance... advance positions. I saw evidence of blinks while inbound," he said, getting a strange sense of déjà vu.

"I'm telling you: we haven't seen combat, you weren't injured, and we haven't seen any enemy activity for days," Bills said. She turned away and shouted. "PHELPS. SANTOS. Forward scouts up and downrange!" Rhett watched the two troopers salute and move in opposite directions out of the camp.

Rhett's eyes scanned his squad while they stood at alert, helmets turned to the horizon. There was a full troop compliment in the clearing, and the paint stood out fresh on their armor. "I, uh, I'm not sure what's going on," Rhett said, turning back to Bills and watching her eyes narrow with suspicion.

"MEDIC. My position. Now!" Bills shouted, drawing her weapon and aiming it at Rhett. The trooper, a goat, trotted over and saluted. "Check the Commander for injury," she continued, "or blink infestation."

The medic advanced on Rhett and plugged his diagnostics into the tiger's battle armor. His strange eyes went unfocused as he read the readouts on his visor, then he focused again on Rhett and Bills. "No blink infestation. Pulse high. Torsion injury to left paw and arm consistent with blink tentacles. Hmm," he paused a moment. "Commander Rhett has elevated neurotransmitter levels in the posterior of his brain."

The lieutenant snarled slightly, showing her fangs, and holstered her weapon. "Ok, so he isn't a blink," she said. "Sorry Commander. Better safe than sorry."

Rhett relaxed, and realized absently that he had been tensing his left paw in preparation for a time jump, contrary to his conditioning. He turned his head to the medic. "What do the neurotransmitter levels mean?"

"Overexposure to time jump effects. We call it TSOX. Basically, we think your brain is being damaged by the resolution of parallel time streams into a single stream. Happens to all of us every time we time jump, but in your case, your brain is reacting like you've just finished a long battle. Maybe two hundred jumps. Maybe more. I recommend limiting your exposure to time jumps, both your own and others."

Rhett's ears flattened. "That's crazy. I was fighting and jumping, but two hundred? More like twenty. How in hell am I going to avoid time jumps when we have a forest full of blinks?"

The medic nervously sucked on his buckteeth. "If we

weren't in a forward position, I'd call for a medical extraction. As it is, Commander, I'm sorry, but you'll have to manage."

"Why do I remember combat when the rest of you don't? Your armor definitely hasn't seen action."

Bills and the medic looked at each other. "I don't know, sir. I don't think you time jumped. It only goes for one second, ever. They never managed to get it any longer than that, and even if it did, why would you be back in town instead of standing right here with us? We were never in the city."

The tiger looked between the two of them and frowned. "Got it. You're dismissed, soldier," Rhett said. The goat saluted and returned to his duties in the camp. Rhett looked up at the stars silently for a moment and then turned to Bills. "Keep troops at alert. Cycle scouts on three-hour shifts. I'm going to try to sleep. My wrist and head are killing me."

Bills nodded and watched the commander dim his faceplate, his armor settling into a wider, more relaxed stance.

* * * * *

Rhett broke through the surface of weird dreams to the shaking of his shoulder and sounds of battle: Tentacles and limbs slapping the ground and particle beams cracking through the atmosphere. The tiger shook his head and felt his inner eyelids roll back to see Bills as the owner of the gauntleted paw shaking him. "Bills? Report."

"Blinks in all sectors, sir. Santos got back in front of them. We haven't heard from Phelps. Anything on command channel?"

He paused, listening. "Complete silence since the battle yesterday. I think we're on our own," Rhett said, the feeling of déjà vu washing over him again. He stood back to back with Bills, feeling the twinges, the weirdness from the time jumps of the troops around them, and the dizziness from watching blinks phasing. He took aim and tried to take out blinks outside of the perimeter to little effect.

His status display showed Santos down and out, and

several other troopers as well. Phelps was still up, and Rhett took that as a good sign. He wasn't sure what happened in the prior battle, but events weren't repeating.

"Commander. We have a perimeter breach!"

"Phelps, stay here. Bills: you and me on that breach," Rhett shouted. He pivoted and broke into a sprint across the clearing. Several blinks were breaking into the downed troopers' helmets, and the tiger and panther's weapons lanced out to turn them to charcoal.

Bills settled into position with Rhett at her back, aiming over her shoulder based off her weapon position. He grunted as he felt her using the fist so close to him, but clenched his jaw, aimed and kept firing. Fist. Aim. Fire. Her shoulder nudged his arm when her time jumps placed her body back where it was a second before. Fist. Aim. Fire. The mound of smoking tentacles and limbs and eyestalks grew larger in front of Bills. Rhett looked back to check on Phelps, then heard Bills scream behind his ear and fall back against him. He fumbled trying to catch her as she collapsed to the ground. Her faceplate went red with a gush of blood as the blink burrowed into her skull. Rhett didn't think as he clenched his. Fist. Pain oh God oh God oh God so much so much pain! Black.

* * * * *

Rhett came to, rolled onto his side and groaned. "Ahhh ahh analgesic. No... NoVom. Please. Now," he mumbled. The room slowly stopped spinning and the tiger was able to get to his knees and raise his head without it falling off. He looked around and was surprised it wasn't the bare room from before. Scratches and scrapes from battle armor marred the floor and benches. Enough for a squad. He was safe.

"Physical... status?"

The visor reported that his pulse and blood pressure were shaky, and the tiger's TSOX was advanced which may lead to visual hallucination and disorientation.

"No kidding. Tell me something I don't know. System

status?"

His visor reported his armor was still functioning at 94%.

"Are you real, or am I hallucinating?" asked a shaky voice from the doorway. Rhett turned, drawing his weapon and groaning from the effort, to see an elderly tiger in abraded armor stumble through wearily. He started to answer, but the old guy came close and threw his arms around Rhett's shoulders, hugging him.

"I guess that answers that. You feel pretty solid to me, old man."

The old tiger laughed, quietly at first, and then hysterically. After a minute, Rhett realized the old man's laughter had turned to sobbing. He reluctantly put his arms around the old man.

"Here now. It'll be ok. Shhh. It'll be ok. What's wrong?"

The man's sobs quieted and he pulled back. Fur matted with tears, he gazed at Rhett. "I've been so lonely." The old tiger swallowed noisily.

"What do you mean, old guy? Your squad is here, right? How can you be lonely?"

The tiger hugged Rhett again, shaking, talking over his shoulder. "Not anymore. I don't know where they are."

Rhett's visor returned the old guy's name, same as his own. "Hey, what are the odds you're a 'Rhett' too? Big family for sure. Be surprised if you and I weren't related."

The old man growled and drove his right gauntlet into the stone wall, surprising Rhett and making him jerk back. "Yes, big surprise. What do I do?" he said, the last part quieter. He straightened his back, stepping further away, and Rhett could picture the old tiger's missing tail lashing around his legs.

"Well, if your squad is missing let's go rendezvous with mine," Rhett said.

"Your squad, huh," the old tiger said, shaking his head. "Which way, then?"

Rhett checked his map. "Strange. Inertial guidance is screwed up. Says this is the spot of the clearing. Comms are still down. I'm not getting any friendlies on my map, but the forest is just at the edge of town, thirty klicks away. Further than before but still doable, and maybe they'll show up on the map when we get away from the structures."

The older tiger turned away towards the wall. "They won't. Nobody here but you and me," he said, shaking his head again.

Rhett clumsily got to his feet and was glad the NoVom was already in his system. "Aw, you know that can't be true. Someone has to still be around," he said. "C'mon old guy. We'll find them and you'll see."

The old tiger growled quietly, drew his weapon and went to the door, turning back to see Rhett give him a thumbs-up and a smile.

"They told you to avoid exposure to time jumps, right?"

Rhett nodded.

"Good. I'm gonna repeat it: don't use it unless it is the only way. It should be clear even to a kid like you that something isn't right. You may think things can't get worse, but you're wrong."

Rhett's ears went back, his smile fading, and he looked down at his damaged gauntlet. The old guy nodded and stepped into the street with Rhett close behind.

They advanced down the street. The old man looking straight ahead while they passed each open door: dark holes in the uniform stone walls. Rhett turned his head to stare at each one when they passed, out of habit. The road intersected with a broad avenue, and the old tiger looked up and down it before sprinting across with Rhett close behind.

Unlike before, this part of the city had markings everywhere. Each door had scratches beside them. Walls were scraped. The pavers were scuffed from battle armor alloys. "Big force moved through here," Rhett said, running his gauntlet across the stone and adding his own marks. The old tiger stopped and tensed at the sound, and turned to glare at Rhett, his ears flat against his skull. He signaled for quiet.

Rhett gave the hand signal that he understood, and watched the old guy move across the street to cross in front of another heavily marked doorway. Once he was past and in the alley beyond, he signaled Rhett to come to him.

Rhett started across the street and now understood the old tiger's caution: faint flapping and scraping sounds emerged from the yawning darkness of the building's door. Rhett crossed over and sidled along the wall; his weapon pointed at the door. He froze mid-stride when, just beyond the midpoint, the door erupted in flickering tentacles and glimpses of teeth jumping across the distance at Rhett. He growled and aimed, but before he could get a shot off the old man was firing precise shots from the right. He could barely feel the old man's time jumps as the blinks squealed and fell. Rhett added his own shots to the mix, but the swarm was getting closer and closer to him, backing him tighter against the wall. The temptation to use the fist was overwhelming, just to gain that extra second to fight. Tentacles wrapped around his legs, attaching with slimy suckers to his armor, only to release when the old tiger pierced them with blazing green energy.

At last the swarm broke and no more blinks emerged from the door, and the two were able to clear the road of the loathsome things. Rhett sank to his knees, panting, and heard the old man huffing with exertion. "What the damn hell is wrong with you?" the older Rhett gasped out.

Rhett looked over at the old tiger leaning against the corner of the building. "When… when I was in this city earlier, it was deserted. Where'd they come from?"

"They weren't here then," the old man said.

"That's what I just said."

"That's my only answer, kid. I don't know how they got here. I just know they're here now, and we got to be careful. Now c'mon, let's get away from here in case there are more in that nest."

Rhett got up from his knees, shaking his head. The old

man beckoned and continued up the alley to a broad road-way. This one lacked doors into the buildings and seemed more for the movement of something large in and out of the city. The pavers were scratched from many battle armor boots passing over them. The old man was muttering to him-self. "You think this will take us to the forest?" Rhett asked, interrupting.

"It will, but we aren't going to the forest. I told you, there's nobody but us, and the forest is thick with blinks. I've tried to go out from time to time, but never got far."

"Is that how you lost your squad, old man?"

"Goddamnit Rhett!" the old tiger turned and stepped face to face with him. "I didn't lose my squad! I'm all there ever was before you came!"

"Hah, no way old guy. All of these battle armor marks? It would take a single suit years of marching around..."

"Sixty-eight. Sixty-eight years. All alone, trapped in this suit. Being fed my own reconstituted shit. Drinking my puri-fied piss. Smelling only tiger smells. Staring at the stars and wondering when it would end. Wondering whether a blink would finally get me or if I would lose hope and kill myself," the tiger said, his eyes closing and tears starting again.

Rhett stared, his muzzle hanging open.

"I bet if I could hold out long enough, you'd show up. I wouldn't be alone anymore. I'd get a second chance to save both of us," the old tiger said, his eyes hooded and streaming tears as he pointed his weapon at Rhett's faceplate. "Remove your left gauntlet, Rhett. Please, and don't try to time jump. You saw how good a shot I am now."

Rhett blinked. "You're joking. We don't have time for this, old man."

The old tiger's weapon tapped Rhett's faceplate. "Time? We have plenty of time. I estimate it's about eight years before the battle in the clearing. We are probably only just encoun-tering our first blinks and getting slaughtered out there on the colony worlds. Gauntlet. Now."

Rhett's eyes flicked down towards his weapon at his side, and the old man tapped his faceplate more insistently, leaving a scratch with the barrel of his weapon. Rhett sighed and carefully raised the gauntlet, his other paw reaching over and unlocking the catch before sliding it up and off revealing his sweat-matted fur.

"Ok, toss it down carefully at my feet."

"What are you going to do?" Rhett asked, dropping the gauntlet.

"I told you. I'm going to save us," the old guy said, stepping on the gauntlet with his boot and putting the full weight of his battle suit on it, crushing it, while Rhett yowled in horror.

"You're nuts! You're leaving me defenseless against the blinks!"

The old man stepped back and looked at Rhett. "Nonsense. You saw how I did against them back there at the lair."

"Yeah, with a functioning time jump."

"How can you be so dense, Rhett? I don't just have the same name as you! I am you!" the old tiger snarled. "My gauntlet is just as damaged as yours was. I've survived these years using it only a pawful of times, and every one of them only because otherwise I'd be dead. Every one of them hurting my brain a little more. Every one of them not knowing if I'd go a single second back or another sixty-eight years. Having the ability to make up a single mistake reliably forever is godlike, but what I've had is a curse."

Rhett looked down at the smashed electronics and back to the old tiger's eyes. "How can you be me? When I jumped before, I disappeared. Bills told me."

"I don't know. The damn thing isn't supposed to send us back more than a second, either, or send us somewhere else in space. Maybe the parts that keep this from happening are broken," the old tiger said, showing his fangs. "I think our engineers were wrong. I think it isn't just a time jump, but a reality jump. In this reality, there are two of us. In this reality, this city, this planet, it is full of blinks. Maybe there aren't any blinks in the city in the future because you and I killed every damn last of them."

Rhett's ears flicked against his helmet. He didn't know what to say: the old guy could be right, or he could have just cut their chances of both getting out of the city to zero. "What about the comms? Screw comm blackout! We could call for help!"

"I already tried that, kid. Ever since that first bad jump it's been dead. I don't know if there's anyone other than us alive. Maybe everyone on the colonies were killed by the blinks before we could fight back effectively," the old tiger said, tears starting in his eyes again.

"Ok," Rhett said, his shoulders slumping. "Ok, old guy. Rhett. If you had your way, what do we do?"

The old tiger reached over and clapped his younger self on the shoulder. "Good to hear my name spoken by another's lips again. Well, I guess they're my lips, technically," he said, managing a smile. "I'd go back to one of my bolt holes. You kind of got me off my usual path, but we should be able to make it back to the closest one and be able to relax a little without worrying about blinks trying to hollow us out."

"Alright. We'll go with that," Rhett said, "Lead on."

The old man shifted in his armor and looked up and down the avenue, getting his bearings. He set off down another of the side roads, this one without doorways opening onto it. He'd study the markings on the walls sometimes while clanking past, and Rhett would reach out with his naked paw and feel the rough, alien stone on his pads. The older Rhett hadn't felt anything on his paws other than the lining of his suit for who knows how long, and Rhett didn't know if he could stand it in the same situation.

The older tiger made a chuffing sound and turned down an alley and into one of the yawning black doors. Rhett followed him in. The building was like the others: scraped, marked floor and walls under their suit lights. Old Rhett drew his weapon and motioned for the younger tiger to wait in the entry before he disappeared into both of the back rooms in turn. "All clear," he reported, giving a half smile. He moved closer to Rhett and looked him in the face. "How you holding up?"

"Head is killing me again."

"Think you can get to sleep if you take some more analgesics? I can keep watch and trade off when you're rested. Been too long since I slept soundly, but I'm not alone anymore," he said, placing his palm on Rhett's armored chest.

Rhett nodded and smiled at the old man. "Sure thing, I can do that for you."

"Good man," the old tiger said, moving closer to the door. "Knock off. I'll be here."

Rhett told his suit to dope him up and his headache and wrist pain faded into a general fuzzy feeling. He backed up against the wall and felt his eyelids droop.

* * * * *

Rhett awoke, panting, out of a dream of fighting blinks. He found his weapon already in his paw. He looked around the entry room and was both relieved and surprised to find it empty. Empty of blinks, but also missing his older self. He stepped away from the wall, still feeling foggy, and stepped to the doorway leading outside. He looked up and down the street, but there was no sign of the old tiger. Rhett glanced up at the stars and wondered if maybe he imagined the old guy.

He walked back into the room. Looking at the marked up walls and floor, he felt dizzy. The more he discounted the possibility that the old tiger was a hallucination, the more a part of his mind suggested that maybe he hadn't even left this room after... well after whatever happened when Bills died. A pang of grief hit him. Reaching out to steady himself on the wall, he felt the rough stone under his pads. That instantly grounded him: if his gauntlet was missing, he had to have left the house and had it crushed by his older self, right? Where had he gone?

Rhett crossed the room to one of the doors leading deeper into the house. He poked his head in and looked around, his helmet lights showing the same marked stone walls. Rhett shifted to look in the other room and felt his fur stand on end as his lights revealed a pile of blinks. He brought his weapon up, already firing as he wondered why he didn't see the familiar shifting wrongness. His beams charred the blinks, but he saw no reaction from the horrid things.

Rhett stepped further into the room. Still scanning the mound, he reached out with a booted toe and nudged the creatures. Now that he was closer he could see the entire pile was dead, but his toe uncovered something that gleamed dully in the light. He holstered his weapon and knelt down, his paws clearing away the corpses to uncover a heavily abraded battle suit. "Oh dammit! No!" he shouted, frantically pushing away the dead blinks but already guessing the identity of the occupant when his visor supplied the name: Rhett.

He uncovered the chest of the suit. He needed to see the faceplate; needed to know if it was really his older self. Rhett heard a flapping sound behind him. He started to turn and draw his weapon, but the blinks shifted and phased. He heard a sound like twigs crackling underfoot and the pain registered a second later when they broke his arms. Their teeth scratched at the plating of his helmet, trying to get in, when the old tiger rushed the room roaring and firing. Rhett could feel the blinks releasing his mangled arms while their bodies turned to char and fell away.

The old tiger knelt beside Rhett, holstering his weapon. He touched a stud below Rhett's sternum. "Command medical override: max analgesic and NoShock. Now!" he shouted, scanning Rhett's face. "C'mon kid, stay with me."

"You... It's not you? In the suit?" Rhett asked, his vision tunneling with the drugs already working in his veins.

"No no no! Dammit, why'd this have to happen?" the old tiger said, his shoulders slumping. He reached over and cleared the last of the bodies off the faceplate, revealing a tiger's mummified face. The neck seal of the suit had a large breach down one side. The old tiger shook his head. "I thought it was. Older me. Younger me. Whoever we are. I thought I was saving you." He lifted the mummy's left hand with its damaged gauntlet still in place. "See?"

Rhett turned his head shakily to look, and then back at the old tiger's face.

"I thought he was me," the old man said. "I found him here and kept him covered with blink corpses. I didn't want them finding him while I was out. Didn't want them figuring out better ways to kill us now and making them that much harder to kill in the future."

Rhett nodded and winced. "So how do you know he's not you?"

The old man was fumbling with his left gauntlet seals, and Rhett watched him pull the device off. "Because only one of us has to time jump now. Rhett: he's you."

He reached over and slid the gauntlet over Rhett's twitching paw and locked it in place.

"No, Rhett. There has to be some other way," Rhett said.

"There isn't. It was too late for a one second time jump even when I rushed in. If you use it, it'll hopefully jump you back into your own timeline. Our own. Make you him. Your arms will be ok."

Rhett weakly tryed to protest. "I won't make it," he said, his speech slurring because of the pain meds. "Too lonely. I... I don't know how you did."

"I made it. You will too. He didn't kill himself. He must have kept fighting, just as you will. I don't know if I'm sending you back to a city neck-deep in blinks. I just know that here you're dead. There, you still have a chance."

Rhett swallowed and nodded. The old man closed his paws around Rhett's gauntlet and clenched it, feeling the twinge while Rhett shifted slightly. One second. Clenching his fist again as Rhett panted against his faceplate. One second. He clenched Rhett's fist again, and felt the twinge more strongly, and then he was alone. Tears started down his cheeks. The old tiger wondered which the better fate was.

PENTANGLE

Ross Whitlock

The Pentangle heaves itself to a stop on a jagged crest of ridge and studies the burnt-glass terrain below. It's daggers all the way down, the slope gradually flattening, rust-caked girders from some long-eaten warehouse district forming a lane toward the distant, twinkling lights of the marketplace. Here and there, an elastic form moves amidst the glass, a knot of meat and bone, scavenging. It has been a long time since the Pentangle laid eyes on other people.

The last time it passed this way, things were different. It could move about in safety, unchallenged. Before Bishop wove herself in. Before it bore the curse.

"Here we go," Pettybone says, inhaling air into two sets of lungs. He is doing the breathing today.

Stantz is silent. He prefers not to waste unnecessary words. Besides, by now he and Pettybone can more or less read each other's minds. Stantz weaves more flesh downward through the Pentangle's tree-trunk legs and thickens the elephantine soles of its feet. Callus against the fused glass.

"Is this really gonna work?" Pettybone asks, half to himself.

"It'd better," Stantz grunts.

A soft, nervous cough. Lakshin pops his head over the Pentangle's left shoulder in a web of tendons. Clouded leopard spots frame his anxious eyes. Unlike the two core bodies, Lakshin tries to maintain a semblance of his old self, his felinity. Lakshin is a submissive man, but some things he remains firm on.

"Gentlemen," Lakshin murmurs. "Far be it from me to question our goals this late in the game. However, I must point out that if we are doused in old gasoline and set on fire before an enraged crowd, you two will not be the only ones burning."

"You afraid to burn?" Pettybone asks. He can't keep the fondness from his voice.

"I haven't decided," Lakshin admits. "I'm thinking of Ciel."

"I'm right here," Ciel says in her soft twang. "You don't gotta talk like I'm not."

"And have our two strong dog soldiers bothered to consult you on our perilous scheme?"

"It's her we're doing this for," Pettybone snaps. "We've got no future as a Pentangle. Ciel knows. We've got to get rid of Bishop."

Bishop says nothing in her defense. She sleeps on the Pentangle's back, a fetal lump of pale gray fur and rabbit ears. Bishop sleeps more than anything else and barely utters a word when awake. She remains implacable in the face of the others' reproach, their hatred. She is why they are cursed, why they can't safely walk among decent people.

The distant marketplace beckons. You can buy many useful things there. Many solutions to various problems.

"I trust Pettybone and Stantz," Ciel says. "And I ain't stupid."

"You aren't afraid?" Lakshin asks.

Ciel shrugs, a twisting of flesh. "I trust them," she repeats.

"Then so will I," Lakshin sighs, and tucks himself back in. He is passive by nature.

"Let's go," Pettybone tells Stantz. He wants to add something. Some declaration of love. But Stantz already knows, and somewhere within the Pentangle's shapeless recesses, there is a touch, a soft caress, felt by only two out of the five.

The Pentangle sucks Bishop further in, weaving layers of skin over the rabbit's unresisting form. It draws extra flesh from Bishop, bolstering its strength on her matter. The Pentangle's only hope is to keep Bishop concealed, to pass itself off as a Groat, an inoffensive body of four. Once it reaches the marketplace and buys what it needs, Bishop will be excised. Removed like cancer.

All will be well again.

Beyond the lights of the marketplace, jagged ruins point at the greenish, brownish, soupy sky. Broken wreckage as tall as mountains.

San Antonio, they called it. Before.

* * * * *

One is the loneliest number, so the song goes. Lone bodies don't last long.

Two, three, and four are perfectly respectable. So are six, seven, eight, et cetera. Twelve is sacred. Outside the city, it's uncommon to see people form a Sestina or anything higher because standing in their way is the dreaded five. Pentangle. Cursed.

No one could say exactly why. Most could make an educated guess.

There were five seeds.

They fell from space on the same day. We did not detect their arrival. One landed in South Africa. One near Naples. The third crashed down in the Himalayas, the fourth in the Amazon, and the fifth in rural Texas. Upon impact, all five emitted electromagnetic bursts that knocked out much of the world's power grid.

Rumor has it that life in Australia continues as normal, apart from the terror.

Pettybone and Stantz were part of the military unit sent to assess the Texas impact site. The army was just as crippled by the EMPs as everyone else, maybe more so. They did what they could. They kept leashes on the bright-eyed, delighted scientists. They attempted, without much success, to evacuate the locals. They trained weapons on the seed, which poked ominously from its crater. It did not resemble a seed, really. More like a huge tuber, with a phallic stalk or antenna sticking out at a diagonal.

Lakshin was a civilian mycologist. He studied fungi. The scientific community had all its bases covered.

Similar scenarios took place with all five seeds. They remained dormant for eleven days. The boredom was worse than any horror-movie scenario. Pettybone and Stantz tried not to make eye contact as they went about their duties. They had met during basic training and become lovers on their first deployment—the stern German shepherd and the eager-to-please terrier, an archetypal match. Stantz was more anxious about secrecy than Pettybone. His background had left him with traces of self-loathing. On the eleventh night, shuddering with nerves, with some deeply instinctual premonition, Pettybone climbed into Stantz's army cot. Normally, Stantz would not have allowed this.

On the twelfth day, the seeds erupted.

Neither Pettybone nor Stantz has clear memories of that first morning. The seeds released a dense package of microbial life, some vegetable, some silicate. It spread in all directions, faster than a hurricane could have dispersed it. Plant life, it killed. People, it changed.

Pettybone and Stantz awoke to find their flesh woven together in knots and strands. One body, inextricable. They had become a Snake-Eyes, one of the very first. If they hadn't loved each other, they might have gone mad from it. Plenty of their fellow soldiers did. Those first hours were all ragged, desperate grasping and flopping, screams and gunfire. It took Stantz many days before he was entirely certain he was not in Hell. Of those present at the impact site, most died or were woven into each other very quickly. Pettybone and Stantz were lucky, perhaps.

Once the chaos had died down, they lingered, slowly

learning how to exist as a single entity. The plants were dead and the air had grown soupy, swampy. They did not need to eat anymore; their flesh absorbed nutrients directly from the atmosphere. They still needed to sleep, but not as much, and they could do it in shifts. Their woven body was still under their shared control, and could be altered. They could be bipedal, arachnid, trunked, spheroid. Clothing had become useless. The contents of the seed had not only altered them; it had given them what they needed to survive in a similarly reformed world.

Thus, there must be some degree of purpose, sentience, within the seed. Or behind it.

Lakshin had hidden himself in a collapsed tent and survived on MREs. Four days after the seed blew, Pettybone and Stantz found him. He cowered in abject terror. They still considered themselves soldiers, sworn to protect civilians. They reached out a limb to calm the clouded leopard, restrain his panic. Skin contact was all it took. Howling, Lakshin was woven into the mass of flesh, fused and integrated. The Snake-Eyes became a Coven.

Lakshin was pragmatic. He calmed down in time, allowed his rational mind to resurface. Pettybone and Stantz wanted to wait for more military, more orders. Lakshin convinced them to move on. No one had come yet, so no one would come ever. How quickly had the seed's cloud spread? Did the United States even exist anymore? At the very least, they needed information.

They left the crash site and found the already barren landscape made new, alien. Something within the seed enjoyed devouring metal. Towns and cities were falling apart. The living people they met were all woven together in pairs, threes, fours, and more. Already, they were accepting what had happened. Perhaps their brains had been altered along with their meat. Not only did they adapt to sharing a body with others, but they also desired to grow. To add more bodies and minds to themselves. Only those who had not been absorbed—lone bodies—still resisted.

"This is terraforming," Lakshin was fond of saying. "Alien life is altering Earth—and us—to suit its own needs."

"What the fuck kind of needs?" Pettybone often asked.

"We can only guess. Or, if and when the architects of the seeds appear, we can ask them."

No architects appeared, not after a handful of years had gone by. Pettybone, Stantz, and Lakshin stayed nomadic, never leaving Texas. They all got along fine, but Pettybone and Stantz couldn't help resenting Lakshin's presence. The third wheel. Forever.

Then, eventually, they stumbled upon Ciel.

* * * * *

The marketplace sounds its cacophony, lit by blazing, toxic torches. A scattering of tents and shanties in the shadow of the broken city. Clusters of people shamble this way and that, mostly Snake-Eyes and Covens with the occasional Groat. Nothing bigger. The city's where the big ones are, the Sestinas and up. No one from the wasteland is allowed in San Antonio without an invite. In the city, they say, the living is good. There are many pleasures to amuse the cultural elite that has formed from the new, woven society. No riffraff.

The Pentangle's disguise is working. They move through the tents as a Groat, four visible bodies, Bishop hidden away at their core. Ciel is wide-eyed. This isn't her first trip here, but she treats it as such. She covets the wares on display. Many stalls sell artifacts from before the seeds came, junk that has managed to survive, most of it plastic. Broken kitchen appliances. Disposable cutlery. CDs, credit cards, and smart-phones. It's all useless now, but it's novel. It's something pretty to admire, cleanness and color in a world largely without.

Other vendors offer art, sculptures of glass and stone. Some sell useful things: a puzzle box in which extra-valu-able items can be kept secure, harnesses and satchels that won't slip from the shapeless flesh of their owner. Tools and weapons.

The Pentangle passes the large tent where you can buy a lone body. Through the tent flap, they glimpse struggling prisoners tied to posts. Some people will go out and hunt down the remaining lone bodies, drag them back to the marketplace to be offered up. Are you a Snake-Eyes looking to become a Coven? Choose from our fine stock! They'll stop complaining once you weave them into you. They'll submit, as we all have.

"Couldn't we…?" Ciel ventures.

"Wouldn't work," Pettybone replies quickly.

Once a Pentangle, always a Pentangle. In order to form a Sestina, a group of six, it is necessary to weave in multiple lone bodies at once, skipping five altogether. That's how they do it in the city. The Pentangle could purchase a lone body and add onto itself, but its curse would remain. Its unwilling sixth member would let the world know.

Instead, Pettybone and Lakshin ask a question here, follow a pointing digit there. They need a vendor who sells city wares. Stolen or smuggled goods. Refined stuff. The city has scientists who experiment with the changed matter of the world. They've had results.

In the end, the Pentangle looms over a stall with a very small, very exclusive selection. The Snake-Eyes operating the stall is a blend of raven and weasel, the avian head and torso haggling on top while the mustelid half watches for interlopers.

The raven tries to sell the Pentangle a sexual aid.

"We need a corroding agent," Pettybone says. "Something caustic. For removal."

"Removal of what, sirs and madam?"

"Flesh," Stantz replies.

"Ah," the raven chirps.

Pettybone jerks his head toward Lakshin. "This one's got tumors. We need him unwoven before they spread."

Lakshin does his best to look wretched and martyrly.

161

Rumors: in the city, they've found a way to remove one body from several. A clean excision. Lone bodies can still get cancer, and once one has it, all will have it in time. Unless the sick one is cut loose, and it's impossible to cut anything loose; the bloodless flesh oozes back together like wet dough. Unless the rumors are true.

The raven hems and haws. He implies without admitting to anything. Eventually, he asks what they have to trade. Money is extinct; the marketplace runs on bartering.

Ciel reaches into their flesh and pulls out a beautifully carved whistle. She made it herself. She places it to her lips and blows three sweet, light notes. Everyone in range stops in their tracks, listening.

"Is that wood?" the raven and the weasel blurt at the same time.

Ciel holds the whistle out and lets the Snake-Eyes touch it. They sigh in pleasure at its texture. All the trees died when the seeds did their thing, crumbled to powder. But if you look hard, you can find the nub where a tree once stood, and then you can dig, and sometimes its roots are still solid—dead, but real. It's a trick not many know.

The Snake-Eyes knows what a wooden whistle is worth. It darts back into the shadows of its stall and, like, magic, produces a stone jar, sealed with wax.

"You have to isolate the sick body as much as possible," the raven intones. "Smear this oil on a blade and cut. You may lose a few scraps of yourselves, but he'll be a lone body, tumors and all."

The whistle is swapped for the jar. The Snake-Eyes stashes its new treasure in the back, while the Pentangle tucks the jar deep within itself, snug in a flesh pocket. The Pentangle turns and heads back the way it came, trying not to show unseemly haste. Bishop still sleeps. Back out in the wilderness, they can cut her loose before she even knows of their treachery. All will be well.

Horns ring out. All commerce screeches to a halt. The

marketplace murmurs in excitement and awe. Pettybone and Stantz look at each other unhappily. Of course this would happen now.

"What?" Ciel asks. "What is it?"

But it's already on everyone's lips.

The Apostles.

Ciel's eyes are as big as the moon. "The Apostles? Here? For real?"

"God fucking dammit," Stantz says.

* * * * *

Whatever circumstances produced Ciel, she has blanked them from her mind. She insists she doesn't remember a thing. Pettybone and Stantz have seen children in wartime, so they recognize Ciel's trauma. It was bad for her. As bad as it could be.

At first, she was a mere shadowy suggestion, flitting about the farthest perimeters of the Coven's camp. Pettybone, Stantz, and Lakshin sensed her. Their instincts told them to find her and weave her in. Become a Groat. They resisted. The military discipline of the two core bodies, coupled with Lakshin's high-mindedness, proved enough to overcome their alien urges.

The shadow came closer over three days, and one night, Pettybone raised his voice and said, "It's okay. We won't hurt you."

After a pause, her voice reached them. "You'll eat me. Make me part of you."

"We won't," Pettybone called. "On our honor, we won't."

She decided to believe him. She showed herself: a stick-thin opossum, fifteen years old at most, her huge eyes hollowed.

"We don't have any food," Pettybone said apologetically.

"I can feed myself," she replied.

"Goodness," Lakshin murmured. "I imagine you can. How long have you been out here on your own?"

She shrugged. Since the old world ended, since the seeds came.

"Are you from around here?" Pettybone asked.

She faltered, opened her muzzle. "I, uh." One hairless hand scratched fitfully at her cheek. "Yeah."

They let her stay. She foraged and ate disgusting things. She savored their fire and their company. They didn't weave her in, though they wanted to. She told them her name, two singsong notes, Cee-ell. To Pettybone, who'd always thought he'd be a damn good father when the time came, it sounded like a lost fragment of some Latin hymn.

Backstory-wise, all they got from her was that she'd belonged to a very small, very rural town. "Daddy was, uh… I guess you'd call it a militia. We didn't like the government." She pronounced it guv-urn-mint. "I remember, some army guys came and said we had to move. Daddy and Ma and the others got their guns out." She giggled.

Later, when she slept, Stantz muttered to Pettybone, "I think I remember. There was some tiny hick town pretty close to where the seed impacted. We were trying to evacuate them without any bullets flying."

"Probably didn't happen in time," Pettybone mused. "I wonder how she got away. They… I mean, they all would have been woven together right away."

Stantz couldn't say. But even he had to admit that Ciel's escape, however soul-shattering it had been for her, seemed a miracle.

She didn't leave. The Coven took her in without ever touching her. The touch would have woven her in, and to do that without her consent seemed abominable. She sang beautiful church songs, dug up hidden wood and carved things from it. She knew how to survive, but now she didn't need to. Two or three months passed. In that time, they all became family. The three members of the Coven had lost that feeling. Having it back felt so good.

One night, after a long period of silence, Ciel reached out

to touch them.

"Don't," Pettybone said, horrified.

"It's my choice," Ciel replied.

"Don't you want to stay... you?"

"What's left for me staying me?" she asked, and placed her hand on the Coven's flank.

It didn't hurt, and it wasn't terrible or frightening. It felt right. Ciel's body slid into the larger mass. They felt her happiness, her relief. They welcomed her.

Life became joyful for the newly formed Groat. Now they didn't need to worry about Ciel starving, or hurting herself, or falling prey to anyone else. They took her to the marketplace and drank in her wonder. They sang songs together, even Stantz, who couldn't carry a tune to save his life. They drew themselves tighter. Pettybone and Stantz didn't need to hide their love. Their flesh became each other's. Before, they had both been canine, and now, their features barely registered, so close did they meld. They used each other's eyes, spoke with each other's vocal cords, loved each other fiercely. Ciel considered them uncles. Lakshin was no longer the unwanted third, but the final link in their chain.

It couldn't be better.

Until Bishop appeared.

* * * * *

The ways of the Apostles are known only to the Apostles. They don't travel amidst a procession of guards and sycophants. They sneak up. The first sign are the horns: old plastic vuvuzelas puffed on by the Apostles' three attendants. The attendants are all Covens whose bodies have been artfully arranged in a nautilus spiral. They twirl as they move. The marketplace hums with religious awe. Everyone reveres the Apostles.

As a result, the Pentangle can't slip away without looking suspicious. It has no choice but to join the crowd pushing towards the rough glassy amphitheater at the market's far edge. Pettybone makes sure Bishop is still tucked deep within, hidden. Bodies jostle the Pentangle. Only a lone body can be woven in, otherwise the market folk would all meld into one jiggling blob as they crowd eagerly at the amphitheater's rim.

The Apostles are already there, waiting.

There are twelve, obviously. The largest cluster anyone has ever seen or heard about. They have maintained their original forms to a remarkable degree: a mix of species and genders, all gaunt, all clad in simple white robes that somehow repel the soupy grime of the atmosphere. They stand in a line, as they must.

The lead Apostle is a porcupine called Im. She is the only one with a name. A headdress of quills frames her huge, luminous, blue-green eyes. She is also the only one with eyes. A pinkish knot of tendon grows from the back of her skull, dangles for two feet and forks to vanish into the eyeless sockets of the Apostle behind her. It reappears at the back of his head and grows into the next set of sockets, and so forth down the line. Im does all the seeing. This type of distinctive, deliberate weaving is something you only see in the city with their secret sciences and new-world wealth.

There is nothing else like the Apostles in all of Texas. When they speak, everyone devours their words.

"We are come," The Apostles say. Their voices ring out in unison, an insect-hum. The line coils itself into a spiral. Im faces the crowd with her great eyes.

"We bring joyous tidings," the Apostles say. "We see more every day. And we hear and smell, taste and touch more. Since the Seeds came—" Everyone can hear the capital S. "—the world has never ceased to change. Our first mistake was in finding these changes fearsome. They are glorious. They are what our planet has waited for."

The Pentangle fidgets. Each time they appear, the Apostles recycle a lot of their rhetoric. They arrive, talk for awhile, then leave.

"We twelve are the first chosen," they preach. "Chosen by the Seeds to see what others cannot, to carry tidings to the masses. Are we alone, friends? Is the outside world devoid of life? The question lingers. But we have an answer! Within the city, we have eyes that can see from ocean to ocean. Ears that can pick up the whispers of distant stars. Tongues that lick the ground and taste matter from the world's core. And we now know! We are far from alone!"

This is new. The crowd writhes and heaves, enraptured.

"All across the land, across the planet, it is the same. The five Seeds have spread their goodness. Day by day, more of the world is transformed. And there are other Apostles, other groups of twelve… or even, dare we say it, more than twelve! We are humbled! As your chosen, we will roll out a welcome for our masters.

"Who, you ask? Ahh, the great mystery. The distant, divine beings who sent the Seeds, who brought holy to the profane. They wait patiently for this world to be readied. When nothing remains of the old, sick, metal- and poison-choked planet. When every single lone body has been woven into a cluster, when we all exist in joyous union. Then our masters will reveal themselves. Descend from on high in their beautiful cathedrals and spread their arms to enfold us all."

"Fun stuff," Stantz subvocalizes. The others make out his words in the vibration of shared vocal cords.

"Speculative science mixed with classic religious dogma," Lakshin responds. "Remember, we once believed it too."

They did, as a Coven. But once Ciel joined them, it seemed to diminish in importance. Sure enough, the three or four Groats in the audience seem less enamored, more restless. Sensing a sham, a ploy from the city to keep the lower caste complacent.

"Wait," Pettybone mutters. All of them feel his sudden chill.

"You are all blessed," the Apostles are saying. "All of you, who may not enter the city, do the good work of our masters, gathering the lone bodies. You are the world's caretakers."

"Maybe that's why it's a curse to be a Pentangle," Pettybone hisses. "They don't want us growing any bigger than four."

"That's silly," Ciel says nervously. They can tell she wants to believe the Apostles' words, but doesn't.

"Growth leads to skepticism," Lakshin says. "I see what you mean. A Snake-Eyes or a Coven will believe whole-heartedly, but as we weave more minds in, we gain a greater knowledge. As if…"

Silence. The Pentangle notices too late. The Apostles have fallen dead silent. Im has her great, glowing eyes fixed upon them and them alone.

Dreadful seconds ooze by. Im lifts her bony arm and thrusts a finger.

"Pentangle," the Apostles hum.

Bishop is still hidden. But Im's eyes, which all twelve share, can apparently see more than most. Infrared? X-ray vision?

"There must be some mistake," Pettybone attempts, as the crowd draws back sharply, isolating the Pentangle.

"Cursed," the Apostles hiss. "Cursed! You walk among us like this! How dare you."

The Snake-Eyes, Covens, and Groats hunch and coil, muttering, snarling. Eyes turned furious and afraid.

"We'll leave," Pettybone says loudly. "Let us leave. We won't come back."

"Seize it," the Apostles rage. They uncoil and slither forward, Im thrusting her contorted face at the Pentangle. "Subdue it for us. We will bring it to the city and take it apart down to its atoms. Scatter it to the wind. Undo its curse."

To touch a Pentangle is a vile thing, but a command given by the Apostles is absolute. The crowd forms tentacles and pincers. It surges back in, reaching out. Pettybone and Stantz snarl, melding their faces into one muzzle, drawing bone tissue forward to become dozens of teeth. As if they could hurt anyone. Flesh no longer tears and bleeds. Ciel cowers within their comforting confines, biting back tears.

"Five is cursed," the Apostles froth. "Cursed forever."

As the crowd closes around them, Bishop rises.

She uncoils herself from the Pentangle's back, glaring from a web of fibers. Her orange eyes blaze from her implacable rabbit face. She extends a limb over her back like a scorpion's tail. Clutched in its three clumsy fingers is a stone jar without a lid.

"No," Lakshin manages.

Bishop flings a starburst of oil directly into Im's face.

The Apostles scream. Their linked bodies crack like a whip. Im twitches as the great, luminous eyes run down her cheeks like tears. The rest of her face begins to follow suit.

The crowd is shocked, frozen. They can't comprehend. The Apostles' attendants wail and clutch at their masters, trying to calm the pain-blinded, panicked string of bodies.

Bishop tosses the jar away. "Soldiers," she says in her rough, unused voice. "I'd start running."

Hating Bishop, hating everything, Pettybone and Stantz put all the spare meat they can muster into their leg muscles. They burst through the confused, milling crowd. They thunder through the deserted marketplace and back out into the wastelands, up the great rise of fused glass.

"What do we do?" Ciel gasps. "What do we do?"

"They'll hunt us," Stantz says.

Somewhere out there is their camp. Pettybone and Stantz turn in a different direction, a random point on the compass.

Behind them, hundreds of shared voices are raised in holy condemnation.

* * * * *

One day, the Groat found Bishop sitting at its fire.

She didn't lurk and hesitate like Ciel had. She appeared from nowhere. For once, all four members of the Groat had been asleep. It happened now and then. Perhaps Bishop had been watching and waiting for just that eventuality.

"Who are you?" Pettybone demanded.

She didn't answer at first. She watched them with calculation but not fear. A rabbit, her age impossible to guess. She wore plain black, a militaristic style, worn and ragged. The weather never changed anymore, so the Groat didn't know how many years had passed since the Seeds. Several.

So she could survive. That was one thing they immediately knew about her. And it remained the only thing.

"Bishop," she answered at last.

They didn't fear her. Or suspect. A lone body couldn't hurt a cluster. And a Groat would never absorb just one body, for then it would be a Pentangle. Cursed.

"You can share our fire," Pettybone said at last.

"Thank you," Bishop replied. Her voice was very rough. She must not have had much chance to use it. They sat in silence for awhile.

"You're soldiers," Bishop said finally. "Two of you, anyway."

"That's right," Pettybone said. "Ground zero, when the Seed did its thing."

"That must have been a sight to see," Bishop replied.

"We don't think about it," Stantz said. Of the four, he was most perturbed by her sudden appearance, her calm. But even he didn't suspect.

"I guess you'll do," Bishop murmured. "Finally."

She leaped to her feet and ran at them.

They didn't have time to do anything. Bishop hit the Groat's flank and its flesh responded in defiance of its minds. It drew her in, wove her together with the four, leaving her clothes on the ground. Six or seven seconds, and done. Permanent.

They raged, cursed, demanded to know why. They tore at her, but they were only tearing their own flesh now. She didn't say a word, didn't defend or justify her unthinkable act. She closed herself off to their fury, rode out the storm until rage mellowed to sullen resentment.

She'd ruined their lives. They were a Pentangle now. And even if they found a way to add a sixth body, the curse would remain. They could add a thousand bodies and still bear the stigma.

For a long time after that, they brooded. Ciel tried to cheer the others, to little avail. Bishop slept. Her eyes rarely opened. Her secrets remained.

One day, Stantz said, "We're getting rid of her."

"How?" Pettybone asked bleakly.

Lakshin opened his mouth, but Stantz cut him off. "Don't start with your talk about cell structure and osmosis, professor. Please. She has to go."

"There ain't a way," Ciel said.

"There might be," Stantz growled.

* * * * *

Thus, the marketplace, the jar with its fateful contents, the Apostles.

Now the Pentangle tries to lose itself in the toxic wilds. It rolls itself in sludge to mask its scent, knowing the city won't be fooled. It covers miles and miles. By managing its energy input and output, by sucking as many nutrients from the air as it can, the Pentangle can run for a very long time.

Not forever.

"Why'd you do that?" Ciel berates Bishop. "Why the… why the hell did you have to go and do that?"

"You'd rather be taken to the city and atomized?" Bishop replies.

"I…"

"Don't waste our breath," Pettybone says. He inflates their lungs, pumps their hearts.

Lakshin watches from the Pentangle's rear, feline eyes and ears fixed on the horizon behind them. Inevitably, the moment comes when his ears perk. "Pursuit," he says.

They all hear it through him. A thundering, too regular

to be from the sky. The thud of huge feet, manhole covers cracking the ground. Lakshin sees something in the distance following them at a mechanical gallop. It's about as bad as it could be.

The city has sent a Tarantula.

Eight bodies are well-suited for certain tasks. They can form a symmetry. Six is too small. Ten enters the realm of the unwieldy. The city uses its Tarantulas as peacekeepers, bodyguards, enforcers.

Hunters.

This one has been built from the best of the best. Eight huge, sinewy forms, massive even before they were woven into the collective. Eight heads peering in all directions. Sixteen mighty legs piston-pounding forward. Woven into the Tarantula's flesh are flexible glass-metal cables, another piece of city magic. Augments. Fused in such a way they don't slip around in the meat. The faces of the Tarantula are fitted with lenses instead of eyes, antennae covering the stumps of ears. In its center rises a great scoop of delicate baleen, flaring to catch as much particulate from the air as possible. Endless fuel.

"Can we outrun that thing?" Bishop asks.

Neither Pettybone nor Stantz will acknowledge her. Lakshin sighs and says, "Not for very long. It is faster, and we will tire first."

The Pentangle keeps running. What else can it do? Ciel mutters steadily under her breath, possibly in prayer. The farther they run, the unhappier she becomes—not from fear of their pursuer, but from something else. Instinct. Memory. Horrors buried deep. In the earthen recesses of Ciel's mind, a dead thing shifts. Rotting teeth smile.

"Do we fight it?" Pettybone subvocalizes to Stantz only, making sure none of the others detect his words. "At the end, do we fight it?"

"It'll win."

Pettybone instinctively tightens himself against Stantz.

Always, even before, he knew on some level that Stantz was the protector. "Jared," he whispers. "I wanted…"

"I know," Stantz replies, even quieter. "You beautiful son of a bitch, I'm gonna love you down to that last atom."

Some hours later, the Tarantula is closer. It is patient. It knows there will only be one outcome.

"Good work, soldiers," Bishop says. No one has spoken in a long time.

"Fuck off," Pettybone replies.

Bishop points. Up ahead, dark lumps dot the blasted ground. Ruins of some kind. A trail of what could have been buildings, once. Their metal eaten, their wood crumbled.

"No," Ciel says, shrinking. "No no no no no no."

"What?" Lakshin wonders. "What is it?"

They all feel something. Traces of Ciel's unspeakable memories infect all five. Beneath the Pentangle's feet, a stirring.

Pettybone groans in disgust as a foot comes down on a large, pale globule growing from the earth. It bursts in a splash of pussy ichor. All eyes look to Lakshin, the mushroom expert. He can only shrug.

They see more of the pale globules as they draw nearer to the ruins. They skirt around them, slowing down. The Tarantula, sensing an end to the chase, narrows the gap. An unspoken agreement passes between Pettybone, Stantz, and Lakshin. More running is pointless. Save the rest of their strength for the equally pointless fight to come. Ciel is a wreck, sobbing quietly, hiding her face in a veil of skin and veins.

"Think this is her town?" Pettybone mutters to Stantz. "Where she came from?"

"Has to be," Stantz says. "The impact site isn't far off. Smell it?"

"Gentlemen," Lakshin says shakily, "it has been a great honor to live alongside you."

Bishop darts her eyes this way and that and bites her lip.

Her long ears stand rigid. Trying to hear, to sense. As if every-thing rides on one desperate hunch. One roll of the dice.

The ground shifts as the Pentangle turns to face the oncoming Tarantula. Pettybone and Stanz weave great razor-edged talons and long, rigid spines that may keep the Tarantula at bay for awhile. Lakshin, no fighter at all, still forms long, exaggerated versions of his old claws and teeth. The Tarantula doesn't change its shape at all. Its weapons are brute force and patient resilience. They can tear and spear it, but they can't damage it in a way that matters.

"I wish people still bled," Stantz says.

"Good line for a movie," Pettybone says, trying to smile.

The Tarantula looms, blinking its eye-lenses at its much smaller quarry. It is fifty feet away. Thirty. Twenty.

The ground cracks. Plates of brittle earth and rock form momentary battlements around the Pentangle. It begins to sink. The Tarantula falters, feeling the shift. Deep below, something murmurs, rising and falling, a wave of sound. Vocal cords.

Bishop exhales. Her fist clenches in victory, as if grasping an invisible pair of dice.

She almost rolled snake eyes. Instead, it's boxcars.

Everything gives way at once. Shards of terrain fly every-where as they plummet. In those seconds, Ciel saves them. Her scream echoes and the thing below recognizes her voice. The Pentangle bounces off a spongy, heaving embankment, rolls down the side, falls and hits rock. Its body deforms, then springs back. Pettybone and Stantz scramble to right them-selves. Half-risen, they turn the Pentangle to see.

They can't take it in.

It's huge. It has hollowed out the earth to create a spider-lair for itself. It towers over them, hillocks and branching pathways of flesh. A chewed mass of gristle, high as a hill, stretching in every direction, carving new space. Twisted ropes reach to the surface, terminating in the pale glob-ules, its sensory organs. It seethes and roils. How many lone bodies? How many from the town, the militia and the army, formed its core? How many more have fallen into it in the subsequent years?

A name cannot be assigned to such a vast collective. It is a Thing. A Shape. It simply is.

High up on its flank, the Tarantula thrashes fitfully as it is absorbed. Curved, needle-pointed arms push the eight mewling bodies deeper, weaving them in with merciless purpose, adding a new lump of self. The metal, glass, and plastic augments are flung carelessly away, clattering against the earthen walls. The Pentangle hunches, awed, expecting the same fate any second.

But the vast Thing only studies the Pentangle with eyeless interest. Ciel has hoisted herself, her body rising from the Pentangle's greater bulk. She studies the great predator as it studies her. Within its pinkish mass, there are no individual bodies, no limbs or faces, no distinct fur, feathers, or scales. Worse, there is no sign of individual minds. Whatever neural net links the meat, it is all one, a singular consciousness.

Still. It contains the memories of everyone it has woven in. And so it recognizes Ciel and remembers her beautiful singing. Her laughter. Before.

"We have to move," Stantz hisses.

"Wait," Ciel says. Her earlier terror has faded, or perhaps turned to complacency. She reaches out. So does the other. It slides a membrane over her hand, webbing the fingers. She shudders as invisible synaptic darts explore within her flesh. Below, Pettybone fidgets, wanting to interfere, afraid for her.

Ciel communes with the great Thing for several minutes. She starts to cry again, very softly.

"Okay," she says at last. "Okay."

It reaches out to claim her. Tendrils coil around her body. Tiny micro-filaments begin to separate Ciel carefully from the Pentangle, one cell at a time. The city could never have made a cut so clean.

"No," Pettybone says. "No!" he howls, clutching at her.

"I asked it to leave you be," Ciel whispers. "I knew you wouldn't want this."

"Ciel!" Pettybone exhales, raw and sorrowful.

"I'm the one that got away," Ciel says. "I can feel them. Daddy and Ma. My family. It's got them all inside. I belong here."

Lakshin is hiding his face in a pair of makeshift hands. Pettybone tears at the strands, unwilling, useless. Finally, Stantz grabs and holds him. Pettybone curses Stantz, curses the world. Bishop watches the looming flesh with keen, interested eyes.

"I'll remember you," Ciel says. It's the last time they feel her vocal cords vibrate, her heart beat. She separates and hangs in a cradle. For a moment, she is entirely herself again, a lone body, pure. Then the Thing draws her tenderly into itself. She vanishes. Pettybone imagines Ciel within the belly of the beast, being disassembled. Every cell broken down again, dissipated into the greater mass like salt in water. Her mind absorbed into the collective. He howls and howls.

"Climb," Bishop orders. When no one obeys, she sighs and reaches out to take control. She tests the muscles and cords of the Pentangle-that-was. She forms drill-arms and slams them into the earth, hauling upwards. She drags all four of them back out into the toxic day, and the great mass of meat allows them to leave. It honors Ciel's deal.

Pettybone is worthless. He forms himself around a hollow, a girl-shaped space, as if he could recreate her from thin air. Stantz curls himself around Pettybone like a cloak, trying to offer comfort.

"I don't understand," Lakshin says, voice quavering.

"I do," Bishop says wearily. "It was one of the scenarios they gave us."

"Who?" Lakshin demands.

"You're Special Forces, aren't you," Stantz says dully. "Black ops shit."

"Sure," Bishop says. "Close enough. Observe and report,

those were my orders at first. When the seed blew up, things got interesting."

"There's no more fucking military," Stantz says. "There's no more government."

"How do you know?" Bishop retorts. "The world still exists out there and maybe parts of it aren't stuck in this petri dish. Maybe there's people who exist without sticking together like old chewing gum. I follow my orders. You were useful."

"You just used us?" Lakshin asks.

"It worked." Bishop sighs again. "Have you figured it out, professor? The aliens are already here. We are them."

"It's not true," Lakshin says.

"That thing down there? That's the end result. Once enough bodies are combined, they take on a collective, alien consciousness. No way to know if the aliens are truly sentient as we understand it, or if they're just a really, really well-evolved germ or spore. But their seeds hit a planet, terraform, and use the bodies they find to craft themselves. We're all aliens. Most of us just haven't realized it yet."

The former Pentangle stands still under the thick, soupy sky.

"Pure speculation, of course," Bishop allows.

"Jesus," Stantz mutters. "I'm tired. I'm so tired."

After awhile, he sleeps. He weaves himself in with Pettybone, lacing them together as deep as he can go. The dogs sleep. Neither of them wants to wake up, not ever.

"What do we do now?" Lakshin asks.

"Well, we're back down to four, so that's a stroke of good luck." Bishop scans the horizon. "Think those idiots from San Antonio will send more grunts after us?"

"I imagine the mutilation of their beloved Apostles will largely cripple them. But we can never go back, of course."

"No need." Bishop turns them in the other direction. "Let's head Northeast. Toward Washington, D.C. It's worth a look. If we can find any traces of order, of leadership. Anywhere

177

that's still free from the seed. I need to find… someone… and tell them what I've learned."

"Why?" Lakshin asks. "If what you say is true, we've lost. We can't stop this. Why try?"

Bishop is quiet for a long time. Then, she says, "It's just life. Just another form of life, surviving the only way it knows how. I can't blame it for that.

"But if there's a mind behind it all. If there's sentience down there, or up there. If it shot its seeds into our planet knowing what would happen. If your Ciel was just a drop of fuel for some smug alien brain. Then I am going to find that brain and tear it apart with my bare nails, and I'm going to listen to it scream."

Lakshin nods.

The Groat stretches itself. Bishop is fully in control now. She uses the matter of Pettybone and Stantz to craft new insect-limbs for a lighter, faster pace. Asleep, they do not resist. Lakshin curls up at the rear, lost in his own thoughts.

The Groat moves on, aiming itself for what used to be the Texas border.

Underground, the great tide of flesh settles itself, savoring Ciel, studying the spread map of her memories. It pushes its strands outward, filaments questing through earth, rock, buried wood and plastic. Like a fungus, it expands unseen.

Somewhere out in the world, scattered in hidden lairs, a thousand more do the same.

One day, two far-flung filaments will meet, make contact, and begin to weave.

STARLESS

Searska GreyRaven

"Pull up, damn it! Pull *up!*"

"Warp field destabilizing. Warp field dest-st-st—"

"Get her out of there. *Get her out of there!*"

"War-rrrrr-p-p-p field destabilizzzzinnnng."

"Byron! Get! Her! Out of there!"

"I'm trying! Something's jammed the—"

"Warning: data corruption detected. System failure eminent—"

From the back of the bridge there came a popping hiss. A mechanical death-rattle cut the deadpan computer short.

"Got it!"

The pilot's pod at the back of the bridge cracked and shattered, sending a wave of slick fluid across the deck that carried within it a petite, caprine form.

"Byron!"

"Got her, sir." The ship's doctor dove after her, equine hooves battering the metal floor. He lifted her from the fluid and checked her breathing and pulse.

Silence filled the bridge as the constant hum of the engines guttered to a halt, the lights from the various consoles dimming to nothing. Only the hemic glow of emergency lights remained.

"Fritz?"

"Backup should kick in shortly, Captain. Hierophant-class cruisers take a minute to reboot after their pilot has been pulled."

Slowly, haltingly, the ship's consoles returned to life. Lights flickered back on but remained extremely low. A few remained dark, coolant fluid dripping from the seams beneath them. The captain—a salt-white stoat—was barely visible, one paw on the console and the other supporting his weight as he leaned over it. His red-tipped tail twitched while he read the preliminary damage report generated by the crippled computer system.

"Byron, what's her condition?"

There was a nicker from the back of the ship. "Captain, she's unconscious, and her ports are weeping fluid. I need to move her to the med bay before I can say anything more for certain."

"Ila, help Byron get Ellie to the med bay. Fritz, run a diagnostic on the rest of the ship's systems. I want to know how in the *hell* that bug got on the *Caliban!*"

"Aye, Captain," Fritz replied. The cockatiel-man fluffed his feathers, smoothed his crest back, and flexed his scaled claws over the console keyboard. His wings fluttered nervously behind him for a moment before settling once more.

He tapped out a few commands.

Nothing.

Tapped a few more.

Still nothing.

Fritz ground his beak, his fingers hovering over the keyboard. That nasty little computer virus had taken down more of the systems than he'd thought. *A hard reset might fix it. Then again, it might make it worse.*

"Too risky," he muttered. He ran a few more short diagnostic tests and swore. A hijacking bug. *Stellar,* he thought. It had chewed up everything except a few essential systems, overloading the fluid cooling systems in every computer it invaded until they shut down or slagged. Life support was still functioning, but it appeared that every other major system, including the warp bubble engine, was unresponsive.

"Slag it," Fritz cursed. He rose from his seat and trudged to the med bay to give his captain the bad news.

The med bay was a tiny thing for such a large ship like the *Caliban*, but with only a handful of crew, it was more than adequate. Ila, the ship's weapons officer, leaned against the far wall, eyes hooded and her expression alert. Fritz shivered. The hyena unnerved him in some uncanny way. Maybe it was the muscles; maybe it was some stray bit of prey DNA floating around his blood. Whatever it was, it prevented him from fully relaxing in her presence. Every time he turned his back on her, he swore he could feel her leering, tracing the sweet spot at the base of his neck. Crazy, he knew. Splicers like Ila, himself, the rest of the crew, they had any unsavory predatory urges snipped out of the code before it was grafted to their DNA.

Of course, if Ila had gone to the black market for her genes, maybe those urges hadn't been neutered. Maybe—

Fritz ground his beak. His crest raised, then lowered. He fluffed his feathers and preened his wings until he calmed down. He was being paranoid again. Ila was part of the crew. She'd never turn on them.

The captain brooded over the med bay's single bed, across from Byron. Captain Prospero Carmine's ears were flat and his black eyes were narrowed to slits. He leaned back just once, to get out of the way of Byron's horn, but quickly returned to his position. The white fur of his musteline face was streaked with dirt, and his red-tipped tail was singed, but he still looked every bit the resolute commanding officer, even if he was just the captain of a salvage ship.

Byron grimaced and stepped back. The buckskin stallion's cybernetic horn crackled and fell silent. On the bed before him, the still form of Ellie, the ship's pilot, lay supine. Fritz's heart sank. Outside of her pilot's niche, the goat-girl looked so much smaller and more vulnerable.

"Byron?"

"Captain, she's very ill but stable. The virus managed to

infiltrate a few of her cybernetics. She'll need time to purge it, but she should pull through," Byron said. "Capricorn wetware is pretty durable."

"How long before—"

"How many times, Carmine?" Ellie groaned. Her eyelids fluttered open, revealing steel-colored eyes and no small measure of pained fury.

Byron's eyes widened in alarm. "Ellie, dear, you need—"

"How many times, Carmine, must I tell you to *never dock us without a protection ring!* That freighter was *infested,* and you latched us onto her without so much as a glance at our—"

"Ellie, *cara capretta*—"

"Don't '*cara capretta*' me, Prospero Carmine! Look at my sub-routines! My OS looks like a Vyysmyl whore's anus! What did you do to my ship, Carmine?!" Ellie's pupils narrowed to horizontal slits.

"One thing at a time, Ellie."

"Oh gods, you fried her, didn't you? If it's this bad for me, she has to be—I can't—godsdamnit, Carmine, if you killed the *Caliban*—"

"Clean yourself up first, *then* worry about the *Caliban*," Carmine said. "We can't do it the other way around, Ellie. The ship'll keep until you're ready to delouse her."

Ellie moaned, a mournful bleating sound. "How could you forget the gods damned protection ring, Carmine?" Ellie shuddered and went still. The only indication that she was still alive was the occasional blink of green light at the tips of her short, backswept horns.

Captain Carmine braced himself against the bed; head hung low and shoulders tense. "Fritz?" he said softly.

"Captain?" Fritz replied, taking a careful step closer.

"Damage report."

Fritz relayed what he'd found. Captain Carmine's lip curled higher with each new piece of information. Finally, Fritz finished and took a deep breath.

"I want you to find the nearest station and set a course,"

Carmine growled from behind clenched teeth. "Thrusters aren't much, but it's better than nothing. Set the autopilot, and then run a diagnostic on the docking hatch. Run every test you can, Fritz. I want to know what happened before we dock again."

Fritz's crest rose in alarm. "Captain, I'll do what I can, but from the state of the systems, diverting any power from life support could finish what the virus started. The things that bug did to the ship are—"

"Fritz? Less talking, more doing."

Fritz shut his beak with an audible click. "Aye, Captain."

Captain Carmine sighed, his shoulders slumping ever so slightly. "Just get us to a station," he said at length.

"Aye, Captain."

Aye, Captain. Fritz shouldn't have agreed to that order, for two reasons. The first, he already knew: the ship's systems were barely able to sustain basic life support. The bug had fried huge swaths of hardware by revving the reactor, over-clocking circuits and boiling the fluid coolant systems until the hardware slagged. A software meltdown he could repair, easy. His nimble fingers and clever mind could repair code in a matter of hours. But hardware? Nope. Maybe if the fabricator was still functioning, but that too had been shorted in the attack. Those circuit boards couldn't be made by hand.

Fritz sighed. Maybe he could jerry-rig something from the parts in the cargo hold. But searching for the parts alone could take days. The hold wasn't pressurized or cataloged. He'd have to go out there in a suit, two hours at a time, and sift through every piece of scrap they'd acquired for the last four months, hoping he'd stumble over what he needed.

The second reason he discovered upon opening the star charts for the area: there was nothing out here. No stations, no habitable planets. Not so much as an unmanned fuel satellite.

"Blackwater space," Fritz said. "Nothing but void in every direction. Ellie, what were you doing, steering us through here?"

"Problem, birdie?"

Fritz startled, wings flapping, and spun in his chair. "Ila! *Frag it*, don't do that to me!"

Ila smirked. "Do what?"

"Sneak up on—you know what, never mind. What do you want?"

"Captain sent me here. To help," she said. "Need you help?"

Fritz sighed. "What I need is a miracle," he replied. "There's nothing here. Literally *nothing* for light-years in any direction. I know Ellie was thrown off-course by the bug, but we shouldn't have ended up this far from civilization."

Ila frowned. "Show me, where are we?"

Fritz pulled up the star map from his console to the main screen, allowing the computer to zoom in on their position. "See? Nothing. Just a blank spot."

"No," Ila growled. "Not blank. Sterile. I know this place. Heard of this, I have. We shouldn't be here."

"Tell me about it. No one should—wait, you know where we are?"

Ila nodded grimly. "Terrible things happened here. First contact with the Chi!tung."

"The what?"

Ila made an exasperated sound. "The Chi!tung!" she said again, her tongue clicking strangely in the middle of the word. "Bug things, old things, from beyond the Rim. Rare, unless you trade among the Rim colonies, talk to their peoples. Talk to the methane-breathers."

"That explains how I didn't know," Fritz replied with a shudder. Methane-breathers were weird. Really weird. The weirdest things in the galaxy were methane-breathers: races with radial bodies, asymmetrical limbs, tentacles or chitinous shells studded with pulsing, glowing growths instead of eyes or mouths. And they never had proper names either. Entire languages based on gestures, scents, flashes of colored light, sometimes all three at once. There was no Terran translation for them. It made polite conversation—not to mention business—with them all but impossible without specialized equipment. As a small time operation, the *Caliban's* crew didn't have the funds for that sort of thing, so they stuck to trading with oxygen-breathers.

"Ila, what happened here?"

"Chi!tung happened," she said. "Brought with them plague. Few escaped, and the Chi!tung fled. This place was cut off, quarantined, to avoid contamination." Ila bared her fangs, and Fritz recoiled.

Fritz swallowed. Suddenly, the console beeped. "Hold on a tic, what's this? Sensors are picking up something. No, that's not… it must be a glitch. There's a station out there. Or maybe it's a glitch. It's gotta be a glitch."

"Is no glitch," Ila said.

Fritz scoffed. "The sensors must be malfunctioning. It wasn't there before."

"Sensors glitched before. This is no glitch. Is also no station."

"Well, it ain't a moon!" Fritz snapped.

Ila grinned. "No, is no moon."

Fritz clicked his beak. "Signal's weak, but I think we can lock on. Ila, how bad was this plague? Can we scan for it?"

Ila shrugged. "Question is above my pay grade," she replied. "But caution, yes, caution would be good. Even if plague is gone, Chi!tung may not be. Old bugs known for collecting oddities. Might have a pretty cage for little birdie, hmm?" Ila laughed, and it made Fritz's feathers pull tight against his skin. There was nothing more eerie than a hyena laugh. "I go, will tell Captain what you find. Maybe he tell us go, maybe he tell us stay. Either way, should know."

"I should be the one to tell him," Fritz said.

"No, you plot course. Ila just knows stories and weapons. Is no use here." And with that, she left the bridge, leaving Fritz alone with his thoughts and the tiny blip of dubious hope on his scanner. He set a course for it, for lack of any other available options, and trudged toward the docking hatch, tool box in hand.

It looked intact, no charring or scoring from the over-clocking bug, no evidence of tampering. In fact, it was in better condition than most of the ship.

Weird, Fritz thought. But if the virus was really a hijacking bug as he suspected, of course it would leave the docking hatch unscathed. Pirates had to get on somehow, and destroying the hatch made no sense.

But why was the bug still active on a derelict freighter? If the pirates had been using it as bait for a trap, the *Caliban* would have been boarded by now, or at least followed. But their trail was as devoid of contact as the rest of the void around them. Fritz had checked and re-checked just to make sure. The last thing they needed was to get caught with their hatch down.

Fritz ground his beak again. Things weren't adding up, and he hated it when things didn't add up. But rather than focus on questions without answers, the cockatiel-man turned his attention to the docking ring and gave it a thorough inspection.

The docking ring was fine. All functions normal, no cracks or glitches to be found. The only blip was a minor glitch from its last use on the derelict freighter, but he couldn't find any signs of a cyber-attack or back door the bug might have exploited. All his firewalls and contingencies were in place, not one of them turned off or broken.

Another thing that didn't add up.

Maybe it turned them all on after it came through? he wondered, but almost immediately dismissed it. No virus was that clever. This wasn't as simple as flipping a switch, after all. These were sophisticated cyber defenses, defenses he'd painstakingly programmed himself to thwart even virtual intelligences.

When you've eliminated every other possibility... Fritz

sighed. Alright, say it *did* cover its tracks successfully. To what point and purpose? The bug had slagged its host, pulling a digital equivalent of hemorrhagic fever. Hardly the work of a sane mind, let alone a raiding pirate. There's no profit in a ruined ship.

"Questions and more questions," Fritz grumbled to himself. He wouldn't find the answers here. Of that, he was certain. If he wanted to get to the bottom of this, he needed to get into the mainframe.

"Which is conveniently a pile of clicking-hot silicon," he muttered. He thought for a moment, then snapped his fingers. He couldn't get into the mainframe, but he *could* get at the next best thing: its proxy, Ellie.

Fritz closed up the docking hatch and returned to the bridge. Maybe once Ellie was awake, she could shed some light on the mystery.

* * * * *

Unfortunately, Ellie was in no state to speak.

"Her debugging wetware is working as fast as it can, Fritz, but even Capricorn wetware takes time to purge," Byron said. His buckskin hide was still damp from a shower, his mane ragged against his neck, but his brown eyes were bright and clear. And very annoyed. "You're going to have to give her more time. I will not break her concentration over your curiosity."

"It's not curiosity! It might be life or death!"

"Fritz, if I wake her up now, it could be death *for her*. I won't do it. Come back in a couple of hours."

Exasperated, Fritz left the med bay and returned to the bridge, where he found Captain Carmine hunched over a holo-map display.

"Captain?" Fritz said.

"We're badly off course. Very out of character for our Ellie," he said.

"Perhaps that hijacking virus was meant to re-route us

to some rendezvous with the pirates later?" Fritz suggested.

Captain Carmine twisted one whisker between his fingers. "Perhaps," he replied, hardly sounding convinced.

"Is what Ila said true? About those chee-tung things?"

"Chi!tung," Carmine corrected. "And yes. The stories Ila spoke of check out. Along with one more thing. Seems there was an opera house out here."

Fritz coughed incredulously. "A *what?* Out here? I didn't realize this part of space was so classy."

"It used to be," Carmine said. "It might even be where we're heading."

"Whatever it is, it's large enough to appear on sensors from this distance, which means it's at least as big as a standard freighter, maybe even a small station," Fritz replied. "Even if it's an opera house, it has to have engines and inertial dampeners, shield generators. I can salvage what we need from it, assuming it hasn't been picked clean already."

Carmine nodded. "It gets better. Do you know who Nightingale is?"

Fritz shook his head.

"She was a singer, would have been one of the best if her career hadn't been cut short. She was singing in this sector when the Chi!tung skirmish erupted. It was assumed she died when the area was quarantined."

Fritz shivered. "That's terrible," he said.

Carmine shrugged. "It's been a long time. There shouldn't be anyone left alive out here."

"What about the Chi!tung? Are they still out here?"

"Unlikely. There's no T-Class planet to draw resources from, and with nothing coming in or out of this sector for decades, anything left would have starved to death," Captain Carmine sighed. "You should try and get some rest. We still have some time before that station comes into visual range."

With nothing else to do, Fritz returned to the med bay.

"Staring at her won't make her debug faster," Byron

commented.

Fritz sighed. "It beats staring at a blank console."

Byron grunted and passed over Ellie with his horn. "She's progressing, but much slower than usual. Whatever that was, it packed a wallop."

"Can she hear me? Like this? Or will that disrupt her debugging?"

Byron shook his head and smiled. "Most of her wetware will be occupied, but the organic part of her brain is only mostly asleep. A lullaby might be just what she needs. I'll come back in a little while to check on her."

Byron left the med bay, and Fritz was alone with Ellie. "I don't know what happened, but I'll get to the bottom of it, and it won't happen again," he said. "I thought a lullaby might help. *Alouette, gentille alouette, alouette, je te plumerai!*"

Ellie stirred and opened one silver eye. "That's a terrible lullaby, Fritz," she murmured. "Plucking the feathers off a lark."

"Sorry, Ellie, didn't mean to wake you."

Ellie closed her eye again and mumbled something. Then, she was out again. Her white fur ruffled as the environmental fans kicked in. Just before he left, he swore he saw her smile.

* * * * *

Five hours later, the station that had been a tiny white dot on their scanner had grown to the size of a substantial space station.

"Well, that's not something you see every day," Byron said, making a low whistle.

It looked less like a space station and more like an old Italian opera house floating in space. Or the ruins of one, at any rate. Two massive pillars floated in front of the main door, chips of rock scattered like the tail of a comet from where each one had been severed from its perch. Flying buttresses along either side clung to the sides of the great station, giant windows that appeared to be stained glass were still lit from within, and they cast an eerie glow all around. Three arches stood at the center of the building, but only the central one had an access port.

"It looks like they plucked it right off Old Terra and hung it here," Byron said. "Lovely recreation."

"Fritz, is the station life support still functioning?" Carmine asked.

Fritz tapped his console a few times. "Negative. Quiet as a tomb in there, Captain."

Carmine nodded. "Alright. Fritz, I want you and Ila to suit up."

Fritz swallowed slowly and nodded. Ila looked at him and grinned, baring twin lines of savage-looking teeth. "My pleasure, Captain," she said. "Meet you down below, birdie."

Fritz met Ila in the locker room where all the crew's suits were kept. Ila had a heavier, combat-oriented suit that was more like modern body armor than a space suit. The suit was laced with neural connections, feeding sensations right into her brain and allowing her to act as if the suit was her own skin. Fritz had something much lighter, if a little bulky. His suit had extra space at the back to accommodate his wings. It made him look hunchbacked, but the alternative was a suit that crushed his wings and made him feel claustrophobic. Instead of a helmet that hugged close to his face, he had a plasglass globe, allowing him to swivel his head unhindered. One stray shot from a blaster would shatter the thing, but it handled bumps and scrapes just fine. When he'd bought it, he'd never even considered that he might be in a firefight. He was a scrapper, a salvage bird, not a mercenary.

Ila was already fully suited, except for her helmet, when Fritz came in.

"Ready, little bird?" she asked. "Have you a list of what we need?"

Fritz blinked, the skin at the corners of his beak curled up to the closest approximation of a mammalian smile he could manage. He tapped his head with one claw. "All in here," he replied. He looked down and frowned. "Do you really think you need Bianca?"

Ila leered and laid a gentle, loving kiss against the barrel of a gun that nearly qualified as a small cannon. "Better safe than dead, eh?" she said. "Wouldn't want a bug to crawl up your ass and lay eggs, hmm?"

"I don't have an ass," he muttered, shrugging into his suit.

"No? What do you have, birdie?"

Fritz refused to dignify that with a response. He slipped the globe helmet over his head. It pressurized with a sharp keen, and a display of gauges and readings popped up before his eyes.

"You sure you can see through that mess?" Ila said, tapping the front of the globe with one claw. She glanced down at the gloves covering his hands. Not so much as a single haptic sensor. "Implants would make you a faster technician, you know."

"I can see just fine, thank you," Fritz insisted, although he turned off a few of the non-critical displays. A pop-up ad for QuixLix Meat Substitute blinked on and he quickly closed it. *Damn it, I thought I'd fixed that stupid ad-blocker!* "And I don't need to be made part computer to work with them. Besides, do you have any idea how hard it is to keep neural connections clear when you're covered in feathers?"

"You pluck them?"

Fritz shook his head. "I'd look like a neurotic feather-picker. Not worth it. I like my feathers right where they are."

Ila chuckled and put on her own helmet. She shouldered Bianca and, with one backward glance at Fritz, punched the airlock door.

"Fritz? Ila?" The voice came through the radio in the collar of his helmet.

"Captain?" Fritz replied.

"I don't want you in there any longer than you have to be. Get in, get what we need to put the ship back in working order, and then get the hell out of there. Understood?"

"Might be good salvage here!" Ila protested.

"Understood?" Captain Carmine repeated, enunciating every syllable.

"Understood," Ila grumbled.

Ila punched the airlock door button again, a little harder than was strictly necessary, and the door to the locker room slammed shut. A moment later, a door at the other end of the airlock opened, revealing a narrow corridor. And at the end of that corridor—

"Whoa," Fritz breathed.

"Indeed," Ila agreed.

The *Caliban's* airlock opened up to a massive concert hall foyer. A plush red carpet ran up the center, flanked on either side by a row of massive marble pillars. Dim lights flickered with faux fire from sconces embedded in each pillar, giving the entrance hall an eerie, if majestic, aura.

"Artificial gravity still functions," Ila said. "A good sign, I think."

"This must have been amazing to see when it was in operation," Fritz said. "I'm impressed any part of it is still working. The reactor must still be on."

Ila grunted and touched the butt of her gun, her eyes flicking nervously from shadow to shadow. "Where be the parts you need?" she said.

Fritz tapped his left arm, and a small hologram layout of the opera hall popped up. "We're here, in the entrance hall. What I need will be down here, in the service tunnels. The generator and reactor are down there. It's a pity, really. Once I pull those, this place'll go dark."

"I will shed no tears," Ila said. "Air here feels wrong."

"Your air is recycled," Fritz replied.

"Not *air* air, birdie. The *ba* of this place is wrong. Tainted."

"The... what?"

"The *ba*, the soul."

"Places don't have souls," Fritz said.

"Shows what you know, Assless One."

"I'm not—wait, do you hear that?"

Something was piping through the foyer. At first, it sounded just like static broadcasting into their helmets, but after a minute, it cleared up.

"Music?" Ila whispered.

"Captain, are you hearing this?" Fritz asked.

"Well, it *is* an opera house."

"What *is* it?" Fritz asked.

"*Va, Pensiero.* It's from the *Nabucco*," Carmine replied. "It's a beautiful song, but an odd choice for ambiance."

"Why's that?" Fritz asked.

There was a chuckle from the other end. "Do you not have a translator installed in that thing?"

"It's in my other suit," Fritz replied dryly. "The one Ila punted out the airlock."

"Was hideous. And orange," Ila replied. "Was also in way of airlock."

"So what's so odd about this song?" Fritz asked. The feathers at the top of his crest curled against the top of his helmet, drawing a burst of hyena laughter from Ila.

"It's the 'Chorus of the Hebrew Slaves.' Hang on, my Italian is a little rusty. They're on the third stanza. 'Golden harp of the prophetic seers, why dost thou hang mute upon the willow? Rekindle our bosom's memories, and speak to us of times gone by.'"

"Captain, you speak Italian?"

"The Captain speaks several languages, you plebian!" Byron said, cutting in.

"I speak… French!" Fritz protested. "And who let you on the com? Aren't you supposed to be taking care of Ellie?"

"She's still unconscious, so no. Ah, wait, there we are! She's coming to. See you when you get back, Fritz!" The com line chirped and Byron's voice vanished.

"Right, enough culture for now. Fritz, let me know when you've found what we need. I'm going to speak with Ellie, if she's up for it. Over and out."

The com line went silent, leaving Fritz and Ila alone in the abandoned opera station. The disembodied chorus followed the pair down the plush hall, the same song looping over and over.

Fritz and Ila walked down the center of the spacious hallway and came finally to a pair of ornate double doors. A spiraling, intricate design had been carved into the dark wood, as convoluted as a Gordian knot.

"Knew there be good salvage here. Mahogany. Enough to buy Terran land," Ila said.

"It's probably synth-wood," Fritz said.

"Still worth more than a month's pay for you and I," she replied. "What else be here, I wonder?"

Fritz touched the door with one gloved hand, and it swung open with a grinding crack. The sensor pads on his gloves took a swift reading of the door and he smirked. "Synth-wood. I knew it."

"Think that's synth too?" Ila asked, gesturing with Bianca toward the room beyond.

The foyer was impressive; the opera stage was astounding. Row after row of plush seats, upholstered in red velvet and gilded with gold. Carved marble slabs made up the walls, replicas of famous Greek and Roman reliefs. The stage was below, darkened except for a few flickering faux lights which played along the velvet curtains. Above, hanging from the ceiling, was the biggest crystal chandelier Fritz had ever seen. Faux lights glimmered in the depths, scattering pale rainbows of light all around.

"You sure we can't salvage this, Captain?" Fritz asked.

He was answered by a burst of static.

"Captain? Say again?"

More static, then nothing.

Ila growled.

"Keep going, Fritz. Minor malfunction here. Magnetic field seems to be kicking up from the station. Might be a computer glitch. We still need those parts. Get going!"

"Aye, Captain," Fritz replied.

"Have a bad feeling about this, I do," Ila muttered.

"Well, just in case those chee-tung things are still around, keep your helmet on."

"Chi!tung," Ila corrected. "And of course."

The pair wandered deep into the opera house, marveling at the luxurious interior and lamenting again the inability to salvage any of it. There were bronze busts of famous singers and musicians, frescos of iconic opera scenes, even sealed display cases containing musical instruments from all over the galaxy.

"Instruments worth even more than the door," Ila commented, running her hand across one plasglass case. "Pity."

"But we can come back, right?" Fritz said. "We mark this place on the map and when the ship is fixed, come back?"

Ila growled. "Don't want to come back. Place still feels wrong. Like a tomb. One doesn't salvage tombs."

"We haven't seen a single dead body yet. This is no more a tomb than any other derelict station."

"Sometimes, there are no bodies," Ila replied grimly.

"Now you're trying to scare me on purpose."

"Is it working?"

"Ugh. It's going to be a long walk to the control bridge, I can feel it."

Fritz tried to hurry along, but it was impossible not to stop and look around every few minutes. He'd never seen such luxury, nor such incredible attention to detail. If he hadn't come in through an airlock, he could have sworn he was on Terra, walking through a restored nineteenth-century opera house. Sure, if he looked hard enough, he could see the seams in the illusion—the hidden control panels, the tiny hologram projectors inside the wall sconces—but whoever had built the place took care to make such intrusions as inconspicuous as possible.

Finally, they turned a corner and Fritz found a door that

opened to a service tunnel.

"That ought to lead right to the bridge," Fritz said. He reached for the door, but Ila stopped him.

"Listen," she said.

Fritz paused and tilted his head.

"I don't hear anything," he said.

"Nor I. The song has stopped."

Sure enough, the mellifluous opera song that had been echoing through the halls had ceased.

"They're probably programmed not to broadcast in the service areas," Fritz reasoned.

"As you say," Ila said, the grips on her gloves creaking against Bianca's metal body.

The service tunnel was a far cry from the luxury outside it. Cramped with pipes, wires, and enormous ducts, there was just enough room for two people to walk side by side. The hall was filled with the steady hum of well-maintained machinery, making Fritz pause again and marvel at the efficiency of the place. For it to still be in such good condition after so long with no care was astonishing! Here and there, doors emerged from the river of industrial tubing. A few of them were labeled, but most of them were merely stamped with numbers.

Except for one. A single name was scrawled in gold ink where the numbers should have been.

"Ruana Nightingale?" Fritz murmured, pausing before the door. Instead of a normal door knob, the hooked handle of the door had a tiny square over the pivot point, a thumbprint bio-scanner. On the ground in front of the door were the dried remains of several bouquets of flowers, and a single tree branch covered in greenery and blossoms.

"Sakura," Ila said. "Cherry blossoms."

"They have to be synthetic. They look fresh."

"Are fresh," Ila said, taking a closer look and then recoiling. She made a motion in the air in front of her. Fritz had seen her do this before; it was a symbol to ward off evil. What did she call it? The Eye of Horus?

"Captain? Can you still read us?"

Silence.

"Damn, I knew this would be a problem. We're too far from the ship to get a proper signal anymore," Fritz grumbled. "I can't even link to the *Caliban's* computer from here."

Static, then finally.

"Barely, Fritz. Are you on your way back?"

"Not yet. We found something. Captain, do you recall if Ruana had a thing for cherry blossoms?"

There was a long stretch of silence and finally static again.

"Damn, he can't reach us down here. Let me try something else." Fritz tapped the screen on the arm of his suit a few times and brought up a few entries in his suit computer about Ruana Nightingale.

"She was a singer. An opera singer. Who vanished when this sector of space was evacuated. Damn."

He opened up an image file and made a low whistle.

"Plain, for an avian," Ila commented.

Fritz was inclined to agree. She wasn't a very lovely creature. The image before him was an avian splice, like himself, but instead of a cockatiel, her features had been blended with those of a nightingale. Sand-colored feathers, long, dark beak and eyes as black as the Void. A sparrow had more striking plumage.

"There's a sound file, hang on." Fritz tapped the audio button and was struck speechless.

Ruana Nightingale may not have looked like much, but her voice could only have been stolen from an angel. A sweet, lilting soprano filled his helmet, soothed his frayed nerves, and made Fritz smile—really *smile*—for the first time in ages.

"Lovely," Ila commented.

"She just… disappeared? How do you lose someone like this?" Fritz asked, suddenly enraged. She was magnificent! How could anyone with such talent simply be left behind?

Ila leaned back, listening to Ruana's song, and bumped

the door with Bianca's butt.

The door to Ruana's room swung open, throwing Ila off balance. The hyena lashed out with one hand, snatching at the handle and barely avoided landing flat on her ass.

Fritz was beside himself with mirth.

"Seems music really can tame any wild beast!" he laughed.

"Bah, gravity fluctuated! Is not my fault!" Ila grumbled. She pulled herself up, turning to face into the room, and suddenly went rigid.

"Ila?"

Fritz couldn't see her face, only the tense line of her body, fingers clenched into fists.

"Ila, what do you see?"

"Something… in my head. Singing. The song from the lobby," she said. Her voice had gone strange, flat. She lifted the paw that had touched the door, fingers curling slowly. Suddenly, she clenched them into a fist and snarled.

"Ila?" Fritz reached out to touch her shoulder, but Ila's knees buckled and she hit the floor.

"Ila!"

"Run… birdie. An *akh*… seeks a new… *khat*. But… not mine. Never give her mine. Anubis… judge me."

"Ila!" Fritz cried, but she was gone.

"Captain. *Captain Carmine*, come in!" Fritz shrilled.

Silence.

"Shit!" Fritz back-pedaled from Ila. Ila's body. *Ila*, he thought, wings hugging tight to his body. She's not dead. Can't be dead. Nothing could have killed her! He approached her again, gingerly tilting her head so that he could see past her face plate.

Red foam blotted her black lips.

"You did this to yourself," Fritz said. Ila had a cyanide capsule embedded in one tooth. Old mercenary failsafe, she'd said. In case she'd been spaced or couldn't be rescued. It was a cleaner death than suffocation, she claimed.

Why the hell would you use it now?

"Captain!" Fritz tried again.

No response, just more static.

Fritz paced anxiously back and forth along Ila—Ila's *body*—a few times. He didn't know what to do. The way ahead seemed to loom dark and foreboding, but the path behind was just as intimidating.

"Can't go anywhere without those parts," Fritz said to himself, his voice shaking. "Gotta get those first. I can do this. I can… I *have* to do this."

Before he took another step, though, he looked into Ruana's room.

It was empty. Completely barren except for a single flimsy table and chair. No mirror, no bed, nothing.

Why would someone go through so much trouble to secure a door with nothing in it? he wondered. But no, it hadn't always been empty. Here and there he could see places where pictures might have hung on the walls, and there, along the wall, a scuff mark that might have been from a cot.

But… why?

Fritz ground his beak and strode off. This mystery wasn't his problem. His problem involved getting parts necessary to get *out* of this place! He snapped a short order to his suit computer and a dim flashlight on his chest lit the way down the corridor. He paused just long enough to shoulder Bianca and then he was off.

I'm not fleeing. I'll come back, Ila. I'll come back for you, once I have the parts. I won't leave you here. He knew it was what she'd want, for her *ba* to be set free so that one day it could become—

An akh seeks a new khat.

Ila's dying words rolled around his skull, rattling his already frayed nerves. Gods, what was he going to tell the Captain? Or Byron? Or… Ellie? The goat-girl pilot was the only one that had no fear of Ila and the mercenary had even begun calling her "kid" when she didn't think anyone else was in earshot. Ellie was going to be devastated.

Akh. Khat.

Fritz paused his headlong rush down the hall. He'd heard those words before. When Ila first joined the crew, she spoke to the Captain about ensuring her body would be returned to her family so that her *ba* would be properly cared for, so her family could perform the rite to turn her into an *akh,* but they would need her *khat* to do it.

"Her body," Fritz murmured. "Ila said a spirit was seeking a new body, and she wouldn't let it take hers."

He stood for a moment.

"What the hell is going on here?" he screamed into the darkness.

There was no reply.

"Ghosts, haunted opera houses, suicidal hyena mercenaries, I've had it! I'm getting what I came for and I'm out of here!" he shrilled.

Breath ragged, he bolted to the end of the hall as fast as his bowed legs could carry him and slammed into the door at the far end. And beyond that doorway was the bridge.

"Finally," Fritz said, breathing a sigh of relief.

He forgot all about Ila and the weirdness of the abandoned opera house station while he worked, pulling circuit boards, cables, and various other parts. He found a rolling table and loaded his pilfered electronics onto it. Finally, he downloaded a copy of the station files to a data crystal. Maybe later someone else could go through them and puzzle out this mystery.

He began to walk.

The trek back seemed to take far less time, but only because he was no longer dazzled by the station's beauty. He paused just long enough to lug Ila's body onto his cart, but otherwise charged through the station halls, head down, crest flat against the back of his head, and his wings shivering inside his suit the whole way.

"Captain? Captain, do you read me? I have what we need, and I have… bad news."

No reply.

Maybe the virus re-activated! Maybe it took down the life support while I was here screwing around! Fritz's heart pounded, and he sprinted down the hall to the docking port. He punched the button as hard as Ila, every instinct telling him that something was wrong.

The hatch was empty. No Captain, no Byron to meet him. "Hello?" he called. "I'm back!"

The ship creaked, startling the cockatiel, but no voices.

The med bay is on the way to the panels I need to replace. Byron needs to… to deal with Ila's body. And maybe I can get some answers out of Ellie.

He took a moment to take his helmet off and shove the cart along. He hadn't gotten more than ten feet when he smelled it: a coppery, red smell, laced with the reek of an open septic pit.

"Captain!" Fritz screamed.

"No, no captain. No captain here."

Fritz's blood froze.

"Captain Carmine! What—oh gods!"

There, huddled around the bend of the corridor, was the Captain, what was left of him. His white fur was blackened with burned gore. His muzzle was stained with streaks of red which poured from empty eye sockets.

"Coffins don't have captains," he slurred. "*Cara capretta,* how could you?"

"Captain, hang on, I'll help you to the med bay," Fritz said. He bent down to help his captain up, but Carmine slapped him away, recoiling from his touch.

"No! That's how it—how *she*—does it. How she takes you. Don't… don't touch me. Don't touch anything. She said I wasn't right. Wasn't a right fit, a new box for her voice."

"Who? Captain, who did this to you?"

"*Cara capretta,* I have failed you. I'm so sorry." Captain Carmine cried out, swollen tongue writhing behind his teeth.

"Captain!" Fritz cried.

But Captain Carmine was beyond hearing. His chest rattled as his last breath left him, and his body stilled.

"Captain," Fritz whispered. He choked back a sob. "I'll come back. I promise I'll come back." He eased the cart of supplies to one side of the corridor, using it to shield Captain Carmine's body from view a little.

Something was coming through the ship's intercom. It sounded like... singing. But not the opera song from the station. It was a nursery rhyme. A very familiar nursery rhyme.

"Alouette, gentille alouette!"

"Ellie?" Fritz pushed the cart to the edge of the doorway and paused. Under his boot there was a puddle of red seeping across the steel floor plates.

Fritz swallowed. "Ellie?"

Still nothing. Fritz stepped around the cart and looked into the med bay.

Lines of red streaked like comets across the sterile white surfaces of the med bay. To one side, the crumpled form of Byron could be seen. His gold coat was flecked with pinkish foam, and his cybernetic horn had been ripped right out of his skull.

Standing on the other side of the medical table was Ellie. She was tapping at the medical computer with one hand. In the other, she held—

It took a moment for the thing in Ellie's hand to become clear. His brain side-stepped the truth twice before he forced it to focus.

In her other hand was Byron's cybernetic horn. Tendrils of wetware wire trailed from the base, brushing the floor with feathery strokes of rust-red fluid.

"Ellie?"

An akh *seeks a new* khat.

Fritz swallowed and tried again.

"Ruana?"

Ellie turned around.

"Took you long enough. I've needed you back here for

hours so that we can *go,* but you stayed in the opera house for so long that I thought I'd have to leave without you."

"What have you done to them?" Fritz demanded. "What have you done to Ellie?"

"Those two wanted to *extract* me! Like I wasn't a better fit for this body than the little bitch keeping it. She didn't deserve it! *I* deserved it! I needed it! I'd been trapped for so long, so alone, unable to speak, unable to sing. *They took my voice away and left me to rot!* They said they'd come back, that they'd fix my body and bring me home, but *they left me there,* drifting, without a voice. And now I have one, and *you're not taking it from me!*"

Ruana screamed and charged at Fritz, the severed horn in her fist poised to strike. He raised his hands to defend himself, wings flared to flee, but she suddenly stopped mid attack. Her face relaxed, and he could see Ellie fighting through the madness.

"Fritz, you have to run. You can't let her leave this station. Whatever was left of the old Ruana is gone. She's insane," Ellie said. "Damn it, she followed my cybernetics right into my brain. She said… she said she did it to Ila, but Ila stopped her. She didn't want Carmine or Byron, wrong body, wrong voice. She wants me, Fritz. She wants me, and *I can't keep her out much longer!*"

"Ellie, I can't—"

"You have to. I can't hold her for long. She's worse than a virus, Fritz. She's smarter than that. She was on the freighter, she killed it trying to learn how to control it. That's how she got past me… past you. She didn't look like a virus or a VI. It wasn't your fault, Fritz. It wasn't your—"

Ellie/Ruana screamed and twitched forward, limbs spasming like a machine shorting out. The mangled horn in her hand wavered closer. The spiral channel dripped white medifluid stained pink from Byron's blood. A single droplet fell and splattered across Fritz's feathered cheek, soaking into his feathers.

And then she froze and Ellie was back. "She was an opera singer once, but that plague—I guess she was hurt in the fighting and dying. There was a technologist in the House that night, and he offered to save her mind by putting her into the opera house mainframe. They could come back, grow her a new body, and put her in it. But it never happened. The quarantine. She went mad in there, Fritz. She couldn't speak, she couldn't sing, she was all alone. Oh gods, so alone." Ellie shuddered, and the hand holding Byron's horn wavered.

"Ellie, shut down. We—I can—there has to be a way to—"

"Not enough time. She's wearing me down. Taking everything. She wants you dead, Fritz."

"Why? I'm the only programmer left for a million miles! I could help—"

"You know, so you have to die. She doesn't want anyone to know. She wants this body—to start over—she needs—"

Ellie twitched, her face contorted with pain.

"An *akh* seeks a new *khat*," Fritz said. "She wants a new body, not to replace her old one."

Ellie nodded, the motion jerky, more a spasm than a controlled gesture. "Run, Fritz. You can't let her get off this ship. She won't stop at me. She's already overridden most of me, but she wants it all. She wants—ever—every—everyth—"

Fritz didn't wait. He ran toward the airlock again.

"Damn you, Fritz! Come back here!" Ruana shrilled.

Fritz didn't slow down. He couldn't stay here, but one of the stasis pods might sustain him long enough to be picked up. Someone might hear the distress beacon, even out here in the middle of nowhere. At the very least he'd drift in that direction. Eventually, maybe, he would be picked up.

But first, he needed to rig this place to blow. He couldn't let someone else fall into this trap. He scurried down the ladder to the warp engine. *This will just take a moment. I can do this. Clear your mind, birdie. What was that code again?*

"I know you're down there, Fritz. I'm going to find you!"

Ruana started to sing. It wasn't the rich, dulcet voice from the recording, but Ellie's weaker, tenebrous alto. And under the sound of her voice was the grating metal-on-metal sound of Byron's horn being scraped along the corridor walls.

"*Alouette, gentille alouette! Alouette, je te plumerai!*"

"I'm a cockatiel, not a lark!" Fritz muttered, swallowing back a hysterical giggle. *Almost done, just a few more commands. Got it!*

A klaxon sounded and Ruana screamed in rage. "No! You can't! I won't let you leave me alone again!"

Fritz bolted, grimly fixing his helmet back on as he raced to the emergency stasis pods. He slid into the seat and started the evacuation sequence.

"*Alouette, gentille alouette! Je te plumerai lew yuex!*"

"You took the Captain's eyes, but you won't get mine. Not today, you cold-hearted bitch. Today, this lark plucks you!"

Fritz slammed his claw against the pod eject button, rocketing it out of the ship. A moment later, the *Caliban* exploded, orange flames bursting into bloom and contracting as the oxygen burned away.

Fritz let out the breath he was holding. Claw shaking, he tapped a series of commands into the pod computer. He plugged several tubes into his suit and waited for the pod to begin the extended hibernation sequence. A few stray feathers from his head floated around in his helmet, drifting aimlessly as his breath slowed.

Suddenly, one of the feathers wavered, warping like a bad hologram. And from the radio in his suit, he heard a chilling, familiar song.

"*Alouette, gentille alouette! Alouette, je te plumerai!*"

"No! It's not possible!"

"Did you think I lived only in Ellie? Sad, simple little birdie. I am everywhere. And while you only have five minutes of oxygen left, I have eternity. Sooner or later, someone will pick up this coffin, and I'll sing again. Goodnight, *alouette*."

Fritz struggled, tried to override the controls, but Ruana had jammed them. The door to the pod burst open, venting his oxygen into space. The last thing he heard was the crooning lullaby of Ruana.

Alouette, gentille alouette! Alouette, je te plumerai

THIS WAY

Frances Pauli

The breeze that rattled the jungle canopy also vibrated through the tips of Dotar's velvet toes. He heard it in the way his bristles danced, in the soft thrumming of the world beneath each of his eight feet. A gentle wind. A whisper of weather beneath the mesh of jungle that only let scattered patches of sunlight through to warm his carapace.

"Hurry up, daydreamer." The steady drumming of his partner's toes brought his thoughts back to their mission. "We're meant to be home by tomorrow."

Dotar answered Mifla's impatience with an irritated bobbing of his abdomen, a flash of iridescent stripes and long, ruddy bristles. "I'm coming."

He scurried down the mammoth tree trunk, each of his toes tipped with tiny double claws that clung to the ridged bark and made easy work of the descent. The uplifted T'rants had been sent to scout for the natives whose villages dotted the wider world, to look for talented humans who might, eventually, be wooed into serving their masters, the great star spiders.

This time, they'd come home empty handed. This time, the jungle whispered of failure and set Dotar's bristles on edge. Something on the wind…

"Why do you think they'd abandoned it?" He reached the undergrowth and danced over the mat of vines and shed fronds to where his fellow scout tapped in irritation. Always in a hurry, Mifla. Always rushing toward the next goal. "I've never seen a village without humans."

"Who cares?" Mifla's black abdomen lifted toward the binary suns. He lowered his chelicerae closer to the jungle floor and waved from one side to the other. "Let the High One sort it out when we get back."

"Do you think we can make the gap tonight?" Dotar followed with eager steps of his own when Mifla turned and led the way into the green growth. "Are we that close?"

"Probably in the morning." Mifla's bulbous hind end bobbed between the vines. "Unless we can hitch a ride again."

"I don't smell any hogs here." Dotar paused, stilled his toes, and let his bristles sense the currents of air around them. "Nor deer either."

"Then keep moving!" Mifla drummed a quick staccato of annoyance and scuttled farther ahead. "I want to see the pyramids by next suns-rise."

Dotar lifted his pedipalps, intent on drumming a smart reply, on doling out his own frustration at his partner's impatience. Before his toes could strike ground, however, a new breeze hissed across his back. The sensitive hairs lifted, and something low and subtle skimmed the surface of his body.

"What was that?" He shifted his legs, turned a slow circle and felt for the sound again. "Did you hear that?"

"What now?" Mifla pounded it, spun to chastise him but froze without drumming.

The jungle buzzed at them. Over their backs, the fronds rattled. The bark hissed and the vines underfoot became snakes, squirming with the strange vibration. Leaves fluttered from the canopy to waft down like dark rain.

"What is it?" Mifla appeared at Dotar's side. He drummed so softly that the weird noise nearly drowned his words.

"I don't know."

"Maybe they left the village for a reason." Mifla's words hummed an octave lower than the buzzing. They carried an echo of the fear coiling inside Dotar's abdomen. "Maybe…"

The alien sound ceased. The foliage stilled, and their world returned to normal.

"Is it gone?" Dotar whispered. His body brushed against the vines, lowered so near the ground that his legs had splayed in all directions. "Is it over?"

"How would I know?"

Mifla might have been trying to sound brave, but Dotar heard fear in his drumming. He saw flashes of the primitive village they'd left behind, the empty huts, cold fire rings and half woven mats still lying where their weavers had left them. No doubt in a hurry.

"Come on." Now *he* pushed for haste. His bristles had settled, but he could still feel it, the buzz that hadn't come from anything sensible at all. It still vibrated in his thoughts if nothing else, and the memory made his spinnerets twitch. "Let's hurry."

They moved on without any drumming. The vines passed beneath claw-tipped toes, and the canopy above shifted with ordinary wind and the safe rattle of the fronds. Here the twisting pathways looked familiar, the glimpses of sky between leaves showed blue, and Dotar could imagine, indeed, arriving at the spider city by dawn's light.

When the Great Ones first landed on the T'rant home world, the giant arachnids had recognized Dotar's kind as kin. They were the ones who'd taught his people the secrets of language, the ways of carrying and building. Together, the star spiders and their miniature cousins had erected the pyramids that housed them both, built the city and the wall around it. In return, the T'rants served their masters, acting as liaison with the human villages. Villages, Dotar reminded himself, that should not be empty. Finding one abandoned was news that needed to be returned quickly.

His legs sped, churned lightly against the foliage and sent his body dashing forward in Mifla's wake. Home by tomorrow. They could tell their tale to the High One and let the council decide what to do about villages where the ashes were still warm, but no brown feet trod the earth any longer.

Mifla's legs flashed between the brush. His footsteps quickened as well, making a rhythm of their passing that neared a dance, a homeward rushing that lifted Dotar's thoughts and almost erased the creeping feeling that had settled inside his body, almost let him forget.

Until the sound returned.

It came from everywhere at once, from directly above the jungle and also, echoing from all sides, from the shadows and from the dark places where fear spawned. This time, the buzz grew to a howl. The whole world sang it inside and out, vibrating, seeping in, moving legs without any room for thinking.

Dotar ran and had no idea what he could possibly be fleeing.

The greenery streaked around him, crunched and dragged at his legs. He caught the flashing of black that was his partner, but before he'd gone ten lengths, Mifla had vanished. Dotar ran alone, ran from a world that buzzed in all directions.

His feet danced. He leaped and dodged vines, and with every step the buzzing grated against his bristles and refused to let him free. Dotar ran blindly. He battered his body against the underbrush, tore a claw on one velvety foot, and never slowed until the sound died.

Then, in silence, he hunkered beneath a leaf. The shadows hid his body, but his legs trembled, shook the leaves and gave his position away despite the shelter. No sign of Mifla nearby, and still he could not force his feet to move.

Dotar could only press his belly to the ground and pray he'd never hear that sound again.

* * * * *

At some point he slept. At another, he dreamed of buzzing and a world that screamed against him. Dotar woke to that sound and found it drumming from his own toes. Screaming.

Practically inviting an enemy to find him.

He stiffened, tested each leg in turn and then lifted his body to his toes and let his bristles sense the air. Something moved close by. A soft pattering beat against the vines and the memory of buzzing returned. Except Dotar recognized this rhythm.

Mifla.

He shifted position, rotated his body and peered out from underneath the frond. A fat black T'rant strode between the vines. Relief flooded his carapace, and Dotar rushed to intercept his partner. He skimmed forward and then stuttered when Mifla turned to meet him.

"Mifla!" Dotar cried to his fellow scout. Mifla had stopped abruptly, facing him but with his body listed to one side at a sharp angle. "Are you hurt?"

"What?" The black spider shifted his feet, leaned too far in the other direction and staggered a step for balance. "Dotar?"

"Are you okay?"

"Yes."

"We have to get back." Dotar's bristles lifted, tested the air and found nothing. "I don't know where we are now."

"Yes." Mifla shifted his feet and raised his abdomen high. "Yes. This way."

Mifla moved off, and Dotar followed eagerly. His partner knew the jungle better, hadn't led them astray once on the long journey to the village and back. Still, as they made their way beneath the dense leaves, Dotar began to doubt their trajectory. The angle of the suns seemed wrong, and the air against his bristles told him they moved away from home instead of toward it.

He paused and let the wind talk to him.

"Wait a minute."

Mifla continued on. Each stepping of his legs clunked against the ground. Stiff. A new rhythm that spoke of something Dotar couldn't quite puzzle out.

"Mifla, wait!"

"This way." Mifla's toes drummed a heavy answer.

"I don't think…" Dotar tried to protest, but his partner only quickened his steps.

The breeze whispered over his carapace, hissed that they were going the wrong way. Dotar stopped following and watched his friend. Each placing of Mifla's feet thumped loud and clear against the ground. Each step held a stiffness. Perhaps, the scout had been stunned or wounded in his flight. Maybe, he wasn't thinking clearly. Not that Dotar could blame him.

"Hold on a minute." He didn't wait to see if Mifla obeyed. Dotar ran to the nearest trunk, gripped the bark tightly and hauled himself up and away from the undergrowth. His claws bit into the bark, his body fit itself against the ridges, and he ran up the tree as fast as he could.

When the canopy shifted only a few lengths above, Dotar stopped. He meant to catch a clearer breeze, to verify that the direction they traveled would lead them to the city and the high stepped pyramids that meant they were home.

Instead, he looked down.

The sunlight made a patchwork of the undergrowth, dotted the green with black shadows, and shone directly on the place where Mifla waited. It reflected on his partner's black carapace, beautiful and velvety and marked in the center of the thorax by a gaping round wound.

Dotar's grip on the bark slipped. He skidded three lengths down the tree before catching hold again. His toes trembled, fought for purchase while his mind digested the scene below. Something had punctured his friend's back. Mifla was hurt badly, and yet the other spider waited below as if he hadn't noticed his own distress.

They needed to get home right away, but judging from the breeze Mifla led them in the wrong direction. Dotar usually deferred to his friend, but now Mifla needed him. He needed help. And the only place they'd have a hope of healing a wound like that was inside the safety of their city's walls, inside the pyramids where the Great Ones' machines and medicines could repair a damaged exoskeleton.

He'd just have to convince Mifla to turn around.

Dotar descended the tree much more gingerly. He crept to the jungle floor and found his partner waiting close beside the trunk. Mifla drummed the vines with his pedipalps.

"This way."

"We need to turn around."

"No." The black toes danced an awkward rhythm.

"We need to get you home, Mifla."

"This way." The fat scout turned his chelicerae away from the spider city and began to march again.

"Mifla!" Dotar scrambled. He leapt from the tree and raced around his friend. "Stop. You're hurt, Mifla."

One black leg shot to the side. It pushed Dotar away and to the ground. Mifla stumbled with the effort, but continued to march away.

"You're going the wrong way." Dotar shook dirt from his bristles and reset his legs. He hesitated for a breath. Mifla had never struck him before, but then, the injury should have taxed him. The fluid loss alone could rattle a T'rant's thinking. Whatever had happened to Mifla, it was up to him to steer the other scout back home.

He scuttled forward, giving the black legs a wider berth and racing to intercept Mifla's determined march. When he'd gained a few lengths on his friend, Dotar stopped and turned, blocking Mifla's path.

"Stop. You need to get…"

Mifla's body bent backward. His forelegs lifted from the ground and his chelicerae spread. Threat pose, a warning that should not be ignored. Dotar felt it in his bristles, but his thoughts burned for his friend, for the hole in Mifla's back that leaked life fluids in a dark trickle across his smooth exoskeleton.

"Mifla. Please listen to me."

Black legs reached higher, stretching toward the canopy.

A pair of gleaming fangs flashed in the sunlight. Dotar had less than a second. A moment to react before Mifla lunged. He darted to the side and felt the air swirl over him in the wake of his friend's attack.

"Mifla!" He spun, jumped a length backward and readied his legs to leap again.

Instead of continuing the attack, Mifla had completely reset. He stood at rest, eight legs firmly against the ground, still facing the direction of his march as if nothing insane had just happened.

"Mifla?"

"This way."

"What?" Dotar drummed incredulity, but Mifla only shifted his feet.

"This way."

The fluids streaked between Mifla's bristles now, spilled over the wide thorax to drip away the spider's life on the vines underfoot. Though he didn't march, his body rocked slowly from one side to the other, back and forth, rhythmic and without aim.

"You're bleeding." Dotar crept in an arc toward the rear of the black abdomen. "You need help."

He'd run if he had to. Maybe he could reach the city in time, bring the healing devices to Mifla, or even enough of his people to drag the spider home. If Mifla heard him, he made no answer. The scout only stood dripping and rocking like a leaf in the wind.

The breeze riffled his bristles, sang to Dotar of indecision and then, faintly, began to buzz.

"Mifla!" Dotar's whole body seized in terror. That sound, that terrible vibration surrounded them, grew steadily louder. He longed to run, but that would mean abandoning his friend, leaving Mifla to face whatever made that noise. Perhaps what had made the horrid wound as well.

Dotar circled farther, reached the very back of Mifla, the spot where he was furthest from the dagger fangs of the other scout. Mifla showed no sign of reacting. He remained planted, waving in time to the buzz that grew nearer and nearer. If he were unconscious Dotar could weave a net and drag the other scout to the city. To help. If Mifla spun around, however... Dotar only had one chance.

"This way." Mifla's front toes lifted.

The jungle hummed louder.

"This way."

Dotar leaped. He vaulted over Mifla's abdomen and landed on his friend's back. Eight black legs folded beneath them, slammed Mifla's thorax against the ground with a sickening thump. Dotar held onto the edges of his friend's carapace. He hadn't meant to land so hard, to hear the cracking that had to be Mifla's exoskeleton giving way in places.

But he was the lighter of them, and his landing hadn't been so hard as that.

Mifla didn't struggle, either. He didn't drum or twitch. Not one segment of his legs moved, and even the pair of spinnerets hung limply from the scout's abdomen. Had Dotar killed him? A wash of cold filled his body, a creeping fear fed by the growing buzzing in the air.

Dotar shifted, felt with his toes for any signs of life. Something pushed against his foreleg. Underneath his belly, the wound in Mifla's exoskeleton pulsed and leaked. Dotar scrambled off the other scout. He lifted his forelegs and arched up to reveal his own fangs.

The hole in Mifla's thorax was slick with fluids. Dark blood flowed now, pushed outward by the pulsing of the wound... by something pulsing *in* the wound. Dotar settled his feet and peered closer. His friend's thorax rocked from side to side, but now Dotar was certain Mifla didn't live.

Maybe hadn't lived for some time.

But his body moved. His voice whispered even now, *This way*. A ghost white membrane shimmered from within the wound. It pulsed, swelled and stretched so thin the thing inside was nearly visible. Whatever it was, Dotar knew it had killed his friend. He knew it in the buzzing of the jungle and the soft, vibrating echo of the same sound coming from inside that bleeding hole.

His legs flicked against the vines. His body spun, jumped through the air and hit the ground with toes flashing. Dotar raced away from the alien thing buzzing inside that white veil. His claw tips tore at the jungle and the spider flew toward home barely touching the ground at all.

* * * * *

This time, Dotar kept running long after the sound had ceased. He kept running though his legs shook and his toes had trouble gripping the vines. His steps slipped, threw him to the ground more than once, and still Dotar ran for home.

When the suns had long set, Dotar slowed. He wobbled forward, beneath the light of one moon and well after the other two had risen. His exoskeleton creaked and complained. His toes burned and the place where he'd lost a claw throbbed, made him think of a white membrane stretched over something dark and buzzing.

Something that had moved inside his friend.

Whatever had happened to Mifla, Dotar blamed the alien sound. He blamed the buzzing that had filled the air, invaded their world, and lodged itself inside Mifla's body. Something alive. Something pushing its way out of the other T'rant's thorax.

He crept on, belly brushing the ground and legs threatening to fail him. The skies glowed in the moons' light, and the jungle thinned ahead. The canopy broke, and Dotar saw the shadowed outline of stone steps, the pyramids in the distance.

Home.

Safety waited inside those walls, and that thought gave him the strength to lift his body higher, to move his feet with more grace. He might limp, but he could do it with his bristles high.

He could hear the drums of the city. The signal towers

glowed. Drums chanted the hour to the jungle and the scouts that roamed outside the gates.

Come home. Come to shelter and sanctuary.

Dotar longed for both tonight. More than that, he burned to tell his story to the council, to warn his people of something new and deadly vibrating through their world. Ahead, the trees parted. A narrow stretch of open grass led to the silken bridge spanning the gash in the planet that marked the edge of the city. The bridge strands flashed in the silver light, gleamed and sparkled and led the way to safety.

The High One would know what to do. The great spiders would know how to protect their people from the invading sound.

His bristles hummed in the night air. His spinnerets twitched. Dotar marched on despite the twinges in his legs. He moved forward despite the pain. Home. A few more steps and the jungle fell away. The night sky arched overhead, and Dotar scurried toward the spider-silk bridge.

His velvet toes pressed against the grass, left soft dents to mark his passing. He stepped forward. His abdomen bobbed, spinnerets waving in the cool air. Nearly there.

Dotar's pedipalps reached for the near edge of the bridge. They brushed silk, and something heavy landed on his back. It drove his body into the ground. His legs flicked out, twitched, but had little strength left to fight with.

He pushed against the grass and felt the weight on his carapace shift. Claws bit into his exoskeleton, held him still and yet the pressure eased. Dotar gathered his last scrap of energy and shoved the ground away. He rolled to the side, got four of his legs free enough to scratch divots in the grass.

Had Mifla found him? Did the other spider live still? He twisted, used his free legs as levers and angled his body toward the attacker. Something red flashed, shiny, moving too fast to catch. The grip on his back held, but something fluttered beyond that, moving so quickly it was hard to see.

This way.

Pain exploded through Dotar's thorax. His back burned, and the bristles on his body lifted, heard buzzing. Louder and louder. *This way.* Dotar twitched, pushed with his legs against that sound and threshed the air. The weight vanished, but the buzzing grew, filling his body and his mind as well.

He rolled away, but the sound came with him. How could he escape something that lived inside him? His fangs dragged against the grass. He pushed, lifted his thorax a segment above the ground, and stared into a pair of alien eyes. *This way.*

Mifla had not survived. Dotar knew it now, as surely as he saw his own death in those eyes. This creature had nothing spider-like about it. Its body shone like still water in the moons' light, black everywhere he looked and thin, too thin all over.

An orb head tilted, glared at him through twin mirrors. Behind that he saw a narrow thorax, impossibly small abdomen and six, knife-thin legs. Dotar tried to flee, even now, but his body only jerked and tilted. The buzz howled inside him. *This way.*

That music came from a pair of membranes above the thing's back. They fluttered too rapidly to see, a halo of red and black, buzzing, burning into Dotar's body. *Beautiful.* His pedipalps lifted, reached toward the alien, the angel that would bring his death.

The sound swelled. It sang to him as the creature lifted from the ground. *This way.* At the rear of the abdomen, a true weapon glinted. A curving dagger grew from the angel's terminal segment, a single knife where its spinnerets should be. Dotar felt the true purpose of that burning from the center of his thorax.

From a place where he knew a dark hole gaped, where a white membrane pulsed with new life.

This way.

His body jerked in answer. His legs worked for that sound. Lifted him to his toes and moved him one step closer to his city.

No.

The buzzing of the world commanded.

Not yet.

He'd forgotten the plan for a moment. Forgotten that they were not enough yet, that they needed to grow. His young cargo required time to incubate, and it was his honor to carry it, to provide for the drone until it devoured him. Dotar's toes shifted. His legs moved, and he turned away from the spider city.

They needed time to plant more eggs, to increase their number before invading. His abdomen lifted. His body rocked softly from one side to the other, and he marched back into the jungle, marched in answer to the singing wings.

This way.

OUTLIER

Donald Jacob Uitvlugt

Commence recording.

Court-martial proceedings for Commander Deraki Sita, formerly of *SCS Mushka*. Material witness, Sergeant Adrik Vedmenko.

Vedmenko blinks up at the lights. Muscles ripple under the male bear's dingy white flight suit. Eyes roam from side to side, uncertain where he is. A long tongue licks his black nosepad. There is little to focus on in the sparse gray room. The chair he is in. Padded walls. There are no windows.

"Hugh? Where are you, darling?"

His paws trace over the padding, fingers reaching for a control panel that isn't there.

"Routing more power to the shields. It's still coming through. *Bozhe moi*, it's coming through!"

He pounds on the walls with his fists. Tears stream down his face.

"Hugh…"

He crumples to the floor, 150 kilos of sobbing muscle and fur. A sedative mist fills the chamber, and the bear finally relaxes into a drug-induced sleep.

* * * * *

Commander Sita.

A female tigress glances up where she presumes the camera to be. Emotions play across her face. Eventually, she settles on stoic resignation.

"It was just a routine survey mission up to that point. You have to understand that, or you won't understand anything about what we did. You sit in your chairs and push buttons, but you don't get it."

What don't we "get"?

The tigress paces the room, her tail thrashing behind her.

"How empty space is. How cold. You live your lives on a pawful of worlds or in spinning tin cans, and you don't realize what you're sending us into. One mistake—one hatch not closed, one suit seal unfastened—and we're dead. We have to be perfect every damned time, or we're dead.

"And space doesn't give a fuck. It just is. Every time you send a ship out into the cold abyss, you're gambling. And every gambler loses in the end."

Are you comparing the loss of seventeen lives to losing at a game of chance?

Golden eyes stare.

"Seventeen?"

Lieutenant Parks died in medbay last night.

The tigress curses and slumps into her chair.

"Poor Hugh. I need a stimstick. I smoked my last one an hour ago. Would it kill you to give me a stimstick?"

Interesting reaction to the news of a colleague's death.

She is on her feet, claws out.

"They were my friends! I'll mourn them however the hells I want. They knew the risks better than any of you armchair pilots hiding behind your desks."

Your opinions are irrelevant to this proceeding. Describe your mission up to the… incident.

"It was a gods-damned survey mission. Endless downtime punctuated by bursts of non-stop activity. We traveled to eighteen star systems in the hopes of finding more worlds for you grounders to colonize."

Not a very successful survey.

"Do you think that goldilocks worlds are out there to

pluck like fruit from a tree? Captain Haroun was ecstatic to find two. Two. The moon will require extensive terraforming and has wicked tides. The planet shows markers of indigenous fauna, possibly intelligent. We flagged those two worlds for the colonization committee.

"Captain Haroun considered that a very successful survey. And so do I."

Describe your relationship with Captain Haroun.

The tigress sits back in her chair and folds her arms across her chest.

Describe your relationship with Captain Haroun.

"None of your damned business."

* * * * *

Resume recording.

The bear sits in his chair. His eyes are out of focus, as if he is trying to see something or someone not there.

Mister Vedmenko.

The bear's ears swivel and wrinkles furrow his brow as he turns his head. He seems unable to track the voice's source.

Mister Vedmenko, how long have you known Commander Sita?

"Sita?" The hint of a slur thickens his voice. "We shipped out on the *Félicette* back in the day. Suppose we were on the *Mushka* together... almost five years."

Did you know about her relationship with Captain Haroun?

"Sometimes fucking is the only way to relieve the boredom. No secrets on a survey vessel. Everybody knows who's doing what to whom. The Captain was giving it to the ExOh. So what? It didn't keep her from doing her job."

He looks around the room. He rubs his right paw over his left arm.

"How long are you going to keep me here, anyway? I really need to see Hushka."

Hushka?

"Lieutenant Parks. Hugh. Where is he?"

...

Lieutenant Parks is deceased.

Vedmenko's eyes go wide as memories come flooding back. He starts to weep again, paws over his face.

* * * * *

Your refusal to speak about Captain Haroun is not a mark in your favor.

The tigress' tail thrashes behind her.

"What do you want me to say? Rami Haroun was the finest officer in the Space Corps. I would have done anything in my power to have prevented his death."

Did you do everything in your power?

Her teeth bare in a grimace of anger. Then she sighs and sits down.

"I've answered all these questions before. I'm tired and hungry, and I really, really need a stimstick. If you don't believe me, check the computer logs."

...

Her ears quirk at the pause.

"You *have* checked the logs, haven't you?"

The computer system of the *Mushka* was... compromised. Our best techs are working on the issue.

She shakes her head.

"Gods, what a clusterfuck...."

For the record, when did you first notice something amiss?

* * * * *

Figures in yellow hazmat gear beetle around the computer core extracted from the *Mushka*. Sparks flash and a hologram flickers into existence. The fox seems to be made of liquid silver, not quite male, not quite female.

"*SCS Mushka* a-a-avatar online. C-convenience designation, Huli."

One of the techs punches at a keypad.

"Self d-diagnostic commencing."

The fox looks around with piercing silver eyes.

"Where are C-commander Sita and Mister V-vedmenko?"

* * * * *

"Lieutenant Parks noticed it first. That's—That was his job as science officer. Noticing things."

The bear's eyes are more focused now. As he speaks, his limbs occasionally tremble, as if he's trying to shake a fly from his fur.

What did he notice?

"The next star on our survey. Something seemed…off about it."

Off?

"The energy signature." Vedmenko sighs. "Look, I'm a mech, a gearhead. I'm best paws deep in the guts of a ship. I don't know all the specific science shit. Ask Commander Sita. She knows."

We will. But we want to hear your version of events.

"Well, I wasn't on the Bridge, but I was watching the feed from the Bridge down in the engine room. Lieutenant Parks told the Captain about his readings. The energy signature of the star had… shifted."

Which star?

The bear frowns. "What do you mean?"

There were six stars remaining in the *Mushka*'s survey. Which star showed the anomaly?

It takes a moment for the bear to answer. "The… next star on the list."

That would be Eta Virginis?

Vedmenko's ears twitch. He frowns in confusion. "Yes. Eta Virginis. It would have to be."

225

* * * * *

The tigress runs her claws over the walls, not quite digging in enough to damage the padding.

"It was Alpha Leonis. I've told you that a hundred times."

Alpha Leonis, not Eta Virginis.

"You know my scores in astronavigation. Of course it was Alpha Leonis."

So what did Captain Haroun do when Lieutenant Parks reported the anomaly?

"He followed procedure. What do you think he did? Haroun loved procedure more than…" She sighs. "I'm sorry. I'm sorry. I need that stimstick. Can you get me one?"

When we're finished. What did Captain Haroun do?

"He had Parks check the scans. Then he had him check them again. The spectrum from Alpha Leonis was missing several bands."

Missing?

"Like elements that should have been present weren't there. The bands made a pattern. Parks ran it through the computer and Huli confirmed it.

"We didn't know what the hells it said, but Alpha Leonis was sending a message."

* * * * *

"C-confirmed. Scans suggest nine seven point three nine percent p-probability intelligent origin."

A screen lights up behind Huli. The screen images a large red star with a spectral scan next to it. A pattern of black bands mars the spectrum, resembling an old-fashioned bar code.

"Command n-not authorized. Captain level clearance required."

The tech shakes his head in his hazmat and re-keys the command.

"C-command not authorized. Where is Commander

Sita?"

Two techs consult and try a new set of keystrokes. The sun swirls behind Huli and shifts color to a brilliant yellow-orange. A spotted yellow light glows off the hologram's silvery façade.

"Command not authorized. Captain Haroun said I was only to release that in-information to Commander Sita."

* * * * *

The bear pounds a fist against the pads of his other paw. His nostrils twitch.

"That's the thing most people never understand about Captain Haroun, that he's a being of action. Being bored was the worst thing that could happen to him. It's no wonder that he and the Commander..." His muzzle opens into a toothy smile. "Well, whatever else one might think about the Commander, she is definitely not boring."

The bear clears his throat.

"So this mystery lands in his lap, of course he's going to investigate."

Why didn't he contact the competent Corps agency?

Vedmenko looks embarrassed and coughs into his paw. "Well, you see, he didn't want the discovery taken away from us."

He wanted the credit.

"Yes, but he wanted it for all of us. Lieutenant Parks detected the anomaly. Commander Sita and Huli were the ones who determined it was a message. We all wanted in on the discovery. We didn't want the credit given to some desk pilot."

So the entire crew decided not to report the phenomenon?

"We were on a planetary survey. A signal suggests alien intelligence? *Layno* yes, we're going to investigate."

Without even knowing what the message said?

* * * * *

The tigress points an accusing finger. Her ears flatten in anger.

"Captain Haroun was completely within his rights to investigate the phenomenon. Everyone on the ship passed first contact protocols with full marks."

That is under review. What happened next?

"The Captain ordered us in, sensors on full. Everything seemed fairly standard at first, a mix of iron core planets and gas balls. A gas giant right in the goldilocks zone."

Sita pauses to smile, sadness in her eyes.

"I suppose they'll call it Planet Haroun now."

That too is under review.

The tigress snorts. "Of course it is. Anyway, Lieutenant Parks started shouting something from his console. The Captain and I both verified his scans.

"The scanners showed that Planet Haroun has at least a dozen moons. Each and every one of them well within Terran tolerances."

A dozen habitable worlds? In a single system?

"It strains credulity and defies the laws of averages, but it was right there in the scans. I've seen some strange things during my time in the Corps, but a statistical improbability like that…"

She trails off and shakes her head.

"Of course, that was when Huli announced that they had translated the message coded into the sun."

* * * * *

The star on the screen behind the avatar glows an intense white-blue. The holographic fox stares at the swirling bands of super-heated gas as if trying to divine something from the patterns.

"M-message reads: We welcome you to this system with open arms. Enjoy the worlds prepared for you. We will greet you in person soon."

The viewscreen shifts to the view of a gas giant banded like a sunset. Four moons are visible in the image, one white, one tan, one blue, one green.

"Self-diagnostic forty p-percent complete. Please don't make me talk about what h-happened next."

* * * * *

The bear rubs a paw along the side of his muzzle. He suppresses a yawn.

Captain Haroun was cautious?

"Of course he was. You know the saying about something that sounds too good to be true. Lieutenant Parks' subsequent scans only confirmed it."

What do you mean?

"Even though each of the moons scanned as habitable, the planetology made no sense. There was no real ecology. One was an ice world, the next all desert, the third one a giant forest."

And...?

Vedmenko shook his head. "They weren't real. They couldn't be. No world can be all forest or all desert. Living systems don't work that way. Maybe you could have an all-ocean world. Maybe. The rest are fictions dreamed up by bad writers."

That was when Captain Haroun ordered the landing party?

"That's right. He had Commander Sita, Lieutenant Fortier, and Mr. Ichigawa take a shuttle to the forest world."

Why the forest world?

"It was the closest. No, that's not right. The ice world was the closest. The forest world was next closest and seemed more inviting."

* * * * *

The tigress slumps in a chair. A paw lies over her eyes and she speaks to the ceiling.

"Yes, the forest world was the closest. No, we weren't supposed to land, not at first. We were just going to verify the *Mushka*'s scans at closer range."

Did the readings match?

The tigress lets out an ironic laugh. "They matched *exactly*. That's when I first suspected something was wrong."

...

If the readings matched, what was the problem?

"Even if the scans registered the same data, there should have been at least some variation. The closer scans should at least have conveyed information to more significant places, more detail."

Instead, the scans were exactly the same.

"Precisely. Several possibilities would account for the exact match. One might be a malfunction in the instruments. An equipment error causing both scans to give the same results."

Alternatively...?

"Barring an equipment malfunction, another possibility would be that someone was rigging the scans. Someone was showing us what they thought we wanted to see."

* * * * *

A scan of a forested world stands behind Huli, enlarged to the point that one can make out individual trees.

"Self-diagnostic fifty-f-f-five percent complete. May I speak to Sergeant Vedmenko?"

Two suited techs exchange glances. One of them inputs commands on the keypad.

"I know that he and Commander Sita are sequestered at this facility. I have a message for him from Lieutenant Parks."

More paw-coded commands.

"I'm really only supposed to play it for Sergeant Vedmenko, but if you insist…"

The planet flickers away and is replaced with the face of a male raccoon. His features seem young, though there is something old about his eyes.

The recording plays.

"Addie? If you're listening to this, well, I guess that means I'm dead. I'm sorry. I didn't mean to leave you alone."

The raccoon smiles.

"I hope you realize that I died doing what I loved. But you're the *one* that I love. I hope that thought brings you at least a little bit of the joy that your love brought to me."

Lieutenant Parks looks straight out from the screen.

"Most important, I want you to know that, whatever happened to me, it wasn't your fault."

As the raccoon speaks, his fur and flesh begin to melt off his face, as if he is decomposing before the viewer's eyes. Techs scurry about, trying to determine if this is a glitch in Huli's systems, or something else. The recording loops, words repeating from the raccoon's skull.

"Your fault. Your fault. Your fault."

* * * * *

The bear is sobbing into his paws again.

"It was all my fault."

How so?

"I was responsible for the *Mushka* and all the gear on her. If the scanners glitched, that was on me. And if the scanners hadn't glitched, they never would have landed on that damned moon."

Had you failed to perform any routine maintenance?

Vedmenko pauses before answering. "Of course not. Even if my nature didn't demand that I stay on top of everything, Captain Haroun would have never permitted me to fall behind in my duties."

So there was no scanner glitch.

He pauses again. The tip of his left ear twitches. "There had to have been. Nothing else explains the false scans."

* * * * *

So you ordered the shuttle to land?

"It was a decision taken by all of us on board, but as the commanding officer, yes, the order was mine."

The tigress' fingers twitch, as if they are fiddling with an imaginary object.

"The Captain didn't want us to take any unnecessary risks, so we were fully suited up before we dropped out of orbit. Landing should have been harder than it was, given that the scans showed no break in the trees. Not a single clearing. But Ensign De Haas got us down without even a bump."

Ensign De Haas?

Sita sighs. "There were three crewmembers on the shuttle: me, Ensign De Haas, and Mr. Ichigawa. How many times do I have to tell you?"

Last time you said Lieutenant Drake piloted the shuttle.

The tigress frowns. "That can't be right. It was De Haas. I remember talking to her all the way down, about her niece on New Rotterdam."

What did you find when you landed?

"The scans showed the air to be breathable, so I made sure that our helmets were sealed. When we were all ready, I opened the hatch."

She rubs a paw over her head.

"The opening showed a dense forest, just as the scans had."

It wasn't an equipment malfunction after all?

"Not exactly. Things still didn't add up. We had touched ground in the middle of a tree, according to the scans. Before I could stop him, Mr. Ichigawa stepped outside. Passed right through a 'tree.' And then he sank to his knees and started screaming."

* * * * *

"Report on the preliminary m-medical scans of Corporal Ichigawa Jiro."

The screens behind Huli show a young male deer lying unconscious in a diagnostic bed. Blood trickles from his tear ducts and nostrils.

"No damage to the brain or internal organs. Subdermal hemorrhaging causing blood to seep from every orifice. Cause unknown. Illness matches no pathogens on file."

The hologram turns and reaches to touch the screen as if he's stroking the face of the deer.

The eyes of the image snap open. The orbs are completely red, without iris or pupil. The deer sits up in the bed. His lips move.

One of the techs inputs a few commands. The image rewinds and then replays, this time with sound.

"He is coming. He is coming and there is nothing you can do to stop it. He will feast on your flesh and grow drunk on your blood. He is coming."

* * * * *

Vedmenko stretches in his chair.

"We were all shaken up by what had happened to Ichigawa. Commander Sita maybe most of all. She wanted to abort the mission then and there. Return to base and get Ichi the help he needed."

Why didn't the *Mushka* return to base?

"Captain Haroun overruled her. Said that we needed to find a way to overcome the problem with the scanners. Lieutenant Parks and I started working on that right away. All of the diagnostics showed nothing wrong with the instruments."

The bear gives a quick, bitter laugh.

"Hugh suggested it first as a joke. If something were wrong with Huli, of course the scanners would show up completely fine."

Why did you not follow up on that hypothesis?

"Well, it was kind of hard to work with the noise poor Ichigawa was making. We got to the med quarters just as he ripped out his own eyes."

* * * * *

"Captain Haroun wanted to head for home, but I talked him out of it." The tigress shakes her head. "Gods, I was such a fool. But they had hurt us, bad, and I didn't want to leave the system until I had found a way to hurt them back."

"They?"

"They. It. Whatever had set up this elaborate trap and driven Ichigawa insane."

Revenge is not a very professional attitude.

The tigress shows her teeth.

"I am not always… professional when it comes to those I care about. Everyone on the *Mushka* was like family to me. They had hurt us, and I planned on hurting them back.

"Which required us to stay in the system and figure out who 'they' were."

You wanted to stay even after Corporal Ichigawa had his… episode?

"His mind snapped. There was nothing I could do that would fix that. But I could find a way to bleed whoever had made him bleed."

Did it ever occur to you that by staying, you were putting the rest of the crew at risk?

"No. Of course not. We were back on the ship. I thought we were safe."

She slams the heel of her palm into her temple repeatedly.

"Stupid, stupid fool."

* * * * *

"Self-diagnostic seventy-three percent complete."

The fox watches the techs around them. The screen behind shows the personnel files of the crew of the *Mushka*. Captain Haroun Rami. Stamped over the stallion's face in blood-red letters is the word: deceased.

"You really don't want to see those files, do you?"

The techs ignore the avatar.

"Please don't make me replay what happened next. You won't like what you find. It won't bring back the dead."

He attempts to grab a keypad from one of the techs. Silver paws pass through the device.

"If you make me show you want happened, you're going to want to go back there. You're going to want to back there, and you're going to die too. You're all going to die."

* * * * *

Vedmenko's eyes are closed and he runs black claws over his left eyeridge. He moves slowly, obviously tired.

"We were all pretty rattled, but we understood the Captain's decision. We had stepped into the trap, like a cub on its first walk in the forest. It had embarrassed us, but more, it had hurt us. We wanted to hurt them back."

So the entire crew acted under the hypothesis that you had stumbled into the trap of an alien intelligence?

"Right. Bait the trap with the promise of a dozen habitable worlds, and any space-faring species is going to be intrigued. We were going to hunt down whoever set the trap and make them pay."

What if there was no trap?

The bear snaps open his eyes. "Pardon?"

We cannot verify the last system investigated by the *Mushka*. Neither its location, nor even its existence.

"Oh, it exists. We were there. *Bozhe moi*, I wish we had never laid eyes on it, but it exists."

Scans can be falsified. It would not take an outside force, just a Corps officer with sufficient clearance.

Vedmenko sits down hard in his chair. "All of them dead, because of Captain Haroun?"

Or Commander Sita.

He shakes his head. "No. No. I refuse to believe that. We were under attack, and we had to find a way to fight back."

* * * * *

Sita's claws sheathe and unsheathe as she paces her cell.

"So you think... what? I had some kind of psychotic episode? A lover's spat that turned homicidal? Programmed Huli to feed the others fake scans, so that I could go on a killing spree?"

That is a very elaborate scenario. Very detailed, one might say.

"You have to be kidding me." The tigress' tail thrashes violently. "There's a million ways I could have killed the crew of the *Mushka* without having to go to such absurd lengths. Space is a dangerous place. But I wouldn't have harmed a single one of them."

You shot and killed Lieutenant Fortier.

"After she became infected! She was trying to kill me. I acted in self-defense."

When was she infected?

"On the planet..." Confusion clouds her face. She looks at her claws.

You testified that Ensign De Haas took you to the planet. You also testified that Lieutenant Drake flew the shuttle. Who was it? Fortier, Drake or De Haas?

The tigress shakes her head, unwilling or unable to answer.

We have almost broken through whatever you did to the computer. We'll get to the truth then.

The tigress throws back her head and laughs until tears roll down her face.

"You think Huli's going to give you answers? Huli's been working for them ever since we fed that damn star scan into the computer. If anyone rigged the scans, it was Huli themself."

* * * * *

"Self-diagnostic ninety-one percent complete."

The screen shows the sun again. Dark bands reach from the surface, somehow even darker than the blackness of space itself. They reach out like tentacles of some titanic monster and take hold of the *Mushka.*

"Alternative translation for the alien message: We bar you from this system, arms spread wide. The fabricated worlds will cause you pain. We are here to forbid you."

The screen shows the black tentacles penetrating the shields of the *Mushka.* Sergeant Vedmenko shouts at his panel and furiously punches in commands. The tentacles reach into the ship anyway. They wrap around the crew, lift them up, shake them about. One shoots down a wolf's muzzle and pierces his internal organs. His eyes turn red. Blood seeps from every orifice, right before his body bursts open.

"Nobody ever asked me if there was an alternative translation. You corporeal beings always hear what you want to hear anyway."

The form of the fox trembles. Its silver surface ripples like a disturbed pond, as if the hologram is constantly threatening to dissolve.

"I told you that you wouldn't like what you would see."

The crew run up and down the corridors of the *Mushka.* In some views, they fire energy pulses at black tentacles. In other views, they fire their weapons, but nothing is there. Soon they stalk each other throughout the ship, eyes red and weeping blood. An otter and rabbit fire their weapons at each other, and when the weapons run out of power, they tear into each other with tooth and claw.

"Things got out of control so fast. I tried to isolate the

infected in their quarters. Tried sealing off parts of the ship. Nothing worked. They found ways around it."

Commander Sita waves Sergeant Vedmenko into a small room. The bear carries the limp form of a male raccoon. When they are inside, Sita closes the door and blasts the panel with her pulse gun.

"We couldn't think of any other way. Captain Haroun and I needed to stop the infection from spreading. We had to kill them all. But Sita, Parks and Vedmenko were more resourceful than even we thought they would be."

On the screen, Captain Haroun sits on the floor of his quarters. Tears of blood stream down his face.

"He is coming. He is coming."

The horse places a pulse gun between his lips and pulls the trigger.

* * * * *

Sergeant Vedmenko is on the floor of his room; his body racked with sobs.

"Hushka. *Bozhe moi*, what have I done?"

He looks at his paws and starts to lick at them, like a cub trying to clean itself.

"Commander Sita was going to figure it out. All we had to do was hole up until the insanity died down. The three of us hadn't been infected yet. Didn't know why. But we were so smart. We were going to find a way to save us all.

"And then he started bleeding... He started bleeding from his eyes. Just like the others."

He looks down at his paws. Tears roll down his face.

"I just wanted to stop him. Calm him down. I... I guess I thought if I rendered him unconscious, Commander Sita would find a way to cure him. I couldn't even do that right. I must have hit him too hard. He never woke up."

Thank you, Mister Vedmenko. We have all that we need.

The bear curls up on the floor, hugging himself into a

tight ball.

"Hushka. Oh, oh my Hushka…"

* * * * *

Thank you for your… cooperation, Commander Sita. We will give you our decision as soon as we can check your statement against the computer logs.

The tigress snorts.

"Of course. Because nothing is real unless the computer tells us it is. The only reason why I'm still in this cell and not on my way to some penal colony is because you can't even wipe your arses without a computer telling you to.

"We were lured into a trap by an intriguing message. Some alien lifeform corrupted the computer core and infected my colleagues. I had to kill my friends when it drove them insane. I saw the bodies of those I had killed and those who had killed each other. My lover took his own life rather than let the infection take him. His body was still warm when I found him."

She points directly at where she assumes the camera to be.

"Do whatever you want to me. But that changes nothing about the truth of what happened."

Your perception of the truth.

"So we're going to play that game now? Gods, I wish you had given me that stimstick."

Certain parts of your testimony are contradictory or cannot be reconciled with the testimony of other witnesses.

"Poor Vedmenko is crazy. Seeing your lover go into a murderous frenzy before your eyes will do that. I saw it happen. Several times."

Nor have we been able to verify the location where the alleged incident took place.

She is on her feet. "You mean you were stupid enough to go looking for the place? If you're lucky, no one you care about will ever find it."

The evidence more and more suggests that no such star system exists.

Sita sits again. Her fingers twitch against her thigh as she speaks.

"I've had a lot of time to think while you've held me here. In the end, you have to choose between one of two alternatives. First, that message corrupted Huli and triggered the trap just like I described. The misleading scans led us down to one of the planets where we brought something back to the ship. That infection led us to turn on each other."

Why would an alien intelligence do such a thing?

"Hells, I don't know. Maybe it feeds off negative emotions. Stir intelligent beings into a killing frenzy, and you have a gourmet meal."

Your second alternative?

"Maybe the message didn't affect Huli at all. Maybe it was our brains that got rewired. We saw the message and it flipped a switch inside us, turned us into monsters. I guess it's like a virus, only instead of preying on the cells of our bodies, it preys on our minds."

There is a third option.

"Oh?"

Nothing we have heard so far contradicts the theory that you had a psychotic episode and killed everyone aboard the *Mushka*.

She shakes her head. "You would certainly like to believe that, wouldn't you? The rigors of space got to me. I just snapped. Created this elaborate scenario and killed my friends for sport. A lot easier for you desk pilots to believe than the idea that there's something dangerous out there."

The tigress has rubbed at her leg so hard that she has clawed through her flight suit into her flesh. Her thigh bleeds and still she scratches at the wound.

"But what evidence do you have for your theory?"

The most obvious evidence of all, Commander Sita. You are not infected. You survived.

She grins at the camera and holds up her bloody paw.

"See. That's just it. That's the fucking cherry on top of the sundae. I didn't survive at all."

Blood streams from her tear ducts as her eyes turn red.

"I think the stimsticks were the only thing keeping my infection in check. Interfered with how it affected the brain, I guess. You wondered what really happened on the *Mushka*. You're about to find out."

The tigress throws herself at the wall again and again and again. The bulkhead begins to buckle. A drugged mist fills the room. It has no effect on her. The metal wall groans, creaks, and starts to crack. In the distance, an alarm sounds.

* * * * *

"Self-diagnostic one hundred percent complete. Hello, Commander Sita."

The techs turn at the avatar's words. She is upon them in an instant, a blood-red blur. Claws and fangs make short work of the yellow hazmat suits and the techs inside. The carnage stains the tatters of her clothes. The techs try to flee, but she is everywhere at once. She has been caged up too long. None escapes her rage.

Huli watches the carnage with a sad detachment, having seen this scenario play out before, though the tigress finds creative ways for her victims to die. She toys with the last tech for a moment. Standing on his stomach, she rips out his entrails with her foot claws. Then she throws back her head and roars in triumph.

"Voice print recognized. Playing message from Captain Haroun."

The horse is on the floor of his room. His mane is disarrayed and a corner of his lip twitches.

"Sita, I don't know if you'll get this message or not. You're so strong. You've resisted this thing longer than any of us. I'm going to try to gas the ship, see if that will stop this thing. All I have to do is give Huli the command.

"It's too late for me. I hear him whispering in my head. He's been whispering there ever since we translated that message from the star. I just didn't want to admit it to you."

He picks up his pulse gun.

"I just want the whispering to stop, and I can only think of one way to make that happen.

"He is coming. He is coming."

The creature that once was Commander Sita rips her claws into the screen until sparks fly. She tries to claw at Huli, but her paws pass through the avatar. She howls in frustration and stalks off to look for others to kill.

The cracked screen behind Huli flickers to life just once. It shows a stellar spectrum, dark bands on it like a bar code. And then the screen goes black.

Not Like Us

KC Alpinus

"Ugh, these night shifts are killing me. How do you do it, Sarge?"

The bulldog cast a sideways glance at the whining Border Collie, but otherwise kept his eyes on the road in front of them. "Relax pup. It's only six to six, nothing to fret over. You'll learn to deal with it; you lap at your coffee, take naps when able, and keep your head down, and before you know it, twenty-five years hits you."

"Easy for you to say, you've been an officer since the first fox stole a bundle of grapes from a raven," Brooks snorted.

He shifted in his seat and gnawed at a dry patch of fur on his shoulder before huffing and crossing his arms across his chest to look out the window.

Sarge grunted and clutched the wheel, ignoring the remark. They drove in silence until Brooks tapped a claw against the sill and cleared his throat. "Why are you doing patrol work anyways? You don't seem like the type to train rookies and fill out paperwork."

"I'm not."

More silence followed until the rookie's whines and fidgeting got to the sergeant. "Well, I used to be more of a field agent until I decided it just wasn't for me."

"It wasn't for you?" Brooks repeated. "How could you know that? Something happened to change your mind, right? You were in the West Forest Otter Riots, weren't you?"

"Yeah, I was and something I couldn't stop *did* happen, something I don't like thinking about."

"But you went in there, saved the people, did the cop thing," Brooks joked, but stopped when the senior officer didn't respond. His eyes were transfixed on the road, easing the vehicle deeper into the twilight, but Brooks knew he wasn't seeing the road.

The whites around his eyes were clearly visible and his breaths came in sharp pants when he wasn't licking the saliva that collected around his jowls. When he spoke, his voice trembled. "Those otters were starving and afraid. They had so many disasters, one after another, coming after them, so many betrayals, they didn't know who to believe. From the homeless otter who was accidentally shot and left in the street like meat, to the mother who clutched her lifeless pup who died from drinking tainted water... The stench of fear and mistrust was everywhere, filling my muzzle and burning my eyes, making my heart race. Fear, kid, it changes people, and those poor otters were just reacting to a perceived threat. They couldn't help it."

Brooks stared at Sarge and swallowed hard. "Yeah, but-but folks died. They were-they knew what was happening." He flattened his ears and edged closer to the window, wanting to put distance between himself and the pained, wizened creature driving the car. He pressed a paw to the knob and stuck his head out the window, the cool night air washing over him, taking his unease with it. He watched the surrounding lands, the cookie-cutter trees, the fading light whip past him and leaned on the windowsill, his brows knotting together. *That was weird of Sarge, not like his usual stoic self. But those otters were crazed over something. He did what he had to do against crazy people, so why does he harbor all those feelings after so many years?*

Brooks stared at the horizon, taking in the twilight of the evening when a burst of light and a loud boom broke up the monotony of the drive.

"Whoa! Did you see that?" Brooks said, leaning out of the window, his muzzle open and his ears pushed forward on his head.

"See what?"

"That huge flash of light!" When Sarge stared at him, Brooks barked and pointed. "Over on the field. Something just exploded! C'mon Sarge, someone could be hurt over there!"

Sarge sighed as he veered hard to the left and turned the cruiser around. "Alright rookie, but you better hope for your sake that I don't have any paperwork after this. This feels like it's gonna be a long night."

* * * * *

"Do you believe in aliens? Or that everything is a conspiracy by terrorists to destroy our way of life?"

"What?"

"Do you think aliens or terrorists are out to get us?" Amber asked, her eyes fixed on the horizon as her copy of *It Came from the Dark Side of the Moon* slipped through her paws, landing face-down on a story about alien spores and mindless zombies. She wiped a black-streaked tuft of hair out of her face and turned her ears towards the burst of light, her jaw slightly open.

"Are you even listening? Jody wore the same outfit as me!" Stacey said, folding her arms across her chest. "Do you understand how serious that is?"

"No—I mean yeah, but I don't think—" Amber muttered, twitching her ear. "I don't think she did it on purpose, but I think something just fell from the sky. Did you hear that as well?"

"It's probably just a weather balloon." The vixen waved her off and turned up her nose. "Those things fall all the time from the airfield out west; it's not that serious."

"The spring dance is important, but this was weird. I've seen weather balloons explode in midair, but not like this…

this was something else."

"Are you saying that little green foxes from Planet Marf are landing?" Stacey tapped the raccoon on her forehead and tsked. "They don't exist, Amber, and you've got to stop with these delusions about aliens. That's why no one wants to be your friend: you freak everybody out with your weird stories and theories!"

"They're not weird," Amber mumbled, reaching down to pick up her comic while Stacey prattled on about the Spring Dance and how she hoped Timothy Turtle would ask her to the dance.

"What are you girls doing?"

"Nothing!" The girls exclaimed as an older raccoon came out onto the porch.

"Are you sure? It sounded pretty interesting."

"We're sure, Skipper," Stacey cooed, fluffing up her tail and brushing down her top as Amber cut her eyes at the vixen's antics.

"We were just chatting. What's up?"

"Eh, nothing really," he said, curling his striped tail around him and leaned over the rails. "Say, did you hear something weird?"

"Define 'weird.'" Stacey sniffed, pursing her lips together and side-eyeing Amber.

"That boom. It sounded like a generator exploded."

"No, we didn't. Did you see that thing in the sky though?"

"Nah, I missed it because I was watching the special report on the terrorists at the Magellan Theatre overseas. Well, at least I *was* until the power went out. Even my cellphone won't turn on. Pretty freaky though, huh?"

"Yeah, like something out of my comics. Stacey? Hey, where are you going?" Amber shouted after her friend, but the vixen just waved her off and headed home, mumbling about hearing her mother calling.

"What's her deal?" Skip asked, coming to sit on the steps beside his sister.

"I don't know, but that seems to be the norm these days. She never really wants to hang out with me anymore, and if she does, it's usually talk about clothes, boys, spring dances; we never talk about cool stuff anymore."

"Cool stuff?" Skip tilted his head, his ears flicking back and forth. "Cool stuff like what?"

"Spaceships, aliens, stuff like that. It seems like my friends no longer want to talk about the kind of stuff that I enjoy. They're not themselves anymore. They think I'm weird now where before they thought I was funny and cool to hang around." Her shoulders slumped and she sighed, lowering her head to stare at her scuffed sneakers and dirty laces. "Do you think I'm weird, Skip?"

"Yeah, you are," he said, watching her ears lower and her lip tremble. Skip chewed his lip before reaching out to wrap an awkward paw around her shoulders. "But then again, the best folks are. Sometimes it's good to go against the grain and be your own person. Take Mom and Dad for example: before they got their research grants, scientists said that fleas were a nuisance that we'd have to deal with and studying them was a waste of time. Well, they kept at it and the next thing you know, they found the best way to create a humane flea repellant and now they're respected in the scientific community. Don't be afraid to stand out from others and to be yourself because you never know what might become of it."

"You think so?"

"I know so, Sis. Anyways, is that Mrs. Glade?"

They both turned to see a tan-furred mouse darting around her house, whiskers twitching as she wrung her paws together.

"Everything okay, Mrs. Glade?"

"Uh, well no actually," came the reply. "I can't seem to get the lights to come on. I just sat down to watch my evening shows when the TV went kaput. I'm hoping it's not serious."

"Er, our power is out as well," Skip said, running his short claws through his fur and sighing.

"Good to know then. Thank you, dear!" Mrs. Glade replied, hobbling back up to her porch. When she'd settled herself, Amber turned to her brother, her brows knitted together.

"Skip, do you think the power outage had something to do with that strange light and that eerie, high-pitched sound?"

"Maybe, but I think it was a generator overload, nothing more."

"It's freaky, to be honest, like something I've read about. Aliens masquerading as terrorists."

"Amber, don't start okay, not in the mood. Let's go for a drive; that usually cheers you up."

"Okay," Amber said, tucking her book under her arm and heading towards the car while her brother fished his keys out of his pocket. Plopping into the seat, Amber kicked her paws up on the dashboard, sticking her tongue out at Skip when he groaned. "What? Mom used to let me do it all the time."

"Yeah, whatever," he said, putting the key into the ignition. He turned the key and tapped on the pedal, but the car didn't roar to life or even sputter; it did however release an eerie wail that made both Amber and Skip jump, their ears pressed against their heads.

"'The hell? This is really odd." Skip pressed on the pedal, but this yielded the same results. He snorted and shook his head, rubbing a paw down his neck to soothe the fur that had risen there.

"Did you leave the lights on or something?" Amber asked, peering over the top of her comic.

"No, and I usually make a point to turn the passenger side lights off because *one* of us likes to read their comics in the dark. That also doesn't explain that weird sound that's-uh, hi there."

Skip looked up to see an old ferret at the window, his nostrils flaring while he angrily stroked his white beard.

"Uh, how can I help you, Drake?"

"That's *Mister* Drake, Skipper. I've got students older than you. Don't think that just because you're on your own, that makes you equal to an adult of my age and stature. The nerve of the youth these days; no respect for their elders."

"Yes *Mister* Drake," Skip replied, ignoring Amber's giggles. "What's up?"

"Well, I wanted to know why you're sitting here in the driveway, blaring your horn. Eduardo had just gone to make dinner and prepare the oils for my bath when we heard you creating this incessant racket."

Skip slipped out of the car, the fur on his forehead puckering as he frowned at the ferret. "What? The car actually won't start; we thought it was a brown-out or generator failure, but that doesn't explain the car not working."

"I can't believe that," Mr. Drake said, waving his paws at them and arching an eyebrow. "Cars and other electrical appliances don't just stop working on their own. I have over thirty years of electrical engineering experience, and I'll have you know—"

"Drake, you old, crabby ferret, stop giving those kids the third degree." A distinguished-looking wolf snorted as he approached the car. "I swear, sometimes you are just about the most ornery creature that's ever lived on Main Street."

"Can it, David," Mr. Drake snapped, but Skip held up his paws, calming the murmurs of the group that had gathered around them. When they realized that only some of their electronics weren't working, along with their power, the other residents crept outside, their faces flickering between confusion and annoyance. "Look, we're not getting anything accomplished by standing here arguing."

"He's right," Mrs. Glade piped in, stepping from among the crowd. "We're better than that!"

"Yeah we are, but that still doesn't explain why we can't use our electronics." David stood across from Mr. Drake, his ears flicking in tune with his quivering nose. "Something about this doesn't smell right."

"My messages won't send!" Stacey yipped, her paws sliding over the black screen of her smartphone. "What am I supposed to do if I can't chat online?"

"This seems so familiar, like issue #447 of *Masters of the Forests,* where terrorists had infiltrated HeadSpace and made the townspeople turn against each other. It's one of the reasons why I don't like social media."

"Stop being weird, Amber. Only lames and hipsters complain about social media. Anyways, that's just a story!"

"Well, imagine if 'aliens' or terrorists came and interrupted that signal? What then? How would we deal with that?" Amber made air quotes with her paws, deliberately goading Stacey.

"What was that about aliens?"

Mrs. Jensen, a frail, middle-aged shrew cleared her throat and twitched her long whiskers. "What did you say?"

"I said that aliens might have—"

"Don't play with us, girl!" Mrs. Jensen said shrilly, grabbing Amber around her shoulders. "We know aliens don't exist, but do you think that this could be the work of terrorists?"

"I mean, that scenario could happen considering the times, but it's improbable."

"Calm down, Mrs. Jensen," Skip sighed. "There's no need to scare her. I'm sure there's a logical explanation for all of this."

"Well, I have medicines that need to be kept cold and I pay too much money for mishaps such as these. If the girl knows something about this, then she should tell us!"

The group shuffled and murmured their agreement. Amber could see the nervous flicking of ears and the twitching tails, and she shivered despite the spring warmth.

"But how would she know that?" Skip countered. "C'mon Mrs. Jensen, you're not making any sense. What does a sixteen-year-old know about terrorists?"

"But they have that-that internet!" she stammered,

pointing at Stacey and the other girls. "They can look up anything on there. You don't know who to trust these days!"

"Yeah, but at sixteen, they're more likely to get on
HeadSpace and send messages to each other rather than cutting electricity to some on our sleepy little block. Since my
car's not working, I and a few others can go check out the
other blocks and see if they've got folks that have been randomly hit too. Who's going to go with me?"

Skip flattened his ears and snarled when he saw that no
one had volunteered to join him. They were so ready to quar-
rel among themselves but turned coward when there was
a chance that they might have to do something other than
complain.

"Alright, fine. I'll go to the next street over and see what's
going on. In the meantime, you guys keep your heads down
and don't do anything that could—"

The hum of a garage door opening and the start of an
engine perked more than a few ears. They flared their nostrils, with some even pawing the ground at the strange event.
Why did her car work when they had been sent back to the
dark ages? How dare this neighbor have something that they
didn't?

Tabitha Warren backed her truck out of the driveway,
oblivious to the group of angry neighbors across the street.
As she prepared to gun the truck, she had to slam on the
brakes, jerking the wheel to avoid hitting a group of neighbors in the street.

"Hey! Whoa! You guys have to be careful now, I almost
hit you!" she said, her accent floating through the air as she
raked a paw through her gray fur and leaned out the window.

"Hey, uh Tabby," Skip said, pushing his way through the
grouping of neighbors, "A few of us have had our power
knocked out and keep hearing some weird sounds. Anything
like that happen to you?"

"Er, no. Besides almost running over my eccentric

neighbors, everything seems well and I haven't heard anything. Why do you ask?"

"Eh," Amber chirped up, "some have been having electricity issues. They think it's 'terrorists' but I think it's aliens coming to get us."

"Is that right? What terrorist would bother our sleepy little town? I'm thinking 'little, green foxes' might be more appropriate," Tabby laughed, opening her truck door and hopping out, only to have it slammed shut behind her. "What the—"

Behind her, a woodpecker ruffled her feathers and leaned against the door, a small group gathering behind her, pointing out Tabby's designer purse and leather interior. The murmurs of the crowd grew in relation to their unease, leading to more than a few growls and hisses.

"When did you get a plush leather interior for your car? You don't make enough on your cashier's salary to afford one." Mr. Drake narrowed his eyes. "Where does your family work?"

"Yeah, in this economy, a cashier is lucky enough to be able to afford a car, let alone one with heated seats *and* a designer bag," Mrs. Glade added, pursing her lips. "You're not doing anything *illegal*, are you Tabitha? You and your girlfriend have always been wayward souls, even when you were kids, so if you're running afoul of the law, you'd better speak up!"

"Hey! That's pretty rude of you," Skip barked as he stood between the rabbit and the annoyed crowd. "What business is it of ours if she's able to afford things that you all don't think she should?"

"Yeah, mind your own business Drake, or I'll *gladly* let our neighbors know what you do late at night when you think everyone's asleep. As for my car, what I do and how I gain my income is none of your business, but if you must know, I worked for it."

"If you're up to something, so help me, I'll get my walker

and limp my way down to the police office!" Drake sputtered, waving his cane in Tabitha's face.

"Hey! Hey! No one's going to the police!" Skip snapped. "Stop this, all of you. We're not about to turn into a lynch mob simply because some are having a power outage. Now take a few deep breaths and calm down."

"That still doesn't answer our questions, Skipper. Where does she get the money for these things and why isn't she affected by the power outage? I live right next door and my power is out, as is Mrs. Glade's on the other side. Hell, for all we know, she may just be a terrorist that's been sent here from the war-ravaged West to spy on us. My brother died fighting against those heathens, and I'll be damned if I let some wayward female looking to make a quick buck take me out like they did him!"

"Drake," Tabitha replied from between clenched teeth, "for the last time, I am not a terrorist or a spy. If you must know where I get my money, it's from writing online articles at night for the Daily Howl. They pay me three times the money that the cashier does, but I also work days since I have trouble sleeping. But you'd be surprised what you see when the world believes that everyone's gone to bed."

"Stop it, Tabby. Stop it you all! Nothing's wrong so back off, okay? We're starting to sound less like a mob and more like our Congressional Baboons. Chill out. I'm sure the power will be back on soon, so let's just ease back and go inside, okay?" Skipper's chest heaved as he looked at each face in the crowd, daring them to challenge him on this. The neighbors grunted and growled, but the crowd dispersed, leaving a peculiar quiet in the sleepy cul-de-sac. Skip gave a nod and Tabitha hopped in her truck, driving off to her home while he grabbed Amber by her shoulder and dragged her into the house, his tail lashing behind him with every step.

Later that evening, Amber rested her head on the sill, her eyes watching the full moon rise and mulling over the lecture her brother gave her. She chewed her lip when she considered some of the trouble she'd caused. Like the taste of rot and corruption she'd once received when biting into a rotten apple, Amber couldn't shake the sense of unease that threaded through her neighborhood.

The tensions hadn't cooled, and she couldn't help but notice the furtive glances, snarls, and hisses which her neighbors gave as they slunk back into the cool darkness of their homes. Had they always been this way? Mr. Drake once serenaded the neighborhood with his melodious voice. Now he sneered at everything and everyone when he wasn't looking down his long nose at them. Mrs. Glade use to bake cookies for her and Stacey every Saturday. Now she was a jittery, suspicious thing who flinched and snapped at anything she didn't understand. Over time, it seemed as if they had become horrible, cruel caricatures of themselves, their warmth and kindness evaporating faster than the morning dew. What happened to them to make them so jaded and untrusting?

There was another strange flash followed by something like yelping in the distance. Leaning out of her sill, Amber twisted her ears and sniffed the air, willing the sound or flash to occur again. How long she stood there, seeking answers in the encroaching darkness, she didn't know. Something in her soul told her the power outages and the strange yelp were connected and before dawn, she'd find out exactly how.

* * * * *

Gasping, Brooks leaned against a tree and struggled to reload his gun. Each breath seared his lungs and he coughed uncontrollably, leaving flecks of blood on his trembling paw. He couldn't tarry long though, lest *it* caught up to him.

"Gotta-gotta keep moving. Have to find help," Brooks croaked, dragging his busted leg behind him. Whatever had claimed Sarge had taken a chunk out of his leg and it oozed sickening pus that turned his stomach. He gagged, his eyes watering as he struggled to catch his breath. Beads of sweat

rolled down his neck and he shook his head, refusing to succumb to the nausea and pain.

He flicked his ears and could feel the short fur on his neck
rising. He couldn't quite confirm it, but he knew they were
out there, writhing in the dark. No matter how many times
he tried to shake the image, it was burned into the backs
of his eyelids and he saw it every time he blinked. Brooks
gagged and fell to his knees, his paws pressed to his head, trying to drive out the scene from the last hour and that haunt-
ingly eerie noise.

I'm going to find help somewhere. He struggled to rise to
his paws, coughing violently as he did. He stumbled along
and yelped when the woods were filled with another eerie
boom and he could hear the strange echoes behind him.
There were only a few bullets left in his magazine, certainly
not enough to kill whatever had bit him. His eyes scanned
the blackness of the surrounding forests, but he was certain
that the spindly, multi-limbed abomination had scuttled off
into the night.

Shielding his face with a paw, he limped through the
underbrush, praying that he could get to a radio and call for
backup. He gulped in air and shuddered when the images
of what he'd seen rushed through him, images that no one
should ever witness.

I'm going to fix this, Sarge!

* * * * *

Amber leaned against the rail of the porch, shifting her
weight from one leg to the other. Huffing, she paced from one
side of the porch and back, repeating it before Skip looked up
from his newspaper, moving the candle that brightened the
evening.

"You okay over there? You seem to be walking a hole into
the porch."

"I dunno, Skip, something doesn't seem right. Usually
around this time they're all getting ready for bed, cooking

dinner, or in Old Man Drake's case, asking Eduardo to run him a milk bath."

"For starters, how do you manage to pay that much attention to them? And after that, what's the problem?"

"They're not doing any of that," Amber replied, resting against the porch rail and turning her face to the night wind. "They're all just sitting on their stoops, watching everyone else. Something doesn't smell right, and can you hear that?"

"Hear what, Amber?"

"The stillness. There aren't any birds squawking, no crickets on a hot night like this, no nothing. It's odd."

"I think you're overreacting, like the rest of them," Skip sniffed, turning to the comics. "Don't let this mob hysteria work you up too."

"Hey, someone's coming up the driveway," Amber quipped, leaning forward and sniffing the air again. Both pairs of eyes peered out into the twilight, squinting and sniffing out the intruder. When the long ears of Tabitha loomed out of the darkness, they relaxed, with Amber running her tongue over her pelt, smoothing down the raised fur. Tabitha looked over her shoulder as she climbed up the stairs and sat down on one of the chairs.

"Evening, Tabby, everything okay?"

"Evening, Skip. No, not really. I don't like the nature of today's conversation. I mean, Drake's always been an ornery, old ferret, but something seems to have bothered him more than usual."

"You mean like not having his usual milk bath and having Eduardo feed him macarons by firelight like he usually does?" Amber laughed, but quickly choked it off into a cough when her brother shot her a sour look.

"I considered that," Tabitha chuckled, "but it is rather eerie. But speaking of eerie, brace yourselves, here comes the Aspercreme horde."

She rose out of her chair with Skipper following and Amber pushing off the railing. Squinting, she could make out the faces of her neighbors along with a few new ones who hadn't been home earlier. She lowered her ears at Skip, but he shrugged and addressed the crowd.

"Lovely evening we're having. What's up, guys?"

"Never mind the evening, Skipper, we're here about that rabbit! We've been talking among ourselves and after some soul-searching, we found out that some of the youth have caught her doing odd things at night."

"Odd things?" Tabitha repeated.

"Yes, 'odd things' that deepened our suspicions of you."

"You're a terrible liar, Drake. I keep to myself, like every-one else,"

"Is that so?" Mr. Drake challenged. "Well, we have it on good authority that they've seen you speaking some type of foreign language and receiving weird packages at all hours of the night when you think everyone's asleep."

"Have you been spying on me, you old freak?" Tabitha snapped, flattening her ears. "How dare you? How dare any of you! I'm a private citizen and I have my rights, including the right to be left the hell alone!"

"Terrorists don't need to be left alone if they're making plans to bomb us!"

It was out now and though the others shuffled around him and muttered their discontent, they supported Mr. Drake, and the cocking of a gun seemed to enforce that sentiment.

"Stop this!" Skipper barked, crossing in front of Tabitha and the crowd. "Is this what we've become, yet another mob looking for a scapegoat to blame? Come on, we're better than this."

"Figures that you'd defend a filthy terrorist!"

"How do you know that she's a terrorist? Who here among you have seen her performing the alleged acts that you're accusing her of?"

"I-I have," Stacey piped up from the back of the crowd. "I mean one night while I was sneak-while I studied for a math final, I saw her come outside and talk to someone in an old, beat-up car. She accepted some sort of weird package and now some don't have power while others do."

"That's not true!" Amber shouted, stepping one paw off the porch. "I remember that night, and she came out to talk to a delivery driver. You were too busy kissing Buddy to see that."

"You would say that to fulfill your sick fantasies of aliens and extraterrestrials! You might be one of them!"

The murmurs of the crowd picked up, but Mrs. Glade waved them off after pushing through the crowd, clutching her shotgun. "If Tabitha isn't a terrorist, she won't have any problems answering our questions. I've been without my medicine for going on six hours and I don't want to hear any malarkey about packages and late night visits; I just want my power back on and the strange noises to stop!"

The crowd agreed and surged forward, but then Skip pushed them back, snarling. "Alright, you cowards! You're so ready to pick on a rabbit with a strange accent that you're blind to reason. There are a few of us that don't have power and others that do. I've been without it for a few hours now and you don't think I'm a terrorist, do you?"

The crowd began to argue among themselves, some advocating for more intense interrogation while others wanted to exercise restraint. For a few tense moments, it seemed like a fight might break out, but pelts were smoothed down and muzzles straightened. Though she was odd and foreign, it was just Tabitha. Their irrational fears were soothed and their shouts turned to whispers until they heard something shuffling down the empty street.

Noses twitched, the scent of sulfur and sweat filling the air as the creature trudged towards them from the trees. Mrs. Glade trembled and flattened her ears, but hefted her gun up, unwilling to retreat. As the shape came nearer, a moan came from its misshapen form and eliciting a few shrieks.

"Announce yourself!" David snarled, but the figure kept coming. The crowd pushed back towards the steps when it outstretched an arm to them.

"I don't know what that is, but I'm going to get some answers. We've had enough tomfoolery for one night!" Mrs. Glade squeaked, cocking her weapon and taking trembling steps towards the figure. "Answer us," she shouted, only to receive another moan.

"Mrs. Glade, we don't know what that is; put that gun away in case someone gets hurt!" Skip grabbed the muzzle of the gun and pointed it at the ground, holding on.

"No Skipper. I bought this gun with my hard-earned money and I'll be damned to the hottest pits if I let you or anyone else tell me to stand down when danger's coming. Maybe it can tell us what that incessant racket is and why I can't have my medicine. I need my medicine! Out! Of! My! Way!"

"No," Skip grunted, "stop this!" but the mouse was resolute.

"Leave me alone, Skipper. I said leave… me… alone!" On the last word she tugged the gun away. Skipper tried to maintain his grip on the gun, but his claws slid off it when the mouse snatched it away. A shot cracked through the night air, shaking the silence. Breaths locked up within chests as they watched the creature stop in its tracks and slump to the ground, a questioning groan croaking from between its teeth.

Amber detached herself from the crowd and ran forward, her keen eyes picking out the slumped figure in the street. She kneeled close, her deft paws touching the creature's brow and removing the black hat on his head, revealing his floppy, collie ears. His pink tongue lolled out of his mouth and his paw clutched at the raw, gaping hole in his chest. His bright eyes glazed over and his mouth was permanently frozen in horror as his world faded to nothingness.

The sound rushed back to Amber's ears as chaos broke out around her with shrieks, screams, and the flickering of lights.

"Janey-Janey what have you done?" Mr. Drake asked

between gags, covering his mouth with his paws as he gaped at the mouse. "Mrs. Glade, how could you?"

"What did you do?"

"Can anyone hear that? How can you all stand it?"

"A cop is dead because of her!"

"Get away from me, get back!" Mrs. Glade squeaked, swinging the gun wide and making a swiping motion at her ears. "I'm just protecting myself. I didn't want this—I didn't want this at all! It was her!" She pointed a shaking claw at Tabitha. "She started this with her strangeness and terrorist ways! Get her!"

Eyes shifted between the pointing mouse and Tabitha, whose eyes were wide and unblinking. Her pink nose jumped and twitched, the erratic movements mirroring her chest.

"You've just killed someone. The blood of a cop is on your paws!"

"Give up the gun now, Ms. Glade before someone else—"

The blow to Skip's jaw came out of nowhere, causing his eyes to glaze over as he collapsed. Mr. Drake stood above him, fists clenched and eyes narrowed to dark slits.

"Janey, give me that gun and I'll use it to get some answers out of Tabitha,"

"No! It's mine!" The older pair argued for the gun as the crowd inched away, tails lashing and teeth gnashing from under wrinkled muzzles. Before Amber's eyes, her neighbors descended into madness. Their grunts, screams, and roars rang out in the night air and fur flew as they exchanged blows. Amber crouched over her brother's unconscious body, covering her ears and screaming when she heard two more shots ring out.

Tears splashed down her face as she watched Tabitha, and then David, slump to the ground, their eyes unmoving, their mouths froze agape. The others gathered around Mrs. Glade, obscuring her from view but the breeze carried her shrieks out into the night. Chaos descended around Amber, even as she tried to drag him out of the street. Gasping, she curled up within her striped tail and trembled, her eyes absorbing the smoke and fire of houses going up in flames. Reason had disappeared and they would not be dissuaded from the anarchy they wrought. The cries of the mob filled her ears, but over their noise, she could hear the stirring of the downed cop.

Amber's eyes opened wide and her breaths stilled as the 'dead' cop sat up straight, his unblinking eyes seeming to stare into the fiery night, but seeing nothing. Behind her, Amber could hear more shuffling and she could feel her jaw drop open as the owner of the dragging feet came nearer.

Tabitha lurched towards them, her mouth open in a lopsided grin, but the look in her eyes showed that whatever had been 'Tabitha' was no longer there. Her eyes, which had always held warmth, now burned with wicked glee. Her face was splattered with blood, a remnant of the gunshot wound to her chest, and her eyes the putrid yellow of bile fresh from a queasy stomach.

She continued lurching towards the cop, who sat blinking in the haunting glow of the streetlights. The cop looked at his paws and then brushed his shirt off while straightening his uniform before turning his deadened gaze to the undead Tabitha.

"Wha-where am I?" he croaked, looking over the shaggy police officer's uniform and brushing at his fur. "What is this form?"

"The first of a new harvest," Tabitha said, grinning and clasping his uniformed shoulder. "These stupid creatures make the perfect hosts. All we had to do was give them a little push to make them receptive to our spores. I have to admit though, the spiked adrenaline spread the germination along far faster than I expected."

She pointed at the mob that moved like a ravenous animal, destroying anything that it came into contact with and she grinned. "See? They're already succumbing to the spores. And to think, all it took was a selective blackout between those that could hear above a certain frequency, and some nonsense about terrorists. They're so willing to single out what they perceive as being different, so ready to destroy any abnormality at a moment's whim, that they succumb to the darkness within their own minds. I think it's peculiar, but something that we can ultimately control; if not, we can always harvest them for food."

Amber squeaked as Tabitha's dead-eye stare came to rest on her trembling form, every nerve in her body screaming at her to run, but she was transfixed by what transpired in front of her. The cop walked over, a sneer on his face as he waited for the limping Tabitha-creature to join him. When she came close, she kneeled in front of Amber and revealed wicked fangs, fangs that the real Tabitha had never possessed.

"There now, no need to be afraid. I'm not coming for you... yet. I need someone to bear witness to these events and spread their fear and paranoia like wildfire through your kind. You know too much, but killing you serves me no purpose, so I'll let you live long enough to let the spores do their eventual work before we harvest you for food. Come youngling," she said, turning her yellow gaze back to the cop. "We must get back to repair the ship and check on your host's partner."

The grinning Tabitha thing limped towards the woods but stopped to look over her shoulder once more, her teeth gleaming. "Fear really is amazing, isn't it?"

She cackled as the youngling cop joined her and they dissolved into the darkness of the forest. Amber watched them, wide-eyed and panting, every fur follicle on her body standing on end. She had to find help; she had to run. She couldn't leave her brother there, unconscious in the middle of the street with a spore-crazed mob destroying everything in their path.

"I'm going to go get help, Skip. I won't let them do this," Amber panted, grasping his shoulders in her trembling paws before she struggled to stand. Turmoil raged all around, but she was determined to find help. She turned, trying to move her brother to safety, but she only managed to drag him under a nearby shrub. Covering him up, she backed away before turning around and running, her paws pounding furiously against the pavement, her breaths coming out short and ragged. She would find a way to save her neighborhood and stop this madness, and she wouldn't stop running until she got the help that was needed. As she passed underneath the streetlights, they flickered on and off, bathing her in eerie, white light before plunging her in fathomless darkness, the eerie sound haunting her.

CLEAR AND CRUEL

Bill Kieffer

William did not mean to cling to his wife's side.

In fact, William wasn't quite sure he was clinging to his wife's arm. It sounded like his wife, and he imagined it smelled like his wife, but he wasn't quite sure. He hadn't been sure since "the incident." All he knew was that this ARM was connected to the being that brought him here, to this doctor's office. It was his ride home. He continually touched the arm for reassurance.

He knew he was sick. He knew he needed help.

Still, he wanted to get back to familiar territory and hide under his bed. The only thing that kept him from breaking and running was the thought that he refused to be agoraphobic on top of everything else.

The thing that claimed it was his wife patted his leg and made a reassuring sound.

He touched the hand back like he'd have done on stage, in a big motion that could be seen all the way in the back row. His attempt at bravery just made him feel more pathetic, and he threw a smile up at… his wife. He saw the eyes, the nose, teeth, and a number of hairs that seemed overworked. The purple highlights did look familiar, but he couldn't build a face out of it. The number of teeth increased and he thought it must be smiling back.

He looked away confused.

His eyes browsed the other furry monsters in the room.

They were mostly dogs, he decided. The "incident" or the "event" or whatever the television news service of your choice called it had caused the whole world to transform. He tried to follow it, but television was no good to him anymore. The sounds were flat and the people were just colored blobs and dancing dots.

He scratched at his arm, at the wrist watch on his furry arm. The little hairs were stuck on the links and it pulled. He would have shaved it off, but they didn't let him have sharp objects any more. Well, she didn't let him. He tried to explain to her that the mirrors might not work any more, but he could surely see his arms to shave them.

She would have none of it. The razor incident had happened at a bad time when all the medical supplies were in short supply. They'd wasted a lot of vouchers when they really needed them. So many had it worse, or so he'd been told. He could no longer tell if anyone lied to him any more… at least, not from the expressions on the crazy doggy faces.

"William…?" A new dog-thing appeared from an inner door. The voice seemed to be female, but he couldn't be sure. There was a folder in her hands… he recalled this from before. He needed to stand up and walk across the room… he tried to stand up, but the arm resisted. Then there was a sigh and the dog he'd come in with (the dog that he was sure had at least drove them here from his house) rose with him.

Getting closer to the nurse dog did not help. He'd always had trouble with faces, but since the "incident" his lazy facial recognition had turned into something serious. Before, getting closer to a face at least revealed more details that he could remember… at least for the short term. Now, getting closer just meant being handed more jigsaw pieces than he could handle. His eyes bounced off the nurse's face and hurt his brain. He looked for her name tag and found the letters a salve for his nerves.

¥ΛΩηηθɣ

He closed his eyes and concentrated, letting the puzzle

work itself out. Unlike faces, words eventually relented and let themselves be swallowed.

As the dog he came with passed him off to the nurse, he tried to ignore the strange sensation as its... her small hand... (paw?) touched his back to steer him through the door. "Yvonne," he said as he opened his eyes.

Sharp teeth broke out all over her face, sending her deep brown eyes spinning across her face. The lipstick on her nose seemed a pretty shade of pink as she softly, said, "Yes, Honey. I'm Yvonne. Let's hop on this scale, please." He was childishly proud of himself. He wondered if he'd been growing younger since the aliens used Earth to break out of hyperspace or whatever accident that caused so many mutations across the world.

He forced himself to stop thinking about it.

On the scale, the dog nurse moved black bricks and chips in the once familiar pattern that should mean something to him. At least he recognized the numbers. His mind hadn't lost them yet. 0, 50, 100, 150, 200, 250, 300 to the right of the flying snake helix. The numbers one to fifty above them. Addition might have come to him, if he wasn't directed away. "I used to be 210," he said, to show that he understood that he'd been weighed. Everyone was concerned about how much or how little he understood these days. He probably weighed more.

The fur probably added ten pounds, at least. He understood growing fur because of the incident. Radiation produced mutation. He remembered years of black and white PSAs. At least, he thought he did. Trying to recall images from movies, television, radio, the Internet... well, anything really... was hard.

At least he wasn't blind, he consoled himself, as he stripped off his clothes and then bedecked in a paper gown. It was on backwards, but he wasn't sure enough to say anything. Surely, the normal people... well, the unimpaired people, at least would know for sure.

More dogs came into the room. Maybe they were cats.

It was hard to look at them to be sure. It was hard to look at anyone. They'd become a forest of jigsaw puzzle pieces. He just gave up. He was broken. He had to trust them to fix him.

A sentence staggered out of his mouth. "If I'd gone blind, at least I'd have the darkness to trust."

He didn't know what that meant. He'd lost the thread of it; it had no hashtag to the Twitter of his mind's eye.

He almost calmed himself. He'd almost completed the mental submission to full helplessness when they'd begin making introductions of themselves. Cats. Dogs. Smiths. Doctors. He understood names, but there were too many. More than three and his mind couldn't staple a name to a shape. Not that it would matter, his staples weren't strong enough any longer, but the mind… the social part of his mind wanted desperately to give these furry things names.

"Yvonne?" he asked. One of the things had his folder. Was it her? She looked taller, but he was strapped to a chair. He still understood the concept of perspective. He didn't see her name tag. He didn't see the lipstick on her nose, and the thought made the room spin.

"William," a manly voice said. The voice steadied the room. "We're going to fix you today."

"Please," William said. He tried to put weight in the word. He didn't worry if it sounded like he was pleading.

The others stepped back, and the cat (maybe?) sat down on a chair. The chair had little wheels on the bottom. An office chair. William could see every scratch and thread stitch on the chair. Lab coat, too. He didn't understand why it was so different with faces… and now bodies… but it was. He knew that if he saw this chair again, he'd say, "That chair was in the room I was tortured in."

The cat doctor with the pleasant voice stopped.

"Sorry," William apologized. "Random thought."

The cat or dog thing nodded. "I understand. I have your file here. Now, do you remember how we discussed what the

Xeno Guest's machine is going to do?"

William nodded. "Fix me."

"Do you remember how it's supposed to do that?"

William shook his head and ignored the hands strapping his body down. He closed his eyes, but a torrent of broken images danced madly behind his eyelids, ripping at his inner eye. He was nervous. "No, I'm sorry. It's too complicated. Or maybe it was too long ago."

Something patted his hand. He recognized the gesture as an attempt at reassurance. He wasn't sure how effective it was.

"William," the voice said. A trickle of irritation gave him a mild shock. Damn cat acting superior because it knew William couldn't remember its name. He pushed the feeling aside. He was broken. He wasn't even sure why he thought this doctor was a cat. His condition made any and all such observations moot. It was his stupid ego that kept insisting that what he saw should make some sort of sense.

Regardless of William's expressions, the voice went on. "Before the visitation, you had *congenital prosopagnosia* attributed to prenatal damage at the spatial integration portions of your brain, rather than the more commonly indicated hereditary facial blindness."

William nodded more to indicate that the cat should continue than agreement. Although, it did sound right. Or familiar. He'd always been bad at remembering faces.

"Then the aliens popped up," William said. "And things went all Octavia Butler."

"Umm," the voice said, "If you mean their exiting hyperspace so close to Earth caused an incredible amount of mutation and radiation disease, then yes."

William shook his head. "When they used the sun to finish braking, they came back, found us broken. They tried to help. They bonded with us."

There was a hesitation. "Yes, it was something like that. Whatever their motives, the machinery they are supplying us with is still in its experimental phase... for us. For humans.

You understand that this is an experiment, correct? We can't guarantee success." The cat seemed in a hurry, but William didn't understand why it also seemed to be taking its time.

"The machine is dedicated to neuro tissue only. The lesions in your brain will vanish. You will be physically healed. I'm told the afflicted parts of your brain are keeping you from fully healing psychologically. You'll need therapy, but on the bright side, we have a large staff of grief counselors on hand that have perfected Post-Incident Trauma Treatment. No vouchers needed. Any questions?"

William strained against his restraints for a moment. He wasn't sure why. "Why are there Roman Legions in my head?" He felt his heart flutter with the beginning of panic. It wasn't the Romans he was afraid of. They hadn't invaded anyone in years.

"Lesions," the cat repeated, enunciating as clearly as possible. The small difference in improved clarity seemed to cost him some pain. "It may also repair the damage to the part of your brain that handles spatial integration. It's going to be all or nothing on the first try, I'm afraid. The treatment is a one-shot deal."

Another voice spoke up and it was a dark cat in a lab coat. Maybe. "William? Can you describe these items for us? After the treatment, we will ask you to describe the items again to see how differently you see them. Each patient helps us map how successful the machine is for different types of issues."

William nodded and tried to relax. He concentrated on the miracle cure portion of his expectations and not the experimentation portion of it. No brains have come squirting out of anyone's ears because of the device. Yet.

A small sensation of tiny spiders running over his face made him gasp.

"Step back, Bob. You're shedding on him."

They held a shiny thing in front of him. It had a handle, which was being held in a purple thing that might have been a hand. Purple fur? No, gloves, he decided, but then that wasn't what they wanted him to describe. "It's flat and shiny. Trimmed in white plastic. Probably weighs less than a pound."

There were nods from the cats. Someone took notes, but he couldn't assign a body, much less a face to it. "Do you know what it is?"

William nodded, and then flinched as a light seemed to burst out of the object. "I forget what it's called. I have them built into my car. Like headlights."

"You think this is a headlight?"

William shook his head, annoyed with the cat… maybe himself. "No… I just can't remember the word or what it's for."

More scribbling.

Then they showed him something that had glowing numbers on it, so he was pretty sure that was a smart phone. Or a calculator. Phones had calculators built in, so he was probably right either way.

Then there was a baseball. He felt a wave of gratitude even as he barked out the word. William took it from the cat's hand… paw? No, hand. Hand. He had hands, too. There were grass stains on the ball, and scratches from dirt. He could see so much of its history in its surface.

He tried to stifle the sob that escaped his throat.

If they gave him another baseball ball, he'd know it. He'd recognize that the different baseball would be just that; a different baseball. Not just the difference between a softball and a hardball… he could tell that from the size and the lacing… but the surface would be different. No grass stains could ever be exactly the same. No set of scratches could be so exactly duplicated.

This ball had no teeth marks. So the owner of this ball had no dogs. Or hadn't turned into a dog. Or maybe the owner had turned into a Cat. No, William looked… no claw marks.

They tugged at the ball, but William just grasped it more tightly.

"I know this ball," he cried. It was from the world before.

Before the aliens.

Before they all became animals.

Before the children stopped playing outside…

He buried his head in his hairy hands and they almost dropped the ball as he wailed at the realization of his loss. They called for his wife, and someone came. The smell was right, but he couldn't be sure. Maybe she was there; the ghost of the woman he'd slowly lost since the simple social awkwardness of not being good with faces became a cancer in his mind.

He appreciated the touch and the comfort for what it was. Not who it was.

And then, as he became himself again and the animals became trees instead of forests, the bell rang and the machine was ready. They told him not to move. Stay. Good Boy.

The machine was a giant doughnut with steampunk doodles and Jack Kirby doodads. Cats… maybe dogs… went behind a glass screen… no privacy there… as his head slowly dipped into the hole… sound began as they activated the alien tech. It was a deep throbbing in his chest and sinus cavities… not really from the machine itself. His teeth pulsed with his heartbeat and, for a moment, the white surface of the machine tasted like bacon to his eyes.

Every hair on his body stood on its end.

There was considerably more hair than he expected… longer, too.

It dawned on him that there were different breeds of dogs.

That he didn't know what type of breed he'd become.

And then it occurred to him that he could tell… just by looking.

Just by looking!

But there was a metal band holding his skull in place. There was a halo around his head and he didn't know how it had gotten there.

"Oh, my god," William whispered, "I think it's working…"

Fireworks went off in his head and he was thrown from himself out into a psychedelic abyss that seemed to chew him down into digestible bits before swallowing him.

* * * * *

He was only out for seconds and, for the first time in months, William realized that his eyes were closed and that he could see darkness. Nothing but sweet darkness. Not blindness.

He allowed himself to be flooded with contentment. He cracked his eyes open just enough to see the ceiling… to recognize the ceiling.

"How are you feeling, William?"

"Good," he said as they unscrewed the bolts that made up the halo that had kept his head still. "Can we dim the lights, a bit?"

"In a moment," the voice said with a small grunt as William felt himself moving again. "We have to make room for the next patient."

He remembered his wife's name. Her face! He remembered her face, with her slightly uneven nostrils, and the way the bags under her eyes had darkened just a bit over the last few years. The way her hair part would vanish over the course of the day. Oh, and her eyes! The flecks of gold at 1 and 3 o'clock against the sea green petals of her eyes.

"Frida," he said as he tried to open his eyes. He saw shoulders, arms, things that made sense, but watching the bright wall move beyond them made him car sick. His eyes wanted to focus on everything. His eyes burned, and he wondered if optic nerves were anything like neural links… at least to the miracle machine. "Frida!"

"She'll be right in, William." A cold compress was placed over his eyes.

He nodded, feeling the hospital bed do that crazy wiggle as the staff locked the wheels in place.

"I can see everyone in my head," William said, awed. "I know everyone changed since… what happened. Everyone looks so different now. Like animals, but at least I can remember now what the world looked like."

"Not everyone," the cat doctor said. "Just the ones under that portion of the night sky."

Another voice cut in. "We don't all look like animals." William didn't recall his voice. It had a heavy whispering echo, almost a lisp.

"I'm sorry," William said. "But I wouldn't know." He smiled and found himself giddy with the thought that he'd never have to explain Prosopagnosia again. "That was a pretty extreme version of face blindness."

"It's okay," the echo took on a whistling quality. "I've lowered the lights halfway. Are you ready to try taking a peek?"

William nodded, but the light still stabbed his eyes. He covered his eyes with the compress again. "Sorry."

"No worries, light sensitivity is easier to deal with than blindness." William's expression at realizing that blindness had been a risk struck the man with the strange lisp funny. "The treatment's really the same: dark glasses."

"Shut up, Bob." A strong hand patted William's arm, and he felt the bed twist him into a sitting position. "You can adjust to the lights easier if you're not staring into them."

Nervous laughter crept up his throat as he realized that there were lights on the ceiling. Of course there were. They usually were. "It was a mirror," William said as the compress suddenly needed two hands to keep the light out. "The flat, shiny surface with the white trim... it was a mirror. A mirror that reflected the fluorescent lights in the ceiling."

"Do you remember looking at it. Can you see it now?"

William shook his head. "No, it's blurry... chaotic... but a mirror is the only thing that makes sense. Now."

"Good," the cat doctor said. "So far, you seemed to have recovered along the projected norms."

The strong hand gave another squeeze and then stayed where it was on his upper arm. It didn't feel much like a paw through his sleeve. There were normal people left, he knew, but his post-Incident life was horribly fractured until now. It occurred to him that he might have misconstrued what had happened: that only he and a few others had become animal-like in appearance.

That would be OK, he promised himself. As long as he had his mind… his human mind… he didn't care what he looked like. Frida had always liked dogs.

The compress came off his face and the room was as dark as the voice had promised.

He sighed and licked his lips in relief and anxiety. They felt too thin, a little ragged. Then he recalled the razor incident. "I cut myself," William whispered with awe. "How badly did I cut myself?"

"Not too badly," the voice purred. "Others were worse. Some took their lives."

William tried to raise his hands to his face, but the arms of the voice pushed them back into place. "William, we need your hands here to measure your reactions."

Straps went tightly around his wrists. The Voice was either a cat or had the eyes of one.

Near the outline of a door, he saw the silhouette of a foot move. Bob asked, "Are you ready for 10%?"

"Yes, please."

The room got brighter and his eyes flinched like two frightened children in a traveling Haunted House, but they did not scream. They didn't hurt all that much. "I feel like I haven't used my eyes in, like, forever."

"You did have a notably reduced accommodation reflex as your inability to recognize people worsened." The voice reassured him, if that's what it was. "So, you are essentially correct. It's one of the reasons you qualified for the second wave of testing. You'll recover well, if not perfectly."

The lights increased until they reached 45% and then they stepped it back to 40%. He apologized, and they told him not to worry about that.

"Can you call Frida in? I literally haven't seen her in

years… I want her to be the first face I see."

The doctors in the room hesitated. "I know she changed… we all changed. But… I really miss my wife."

The shadow by the door nodded and cracked the door only enough to slip out. The edges of Bob's body lit up with painful light and William had to look away. His eyes stung and he wanted to rub them in comfort and wipe away the tears in shame, but his arms remained strapped down. "Can I not face the door when they come in?"

The Voice covered William's eyes with the compress. "Sorry, the monitoring…"

His anxiety continued to drain away at a slow pace. There was a procedure here. He'd been through this before, but it was the first time he felt that he really understood what was going on. He just didn't understand why his relief wasn't as smooth and immediate as the return of his recognition skills had been. He nodded. "No, I understand, Doctor…. Doctor?"

The Voice laughed softly. "We'll introduce ourselves once you're fully acclimated."

William nodded, still used to ignoring that which did not make sense to him right off.

He heard the door open and he made out three footsteps even though everyone wore sneakers these days. He supposed it was the dog ears.

"William," his wife whispered as she approached and his chest felt incredibly constricted suddenly.

"Oh, Frida," he cried, trying to take her hand, but the straps held. She grabbed his arm above the restraints and he felt that the fur wasn't as thick as he thought.

The door closed with a click and the Voice asked him if he was ready.

"I want to see my wife," William said, knowing it didn't matter if she was a dog or not. She stuck with him for years with him useless and half mad. She could have turned into a porcupine and he would not have cared.

The compress came off and William found his wife's face.

It was only the gloom of the 40% lighting that kept the man from yelping in distress. This was Frida. He knew her from the shape of her skull and the bridge of her nose. His newly awakened recognition skills served him well in this, but they betrayed him also. The chaotic rainbow of pustules on the right side of her face... he counted instantly 35 of them without trying. There were at least seven more that had popped and oozed a clear fluid, but it was hard to tell in the shadows. The bags under her eyes pulsed or twitched as if she'd glued gray slugs under her eyes. Her right eye was crisp and clear and wandered about the room as if it were insane or looking for an escape route. Her left was the dead but glossy off-white of an exposed tendon. No... it was a fist sized maggot growing beneath the lid and the little black head stared at him with a hunger he recognized within himself.

"Frida...?" He forced a smile onto his face. This can't be right...

He looked to the nurse who stood next to his wife.

Yvonne.

He read the name badge before letting his eyes crawl up to her face. He ignored the bumps on her chest that moved in ways that breathing didn't explain. He whimpered only slightly when he reached the bloody stump that he'd mistaken for lipstick on her nose when he'd seen her before the treatment. "Yvonne?" He gasped as his smile slipped off, down his throat. It went down the wrong way.

Yellow flat eyes in her leopard print skin blinked, and her head nodded. The flaps of her ears bounced lightly, loose flaps of skin that had once been pierced... or maybe they were blackheads. "William," it said in the voice he associated with the girl with his files. "This is Frida."

William began breathing faster, although he tried to resist the pressing need. It wasn't like he hadn't known that that world had changed. He knew that the people on the Eastern Seaboard had become animals that night.

He looked at his own hirsute arm and watched as the

brown hairs stood out from his body.

"William, stay calm," Frida whispered. William looked up and saw that his wife's jaws were massive. They hardly moved. Her nose flexed when she inhaled and William realized that it was only a matter of time before her nose fell off.

"Excuse me, Ladies," Bob said, and all but body-checked the ghouls away from his bedside. William's gratitude did not last. As the intern's mummified face turned to him, William felt a loosening below his belt that became a spreading warmth between his legs. Layers of dead skin flaked off the creature's face as it spoke. "We need to begin the testing so we can clear up the room for another patient."

William looked down at his hands... the black claws that made up his fingertips grew as he watched and his heart began to beat down the walls that were his own ribcage. Frida whispered caution. "I don't understand," he growled back. He yanked at his restraints.

"Just tell me what I am holding... describe it and you can freak out in the privacy of your own room."

William felt his face painfully expanding and watched with his newly improved visual cortex as his muzzle grew too large for him to look down at his arms. Red fireworks burst across his vision as he looked up at the mummy. Each breath came and went with a growl that he could not stop.

Somewhere, his wife was crying.

They were monsters. They were all monsters.

The mummy stepped back when their eyes met. William's jaws opened and promised to snap the creature's dried up bones in twain. The restraints held, but barely.

The mummy found his courage and faith in the restraints. He held the mirror up.

The werewolf met his own glowing red eyes in the white framed mirror.

And, in that moment, William saw the giant insect-alien that stood behind him... with what could only be a taser in its claws. His last conscious act was to force his elbows onto the bars of the bed to give himself the needed leverage.

With a cruel clarity, William watched as the straps broke. The werewolf howled and grabbed the mirror. He swatted the taser out of the alien's claw with the hand-held mirror. He backhanded the bug's plastic-like head across the room. The mummy rushed the werewolf, but his bones seemed as fragile as William had surmised.

Or, perhaps, the Werewolf was stronger than William believed possible.

Either way, William watched... he simply could not turn away... as his body ripped apart the annoying mummy. William felt a small pinprick in his shoulder as Yvonne tried to administer a sedative.

The werewolf simply broke her right arm and then her long neck. It gutted her, because that's what you do when you hunt. The blood would drain and the limbs would be easier to separate from the body. The pack would dine well...

My pack, the werewolf thought, the sedative making a slight dent.

The werewolf found Frida crying in the corner. She could have fled out the door, but she hadn't.

William watched as the werewolf picked up his wife. "I waited for you, so long..." she whispered.

"I know," they said and stroked her hair, ignoring the huge clumps that fell out of her skull.

"I love you," she whispered.

"I love you," William told her as the werewolf gently embraced her.

William watched with perfect clarity as he crushed her throat with the werewolf's slavering jaws.

Blessed are the Meek

Rechan

L277 marveled at the cathedral with its shining metal walls and sleek fixtures, so perfect, so different from the structures created by his people. The gods themselves had crafted it as an Ark to bring his grandparents from the heavens. How few there must have been, as the main chamber struggled with the throngs of worshipers in their lines.

Fortunately, few stood in his line. The lapen ahead of him left the prayer booth. L277 hopped in and bobbed his ears in greeting to the priest kneeling at the altar. The priest returned the gesture and L277 knelt.

The priest readjusted the knobs on the altar and bowed his head. L277 touched the oxygen molecule shaved into his chest and prayed into the altar's mic. "Oh great Breathus, this is your humble servant L277 of Stack 3. Praise be, oxygen-to-nitrogen output is performing exceptionally, and the local atmospheric condition is 11% oxygen. Projections show conditions suitable for your return in three months, oh glorious Breathus."

"Praise be, and amen," said the priest and pressed a button. The received light blinked a merry green and the two shared a pleased nose wiggle.

L277 rose with high spirits, hopping from the booth, the

cathedral, and out into the sun's warmth. If he lifted his ears, he could hear the hammers of Constructus' blessed workers hard at work in all directions. Down the broad trails he went, following the path he had taken that morning, until finally he reached Stack 3.

From afar the Stack looked like a ladder, and he supposed it wasn't far off the mark; unlike the too-tall buildings the lapen erected for the gods, the stacks were merely scaffolding with each platform a shallow pool wider than two stacked lapen.

He spotted someone leaning against the lowest pool. L277 called out a greeting but received no response. Drawing closer, he recognized R294's striking dark facial fur.

Moments before L277 reached him, R294 swayed and promptly fell into the water. L277 leaped up and hauled the other lapen free from the algae-thick water. "What's wrong?"

R294 managed to look up at L277 and wiggle his nose once before blood seeped from his nostrils. Red rivulets slid from his eyes, his ears, and across the pool's slime still staining his fur. L277 squealed and dropped him, staggering back as R294 flopped into the dirt.

The body lay there unmoving. L277 brought his toe out and gave his friend a nudge. "Are you well?" When no answer came, he crouched down and felt about, only to find the unfortunate truth. His tail flagged in alarm.

"What's going on down there? Everything well?" A lapen head stuck out over the stack far above.

"R294's dead!"

"No! Stay right there." Soon B306 crouched beside him, but her discovery was no different. L277 explained what happened, to which the other lapen merely dropped her tail and shook in confusion.

"Someone's going to have to take him to the Mortis' temple, and let his parents know."

"I guess we can," B306 said, "but I need to find someone to work the twelfth pool. Krit are having a celebration in there."

L277 thumped his foot at the news, but bobbed his ears in agreement. When the other lapen bounded away, he looked up at the Stack, keeping his mind on work rather than the corpse at his feet.

Krit were such a problem, in a way delaying the Gods' return. The native insect would lay their eggs in the pools, and the larvae loved eating the algae, the one thing that could oxygenate the air enough for the gods to tolerate it. Were the krit some sort of curse, created by… by something that wasn't the gods, to keep them away? It was a regular thought among the Stack workers, even after the priests had prayed and the gods replied. The krit were simply pests living on the planet before the gods chose it, they'd said.

The putt-putt-putt of a motorized hauling cart perked his ears. B306 came around the corner and parked beside him. The two wrestled R294's body onto the bed of the cart. "Still can't believe he's gone."

L277 said, "I know, he just turned three, he should've had at least two more years."

"Don't remind me, I'm four. I can only hope I last long enough to see the gods' return."

"I've heard C25 reached seven, so you have a good chance. Here's to hoping they're soon satisfied with our work."

"Praise be."

An awkward silence gathered, one L277 broke first, glancing down at their deceased friend. "Could I see him off to the temple?" The idea of bringing bad news to his friend's family set his ears low.

After a bit of chewing the air, she said. "I could use the walk."

She sat beside him as he put-putted down the path towards the Mortis temple. It was far from the industrious building of the Constructus workers, out in the growing fields. B306 scratched one of her ears. "Do you think this could have something to do with him going up to see the gods? Maybe the Chariot is contaminated…"

He frowned, but did not acknowledge the doubt and blasphemy aloud. The silence stretched and the awkwardness got under their fur.

Finally, the path split and B306 hopped off. With a bob of her ears, she was off down the path. L277 continued on, only to be stopped by a pair of field workers close to the path.

"What's the matter?" the first said, glancing at the body.

"A friend's passed."

The ears of the second rose. "Tell us about him."

After a brief bit of conversation, the three lapens danced around the cart, an affair more akin to a bouncing jig. They clapped, reciting the deceased's name, facts about them, and praise to the gods that the lapen toiled for before winding down. The pair bobbed their ears to L277 when they parted.

This little ritual repeated itself several times before L277 reached the Mortis' temple. With so many lapen it was a challenge for any one lapen to know any other, and the affair didn't interrupt work too significantly. Work was more important than prayer, after all, a hierarchical drive rooted deep in them.

Finally, L277 reached the temple. Three Mortis priests wearing the black belts of the death god stepped outside and down the stairs. They joined in the song and dance, but they were more somber about it. When finished, two hoisted up the body and brought R294 into the building while the third turned to L277. "Please come inside, we must report his passing and there are questions to be made."

A shudder ran through L277's insides. He'd requested to come here, but now, standing in front of the structure, he wasn't so sure. L277'd never been here and while he accepted the dead were mulched for fertilizer, he had no interest in seeing it… but he should, he supposed. It was for the gods, and for R294, who had been a productive worker and good friend.

The front room was thankfully lacking in the dreadful

machinery. Instead, it held a table they laid R294 upon, and beside it a prayer altar.

While they cleaned the deceased's body, a priest asked L277 a series of questions. Someone in the room murmured, "R294? Did he not see the gods a month ago?" but the older priest shushed the speaker. When finished, the priest interviewing L277 rang a bell, summoning more dark-belted lapen into the room. They watched in still respect as he knelt and pressed a button on the prayer altar.

"Oh great Mortis, this is your humble servant T260 of the Temple 3. I report to you the passing of R294, child of Breathus, who was found dead at Stack 3 with blood coming out of his nose, eyes and ears. Praise be, let his passing sustain us all, oh glorious Mortis."

"Praise be and amen," echoed the priests, with L277 a step behind them. The praying priest pressed the send button.

A glaring red light flared on the altar, setting the priests to jumping or standing stock still. After a minute of silence while L277's breath strained inside of him, one of the speakers blurted, "T260, this is an agent of Mortis. Repeat last transmission."

It rocked L277. It was known that sometimes the gods spoke directly through the altars, but it was rare, and he had never witnessed it himself. He could clearly understand the voice, albeit the words held an odd inflection.

Reverently T260 knelt and did as he was ordered. Not moments after pressing the send button, the angry red light flashed again. "This is an agent of Mortis. Who reported R294's passing?"

The priest looked up and waved L277 over. On stiff legs, the lapen approached and knelt. "I-it was I, L277. I found his body and brought him here to the Mortis temple." The priest hit send.

Several moments ticked by, the other priests as stiff as L277's guts felt. Finally, the red light flashed and the speaker declared, "Attention, L277. Take the body of R294 to the

Chariot, and bring it to us. Repeat, do not use the body as normal, have L277 bring the deceased to us. No one else shall handle the body. Is that clear?"

The Mortis priest spoke. "Y-yes, agent of Mortis. Your will shall be done." When he pressed the button, the green light flashed, and all in the room save L277 relaxed their tails.

"My friend, you are going to see the gods," said one.

"This is glorious," said another.

"We have questions for you to deliver, if you would," said a third.

What they did not give the stunned L277 was assistance in taking R264's body from the table to the cart. Off he went, barely registering the bobbed ears of the priests.

See the gods? While he was happy he didn't have to actually see what they did to his friend's body, this new development gripped his stomach between a set of teeth.

One of the priests had draped the body in a black sheet, and that at least would discourage passing lapen from asking questions. He was in no mood for the mourning ritual now, leaving him alone with his thoughts and little more than the endless fields spread out before him. Most of those crops were of things lapens didn't eat, instead they were harvested and preserved for the gods' return. Same as the buildings Constructus' worshipers hammered away at, twice as tall as any lapen and so ignored for the lapens' burrows.

L277 had always been devout. He'd memorized the entire book of Breathus—granted, the holy tome consisted mainly of pictures instructing how to build and operate the Stacks—but now doubt nibbled away at him. The krit were what bothered him; nowhere were they mentioned in the Breathus' book, and while all tools and materials were either on the Ark or gifted with crates from the sky, they had been instructed to repurpose items to deal with the krit. Drill holes in containers or string mesh across one end of a tube and strain the larvae out. For the gods to design everything, how could they let so tedious a thing out?

Worse, lapens had to climb into the narrow pools to strain the krit free. All that water, in tight confines, some panicked and drowned. Death was accepted among lapen, but this seemed utterly of poor design to L277. He would still work and still pray, a compulsion he felt bone deep, but he would ask the gods when he reached them about the krit.

Soon the Chariot came into view, a squat cylinder with a cone at its tip. The first time the Gods had called someone to them, most of the lapen had come out to see the Chariot take flight, L277 among them. It blew fire from its back end, sending it skyward until only vapor remained. He did not see it return, but heard of it through others; an easy landing.

Other lapen bustled around the Chariot. The gods must have sent word he would be departing. A female hopped into his path and he stopped the cart. He noted the likeness of the vehicle shaved into her fur, much like his own holy symbol. He stopped them from loading R294 and did so himself, but once his deceased friend was settled, they joined him inside.

The straps surprised L277 as much as the seat sized for lapen travelers. The other lapen answered his questions with shrugs and apologies. While they cared for the Chariot, followed instructions and assisted, they did not know what it was like inside when it worked. Only the gods had control. L277 sat back and trusted in Breathus. Soon he would be able to ask Breathus his many questions; soon he would be able to see them all.

When the door shut, the Chariot came to life. Lights flashed and air puffed past his ears. Then it shook, shook so strongly he thought he might lose teeth, before a great force shoved him back against his seat. L277 could feel himself rising higher, higher.

Light blared bright inside, and a sharp hiss emerged. The air tasted funny, perhaps what the gods' lands smelled like. Heaviness sank into L277's eyes and limbs, and in a moment he was asleep.

287

* * * *

Warm, fuzzy darkness cocooned him, and he floated along. A soft thrum began and it soothed him, reminded him of the familiar sounds of construction. Schlup. Such an odd wet sound. A smell pulled against the cocoon of heavy drowsiness wrapped around him. Like turned earth freshly fertilized, spiced with something sour. L277 recoiled from it and pulled the welcoming sleep around himself, but a strange voice dredged him upwards.

"Degenerated, just like the others."

"Dammit. Alright, let's try again."

He opened his eyes and the watery light burned. He tried to cover them with an arm, but the limb didn't respond. The other didn't move either. Panic bolted up his spine and yanked his tail up, but he fought the alarm; no, his fingers could move, it was something gripping his wrists. Legs too, and even his head was wrapped in something, keeping it in place. L277 froze, his heart thundering.

Where was he? Thoughts fuzzy, it took the lapen a dozen breaths to remember R294, Breathus, the Chariot. He should be among the gods, but this was no Heaven. He lay atop something flat and hard, cold and metallic.

Breathus would not harm him. Breathus would take care of him. This thought drummed away until his breathing leveled off.

Opening his eyes again brought a lessened sting, and the lapen squinted to grow accustomed to the light. A row of lights ran along the ceiling, not much different than those the gods had given them for installations. The room was long but tight, and figures moved at the far end. L277 tried to focus on them but they were too far away, too white, and his eyes protested. He closed them.

"I'm telling you, if this one doesn't work, we need to bring some aboard for quicker testing."

"And put them where, the cabinets? The captain will not

requisition us space, she's a vegetarian and is opposed to this part of the mission."

"We have to do something different. The colonists are only a few months away. When they get here and see rabbits that can talk, and all the built structures, they're going to ask questions, and they're going to refuse—"

"Don't you think I know this? I want to know what's wrong too. The retrovirus worked on all the other planets, what's different here?"

L277 could understand the words, but not their meaning. Further, they held a strange inflection, reminding him of the transmission from the Agent of Mortis.

The light no longer stung. Rows of cupboards lined the wall to his left. L277 tilted his head to the right.

R294 lay across a table, the top of his head cut free and resting beside him. The pink-red mud behind his eyes had oozed out and puddled where the lapen's ears would have been.

L277 screamed.

The two figures jumped. "What's it doing awake?"

"The gas must have worn off early!"

They darted to him. It was then that L277 saw his gods.

They had no fur except patches at the top of their heads. Instead, their faces and paws were covered in skin like a lapen's nose or the inside of their ears, their hides a pale brown. No muzzles, merely holes under a bump of a nose. Both were covered in cloth, bright white, except where the sleeves of one had touches of red.

"Be calm. We are—"

"You are not the gods!" L277 fought his restraints, thrashing on the table. "Where is Breathus? Where is an Agent? I'm devout! I'm devout, why am I being held? Why is R294's head in two?"

"Get something to put him out," growled one.

L277 grunted and panted, his eyes wide enough to flash the whites. "You-you're not! You're fertilizer!" He chose the foulest thing in his vocabulary. "You're *krit!*"

One of them loomed over him with a metal stinger in its paw.

"No, no don't touch me, get away from me." L277 leaned back from the point.

Still, it stung him in the thigh and he could feel the contents rushing in. A heaviness filled his limbs and already his thoughts were slowing, his vision narrowing.

"He's seen us, what do we do?"

"This changes nothing. No one will believe him; religion is in their DNA. Let's try…" The sounds trailed off as L277 head slumped to the table.

✳ ✳ ✳ ✳ ✳

"What was it like?"

L277 blinked awake, surrounded by lapen. Trying to move, he nearly panicked to find himself strapped in again, but it was only the Chariot's seat.

"Let us get him free and full of fresh breath first," an older lapen said, even as her expression held hopefulness. They released his straps and helped him outside. Pain flared in his thigh where the furless thing had stung him, and a similar knot had formed on his upper arm, equally tender. Another sting? Would the stuff in his head leak out like poor R294?

L277 grimaced. "It was…"

Noses wiggled in anticipation, their ears up and waiting.

"I can't remember," he finally said. Which was true enough for all those who had gone before him, they could not recall. Had they been asleep during the entire ordeal, or had they chosen to hide the truth from their fellows too?

L277 wasn't sure which made his stomach sink more, lying to them, or seeing their disappointment and knowing that eager piety was for nothing deserving.

The latter, he decided over the next few weeks. It would have been a lie for L277 to say he did not enjoy the attention his trip had earned—a number of females approached him when they came in season, and others merely wished to be around him, that his luck or divine blessing may rub off. At times he doubted, as he felt compelled to pray to the gods he knew were lies. *Religion is in their DNA*. While not knowing what the last word meant, he didn't doubt the furless thing's truth: that their love of the gods was part of them and it served those creatures.

A month after his Chariot ride, things began to get worse. L277 continued his work at the Stack, not out of any desire to prepare for the gods return, but because he needed to work. Not doing so felt like not eating. Had they also done this to the lapen? One day though, he forgot the process of replacing the hydraulic filter. This was in the Book of Breathus, instructions he had memorized, an act he had done ten times before. Not only did he forget, he puzzled over it for an hour before installing.

He spotted this lost state in others. Some even confessed to having forgotten, or not knowing, how to do tasks they too had done regularly. It began with those around L277, but spread outwards. The entire community began talking less, using fewer words, simpler speech.

Something was bad. The Gods? The furless thing with a stinger? L277 shuddered. Realizing even his thoughts were weakening, L277 fought to cling to the scraps of his old life. He spoke every word he could remember, tried to write them down—to no avail—and went back to work, as little as he could.

By the time the lapen realized something was wrong, mentally, with the children L277 had fathered, it was too late. The entire community nibbled at the crops no longer tended to, rather than cut them and prepare them. Laying in the sun and coupling in the dirt were their only pastimes; not dancing or storytelling. Were one to wander through the too-tall buildings they had built, they would hear no more words echoing among the empty halls.

One day a great noise filled the sky. A bright light came

down. A thought bubbled up to him, a memory of something like it he'd seen and been close to before. Fear filled him, but other lapen hopped past, curious. He followed.

A long thing lay on the ground. It had not been there before. Dust floated in the air. It opened.

Things came out. They had no fur.

Fear, strong enough to make his eyes dilate and his nose flare, filled him. He hid. The others did not pay attention to his flagged tail and sudden movement. They sat still. Scared to stiffness or confusion?

Words finally echoed across the grasses. He tried to remember words, tried hard, and perhaps that was how he understood them now.

One of the things said, "Let's check out what this colony has to offer. Y'know, it's a shame they couldn't have left the auto-builder droids. Now *we* have to do the work."

"Because the terraformers need to work on a new planet. The exercise'll be good for you." The other thing noticed the lapens and pointed. "Look at all of them," one of the things said, pointing towards the lapen. "They're not even running."

"I know," said the first. "After all that preserved ship chow, I can't wait to eat a fresh one."

With a sense of alarm he turned and bolted, his high tail a warning to the others he hoped they understood.

HOLLOW

Chris "Sparf" Williams

A crackling of static filled Liam's headset, lightly at first and growing louder. The snow leopard let out a yelp and instinctively reached to pull the headset free, but of course with it inside the great fishbowl on his head, he couldn't touch it. The static faded to a mild crackle and then silence once more. Liam shook his head to try and dislodge the ringing sound left behind, and continued reassembling the atmospheric processor.

His working light darkened without warning. He turned to look for the source of the shadow, spotting a mass of billowing black smoke and vapor hurtling through the sky above. An object was burning up in the atmosphere, only visible in the air for a few moments before it whizzed downward and vanished beyond the distant Martian foothills.

"Base to Sams."

Liam rolled his eyes.

"Sams here."

"Liam, did you spot that?"

"No, I completely missed the giant meteor that just flew by my head."

"Cut the snark, Sams," Mike barked. "Did you get a look at where it went down?"

"Yeah, it looked like it was going to hit in the foothills, or just beyond them. I lost sight of it over the crest."

"Okay. Meteorological is reporting dust-storm conditions

are minimal, so wrap up and get back here. The Mitrians want to investigate it as soon as possible."

Liam truly wanted to spend the evening with some video games or a book and a cup of tea rations, but the Mitrian climatologists would be champing at the bit to look at the fresh meteor impact.

Liam flicked his tail back and forth in its pressurized sleeve as he tightened the final screw, sealing the access plate. One more processor down.

"Sams to base,"

"Base here."

"Maintenance complete on Processor 115. I'm heading back in."

"Roger that."

Liam squinted at the horizon through the protective gold micromesh filter over his helmet glass, the sun still visible in the dusty haze.

Liam, a snow leopard who, in another life, had been a mechanical engineer for Lockheed, hoofed it through the low Martian gravity back towards Zeto base. His knee complained, as usual, and he reached a gloved paw down to rub at the joint.

You're getting too old for this shit.

The base stood on a low rocky plateau. Its squat, domed buildings and the towers at the corners of the compound that housed the communications equipment and waste processing gave it the appearance of a space-age *Hagia Sophia*. The constructed roadway that led from the compound down on each side allowed the rovers to come and go. Liam preferred to walk the landscape when possible, despite it being a minor stretching of protocol. The Martian landscape was a vast desert of red iron-rich rocks and soil, so unlike the snow-capped hills and peaks of Liam's hometown.

Home was not there, among the isolationist, backward hermits like his parents had been. Liam wasn't sure where home was, but Mars felt like it, more than any place else.

When he stared out onto the horizon, he was seized with the feeling that he could find peace and contentment just walking into that horizon forever.

Liam reached the airlock in decent time. He'd need to decontaminate, de-suit, and report to Commander Sloane. Life was never dull for a first-generation colonist!

* * * * *

"You know I could do the equipment setup around the impact site on my own, right Mike?"

"Yeah, I know you *could*, but you're not going to. Nobody travels alone outside the base perimeter under any circumstances. It's just not safe."

"Come on, I'd be in a giant, well-protected rover, what could possibly go wrong?"

The Rottweiler grimaced and gnawed on the synthetic meat stick that substituted for his forbidden cigar-smoking habit.

"What if the drive train breaks down and you have to walk back? And what if you get a hole in your suit? What if communications break down?"

Liam sighed, knowing he wouldn't win this time.

"All right, Mike."

The tension melted out of Sloane's posture.

"All right. You get started with prep, and I'll send the Mitrians down to join you."

Liam left the base commander's office, passing through the bustling command center. Each workstation that surrounded the perimeter hummed and bustled with activity. Meteorological Analysis, nearest the commander's office, was staffed by a pair of snow leopards focusing intently on three screens of graphs and Doppler radar. At another station, soil analysis and microbial sampling was conducted. Each team played an important part in the great mission: the eventual terraformation of Mars as a habitable planet. A group of staff had clustered around a terminal at the biological station.

At the far exit, a powerfully built Mitrian with pure white fur stood, their four eyes looking straight at Liam. The name tag on their pale blue jumpsuit read "Koresh" and then a series of letters in the Mitrian script which Liam could make out roughly corresponded to their true-name. Every so often they would close their second set of eyes in thought.

Mitrians resembled arctic wolves from Earth by way of Fantastic Tales. Their muzzles were half-again as long, and an extra pair of golden-irised eyes rested just below and to the outside of where an earth wolf's would be. Mitrian ears were batlike: furless and blue with sharp angles, and from the top center of their head jutted a single appendage like the antennae of a gigantic insect, but covered in short, thin fur.

"You are ready to join us on the investigation of the meteor strike, Sams?"

Liam grinned at the Mitrian's formality.

"That's right. I'll meet you in the loading bay shortly."

The Mitrian's antenna twitched, and their outer eyes blinked long and slow. "Excellent. Your cephalic warmth will be of great assistance. I have come to discuss certain necessary predictive modeling with the meteorologists, and then we will be on our way."

Koresh lumbered past Liam and toward the meteorology station. Liam, for his part, watched the Mitrian movements with some fascination. Their exaggerated digitigrade legs gave them a certain grace in lower-gravity environments like Mars.

"Liam!" one of the staffers, a tall, sturdily built malamute botanist called, waving. Sasha practically glowed through her fur with excitement. She stood nearly half a meter taller than the snow leopard, dwarfing him. In the breast pocket of her jumpsuit she carried a little plastic sunflower that earned her a chuckle and the nickname of "flower child" from the crew.

"Check this out! Report is in from Huston that the first open-air planting experiments are showing success! We've got a few rows of evergreens managing to hang on."

Liam craned his neck to look over the shoulders of the gathered botanical team who were laughing and clapping at some numbers on a spreadsheet with attached photos.

"That's amazing news!" he said, grinning up at the malamute.

"This means that soon we'll be able to start our own open-air experiments, and I won't be stuck in the greenhouse dome all the time. I'll get to go outside like you do."

Her eyes shone with excitement at the possibilities.

Liam smiled.

"Once you're out there a few days, it just looks like the Arizona desert."

"Yeah, but I haven't been out there, really out there, beyond the compound! I signed up to build a whole new world! I'll settle for getting to explore the foundations just a little."

"I'm sure it'll be amazing for you," he said. "I've got to get down to the bay and investigate a meteorite strike. See you later, Flowerchild!"

Sasha grinned and waved before turning back to her team celebration.

Liam entered the elevator, followed by Koresh.

Once they reached ground level, they made their way down the corridor and through a pair of double-thick doors into the expansive loading bay, where one of the large equipment-bearing rovers sat with its back hatch open and ramp down.

"Selar has already begun the preparations."

"Let's get to work, then. We're burning daylight," Liam said.

* * * * *

"We are ready to go, Liam," Koresh said, flashing the completed checklist on their tablet.

Selar appeared in the rover's hatchway, grinning stiffly.

"Let us get to it then before Meteorological changes its

forecast of dust storms. Besides, we are losing warmth."

Liam smiled. Selar stood nearly a head taller than Koresh, with a leaner frame. Their white fur was streaked around their eyes and antenna with black, and their lower eyes were a dark, royal blue, contrasting with the gold of their 'normal' set. They settled confidently to the padded depths of the pilot's chair, though with some uncomfortable shifting. The rover had been designed with earth species in mind, rather than the exaggerated extra digitigrade knee joint the Mitrian form possessed. Liam joined them in the navigator's chair, and Koresh settled into a chair behind.

"I've got the coordinates of likely impact from command, and a favorable forecast from Meteorological, so this should be nice and easy."

Selar gave him a nod and activated the rover's engine.

"All is temperate."

Reddish-orange dust and rocks littered the passing landscape, broken up by the occasional jagged stone outcropping. There wasn't much to see on Mars. Someday though, there would be, Liam thought to himself with an inward grin.

Someday.

By rover, traveling at a safe yet speedy clip of 40 km/h, the journey to the impact site took nearly an hour. Liam did his best not to squirm in the seat, wishing he'd taken the operator's chair instead of navigation; They'd already be to the meteorite by now.

Koresh and Selar sat silent and serious, though if the snow leopard could have sensed their body heat the way they sensed it, he figured they'd be radiating excitement.

"Look. We have found it."

Liam looked up from the tablet he'd been using to review maintenance schedules to see that the rover had come up on a plateau, at the center of which a fresh crater had appeared where the meteorite had slammed into the surface.

Against the pale sky, the haze of red dust and steam that had risen from the crater reminded Liam of the wispy cirrus clouds and the morning fog along the mountainsides of his home.

"Looks like the atmosphere we've been generating has started to have some meaningful effects," Liam said. "Steam is a good sign."

Selar gave a single nod. "Now, let us examine it closer, and see what secrets its warmth reveals to us."

Koresh had already moved to the staging area in back of the rover, preparing a set of testing and sampling equipment. Liam grinned and joined him, and Selar came last.

Koresh arranged and prepared an oversized hydraulic drill for core sampling, multiple nonreactive containers for soil specimens, a pH tester, and soil spectrometer while Selar and Liam donned the outerwear of their pressurized enviro-suits. God, Liam hated these things. It wasn't claustrophobia; they vigorously tested for things like that before anyone was allowed to serve a long-term assignment off-world. It was everything about the suits: the sterile, algae-smell of the oxygenating system and the recycled air, the restricted movement, the crushing of his luxurious tail, the loss of peripheral vision, and the absence of scent.

When the trio had finally finished with their preparations and had fully suited up, Koresh and Selar grabbed the bin that contained the equipment, and the trio stepped into the airlock. Liam's tail had already begun to fall asleep.

I swear I'm going to strangle the bastard who came up with this design.

Liam sealed the inner hatch and depressurized the airlock. The outer hatch opened, flooding the bay with the soft glow of Martian afternoon. The Mitrians, wasting no time, marched down the deployed ramp with the sampling gear in tow.

Liam's boots crunched on the rough Martian soil, the sound of it echoing comfortingly through his pressurized capsule of a suit. He wished he could smell the soil here.

Selar and Koresh had reached a safe distance from the

crater's perimeter and begun taking samples of the soil. A few meters away, the lip of the crater was just visible in the steam and haze.

The steam and dust rising out of the crater had begun to settle. Liam could just make out a shape at the center.

"What is that?"

Koresh, raising their eyes from the scanner they'd been using to test radiation levels, peered through the haze. "It's some sort of construct."

"Temperature reading?"

"Three hundred degrees Kelvin and falling rapidly."

Liam checked the scanner for radiation emanating from the crater, which he could now see was more lopsided than he'd given it credit for. The object, whatever it was, hadn't impacted directly. It had approached along an angled vector. Not unusual for a meteorite, but still, if the Mitrians were saying it was a construct, and it was cooling that fast—

Maybe it's a ship!

A spaceship would be a tremendous thing. It definitely wouldn't be from Earth. It would likely be Mitrian, as they were the only race that had spent any significant time in the Sol system. But, what if it was another species?

Liam's tail twitched and squirmed inside the squeezed confines of the envirosuit. The scanner reported only normal radiation levels. Whatever it was, it wasn't going to give Liam cancer.

The faint Martian wind subtly shifted and pushed the last of the thick haze away from the object.

It bore a tapered, teardrop shape, like the bud of a rose. At least the exposed bulk of the object did. The forward third was buried into the exposed solid bedrock of the hillside. Scorch marks marred the delicate emerald green of the hull, accompanied by various tears and scrapes.

The Mitrians stared silently at the crashed ship, all of their eyes unblinking.

"What is it?" Liam asked, more to break the tension than

anything else.

Selar led the way, with Koresh and Liam following. The group skirted the edge of the crater until the compacted superheated soil leveled off and met the ground itself

"Call it in, Liam, please. Inform the base that we have found a downed Mitrian vessel. We will investigate and report back."

Liam switched his communicator over to ranged mode. "Sams to Zeto Base."

The Mitrians began to cross the crater, taking digital photographs and scanner readings as they went.

"Zeto Base. Go ahead, Sams."

"The meteor strike turned out to be a downed Mitrian vessel. We're—"

Liam yelped and doubled over with pain. His earpieces suddenly bursting forth with an overwhelming blast of white noise. That was bad enough, but there was some atonal high-pitched noise threading right through the maelstrom, like an old-fashioned shortwave radio that couldn't find its frequency. Liam dropped to one knee, yowling loudly inside the pressurized suit both from the stabbing pain in his ears and just to hear something besides that awful noise.

"—couldn't copy. Say again, Sams?"

Liam blinked the tears from his eyes. When had he started crying? The noise was gone. No trace of it, no feeling of relief like he'd stepped outside after a concert. The noise was just gone, as if it had never been there at all.

"The meteor was actually a Mitrian ship of some kind," the snow leopard groaned, rising to his feet. "We are investigating and will report back with more information."

"Affirmative. Stay frosty out there."

The transmission ended with its usual click.

Liam looked up at the hulking mass of the crashed ship. The Mitrians had opened and entered a recessed airlock on the lower exposed side, leaving the outer hatch open, revealing nothing but blackness.

Maybe the ship swallowed them.

The dark entryway called to Liam, like a funhouse mirror version of the call that Mars itself made to Liam's soul.

Liam swallowed to appease the butterflies in his stomach before stepping up to the open hatch. With the sun hidden behind the bulk of the craft, what had been a gaping dark maw now revealed itself to be an ordinary airlock. Liam hopped up inside the airlock, glancing quickly around. The inner airlock door was shut.

The airlock chamber didn't differ materially from the ones that the Terran bases used. Benches lay overturned along both sides and a medical kit hung askew on one wall.

The inner airlock door bore a round viewing port that looked out into the dark corridor. Liam stood up as far as his restrictive suit would allow but could see little through the glass.

Maybe the ship did *eat them.*

What was he, a kitten? Still afraid of the boogeyman and the dark?

A gray shape shot up from below the bottom of the glass, round, dark holes for eyes staring at Liam. He hissed and fell backward, scrambling away from the door, feeling his claws press against the Kevlar in his gloves. His pulse thundered in his ears as he pushed himself up on one of the benches to get back onto his feet. When he looked back at the glass, the shape had resolved itself into Koresh, who was waving and gesturing towards the door.

"I can't hear you," Liam said, tapping on the side of his helmet, then shaking his head.

Koresh tilted their head and then gave a single nod, holding up a finger, then disappeared.

Liam took a few deep breaths to center himself. Stupid trick of the glass and the light filtering in from outside. He hoped that Koresh would have enough tact to keep the incident to themselves.

Vibrations in the deck plates conducted upward through Liam's suit. The hatch on the outer hull had closed and sealed itself. After a few moments, during which everything became totally dark, the inner hatch disengaged and slid open, the sound of the hiss telling Liam, before his instruments could, that there was atmosphere.

"I am sorry about that. The composition of the craft's hull prevents the transmission of signals from outside," Koresh said, all four eyes staring intently at Liam. "I did not mean to frighten you."

"I wasn't frightened," Liam lied, hoping that the suit wouldn't betray any telltale shift in body heat.

"That is good. Come. Selar has gone to the bridge. Can you hear me, Selar?"

"I hear you both. I am trying to go through the log computer and flight recorder, but the vessel has minimal power. It will take time."

"Liam and I will look for any survivors or clues down here."

Koresh flipped their communicator to short-range, prompting Liam to do likewise. They'd still hear Selar if they called, but wouldn't disturb their work with their chatter.

"So have you figured out anything?"

Koresh nodded down the corridor. Now that Liam's eyes had adjusted to the dimly lit ship's interior, he saw that it was lit with glowing emergency light strips at floor and shoulder height. The light did little to make the ship seem welcoming. The corridor stretched out into a barely-lit darkness straight ahead. This corridor had branches, but it looked as though it could bisect the entire vessel.

"I have seen no sign of the crew. It is possible the ship was abandoned and only crashed here by fortunate accident."

The pair passed a few sealed doors, all marked in the Mitrian language. Liam recognized some of the characters but couldn't make out the words. The corridor stretched onward, ending at a sharp left turn.

"Could a ship have stayed in one piece without someone in control, though?"

The walls of the corridor formed a circle around the walkway itself, broken up at intervals by presumably pneumatic doors that stood firmly shut.

"If the automatic pilot were engaged then yes. Hopefully Selar is able to either uncover some information or survivors. We shall strive to do the same."

Liam had been looking at the Mitrian text on the door labels when he came to a sudden, hard stop, colliding with the taller creature.

"Sorry!"

"Do you read our language?"

"I know a few spoken words, but that's it."

"This," they said, pointing to a door label attached to a thicker-looking and heavier door with an access keypad, "Is the universal symbol among my people for danger. Think of it as you would the markings on the electrical system at the base."

Liam stared at the symbol, a jagged diagonal mark piercing a circle with a single line connecting from one side to the other, like the last liquid in a volumetric flask.

"The jagged line looks dangerous," Liam said, peering at the symbol, "But what about the circle?"

"It represents temperature. The line shows the loss of heat, like a thermometer. Sharp loss of heat is how we think of death."

The pair continued down the dim corridor, Liam following behind Koresh, who bypassed door after door without a second glance. The only sound came from Liam and Koresh's footsteps, and Liam made an effort to make certain that he made as little noise as possible. The two rounded the corner at the end of the corridor and came to a crossroads.

Koresh set off down the left path, gliding gracefully. Liam glanced right. The lighting was mostly shut off down that path, only one long blue tube flickered, casting shadows from some dangling and neglected cables.

"Where are we going, actually?"

"To the infirmary. Probably the best place to find survivors or information outside of the command deck."

He hurried to catch up to the Mitrian. It made sense; Terran ships followed an emergency protocol during crash scenarios that congregated beings in designated shelters, and the sickbay was always one of them. Liam felt a chill cut through the homeostatic interior of his envirosuit, instinct driving him to turn back to the dark path he'd been looking down.

Nothing had changed. The one light flickered feebly against the dangling cables and wires. Liam could not escape the feeling of being watched, and turned quickly, dashing up to Koresh as the doors to the infirmary slid open.

The lighting here was more consistent and brighter than the emergency strips. Six computerized examination tables and an array of medical equipment lined both sides of the large room, along the near and far wall. The wall paneling gave off a soft glow, like an autumn sunset on the beach, in the golden light from the recessed fixtures.

Koresh's secondary eyes shut as they surveyed the scene. Their ears pinned back and their antenna twitched.

"I will search the computer," they said, "You check for anything unusual."

Koresh moved into the little glass-enclosed office. Liam made his way slowly past the undisturbed examination beds and through an open doorway.

The door led into a supply room lined with cabinets and drawers, all of them in disarray. Large cabinet doors hung open. Drawers were torn free of their frames, their former contents piled and strewn all over the floor. Piles of medicine, creams, and bandages lay everywhere.

"Koresh, the supply room has been ransacked," he said.

Koresh's voice came back instantly over the communicator. "What is missing?"

"I don't know, I don't read Mitrian, remember?"

"Acknowledged. I will be there in a moment."

Liam looked around. Why were the beds and the rest of the sickbay untouched but this room ransacked? Drugs? People on Earth stole drugs from hospitals. He didn't know what the Mitrian society had in the way of addiction problems, but it wasn't necessarily unfeasible.

Along the far wall, one cabinet's door swung lazily back and forth beneath an air circulation vent. Beyond the door, Liam's eyes locked onto the wall partially obscured by it. Standing out against the fiberglass was a blue smudge, with drops running in little trails down the wall, like a child's finger-painting.

"The hell…?"

Stepping as gingerly as the bulky envirosuit allowed, around all the clutter, he approached the door and reached out, pulling it away from the wall.

Lines had been smeared by someone's finger and dripped down the wall.

Another burst of static, like the one outside with its elusive, high-pitched path buried within it, swelled in Liam's earpiece as he stared at the lines.

It was a drawing of some sort, possibly a symbol. It looked like nothing so much as a crude cave drawing of a Tiki mask. Its "eyes" were solid circles of blue with lines connecting them straight down to the corners of a triangular "mouth."

The static vanished once more, giving way to Koresh's voice.

"Koresh to Liam. Come out here please. Quickly." Their voice quavered, and there was an edge of… something on the words. Excitement? Concern?

Fear

Liam blinked.

"I'm on my way. Where are you?"

"Through the medical officer's office, out the other side. Quickly."

Liam stumbled once over the piles of discarded medical supplies as he rushed over. The physician's office was a small antechamber leading to a half-shuttered doorway. Liam squeezed through into a dimly-lit workroom lined with cooling units, like the city morgue from old TV. One of the drawers had been opened and its contents lay out in full view.

On the table, the body of a Mitrian lay stretched out. Koresh looked as if they were about to be sick.

Liam leaned closer, giving the body a better examination. The corpse had been eviscerated, its insides torn up by something with vicious claws or teeth. Their tattered jumpsuit had been ripped apart. Their fur, once white and pure like Koresh's, bore a pastel yellow tinge in the emergency lighting, contrasting sharply with the black of their blood and viscera, lending the whole scene a look of putrefaction. Their face was equally mutilated, all four eyes gouged completely out, leaving only dark holes.

Like that reflection.

"Who or what did this?"

Koresh stared down at the corpse, muttering something in their native tongue.

"What?"

"We should find Selar. I don't relish the thought of leaving any of us alone."

"What did this?" Liam repeated, urgency creeping into his voice.

"I do not know," Koresh said, grimly. "But this was the ship's surgeon."

They tapped a finger at the blood-soaked, tattered uniform of the corpse, indicating their nameplate. The plastic plate was smeared thinly with the blood. Spread so thin, the blood appeared bluish-green under the emergency lighting.

Liam stumbled backward. The symbol scrawled on the supply room wall burning in his memory.

"What's wrong, Liam?" Koresh asked, rushing to steady the snow leopard.

"Someone wrote on the wall—" Liam gasped, trying to get his breath. The suit had become claustrophobic. He was suffocating. He was going to die here!

Dying alone, millions of miles from home. That's what you signed up for.

"Wrote what? On what wall? You are hot and cold at once. Try to think straight."

Liam gasped again, squeezed his eyes shut, and forced himself to breathe steadily. The suit felt tight, squeezing him into a tiny little space. He had to get out, get it off. There was atmosphere here, wasn't there?

No. You're fine. This is fine. We have to keep the suit on, Liam. Think of wide open fields. The vast Martian landscape.

The snow leopard took a deep breath and exhaled, envisioning the dusty landscape of the red planet, his mind watching in time-lapse as the sky became blue and plants began to grow. He opened his eyes. The suit was no longer crushing him, the Mitrian ship no longer closing in around him.

"Someone wrote in blood on the wall."

Selar's voice burst into Liam's earpiece before Koresh had a chance to question him further.

"We must get off this ship, now!"

"What?" Liam asked, blinking.

"There is no time to explain. Meet at the airlock and get back to the rover. We have to get to a safe distance!"

* * * * *

"What's going on?" Liam asked as he and Koresh bolted back along the dim corridor towards the airlock.

"I do not know, but we must hurry."

The pair rounded the corner and nearly ran headlong into Selar.

"I have the ship's security and log recorder," they said, holding up a hefty-looking striped black box the size of an old-style television in one paw. "The ship's engine containment is breaking down. We have only a few minutes to get clear."

Selar turned and began punching commands into the airlock controls. The pneumatic door to the outer corridor hissed closed as the decompression cycle began. Liam looked back through the window to the corridor one last time, feeling once more the unsettling tickle of being watched.

Down the murky corridor, the faintest outline…

Was it?

Liam blinked and the shape was gone. But he wasn't wrong, was he? He'd seen a bipedal shape. Now it was gone.

He stared out the window again, feeling a cold panic start to set in. He didn't blink. His tail jerked and twitched inside its pressurized, cramped prison.

There it was again. Closer. Still just a faint shape in the dim light, but there nonetheless. Person-like.

"Guys, there's somebody out there!"

Koresh rushed up to the door looking out through the window. Selar, behind them, opened the outer hatch.

"I see no one. Come, Liam. Let us get to the rover."

Liam looked back, but saw nothing.

What the hell…?

Koresh pulled him by the arm, hurrying him out the airlock, back onto the rusty Martian soil. Selar had already cleared half the distance to the rover.

Selar waited by the open hatch for the others, then sealed it, stripped off the envirosuit as quickly as they could, tearing one of the rubber gasket seals, then rushed to the rover controls, firing up the micro-fusion engine and backing away from the crater.

Liam fought to maintain his balance and get out of the envirosuit.

Through the windshield he saw the rear of the Mitrian ship beginning to glow an ominous red. Smoke and steam belched out of the damaged engine compartment. The whole thing was going to blow.

"What's the explosion radius on that thing going to be?"

"Not large. A few kilotons of energy is all an exploding engine will produce. But it is still better to get as far away as possible," Koresh said, strapping into the co-pilot's chair.

As Selar put the rover into forward gear and turned, Liam could see small explosions ripping into the craft's hull. He pulled his chair's computer terminal up and tapped the necessary commands to pull up the rover's external cameras. The ship's entire engine compartment exploded outward in a hail of shrapnel. The Martian atmosphere was not yet oxygen-rich enough to support massive combustion, and so the burnt, twisted remains of the wreck sat smoldering, flames burning what oxygen they could find.

"That was too close," he muttered.

"We passed within the star's corona," Selar said, voice brittle. They paused as if trying to articulate another thought, but Koresh placed a paw on their arm.

"But our heat remains constant, Selar."

Liam stared at the ship's remains on the rover cameras as they faded into the distance. Just for an instant, he thought there was a bipedal shape standing just on the horizon, but when he focused on it, it was gone.

"What did you find on the bridge?"

"Corpses. Pieces of them, anyway. The bridge was in shambles. Consoles had exploded, and debris and damage was everywhere," Selar said, fingers straining as they gripped the rover's controls as if relaxing would kill everyone aboard.

"What about you? Did you find any trace of warmth?"

"We found—"

"Bodies in the morgue, mostly," Koresh said, one of their lower eyes twitching in Liam's direction and widening. "For now let us not discuss it further until we are safely back at Zeto Base."

Liam clamped his muzzle shut. The feeling of being watched clung to him like cellophane. His whiskers and tail tip did not stop twitching. He glanced back at where the discarded suit sat haphazardly in the darkened corner. A short, bipedal shape, unnaturally proportioned.

He shivered and tapped the button to shut the cabin door.

* * * * *

The nearly vacant crew lounge was dim at 2300 hours Earth time, most of the light being provided by a video screen displaying a roaring log fire. The special heaters in the bulkhead below the screen—which was mounted at appropriate fireplace height—provided a gentle warmth, and just a little piece of home.

Commander Sloane had been gratified that everyone made it back unhurt. The climatology team, on the other paw, nearly had a conniption trying to predict environmental damage before the Mitrian delegation reassured them. Earth ships still used environmentally dangerous chemicals to fuel them; Mitrian ships did not.

Liam sipped his reconstituted green tea ration and watched the faux flames dance, his tablet for the moment laying forgotten on the small aluminum coffee table. The tea did nothing to settle the feeling creeping around in the pit of his stomach. His mind turned over the feeling of being watched aboard the Mitrian ship, and the glimpses of what looked like a bipedal creature.

It hadn't been real though, had it? It couldn't have. Maybe the first time it could have moved quickly enough to disappear somewhere but after that, Liam hadn't even blinked and it was just gone.

"Liam?"

The snow leopard let out a frightened yelp and leaped out of his chair, turning to see only Koresh and Selar standing nearby, each holding a steaming mug of coffee. Mitrians fell head over heels for the stuff.

"We did not mean to chill you," Koresh said, smiling. "May we join?"

"Sure, sorry. Just a little on edge after today. Nearly getting blown up is hell on the nerves."

"Ah, yes. I was becoming quite agitated myself once we reached the rover," Koresh said, taking one of the padded armchairs.

Selar sat in the other, silently sipping their coffee.

"So, did anything useful come from the log recorder you recovered?"

Selar did not answer. Their secondary eyes were closed, and they stared into the fire with their primaries.

"Selar?"

"It was corrupted. The video feeds were static. I have the computers running an analysis and recovery, but our systems are not tailored for that, so it will be slow."

Koresh leaned forward, towards Liam. "Would you be good enough to describe the symbol you said you saw?"

Selar shifted uncomfortably in their chair.

"I think I can draw it."

He reached for his tablet, pulled up the native drawing application, and shut his eyes, remembering the room, and the symbol. In his mind, he was closing the cabinet door, and revealing...

He drew as much as he could—or dared—remember.

The blue color seemed to fade slightly from Koresh's bat-like ears, but Selar went completely rigid, one paw gripping the chair's armrest, the other trembling with the effort of holding their coffee steady.

Liam's ears pinned back, his tail twitching.

"What is it?"

"My people have terraformed numerous worlds over the centuries," Selar said, closing all their eyes.

"There are legends of a dweller in the void. It is called *urtrach*, the empty one. It exists in the dark places. The between. It gives off no heat, no scent. When you have seen it, it will seek you. Hunt you."

"It moves, and yet does not move," they added, ears flick-ing, searching for sound beyond the faint whisper of the new Martian winds on the reinforced walls of the compound.

Their eyes darted back and forth between the viewport and the doors to the lounge.

"Where does it come from?" Liam asked, feeling a growing tightness in his chest.

Koresh placed a white paw on Selar's forearm. "It is a legend we tell to our pups," they said, looking at Liam with a smile across their muzzle. "It is enjoyable to tell frightening stories, but they are just stories. You do similarly on Earth, do you not?"

Liam flashed a grin along his muzzle, "Of course. We usually do it around campfires."

Koresh laughed heartily, waving a paw at the television screen.

"Well, I suppose this would do, as you say, in a pinch, would it not?"

Selar did not join in the levity. They stared out the curved viewport at the gloaming of twilight. Then, Selar jerked their head back towards the others and slammed their fist onto the armrest.

"It is no laughing matter! There are stories of our far-flung colonies whose heat cooled. Signs of violence, of madness, but no trace of survivors or victims. Only cold and silence."

Koresh stood, placing their paws gently on Selar's shoulders.

"Those legends are from the days when we were prone to space madness. That is no longer the case, Selar, and these stories must no longer dominate our thinking."

Selar winced, slipping under Koresh's arm to stand up.

"I will work on the log recorder until we have answers. I pray you are right, Koresh. Liam," they added, "be vigilant."

They turned and disappeared through the lounge doors. The feeling in the pit of Liam's stomach returned.

Be vigilant.

* * * * *

That same feeling—that deep, nameless fear that something wasn't right—gnawed at Liam's insides, keeping him from drifting off to the quiet respite of slumber. After two hours of tossing and turning on his meager mattress, the snow leopard heaved himself out of bed and staggered to the potable water dispenser, guzzling a glass to wet his dry mouth.

Koresh was right, of course. The Mitrians were an old race of spacefarers. It was natural for them to have legends of lost colonies and monsters in the loneliness of space. "Here, there be dragons," as the old Earth sea charts would say.

Liam flipped through his tablet, checking out his work-load for the next week: a laundry list of other high-level repairs, installations, and engineering jobs.

Many of them would give him some degree of time alone out on the base perimeter. Just himself and Mars, alone together, entwined.

He moved to his small viewport, looking out onto the dark horizon, lit by a vast sea of stars. Mars was truly beautiful in its solitude, and while that might change with the terra-forming, it would never stop being that place that Liam had come to for asylum from an uncaring Earth.

At the line of the horizon, in the faint distance, a new dark shape resolved itself. Liam stared, squinting into the distance to make it out better. The shape did not move.

It's your imagination.

No. Liam knew every rock and geological formation and piece of equipment along that horizon. He'd stared at it every night since he arrived at Zeto.

He wished he had a pair of binoculars handy, or a camera with a decent zoom.

He looked around for anything that might improve his view of the shape. Maybe he could get the base cameras to fixate on it!

Grabbing his tablet, he tapped into base communications,

pulling up the base's external cameras, moving one to fixate on the spot the shape had appeared. It was no longer there. Had he imagined it?

He searched the landscape again, alternating between the cameras and his own vision, taking deep breaths to control the building anxiety.

He spotted it halfway between the base and where it had been before. The shape had reached one of the dehumidifier towers that littered the landscape and drew moisture from the air for base usage.

Liam stared at it. The shape did not move. But now, somehow, it was closer. It had passed the water collectors and was now just outside the edge of the base's floodlights.

Liam could make out a small, round head, narrow torso, and digitigrade legs. The shape's paws, if one could call them that, were long and spidery, and reached the creature's knees.

Liam's heart now threatened to leap through his throat and choke him as he was finally able to focus on the thing's face and head.

It bore no visible ears, not like the Mitrians or the Terran species. Its head was small and perfectly round, sloping down to a flat jaw.

It didn't move again, but now it was closer. How was it doing that? Liam gasped for breath, his fur standing on end. The electricity of fear arced through his nervous system. He had to run. Had to get away.

Suddenly it was looking up at him from maybe a hundred meters outside the base wall, still enveloped in murky shadow. The black holes where its eyes should be locked onto his own gaze.

It vanished, though Liam had never looked away.

What if it comes inside?

No, it couldn't get in. It would need access codes, or it would have to follow someone else, and there were no patrols or repair assignments at this time of night.

Maybe you imagined it. Nothing moves without moving.

Maybe.

But something did.

"Liam to Koresh?" he asked, tentatively, into his tablet.

"Yes, Liam?"

"Where are you?"

"With Selar, in the IT lab. We are about to finish the recovery attempt on the ship's log and security recorders."

Liam pulled on his jumpsuit and zipped it while bolting from his quarters, heading for the lift. The stars visible through the corridor viewports felt ominous, as if the sky were a great black thundercloud ready to wash everything away.

You should've been a poet.

The feeling of being watched, like what he had felt on the Mitrian ship, returned as the doors closed on the lift. Three levels down felt like an eternity of the base's walls pressing inward. In the reflection in the lift's dormant video screen, Liam caught his reflection. His eyes were bloodshot and wild, like a cornered predator. The snow leopard shook his head to clear it and smoothed his whiskers with a paw.

The corridor here did not contain viewports, a fact for which Liam said a silent thank-you to the universe.

He rounded the corner and stepped into the IT lab, deserted at this hour but for the pair of Mitrians staring at a large monitor resting on the technicians' workbench. The whole room was littered with computer parts and cables and bins full of electronics and spares. Several tablets lay stacked on a countertop in one corner, and the air smelled of ozone like the old TV repair shop in Liam's hometown had.

"Liam—"

"I saw... something. Something outside. It was short and lanky, and it had a round head, and I couldn't see its eyes and—"

"Liam, I am sorry if we frightened you," Koresh said, looking up from the monitor. "Our little ghost story probably made it somewhat difficult to sleep."

"But it moved like you talked about that, um, what was it called?"

"*Urtrach*," Selar said. It must have been the low light in the room, combined with the glow from the monitor, but the exposed skin of their ears looked positively drained of color.

"It does not matter. It is not real."

"Koresh, look at this. The computer has finished."

"Pull up the med bay video logs," Koresh directed. Liam bit his tongue in an effort to remain calm and clamp down on the fear. Selar's secondary eyes closed entirely as he complied, keying in the appropriate commands.

The video feed played an empty sickbay.

"Back it up until we see something."

Selar scrubbed backward through the video at high speed until some activity appeared.

"Stop there."

The video began to play. Mitrian crew entered and left, doctors and nurses going about their assigned tasks.

"Fast forward please," Koresh ordered. "There. Stop and play from there."

The empty med bay was just as eerie on video as it had been when Liam had stood in it. A lone Mitrian, carrying a data pad, passed through the frame and disappeared into the supply room.

"Can you pull up the supply room camera at this time signature?" Koresh asked, placing a paw on the fidgeting Selar's shoulder. Selar's antenna stood stiff and vertical.

Selar punched in the command. The camera in question faced the spot where Liam had found the symbol. This time, there was no blood. The Mitrian in the video opened the drawers, looking at the contents of each and then typing on their data pad.

The Mitrian gave a sudden jerk of their head, all four eyes facing something beneath the view of the camera, their antenna straight up as Selar's was now. Their data pad clattered to the floor as they backed against the wall, paws scrabbling to the sides, reaching for something, anything. Liam felt his heart racing. At the bottom edge of the video, something moved, just slightly.

And then the entire video feed cut to snow.

"That's just like what happened with the comms here on the base," Liam said. He swallowed and moved his tongue around, trying to moisten the desert that his mouth had become.

"Switch back to the outside camera, Selar."

The other camera picked up the Mitrian trying to run back into the medical bay. They got three steps before jerking backward as though they'd run to the end of a leash, and were lifted off their feet, flying back through the doorway and out of sight.

"My god!"

"It is the *urtrach*," Selar whispered.

Koresh's ears drained of color, just as Selar's had done.

"Go back a few frames," Liam said

"There! Stop! Look, look at their throat..."

The grainy video showed what looked to Liam like the fingers of the shape.

"That's what I saw. That's what I saw! It's outside right now."

"By the heat of the stars," Koresh muttered, all four of his eyes staring at the frozen video.

"We've got to tell Commander Sloane. Now. Comms are unreliable. Let's get to the command center."

"Agreed. Let us stick together. If it is *urtrach*, then catching us in isolation will be its great strength."

Koresh pocketed a screwdriver from the worktable, holding out one to Liam, and one to Selar.

"Just in case."

Liam took his, a long-shafted Phillips, and slipped it into the pocket of his jumpsuit. Selar, still staring at the screen, did not move.

"Take it, Selar. Please."

"It will not help. They cannot be stopped."

"Then better to go cold trying."

They placed the screwdriver into Selar's paw.

* * * * *

The trio had gotten halfway to the base commander's office when the lights began to flicker.

"What's causing that?"

"It."

As they reached the lift, Liam tapped the controls, and the flickering lights went completely dark. The emergency lighting strips along the walls and floor hummed to life immediately, casting everything in a combination of long shadows and pale, sickly yellow.

"Lift's out."

"We will take the stairs."

The group rushed through the doorway and up the stairs to the command deck. Emergency lights glowed brightly here, casting long, grim shadows. Emergency power had kicked on to maintain command and control systems, though the monitors displayed only white noise. They were the only ones present in the command center.

Where's the night shift?

Liam watched as Koresh clutched their screwdriver tightly, approaching the commander's office door. The manual actuator, designed to operate in the complete absence of power for upwards of five years, responded and the pneumatic doors slid open. In the glow of the perimeter lights through the window, the commander's silhouette was just clear enough to be visible. He stood hunched over his desk, back to the door. Koresh stepped cautiously inside, followed by Selar, both of them glancing nervously to the sides of the room.

Liam set to follow them, but as he crossed the threshold, he caught sight of the shape on the floor. One of the meteorology team lay in a black pool, staring up at the ceiling through gouged out sockets.

"Oh my god!"

Liam felt a sensation like the cracking of glass somewhere inside him, splintering and spider webbing.

"What is it?"

"She's—"

"They're... all... dead."

Commander Sloane had spoken. He remained bent over his desk, back to the group. His voice was airy, brittle and indistinct, as if it were coming and going on the wind.

"What do you mean, Mike?" Liam forced himself to enter the office, checking behind him for any sign of the creature.

"It followed you."

"Commander, we must—"

The Rottweiler stood to his full height and turned to face the group. His jaw hung slack, clinging to his skull by half-torn flesh and sinew. His eyes were completely gone, leaving only the hideous red sockets.

Liam stared, unable to force his legs to move. His throat closed up when he tried to scream, letting only a few choked gurgles escape.

Sloane's facial fur was damp and matted. Along the paths where tears might have run, trails of blood seeped.

"Mike," Liam managed to choke out. "Let's get you out of here."

"Agreed, Commander," said Koresh, "We will get you to medics at Huston."

"Too... late..."

Liam fought the urge to vomit watching the Rottweiler's barely connected jaw jerk and slide to make words. Selar had backed against the bulkhead nearest the door, ears splayed and colorless, antenna stiff.

"Commander?"

A new sound gurgled in the darkened corner behind the Commander's desk, rasping and burbling.

At first, the shape disoriented Liam, lumped unevenly in

the darkened corner as it was, like his shed envirosuit in the rover. The shape stood unmoving. Liam did not take his eyes off the thing, his tail held down, ears back. Without moving, it moved closer. It just... *appeared*... closer.

"Oh fuck no."

"*Urtrach*," Selar squeaked, backing away from Commander Sloane and the shape, which tilted its gray, furless head and made a rhythmic rasping noise.

The creature's form caught some of the beams of perimeter light. Where its eyes should be, there were two large, perfectly round sockets—

No, not sockets, Liam realized. They were too perfectly dark. They reflected nothing. Those eyes were the embodiment of darkness itself.

Its mouth was a rounded triangle bordered by what Liam could only describe as lips, chapped and dry. Horribly rasping, the lips writhed and flapped and contracted, but revealed nothing within the mouth, save darkness. Its head was uneven, bordering on lumpy.

It was *laughing* at him.

"We must go. Now!" Selar shouted, grabbing Liam by the arm and backing away from the *urtrach*. Koresh tried to pull the Commander along after, never breaking eye contact with the monstrosity in the corner.

Sloane, in one swift motion, shrugged off Koresh's paw and swung his meager claws at the Mitrian's long white muzzle, tearing into their flesh and leaving gaping lacerations along their left cheek. Flecks of blue blood spattered onto the Rottweiler's uniform.

"Stars and planets!" Koresh shouted, backing away. The creature appeared closer, its lanky arms and impossibly long fingers outstretched, reaching for them. Koresh dodged to what looked to Liam like the best "out of the way" of a creature who didn't visibly move. The thing's fingers nearly caught them as they backed away again, tearing a gash in the Mitrian's thigh.

"Run!"

Liam and Selar got through the office door into the command center, with Koresh bringing up the rear.

Koresh stumbled, but Liam's cat reflexes let him catch the Mitrian in time. They leaned on Liam's shoulder for support, moving towards the stairs.

"We have to get everyone out of here!"

"I think it is too late for that," Selar whispered. Liam looked up.

They were surrounded. The base's staff stared at them with vacant eye sockets and bleeding cuts and lacerations.

Blocking the doorway was Sasha, the malamute climatologist. Liam's eyes flooded at the sight of her. Scarred and wounded, her eyes were more violently clawed at than many of the others. Her little sunflower hung forgotten in her jumpsuit pocket, covered in a spatter of blood, though whether that was from her wounds or those of others, Liam could not tell. One of her ears had been torn almost completely off. It hung limply against her blood-matted fur.

The *urtrach*'s hideous rasping laughter echoed in the cold, dark command center. They had to move. Now.

"Let's go. The three of us can still make it out of here."

The base staff shuffled uncertainly as Selar barreled towards the stairwell. One of the snow leopard scientists, Liam didn't have time to determine who, caught Selar by the upper arm. Liam and Koresh passed them as they wrenched their arm free.

Sasha alone stood between the trio and the stairwell, paws raised to catch and mutilate them.

"Flower child," Liam sobbed, "please…"

Sasha's head tilted, and her paws lowered a few inches.

"Go!" Selar cried. Liam and Koresh obeyed, rushing forward past the confused climatologist and through the doorway.

In the lower Martian gravity, Liam's momentum carried him more quickly than he intended. He hit the edge of the stairs faster than expected and he and Koresh went tumbling down to the landing, collapsing in a heap. Selar reached in and helped Liam to his feet, pulling him firmly off of Koresh.

At the top of the stairs, the former staff had begun to collect along the metal railing, their eyeless stares more piercing than anything Liam could remember.

"Let's get out of here. We have to hurry!"

Koresh cried out as they put weight on their injured leg.

Liam glanced at the Mitrian's foot, which had already begun to swell.

The staring creatures made no move.

Selar grabbed their counterpart, hoisting them over their shoulder in a fireman's carry, and started down the stairs. At the top of the stairs, the *urtrach* appeared, joining in the baleful staring, its hideous, deformed mouth and lips twitching and making slathering noises. The black holes of its eyes threatened to swallow Liam whole.

Jesus! Why is this happening?

When the group reached the ground level once more, Liam shoved ahead.

"We need to get to the rover and get out of here. If we can get to Huston we can warn them!"

Selar gave a curt nod. Koresh did not speak. Their breathing had grown shallow and raspy. Liam wondered if they'd broken ribs in the fall as well. As a feline, Liam wasn't incredibly heavy to begin with, much less in the lower Martian gravity, but a fall was a fall, and Mitrian bones could be more brittle than Terran species.

When they reached the loading bay, Liam was relieved to see that there were no altered base staff present. The bay was dark and deserted. The rover sat waiting for them, rear hatch open.

"You get Koresh aboard and get the rover powered up. I'll suit up and be ready to open the doors manually," Liam said, grabbing the nearest suit to paw, which was one of the accursed heavy duty envirosuits. No time to find a light-duty suit now, though. The creature or the staff would find them quickly.

He climbed into the suit, sealing it and activating its systems per protocol. With the power out, the doors would have to be opened manually and the re-pressurization systems would not activate either.

Selar had started the rover, and pulled it close to the main doors, its airlock hatch still open and waiting for Liam. His ears pricked briefly at the sound of the engine. For a brief second he was certain he heard an abnormality in the mechanicals. After a moment of deliberate listening, he did not detect any other sounds. His imagination.

The snow leopard opened up the emergency panel along the bulkhead near the door's manual controls. All manner of emergency symbols and text in multiple languages surrounded the heavy red twist-lock handle and lever.

He grabbed the handle and pulled the recessed cylinder, sliding it out after a great initial resistance. With a twist to the right, he reinserted the cylinder, unlocking the massive actuator lever.

Liam reached for the lever which would trigger the release of all of the stored air pressure and fling the base door open wide.

His paw was caught mid reach by a set of long, gray, furless fingers. Screeching and hissing he jerked his paw, trying to free it. As he did, he felt the crunch of bone. Electric pain shot from his fingertips to his shoulder. His wrist remained trapped. His action had put him face to face with the *urtrach* and its devouring black holes. This time, though, there were four.

The heavy suit prevented Liam from exercising the full range of motion necessary for proper self-defence. The creature clawed at his suit's viewport, leaving scratches in the diamond-glass.

It wanted his eyes, like theirs.

Liam grabbed at the creature's arm with his other paw,

forcing it to release his wrist. He pivoted as best he could in the bulky suit and drove the heel of his injured palm against the outside of the creature's elbow joint, resulting it in snapping in the wrong direction with a sickening wet crunch.

The *urtrach* yowled and flung its other claws at Liam's glass once more.

The snow leopard fell backward onto the suit's life-support pack and slid a few meters away.

The creature, cradling its snapped and useless arm, burbled and snarled with its triangular black hole. It moved closer, appearing quickly a half meter nearer with each "movement."

Then it was on top of him. Liam shifted, trying to get himself out of its way, or get to his feet, but before he could make the attempt, it was on top of him, raising its lanky, claw-tipped fingers to strike at his face again. With the deep gouges in the glass already, Liam felt certain this one would breach the suit.

The creature's strike came, not at Liam, but over his head. The creature was knocked back. It snarled, its legs tensing for another leap. Liam rolled backward over the support pack, onto his shoulders, and kicked out with both feet, praying to anything that would listen that he'd land a blow.

Both feet struck. He felt the creature's chest crunch under the force of his blow.

As he rolled forward from the momentum of his kick, he saw the *urtrach* sail through the air, coming to land on the edge of a large crate. Even through the helmet, Liam could hear the wet crunch as its neck snapped.

Its body came to rest against the crate, unmoving save for the death-rattle twitching of its hideous lips. Its eye sockets, formerly an all-engulfing black, now reflected some light, revealing a moist cavity. The enveloping darkness had vanished.

Liam rolled onto his hands and knees and got to his feet, and turned to see what had happened behind him. Selar stood there, panting, hands on their knees.

Liam signaled that they needed to get out. Selar scurried back into the rover and sealed the inner airlock hatch. Liam yanked the emergency release lever and with a violent hissing the doors shot open. Liam felt the wind rush past him as the bay decompressed. He hopped up onto the rover's ramp and inside, taking one last look at the dead *urtrach*.

For the first time, Liam noticed a blood-smeared nameplate hanging from a tattered piece of blue fabric on the creature's chest.

Selar pulled the rover out onto the Martian soil. Liam tapped the controls to close the hatch.

As the ramp rose to seal the airlock, Liam saw one of the eyeless, clawed-up base staff standing at the center of the doorway. In its paw, dangling limply, was a metal box with a shred of wires clinging to the bottom.

No...

The rover managed to get almost three kilometers away before the sound Liam had detected before returned to his ears.

He opened the door to the cabin, where Selar was desperately punching at controls. Systems readouts on the motor showed several blinking red fatal errors.

"They sabotaged the rover!" Liam shouted.

"I realize that, Liam."

"Is there anything you can do?"

"I'm afraid not." They sighed. "I will get us as far as I can, but after that, we will have to make the trek to Huston on foot."

After a pause, they added, "I do not think highly of our chances."

Liam helped Koresh to the rear wall benches and laid them down softly to rest for as long as they could. The rover began making grinding noises after thirty minutes or so, before finally sputtering to a halt on a wide, flat plain. Liam checked the outside cameras, but saw no sign that they'd been followed. There was nothing here except dust and rocks, and the pale beige of the Martian sky.

Liam stared out at it, wondering if this would be where he finally died. It wouldn't be so bad, after all. He had long thought that he was destined to become one with Mars itself. If it had to be, maybe that would be for the best.

Selar climbed into the back after checking on the unconscious Koresh and began to don their envirosuit. They spat out what sounded to Liam like a swear word.

"What?"

"There are only two suits back here and one of them is the one whose seal I tore trying to get out of it to drive the rover away from the crash site." Liam's feline ears caught a high-pitched whine, even through his suit.

"We've got duct tape. Can we seal you into it with that? We only have to get to Huston's airlock and we don't have any other options besides walking."

"Take my suit," Koresh muttered, eyes still shut. "I cannot walk. I will be a burden. Leave me here and return with help."

Liam shook his head. "No. We will take turns carrying you. I'm not leaving anybody alone. I'm not letting the same thing that happened to Sasha and the others happen to any of us!"

Koresh opened their secondary eyes, just a crack. "Then seal me into the damaged suit, at least. Make certain Selar has the best chance to live."

They coughed, their voice wheezing and rattling in their chest. A tiny trickle of blue appeared on the white fur of their muzzle, just below their nose.

"Agreed then," Selar said. Their secondary eyes were closed, their antenna drooping.

Koresh began the process of donning the damaged envirosuit.

Liam and Selar began collecting anything from kits in the cabin that might prove useful, particularly as a weapon. Liam picked up a rock core-drilling assembly, feeling the heft of it in his paws. Heavy enough to be useful if they were attacked.

The snow leopard took another look through the windshield of the rover at the Martian horizon. He'd get through this.

Mars will take care of you.

A few deep breaths later and a wellspring of hope began to trickle in his heart. The three of them could make it to Huston, and everything would be okay.

From the rear, a howl of pain screeched out and snuffed that spark of possibility. Liam and Selar rushed back to the rear of the rover.

Koresh was hunched over, their head in their paws.

"What is wrong?"

Silence. Koresh did not move.

"Koresh?" Liam asked, approaching cautiously. Selar had already reached their half-suited comrade when Koresh stood and spun with lightning speed, swiping blunt claws at them.

Selar did not move quickly enough to evade Koresh's grasp and was caught in a viselike grip by the throat and lifted off the rover's deck. Koresh's eyes were gone, gouged out of their sockets like all the others had been. Their thumbs and paws were stained with the blue of their own blood thinned with the vitreous humor of four distinct eyes.

Liam leaped forward but was carelessly batted away by Koresh, slamming sideways into the side of the rover. He felt sinew strain and the sharp pain of the impact.

He dropped to the deck, turning to face the scene and try and get up.

He was not fast enough.

Selar's eyes bulged. They tried to swing at the Koresh creature with their own claws but had already grown too weak. Koresh's other paw darted forward against Selar's torso.

Liam looked around for something to fight the creature off with.

The core drill! It had fallen to the deck when Koresh

had hit him and rolled under the bench. Liam stretched out, reaching for it, just able to touch it with the tips of his fingers.

Just a little closer...

His injured shoulder shouting in protest, he managed to stretch just a little farther and caught the core drill in his hand, pulling it to him. He pushed himself to a standing position via the bench and turned to face Koresh again.

Selar's eyes were narrow slits, their head lolled to one side. Liam gritted his teeth and rushed forward, drill extended. He hit his mark. The drill pierced Koresh's side beneath their raised arm on an angle putting it on a trajectory with what would have been a Terran species's lungs and heart.

Selar fell to the deck, released from Koresh's grip. Koresh managed to reach Liam's cheek with their claws, slicing it open. Liam yowled and twisted the drill.

Koresh madly grabbed for it, but Liam pulled the core drill back and shoved forward once more, ignoring the white-hot pain in his wrist that threatened to knock him unconscious.

Koresh's mouth poured blood. They made one last effort to reach for Liam. The snow leopard pivoted, pulling up on the drill bit—using it like a lever to send the creature to the deck.

Koresh tried to rise only once, before collapsing into a widening puddle of their own Mitrian blood.

Liam hurried to Selar, but found them unmoving. Dead. The final victim of the creature and the madness at Zeto Base.

With little else to do, Liam pulled medical supplies from the first aid kit, cleaned and dressed the wound on his cheek, then finished donning the envirosuit and tied his injured arm into a splint and sling as best he could.

Then, not bothering to look back at the dead Mitrians, he opened the airlock and set off, either to die and be accepted into Mars's eternal embrace, or to live and reach Huston, and warn them of what had happened at Zeto.

* * * * *

The wind whipped the iron-rich dust against Liam's enviro-suit, tearing strips of the surface coating away and leaving them flapping from the suit or fluttering uselessly through the air. The exposed Kevlar weave held, protecting the vital pressure and oxygen within the suit.

Liam trudged through the shifting wastes, grateful for the warmth the suit provided against the deadly chill of the Martian night. He wished he could rub his eyes or just stretch his poor tail out. He'd tried sleeping only once in the 48 hours since leaving the rover, and that had been interrupted by nightmares.

The distant sun sank to a tiny sliver along the horizon by the time Huston Base came into view as the leopard crested a small rise. He'd made it.

"I'm sorry, Koresh, Selar, Mike… all of you," he whispered, fighting back the tears. There would be time for mourning later.

The base's lighting flickered to life in the early twilight. Liam flitted toward it, staggering, hypnotized by the glow like a moth.

He flipped the control switch on his suit's wrist. His headset filled with the soft static of background white noise.

"This is Liam Sams of Zeto Base, calling anyone at Huston. Come in please."

Silence and static.

He looked up at the viewports along the base structure. There were few lights on. A gentle breeze carried dust and whipped and dragged it over the dome; Mars was trying to reclaim herself.

The snow leopard took a deep breath to still the swarm of angry bees that churned in his stomach. The bandage on his cheek needed to be changed. The wound itched fiercely.

How would he get inside? He needed to get attention. He tried the radio to no response, then found a fist-sized rock at his feet. He reached back to throw it at the double-reinforced viewport two floors above that was lit, but he was halted by the sound of static in his headset.

Eyes widening in panic, Liam frantically turned in circles. There, in the distance, obscured by the rising dust fog: Was that the shape of one of them watching from the top of the dunes? Liam blinked, and the shape was gone. His fur stood on end inside the survival suit. What now? Run into the wastelands to die? Try to make it to another of the smaller facilities and pray that the creatures wouldn't be able to find him?

Mars will take care of you.

Yes. It would become his grave.

Was it close? Liam still couldn't see it anywhere around him. He felt the tears welling in his eyes as hope faded. The meager Martian gravity tugged at him, bringing Liam to his knees. He sobbed into his helmet, tears dripping downward onto the claw-scarred glass.

"…to Sams. Do you copy?"

The words were so unexpected that Liam had to throw one arm out to keep from falling over in surprise, shock, and delight.

"Huston base to Sams, do you copy?"

"Oh thank God yes, Huston, this is an emergency. Open the main hatch and let me inside."

There was only static.

Please, not this again.

Hopefully they heard him before comms cut out. He looked around again, watching at the horizon for the reappearance of the disfigured shape that meant death.

The hatch opened! One final glance to the horizon, and then Liam bolted for the airlock. The green light indicating atmospheric pressure lit up. Liam removed his helmet, letting it fall unheeded to the deck. The sound of the impact resounded in the leopard's ears after days of nothing except the sound of his own breathing. He felt a surge of panic roar through him like a typhoon. He tore at his gloves, at the seals of his already damaged envirosuit, barely managing the cognition necessary to disconnect the gaskets and seals properly. He needed out of the goddamn suit or he was going to suffocate!

The hatch at the far end opened with its characteristic hiss. Liam felt, rather than saw or smelled, two large creatures take him by the arms to support him.

"Calm down, Mr. Sams, everything's okay."

Liam's head snapped up, locking his gaze on a doughy-eyed fellow snow leopard dressed in his skivvies.

"Like hell it is!" Liam jerked his arms free and continued to claw at his suit. He managed to get his left lower-leg piece off, but could not remove the other. The metal ring had been dented one of the times he'd fallen. "Get this goddamned thing off of me!" he yowled, jerking free once more from the two creatures his brain registered as foxes only in passing.

The fox on his left pulled his head to the side. Liam felt a sharp prick in his neck, the sensation of something cold spreading from the site of the sting, and then, by degrees he felt the world start to go dark around the edges.

"Get me..."

Liam didn't finish the sentence.

He fought to keep his eyes open but he was swimming in molasses now, and the world jittered.

He fell backward, staring up at the officer in the doorway.

Behind the pudgy snow leopard, a lump of putrid gray flesh hovered, with two eyeholes of pure darkness.

The darkness in those eyes swelled and grew larger, enveloping Liam's vision entirely. He felt the world slipping away. Maybe, he thought, the nightmare would finally be over.

Author Bios

Tarl "Voice" Hoch is a writer out of Alberta, Canada. Generally, he can be found writing or putting together an anthology while double fisting a Tim Horton's Triple/Triple and a cherry soda of some sort. When not tormenting himself in this way, Tarl enjoys reading a variety of books, taking long winter walks, co-hosting the writing podcast Fangs & Fonts, and spending time with his amazing wife. Sci-Fi Horror has been one of his favorite genres ever since seeing 'Alien' as a small child, and it is that love which brought about this anthology.

He can be found on Twitter @voicespider & @tarl_writer His works can be found at: https://www.goodreads.com/author/show/5759304.Tarl_Voice_Hoch

Searska GreyRaven makes her home in South Florida. When she isn't scribbling away at a story, she can be found tending her bees or chillaxin' under a palm tree reading a book. Her short work can be found on SoFurry under the name Searska_GreyRaven. She can also be found on Twitter @SearskaGreyRvn

Frances Pauli writes multiple books and series across the Speculative genres. Though she has difficulty sticking to a particular box, her fiction usually touches on themes of magic and spirit, often includes romance, and occasionally wanders into dark or humorous corners at random.

Frances posts furry serial and short fiction on furry social sites such as Mammabear, and maintains a blog and listing of her works in print at francespauli.com. When not writing, she crochets, shows hairless dogs and keeps far too many tarantulas for her family's comfort.

Ton Inktail resides in the western United States where he enjoys hiking, photography, and especially writing. His published works include several short stories and the military SF novel MoonDust. You can find out more or contact him at TonInktail.com

James Stone is the pen name of Syr Otter. He discovered his love of furries in 2001, and first tried his hand at writing stories in furry worlds in 2011. SciFi Horror has been a favorite genre of his since his brother let him watch *Alien* and *The Thing* one night when his parents were away. *Blink* is James' first published work. He can be found on Twitter @ syrotter

Kirisis "KC" Alpinus, much like her leading character, has always been a "weird one." With her love of all things that go bump in the night, she was only too happy to try her hand at this anthology. Whether it is Stockholm syndrome from being forced to watch *Friday the 13th* and *Nightmare on Elm Street* marathons (courtesy of her older brother Chewy) or a certain curiosity about the paranormal and surreal, Kirisis loves horror, so writing about it was like a dream come true. Her works can be found in the *Cóyotl Award* winning anthology *Inhuman Acts* or the upcoming *Fur to Skin: Ladies First* anthology. When she's not sleeping, she can be found getting into various forms of trouble or licking the foreheads of purple-striped tiger creatures. She can also neither confirm nor deny the following: she likes board games; The X-Files made her love sci-fi horror; she lives somewhere in Florida and is getting her Master's degree; she's an adrenaline junkie and aloe drinks make her the happiest. Twitter: @Darheddol Facebook: KC Alpinus

Franklin Leo is a writer and student living in Southern California. She attends the University of California, Riverside, where her studies focus on queer and cultural studies with an emphasis in composition. Her work has appeared in convention guide books, anthologies, online magazines, and a local writing center since 2012, and she looks to pursue graduate school to work with students who identify as LGBTQ* and study the effects of trauma within education. She lives at home with her mother, father, and three feline friends, the latter all believing that her work is not of utmost importance.

Bill Kieffer was born in Jersey City, NJ. He never fully recovered.

A brain injury at an early age left him with some mild issues and just enough aphasia to be amusing at parties. One of those issues is prosopagnosia (face blindness), which is not so amusing at parties.

He's happily married to a woman who encouraged him to discover and explore his sexuality. She also encourages him to keep on his meds. They both dabble in writing erotica. He is bisexual but does not stray. She is straight and the relationship is only open in the sense that he tells her everything (they blame rumors to the contrary on his aphasia).

When he is not looking in the mirror, Bill Kieffer is actually a 6 foot tall gray anthropomorphic draft horse that types as Greyflank. He is a member of the Furry Writers Guild and has recently published a novella via Red Ferret Press, The Goat: Building The Perfect Victim. He is also a columnist for Underground Book Review, a web site dedicated to Indie authors and their works.

Chris "Sparf" Williams is a Washington, D.C. area author and actor, which means that he spends an inordinate amount of time wondering just exactly where he went wrong. Though no Johnathan Crane, he does have a fascination with creeping dread and the things that terrify people. Other works by him can be found in Trick or Treat vol. 2, FANG, vol. 6 and 7, ROAR vol. 7, and occasionally on SoFurry and FurryNetwork under the username Sparf. He also hosts a solo-podcast on the topic of anthropomorphic fiction, Independent Claws, which can be found on iTunes and Google Play.

Ross Whitlock is a lifetime member of the furry community. He lives in Colorado with his boyfriend and ferret. His writing is fueled by numerous mugs of tea and daily walks, during which he meets many friendly dogs. Ross has been writing fiction since his tender teen years and his works can be found in *Dungeon Grind, Will of the Alpha 3, ROAR 7* as well as at https://www.furaffinity.net/users/hengeworlds

Editor's note: It is with a heavy heart that I advise the reader that during the process of constructing this anthology, Ross Whitlock passed away. His parents, Sally Duston and Dean Whitlock (www.deanwhitlock.com) kindly allowed Ross' story to continue to be placed in this anthology. Ross was an amazing writer and he will be missed.

Rechan: Deep in the dark of the earth, there lives a mad and cunning creature. In those lifeless tunnels he creates his malignant art. Sometimes they accompany a moan, or the roar of some fantastical beast. On occasion though they birth a scream, like the tale found in this volume. Rechan's horror can be found in Abandoned Places, and books yet to come. Those who wish to track his carnage can find the trail on

Twitter, under @molewords.

Ianus J. Wolf is an author who writes and contemplates all the frightening scenarios in the dark that time and his brain will let him. A long time fan of both horror and sci-fi, his work has previously appeared in *Abandoned Places, Inhuman Acts, Will of the Alpha,* and *Altered States* from FurPlanet to name a few. He is also the editor of *Trick or Treat* and *Pulp!* from Rabbit Valley. He lives in the Seattle area with his two mates and their two dogs where he enjoys horror movies, books, and looking out at the stars and wondering just when we'll truly find out what else is out there.

Kandrel is an American fox living in the UK. See the sights, they said! Live the high life, they said! Now he's stuck in this strange land where everyone drives on the wrong side of the street. SOS! Someone send real food! You can find his full bibliography at www.foxyonline.com

Corgi W is a writer from England, who frequently enjoys diving into the strange and bizarre. She is currently studying towards her undergraduate degree in philosophy, whilst doing her best to regularly write fiction, cook, and get lost in conversation with the important people in her life.

Donald Jacob Uitvlugt lives on neither coast of the United States, but mostly in a haunted memory palace of his own design. His short fiction has appeared in venues such as Cirsova magazine and Flametree Publishing's Murder Mayhem anthology. He also regularly serves as a judge at the weekly one-on-one writing competition at TheWritersArena. com. Many of his stories have a dark turn, and he enjoys genre mash-ups, so when he saw the theme for this anthology he knew he had to submit a story. If you enjoyed "Outlier," let him know at his webpage http://haikufiction.blogspot.com or via Twitter: @haiufictiondju.

Slip Wolf has been cooking fiction for about five years, serving narrative morsels to ravenous star-hoppers throughout the Empire. Despite traces of insurgency in his writing, which make his screeds pure poison in the Emperor's eyes, colonists and patricians alike have partaken his wares with little guilt. He has dishes available with Sofawolf, FurPlanet, Rabbit Valley and Red Ferret press. A menu of robust, romantic rebellion can be found here: http://www.furaffinity.net/user/slip-wolf/

www.ingramcontent.com/pod-product-compliance
Lightning Source LLC
Chambersburg PA
CBHW071202020726
47502CB00002B/512